SHADOW RIDERS

Eileen Vera Schuh

SHADOW RIDERS

http://www.eileenschuh.com

FIRST EDITION paperback

Kastle Harbour Publishing

April, 2016

ISBN: 978-0-9869388-6-3

Cover designed by Avalon Graphics
www.avalongraphics.org

Other Novels by Eileen Schuh:

The ongoing BackTracker series:
THE TRAZ Book 1
THE TRAZ: School Edition
FATAL ERROR Book 2
FIREWALLS Book 3

Also:
SCHRÖDINGER'S CAT
DISPASSIONATE LIES

Praise for Shadow Riders

"Readers will feel Allie's pain in this chilling new psychological-suspense novel from author Eileen Schuh. A riveting plot and dynamic characters will leave you craving more." ~ **Luke Murphy, international bestselling author of *Dead Man's Hand* and *Kiss & Tell***

"Author Eileen Schuh can always be relied upon for profound characters, accurate dialogue and captivating plots. Her writing is clear, concise and descriptive all at once.

Schuh's particular talent for dialogue that not only gives us insight into the characters, but also moves the plot forward, allows the reader to focus on what's happening and at the same time get close to the people involved.

In *Shadow Riders*, Schuh takes us along on a horrifying, suspenseful trip with Allison Montgomery. The journey is not just a physical one, however: it's also psychological. Through flashbacks to Allison's session with a psychiatrist, the writer demonstrates the phenomenon of a "Stockholm syndrome" type of situation. Love for an abuser is a mystery in itself, but Schuh carries us so thoroughly into Allison's mind and her relationship with Carbon, that we almost understand it.

The reappearance of some of the Traz series characters is welcome for those of us who are already fans, though this book also stands alone.

Shadow Riders is interesting, intelligent, and exciting. The plot weaves through dialogue and characterization in a perfect union of anticipation and fear, sympathy and revulsion.

Shadow Riders is a thriller with depth and weight and fully explored characters." ~ **Catherine Astolfo, award-winning author of *Sweet Karoline***

Dedicated to:

Those who cannot
Break free of love
Despite the pain

Acknowledgements

Thank you to my beta readers (and there have been many down through the years that this novel has been under construction).

Thanks to my editor, Elaine Denning, and my proof reader, Velma.

Also, thanks to Velma for letting me tag along with her to South Korea.

A salute to Cathy at Avalon Graphics for the great cover and to Allen at eB Format.

Thank you to Allison and the other staff at the House of Hope for educating me about domestic violence.

Thank you to the authors who so graciously agreed to read and review the manuscript.

Thanks to international bestselling author, Cheryl Kaye Tardif, for giving me permission to include the reference to her paperback in Chapter 1. *Lancelot's Lady* by Cherish D'Angelo, is a real novel written under Tardif's nom de plume.

A very special thanks to my husband, Alvin, for his continuous support.

I Don't Know How to Love You
(Lyrics from the movie, DISPASSIONATE LIES)

I don't know how to love you
It's tearing me apart.
Should I love you with my being?
Should I love you with my heart? My soul?
Love you out loud, let the whole world know?

Tell me how to love you.
Should I love you now or never?
Should I love you here forever?
Should I hold you, embolden you, dry your tears
Care for you, share with you, wash away your fears?
Set you on your feet, teach, preach
Hold out my arms and reach?

I don't know if you love me
In what manner, in what way
I don't know if your loving
Is the kind of love that stays.

Does it bind through time?
Is it strong, is it deep, or
Just a fleeting, painful secret
I'd do well to keep?

I don't know how to love you
It's tearing me apart.
Should I love you with my body,
Should I love you with my heart?

Introduction

Her secret fears were becoming too heavy to bear; to share them though, was a dangerous option. She shivered and hugged herself tighter. "I'm only here because it will impress the parole board that I'm seeing a psychiatrist." She sucked in a deep breath. "You're not allowed to tell them I said that." **Allison Montgomery**

"You're right; what's said here, stays here. Feel free to talk." **Dr. Erica Freid**

"I don't want to talk. I just want to make parole."

"If you don't want help, there's not much I can do, so should we watch a movie or something?"

"You're serious, aren't you?"

"Perhaps."

"But if I talk you'll tell me, just like everyone else has, that Carbon is slime and I've been used."

"What if I say nothing? If I just listen?"

"That could be dangerous for us both."

"As a forensic psychiatrist I get paid plenty to listen to dangerous stories. Start with the easy stuff. When did you first meet Carbon?"

Part I

Noraebang: The Singing Room

CHAPTER 1

"Oh my God! Is that what I think it is?" Fran plucked the photo from Allie's hand and tilted it to catch more of the dim tavern lighting.

"Shh." Allie giggled and glanced at the other woman in their party of three. Missy's eyes were glazed, a crooked smile pasted on her lips. She was tilted a little to the left as if at any moment she may topple off her chair. Allie realized with a blush that women edging past fifty looked silly drunk—and that included her. She pressed the soles of her sneakers to the floor, straightened in her chair and silently vowed to become sober.

"It is! It's a penis." Fran's screechy voice sliced through the din of the late-night drinking crowd.

"For Christ's sake, Fran, act your age."

"I'm never too old for this!" Fran waved the photo over her head.

Allie lunged for it, catching her hip on the arm of her chair and sending it clattering to the floor behind her. She glanced uncomfortably around the dingy tavern. A dozen unshaven men with lustful eyes were staring at her from under bushy brows. A burly bouncer, positioned just this side of the women's can, took three steps toward their table. Allie turned her back on all of them, righted her chair and sank into it.

Fran tossed the picture to Missy and quickly thumbed through the rest of Allie's South Korean snapshots. "There's more of them, a whole effin' field of penises! Look at this one. There's...stuff...spurting out!"

"They're phallic carvings," Allie said, covering her brow with her hand and hoping her low voice and cultured words would damper the conversation.

"Phallic schmallic, it's a field of manly tools," Fran said. "Where the hell did you find such treasures?"

"There's a neat story about them. If you shut up, I'll tell it to you. The carvings are in Haesindang Penis Park. According to legend—"

"Penis Park?" Missy giggled, handing Allie the picture which started the ruckus.

"Penis Park?" Fran screeched. Allie cringed.

"Drinks," the waitress said, setting a tray of bottled *Bacardi Breezers* on the table. She leaned toward Fran, trying to glimpse the photos. "Courtesy of the gentleman in the corner."

Fran eagerly reached for a bottle, giving Allie a chance to snatch back the photos. She tucked them under her purse, offered a quick nod of thanks to the man staring at her from the shadows and grabbed a *Breezer* for herself. The waitress left and someone jacked up the jukebox. A lonely cowboy love song drowned the voices around them.

Fran chugged half her drink and then pulled her sweater off the chair back. The evening with her friends was coming to an end. Allie felt a surge of panic. Missy, who was once again precariously tilting to the left, began obsessively curling back the edges of her *Breezer* label.

Allie's throat tightened. Soon she'd be home, alone. Sobering up for another day in a fancy house that was so quiet that she jumped when the fridge kicked on. "If you think the phalluses were great," she whispered, pulling a couple of photos from under her purse, "take a look at this."

"A vagina?" Fran shrieked.

"For Christ's sake, keep your voice down." Allie slumped into her chair. "Oh, my God!" She straightened and frantically gathered her photos. "He's coming over here."

"A penis gets free drinks and a vagina gets the man himself?" Fran suggested loudly.

The fellow's eyes were fixed on Allie's as he approached. When he reached their table, he bent toward her. "May I join you?"

"Definitely," Fran cut in. She shifted her chair and patted the table beside her.

The man straightened and, ignoring Fran, stretched his hand to Allie. "Name's Carbon."

A tapestry of tattoos accentuated the muscles defining his arms. Allie uneasily looked up at his smooth, tanned face. He had a set of the deepest blue eyes she'd ever seen. She reluctantly touched her fingers to his outstretched hand. "I'm Allie." The man was trouble; she could feel it in her bones. He reached behind him for a chair and slid in beside her.

To Allie, carousing with her girlfriends in the worst dive in small-town Alberta was beginning to feel like a very bad idea. She looked across at Fran, who was coyly tipping her chin and fiddling with the gold hoop earring dangling just above her exposed bra strap. She was openly staring at Carbon, pretending not to see Allie's warning headshakes. Allie coughed.

Undeterred, Fran cast an obvious glance to her cleavage, folded her arms on the table and heaved her ample bosom onto them. "So…thanks for the drinks, Carb."

"My pleasure." Carbon winked at Allie and moved his chair so close to hers she could feel his breath on her neck.

"Screw you, too," Fran muttered.

"Live in town?" Carbon asked Allie.

"Yes," Fran interjected. "I do. Not far from here, actually." She plucked her diamond pendant from her cleavage and pressed it to her lips. Allie could swear she saw the tip of her tongue caress the rock. However, a quick peek at Carbon revealed he'd seen none of Fran's flirting—his eyes were still focused on her.

She shifted uncomfortably. Although she'd argued with Fran that she wouldn't mind another go at romance, if for no other reason than to make her ex jealous, she'd definitely not had a man like Carbon in mind. She'd been thinking doctor, or lawyer or wealthy businessman. Besides, her divorce wasn't even finalized.

The jukebox cut out and the tavern quieted, but Carbon kept up his stare. Fran pushed back her chair. "This is obviously a lost cause. I'm outta here." She motioned Missy to join her. "Have fun, Allie."

"Hold it." Allie hastily rose. "I'm coming, too."

"Stay," Carbon ordered, tugging at her arm. "For one drink with me. I'll take you home."

"Like hell you will!" Allie untangled her purse from the arm of her chair. "Fran! Missy!" Her friends walked out and for a brief moment the noise of traffic carried in on the stiff evening breeze. Then the exit door swung shut and she was alone in a dive with a man named Carbon. Another hurtin' cowboy song filled the evening—heavy, slow and sad.

Carbon gripped Allie's arm and yanked her into her chair. Behind her at the bar, glasses clinked. Drunken laughter from a corner table rolled past her. Allie glanced at Carbon. The fire in his eyes was subdued and he was smiling beseechingly.

Perhaps he hadn't forced her into her chair. Perhaps she'd stumbled. The dimple in his cheek deepened. He was likely more gentle than his tattoos suggested—lots of people got body art these days, although probably not a lot of people Carbon's age.

She set her purse on the table. "I'll finish this one."

He beckoned for service then casually stretched his arm across the back of her chair. Before the waitress had time to walk over, his fingers were brushing her shoulder. Allie glanced nervously to the exit. She suddenly felt very sober. "I've changed my mind. I have to go."

As he pulled himself closer, his hand slid further over her shoulder. "I won't let you go." Allie stared at the fingertips now brushing the fabric over her nipple. The waitress arrived, harried—her eyes on a commotion near the door. "Another *Breezer* for the lady and a beer for me," Carbon ordered.

It had been decades and a marriage since she'd needed to refuse a man's advances; it wasn't easy remembering how. Carbon withdrew his arm and began toying with the cell phone clipped to her purse. "I have to go," Allie repeated. She inched her fingers toward her purse, intent on grabbing it and running.

However, Carbon dropped the phone and caught her fingers in his. "You promised a drink with me. And you don't look like the kind of lady who breaks promises." He was squeezing, too tightly. His hold was too desperate.

"I'm leaving," she said.

"I'm just offering you a drink." His grip intensified. It was soon going to hurt. A tiny bit more pressure and her fingers would be crushed. Tears tickled under her eyelids. She was about to cry. She ought to scream, but that was likely over-dramatic. Her judgment was impaired, perhaps he was not about to hurt her. He was just making a play for her. And she had to admit over the past hour, she'd given him more than one good reason to believe she might play back.

Their drinks arrived and Carbon released Allie's fingers, tossed a fifty on the waitress's tray and generously waved off the change.

Allie slid her hand down the *Breezer* bottle. Its coolness felt good against her squashed fingers. Again, Carbon draped his arm across her shoulders. She took a sip and set her bottle down. "I drank way too much tonight. I just went to the can and I have to go again."

He released her and picked up his beer. Relieved, she grabbed her purse and hurried to the exit.

"Before you met Carbon you were in a good mood. You'd just returned from a vacation. You were having fun with your friends, looking forward to your divorce—feeling strong." **Dr. Erica Freid**

"No. Not at all. I wasn't doing at all well before I met Carbon. He actually saved me from a very depressing life." **Allison Montgomery**

"How so?"

"You can't seriously believe anyone facing old age alone would be happy! My parents were both dead. My only sister lived in Texas and hadn't spoken to me for years. Tim couldn't have kids—low sperm count, so I'm hitting menopause with no kids, no family. Very much alone, actually."

"You had wanted children?"

"I always told Tim it didn't really matter to me—because I didn't want to hurt his feelings. Infertility is a hard thing for a man to accept. Tim suggested

we could adopt, or artificially inseminate, or something—but I don't think he meant it. I think he would always have thought he was raising someone else's kid. Guys are like that. I read somewhere it's an evolutionary thing. Whereas a woman always knows she's the mother of her babies, men can't be sure their partner's offspring carries their genes so they jealously guard their mates."

"Tim jealously guarded you?"

"No. He's not a jealous man."

"You don't think he would've been able to handle raising children who didn't carry his genes?"

"I didn't say that. Tim is very gentle. He likely would've been a good father. I just don't think he wanted to be a father."

"He said he didn't want to be a father?"

"No. Why the hell are we talking about Tim being a father? It's not important, it didn't happen, okay?"

"Before you met Carbon—"

"Carbon had nothing to do with whether or not I had kids. All I know is I definitely wasn't happy before I met Carbon, okay? Carbon—he loved me...loves me, like Tim never could. I think we are soul mates."

"Carbon scared you, though. You rushed away from him—out of the bar."

"No! Well, sort of. I could tell he was a powerful man. That might have been a bit scary. I wasn't used to dealing with powerful men. Tim was...he was...impotent. Besides, I was drunk so maybe I was more scared of what I might do than what Carbon would do."

"Tim was impotent?"

"Well, you know..."

"He was unable to get an erection?"

"That's not what I meant."

"You are calling into question his masculinity. Why?"

"I'm not calling into question his ability to have sex, just his ability to be...manly."

"Was unsatisfactory sex an issue in your relationship with Tim?"

"No. Why are we going there?"

"Did Carbon tell you Tim wasn't man enough for you?"

"I wouldn't talk about an intimate past relationship with a new partner, that would be gross. Tim is just a weak man, okay? When he says I'm the reason our company flourished, he's right because he sure didn't have the drive and guts needed to get it going!"

"Were you depressed, Allie?"

"No."

"Depression can make us vulnerable—"

"If I say I was happy before I met Carbon, you blame Carbon for making

me miserable. If I say I was depressed, you say Carbon took advantage of that. What the hell? Give the guy a chance."

"*Okay. The next day, when you sobered up, how did you feel about Carbon?"*

"*I don't know."*

"*How did you two get together again?"*

CHAPTER 2

Allie slowly folded the divorce papers. Her ex was offering her much more than her share of Mahogany Imports was worth. She had the dreadful feeling Tim's generosity was a last ditch effort to convince her to reconcile. Having been her husband for twenty-five years, he knew exactly which buttons to push to set her guilt ablaze.

She slipped the papers into the envelope and reached for her paperback. There was no good reason not to reconcile; she just didn't want to.

She walked through to the living room, her bare feet warming as the cool of the kitchen tiles gave way to the warmth of hardwood. She glanced out the picture window. Stifling the thought that Alberta summers were short and she ought to be outside enjoying the sun, she glumly curled into the recliner and riffled the pages of her book.

Maybe Tim's generous offer was his way of saying he loved her. Respected her. Wanted her. He'd always said she was the backbone of the company and without her, Mahogany Imports would not have become successful. Perhaps he was honouring those words with dollars because… *because he loves me or is he trying to manipulate me into reconciling?*

She ran her fingers over the embossed lettering on the cover of her book, *Lancelot's Lady by Cherish D'Angelo*. Tim had the dark hair and deep eyes of the handsome hero, but he wasn't rugged like the cover model. Tim was gentle, both in appearance and personality.

The long hours and extensive travel involved in running their business had often kept her and Tim apart. He had offered to change things—sell the company, hire more help, downsize. She'd tried to envision their marriage returning to the way it had been in the early years. However, she knew that it could never be the same. They were no longer young and full of energy and dreaming and sharing dreams and chasing dreams. They were old and worn and destined to walk in separate, dreamless worlds.

Allie traced the firm jaw of the hero on the cover. Love ought to be forever but seldom was. She had fought a dark, churning, growing feeling of doom for what seemed like a decade before they had split.

Some weeks she'd been intensely sad. Sometimes, afraid. What if she died while Tim was in Cambodia opening borders to trade? What if she died and no one noticed, no one cared? No one remembered? What if she died before she'd done anything important? What if there was no heaven or hell–just an empty, endless nothing?

Two years ago she'd walked into Tim's office late at night. He'd been sprawled on the black Italian loveseat, his feet on his secretary's lap. Allie had said nothing. Walked out. Stepped around the puddles in the parking lot and booked into a motel. She'd never returned to the office. Never again went back to the family home.

Strangely, it hadn't been despair she'd felt that night; it had been freedom. Freedom from hectic schedules, million dollar decisions, ringing phones and lost luggage. Perhaps best of all, she'd felt free of fear.

'We were just waiting for a late overseas call,' Tim had protested. 'Time zones and such. You understand such things, Allie. We were waiting. We were tired...' She'd eventually accepted that he was being truthful, but she wouldn't go back. Couldn't. Because the night she left him was the night she quit being afraid.

Dr. Freid said it was the night she'd quit feeling much of anything and went from being unhappy to clinically depressed. 'Sometimes we let those who love us, control us,' she'd said, 'and that feeling of being powerless for an extended period of time is debilitating.'

Had gentle Tim controlled her? Had he repeatedly told her how important she was to Mahogany Imports to ensure she felt compelled to keep up the hectic pace? Was his generous divorce settlement meant to spark her guilt and lure her into reuniting?

There was no doubt Tim loved her. He respected her. Allie thumbed through the first chapters of her book to refresh her memory. Tim wanted her, like Lancelot was driven to possess his lady on the Caribbean island. When her doorbell rang, she greeted her guests with her eyes still on the page.

"Hey, we found you!" a voice boomed. She jumped and squinted up. Carbon was smiling at her, amused. She slapped her book closed. Ten feet beyond Carbon was his buddy, Saber, with his massive arms folded across his chest and his eyes hidden by dark glasses.

"Aren't you going to invite us in?" Carbon asked. Lying just beneath the seductive lure of his eyes was the same threat she'd sensed when she'd first met him.

'Stay away from him, Allie,' a well-placed acquaintance of hers had

warned when she'd mentioned Carbon's name. *'He's known to police.'*

Allie had wanted to get free of him, had even looked into getting a restraining order. However, she'd twice postponed her legal appointment after Missy warned her that throwing legalities at Carbon might ignite the latent danger he was harbouring. And Missy would know, she worked for a lawyer. Yet, something had compelled her to make one more appointment.

"Well?" Carbon asked.

The throbbing in her throat stifled her response. His eyes sparkled. His dimple appeared. He cocked his head. She looked down at the novel in her hand.

For several weeks after their meeting in the bar, Carbon had harassed her with repeated calls and texted invitations to meet. He must have stolen her number from her phone when he'd played with it at the table. She kicked herself for having been too inebriated and too taken with his eyes that night to realize what he'd been doing.

'I'm married,' she'd responded repeatedly when he texted. *'I'm not interested,'* she'd told him when he called.

She quit answering his calls and opening his messages–hadn't replied to any of them for weeks. Last Tuesday, though, he'd caught her downtown outside the post office. He had Saber and two other buddies with him. As he was stepping up to talk to her, his friends were removing their helmets and hanging them on the handlebars of their Harleys.

'Allie, I'd like you to meet Saber—' he'd started.

She said hello without stopping and didn't turn when he called after her. The phone in her purse began ringing and she looked over her shoulder to see him with his Blackberry to his ear, smiling and motioning for her to answer. She didn't.

The very next day, she'd come out of the drugstore to find him leaning against the door of her fire-red Ford F150.

'Allie, how're you doing?'

'I'm not interested. I'm married.' Carbon nodded as if understanding and moved away. However, the moment she hit the remote unlock button, he stepped forward and opened the door for her.

'Are you saying I can come for you in a month when your divorce is finalized? Isn't two years long enough to be alone?' Unnerved that he knew so much about her life, she slammed the door and started the truck.

As she shifted into gear, she rolled her window down a notch. 'Please, just leave me alone.' Those had been her last words to Carbon and now here he was—his muscle-bound buddy with eyes she couldn't see, ten steps behind him.

"You're not coming in." She started to close the door on them, but immediately Saber's hands dropped to his sides and his shoulders tensed. Two of his long strides and he'd be on her, shoving her into her house and down the stairs, muffling her screams with his hand. She decided she'd be safer where others could see her. Edging past Carbon, she closed the door behind her and quickly skipped down the three risers to the sidewalk. Two houses over, a lawn mower hummed and across the way, she spotted the neighbour lady tending her flower beds. Allie stood tensely between the men. Carbon looked amused but she couldn't tell if it was anger or hate emanating from Saber. "My house is a mess," she said, hoping an excuse for her inhospitality would lessen the tension.

At five-foot nine, she wasn't a small woman and a good percentage of her one-hundred and fifty pounds was athletic muscle. Yet both men towered above her and more than doubled her in weight—their steroid-fed biceps bulging beneath their T-shirts. She could almost smell the testosterone.

"How about sitting on the deck?" Carbon suggested. A chill crept up Allie's spine. One-hundred-year-old spruce hid her deck from the street and unless he'd been wandering around out there, he wouldn't have known she had one. Carbon released Allie from his gaze and glanced over his shoulder at his friend. "Saber, get the beer." He took Allie's arm and directed her down the gravel path to the backyard.

"I didn't say yes," she protested, digging her toes into the stones. As if unaware of her resistance, he kept a steady pace. The gravel bit into her soles and her heart pounded in her ears. She had to get him to leave. She had to show up for her next legal appointment.

Her toes snagged a root and she stumbled. His grip tightened and he cast a quick glance down with narrowed eyes, but didn't slow. She must not make him angry. She gave in and matched his pace. When they reached the deck, Carbon dropped her arm and bounded up the stairs. Not waiting for an invitation, he sank into a chair.

Allie slowly followed, reluctantly took a seat opposite in the shade of the umbrella and crossed her arms. In the bright afternoon sun she could see clearly the tattoos she'd struggled to decipher in the tavern. There was a jungle of claws and flames—in a glory of colours, fine lines and interlocking chains.

Saber joined them, set a six-pack of *Canadian* beer on the table and sank into a chair. He unsnapped three cans from the carry rings, popped one open and handed it to Allie. He was totally in the shade of a big spruce, making it hard for her to see his face.

No one had said a word since leaving the front yard, which was eerie. It was as if the men were waiting for something; she wondered what.

Saber opened two more beers, handed one to Carbon, and waited for him to take a swig before lifting his own. Allie thumped her beer to the table and leaned toward Carbon. "They do that in Korea."

Carbon chuckled. "Do what? Drink beer?"

"Well, that too. They actually have very good beer and it comes in one point six litre bottles. However, that's not what I meant. I meant no one starts drinking until the respected elders at the table take their first sip."

"Fuck off," Saber droned. It was the first time she'd heard him speak. His low voice, devoid of emotion, sounded ghostly.

"That so?" Carbon said. "Tell me more of what you know about Korea." Allie wondered if he was gunning for more vivid information on Penis Park. Embarrassed, she looked down at her lap. Again silence fell. It became so quiet Allie imagined the sun faintly squeaking against the azure sky as it slid toward the horizon. She stretched her legs and cleared her throat.

"It rains a lot in July," she finally said.

"What else?"

"Nothing else." Allie stared at the red maple leaf on her beer can.

"Did you learn some of the language?"

"No."

"How did you manage, then?"

She hesitated. He was after something, and because he knew what it was and she didn't, he had control. Years of business negotiations had taught her if she could get a lie past men like him, she could thwart that power. However, if she tried and failed, she'd be handing him double the control.

She set down her beer and squirmed in her chair. She had to try something to prevent the impending disaster she sensed. Given their size difference and the fact it was two against one, physical resistance wasn't a winning card. She lowered her chin and stared at Carbon through her lashes. Verbal skills and mental acrobatics might work. "Most Koreans speak English," she said.

Carbon tilted his head and raised his eyebrows. "Really?" A crooked half-smile softened his jaw.

"Yes."

His smile vanished and he locked onto her eyes. Slowly, he leaned toward her. "You're fucking lying," he growled.

She grabbed her beer and downed a swallow. She had to do or say something or his fiery eyes would consume her. She did her best to hide her fear and sound conversational. "Why are you so interested in Korea?"

"Because I'm going there."

Korea wasn't a hot vacation spot for Alberta boys. Afraid Carbon, too, was playing the lying game, she studied his face. "You're going to Korea?"

"Yes."

She couldn't tell if he was lying. "Why?" Allie squeezed her beer can and the enticing sound of aluminum folding in on itself breached the ensuing silence. There was something dreadfully wrong with the direction the afternoon was taking. She ought not to be drinking beer on her deck with men like these two, discussing vacations and lying about languages.

"Want to come?" Carbon's eyes were deadly serious.

She shivered and wrapped her arms about her tighter. "No."

"Why not?"

The question was bizarre; the man was bizarre. There had to be a way to end it safely. She imagined him a grizzly bear—circling, watching, looking for fear in its prey. She might escape if she remained strong, kept him happy, made his dimple appear. She cocked her head and forced herself to meet his eyes. "I don't like kimchi."

"What the hell is kimchi?"

"If you're going there, I guarantee you'll find out."

He frowned and settled into his chair, as if accepting a challenge. "You liked the beer, though?"

She inhaled, carefully, so he would not see the frantic rise of her ribs. She flicked her tongue to moisten her mouth. "There are," she said steadily, "lots of things to like about Korea."

His dimple reappeared and he caught her gaze with his strange magnetic eyes. Her thinking ceased; her heart pounded. Her soul began swirling toward his. Being with Carbon would not be boring. He was promising her that, and more.

She straightened and glanced quickly to Saber. He wasn't grinning at the banter. In fact, she couldn't tell if the man was even listening. He hadn't taken a sip of his beer since she'd called him on it and it struck her he might be sleeping behind his reflective shades.

"Kimchi," Carbon repeated quietly. The bright Alberta summer sun darkened as a cloud passed over. A robin chirped in the spruce boughs. Behind the trees, a car drove by. "You *are* coming with us," Carbon said. Saber was instantly out of his chair and standing beside her—his right hand moving across his belly and disappearing under his other arm.

"I beg your pardon?" Allie glued her eyes to the spot where Saber's hand had disappeared.

"You're coming with us," Carbon repeated louder as he, too, rose.

"I can't! My passport expires in four months. They won't let you in with less than six—"

"It's been arranged." Carbon and Saber both loomed over her. "Now!"

Saber's hand moved almost imperceptibly further under his arm. Allie drew in a breath to scream. However, before any sound made it to her lips, a hand clamped over her mouth and she felt the pinch of a needle in her shoulder.

Her terror was brief before her world faded.

CHAPTER 3

Allie flicked open her eyes. She was face down on the rear seat of a car. In seconds, the motion of the vehicle coiled in her head, travelled as a knot to her belly and began returning.

Frantically fighting the ties binding her hands behind her, she managed to get her head over the edge of the seat just as a stream of vomit erupted.

"Jesus fucking Christ," Saber said from the driver's seat. Another heave caught at her curls.

"Pull over, Sabe!" Carbon ordered.

Saber slammed on the brakes and Allie flew to the floor. "No," she moaned as her face inched toward the vomit.

"I told you the bitch was a bad idea," Saber said in his monotone voice. "Get her the fuck out of here."

"*You* get her the fuck out of here!" Carbon shouted.

Anger rose on Allie's bile; she was about to drown in her own vomit while the men argued in profanities. "Somebody," she hollered between heaves, "get me the fuck out of here!"

"Jesus Christ." Saber shifted into park, scrambled out and flung open the back door.

Despite her protests, he grabbed her by the armpits and dragged her through the vomit into the summer heat. Before she found her feet he gave her a rough push, sending her rolling into the ditch. She came to a stop, sprawled on her belly, retching uncontrollably.

Saber with his eerie voice, was cussing continuously behind her. Terrified that her vomiting would further incense him, she swallowed hard. As she struggled to her knees, her vomit-coated curls brushed her cheeks and the heaving returned.

"What now, Carb?" Saber asked.

"Now, you clean up the mess in the car."

"Like hell."

"Now you clean up the car!" Carbon roared.

"Tell you what, if you leave the effin' bitch here, I'll clean up the car."

Allie glanced up. Carbon was glaring at Saber's back as he retreated to the vehicle. A sob rippled from her belly, followed by an empty heave. Battling the smell and the heat, Allie concentrated on her breathing. Big breaths in and out. Deep breaths. Just as her stomach settled, the floor mat whistled by, hit the ground a few inches away and spat wet remnants at her. She forced herself to ignore her gagging and once more struggled to stand. However, before she got her feet under her, she was struck from behind and smashed back to the ground. Her lungs emptied with a whoosh as Carbon and Saber tumbled over her. A pair of feet clipped her chin and an elbow dug into her ribs as they wrestled through the summer grasses.

Unable to draw in a breath or move, Allie watched, helpless and terrified.

When the men finally came to a halt, Carbon had Saber pinned a few feet from her. "If anyone gets left here," he growled, a shock of Saber's hair grasped firmly in his hand, "it will be you, not her." He released Saber's hair and pushed his face, dark glasses and all, into the vomit-covered floor mat.

Allie's breath returned with a groan. Carbon abruptly stood and stepped toward her. "Get up." He grabbed her elbow, pulled her to her feet and then looked over at Saber. "Are you coming or not?"

"Fuck you," Saber answered dully.

"Sorry about you getting sick, Allie." Carbon linked his arm through hers and led her up the bank to the car. "Didn't think you'd react that badly to the tranquillizer." He opened the driver's door and began rummaging inside. Exhausted and dizzy, she slumped against the fender. "Here," he offered, reappearing with a box of tissues.

She nodded weakly over her shoulder at her bound hands. "I can't." Carbon pulled a folding knife from his pocket and cut the tie from her wrists. She grabbed a handful of the tissues and began scrubbing at the vomit that was quickly becoming a clinging crust under the heat of the sun. "I need something more than this," she pleaded tearfully.

"It's all I have. Sorry." Startled by his apology, she stopped cleaning to stare up at him. He avoided her eyes, however, and leaning past her grabbed a bottle of water off the dash. "Perhaps this will help." He plucked a fistful of tissues from the box and wet them.

Allie held out her hand but he tilted her chin and began rubbing gently. *Was it my tears that suddenly made him gentle?* Too drugged and dizzy to make sense of anything, she closed her eyes and continued to weep. Carbon ran the damp tissues across her cheeks and through her hair.

"You'll have to take those off," he said. She opened her eyes to see him pointing at her jeans. The sun hadn't dried the denim as it had her skin. The fabric was resting wet and cool against her legs and the stench was rising in thick, hot waves.

"Take them off?" she asked with embarrassment.

"Wait a minute." Carbon remotely clicked the trunk open and disappeared behind the vehicle. He returned with a thin, worn piece of grey carpet and held it out. "It's all I have. Maybe you can wrap it around yourself." Allie glanced about. "I won't look," Carbon offered, walking to the front of the car. He leaned against the hood and pulled out his cigarettes.

Allie slipped off her jeans and wrapped the carpet twice around her waist. The aged rubber backing scratched against her belly and the loose threads from the binding tickled her knees. She kicked her pants under the car. "Okay to look."

Carbon opened the door and pointed to the rear seat. "Get in." Allie held the carpet tightly about her and carefully crawled into the car. Saber hadn't done a very good cleaning job. Drying curds splashed the back of the driver's seat and a dark wet patch ringed the floor where the edges of the mat had been. Shutting her eyes and holding her free hand over her mouth, she sidled to the far end of the seat. Carbon climbed into the front passenger side, turned the ignition key and jacked up the air-conditioning. Exhausted and sweltering, she rolled down the window and pressed her face to the fresh air.

Lulled by the drone of the motor and the hum of the fan, Allie began to doze but was jolted awake moments later when Saber climbed in and slammed the door. He settled into the driver's seat, thrust the car into gear and kicked down on the gas.

Allie eyed up Saber's reflection in the rear-view mirror. Though his stony face and shaded eyes revealed little, she imagined he must be furious at both her and Carbon. She ran her thick, dry tongue over her parched lips. "Carbon, I'm thirsty," she dared, once Saber quit accelerating.

"We'll be in the city in twenty minutes. I'll see to it then." He began speaking with Saber. Allie rolled up her window to catch the conversation, but the two quickly fell silent.

"Are you really going to Korea?" she asked.

"I don't like questions unless I'm the one doing the asking," Carbon said.

"Why would you want to go to Korea?"

"Saber, stop the car!" Saber hammered on the brakes and Allie's seatbelt sliced into her shoulder. Carbon reached past the stick shift and flicked off the engine. A terrifying silence followed. "Which part of my last sentence did you not understand? Should I come back there and make it clear to you?"

"No," Allie managed. "I get the message."

"What did you say?"

"It's clear." Allie put her palm to her fevered forehead and slowly slid her fingers over her eyes. "I won't ask any more questions." She peeked through her fingers. "Promise." Carbon motioned Saber to start the car.

Allie leaned against the window and watched the poplar trees whip past, watched the farms change to acreages, acreages to suburbs... She awoke to find the car not moving and only Saber in the front. "Where the hell are we?" she asked. "Where's Carbon?"

"Getting you some clothes."

A suitcase that hadn't been there before she'd fallen asleep was now snuggled beside her. Through the window she saw the south Edmonton mall that was just moments from the QE2 freeway to the International Airport. Could it be they really were taking her to Korea?

Panic suddenly slashed through her daze. "What the hell is it you want with me?" She wrenched at her seatbelt and reached for the door handle, her hands shaking uncontrollably.

"I don't like questions that aren't mine, either," Saber warned.

She fixed her eyes on Saber as she continued to struggle with both her belt and the door. "How will Carbon know what size to buy me? How does he know what I wear?"

Very slowly, Saber turned to her. His arm inched up between the seats. She quit struggling when she saw he had a gun in his hand, aimed right at her heart. He cocked it and put his finger on the trigger. With his other hand, he raised his sunglasses to his forehead. She froze when she saw his grey, cold, clear eyes.

"Anyone who sees my eyes, dies. Shall we make it now or later?" She didn't breathe; it was such a short distance from the chamber to her heart. "You think Carbon is the boss? You think it's only him you have to listen to? Carbon might talk a lot but, hey, I'm the guy with the bullets. What do you say about that?"

"Gotcha," she managed.

"No, ma'am, not 'gotcha'." Saber shifted position without taking his finger off the trigger. "I'd say a piece like this deserves a lot more respect."

Out the corner of her eye, Allie saw Carbon approaching. Saber must have seen him, too, because he began lowering the gun. "I'll think about that," she said.

"Yeah, you think about that." His gun vanished just as Carbon opened the door and tossed a shopping bag onto her lap. She once more began breathing.

"Water in there and some pants," Carbon said. He closed the door and climbed into the front seat.

Saber pulled from the parking lot and accelerated south toward the airport. As Allie's heartbeat returned to normal, she peered into the bag. Reaching past the one-size-fits-all black fleece joggers, she retrieved a bottle of pure spring water. The cool liquid soothed her throat, parched from the drug, her vomit and fear. She vaguely wondered how she'd survive the humid heat of Korea in black fleece. She emptied the bottle and slid it into the bag.

In the mirror, she could see Saber, his sunshades again hiding his eyes. Hoping he was watching the traffic and not her, she pulled out the pants and slipped them on.

As they exited onto the airport ramp, Carbon turned. He had two small green pills in his hand. "Take these." Allie obediently plucked them off his palm and stared at them. "I meant to swallow them," he said.

"Why? What are they?"

"No questions!" Carbon hollered, half-turning, his flailing arm barely missing her face.

Saber slammed on the brakes and wrenched the steering wheel to the right. The truck behind them honked as it skimmed past. "Get her out of here," Saber demanded, pulling to a stop on the grassy boulevard. "The cunt don't fuckin' listen."

"I'm sorry," Allie said. "I can't swallow them. I need more water. I drank all mine."

"For Christ's sake," Carbon muttered through clenched teeth. He turned in his seat and glared at her.

"Stick them under your tongue," Saber ordered.

"I hope they don't make me sick like your needle did." Allie swished the pills around her mouth. They were dissolving quickly, disappearing into the saliva she was determined not to swallow.

"They won't," Carbon said. "You'll just relax and forget." She wondered what that meant. Carbon kept his eyes on her. The pills were gone. Her saliva sweet. "Swallow!" he ordered.

"She doesn't have to." Saber shifted into gear and pulled onto the road. He signaled to enter the airport parkade. "Absorbs through the mouth. It's better if she doesn't." Her swallowing reflex kicked in and Allie felt the bitter sweetness travel down her throat.

Time condensed, at least in retrospect. She'd never remember parking and would always remember it being mere moments before they were inching their way toward the ticket counter in the terminal. She'd also remember feeling strangely relaxed. Dreamy, knowing she ought to do something but not knowing what or remembering why. Simply standing in line had been so easy; trying to think, so hard. As Carbon slid their passports to the clerk behind the Air Canada desk, an irresistible drowsiness overcame her.

"Are you all right, ma'am?" the woman asked. What happened next would forever be lost in a thick fog—her memories so dreamlike they could not be trusted. It seemed to her she had to fight to answer the clerk. It was as if her eyes wouldn't open and her tongue wouldn't move. She remembered Saber appearing beside her and, afraid she was about to fall, she'd leaned against him and dropped her head to his shoulder.

"She's nervous about flying," Carbon said in a faraway voice. "She also gets air sick, so she's taken two *Gravols*."

"I need you to come to the counter, ma'am." She had vague recollections of Saber pushing her forward. The woman looked from her to her passport. "Are you all right?"

Allie peeked over her shoulder just as Saber lifted his sunglasses and stared down at her—his cold, grey death threat. "I'm...just...drowsy from...the pills."

"Where is it you're travelling?"

"Korea...South Korea." Saber pulled her to him and she flopped her head against his shoulder again.

"How many bags do you have?" a distant voice asked.

"Just the one," Carbon answered. She thought she heard him say, "We're traveling light because she likes the fabrics and fashions of Korea." But perhaps she was just remembering what she'd said to Fran that night she'd met Carbon in the tavern. "She intends to buy what she needs over there," he continued, his words jingling, wavering, softening. "It's fine by me..." His voice disappeared and for Allie, the rest of the fourteen-hour journey was time lost forever.

CHAPTER 4

"Allie, wake up!"

"Leave me alone!" Allie swatted the hand tapping her shoulder. She was so close to deciphering the message the dream spirits were giving her. She fought her way deeper into twirling symbols and slowly they gelled into white rocks and green mountains splashed with shadows and red. A canyon. A stream. Bones–her bones laid on white rocks beside a river of cool mountain water at the bottom of a great Korean canyon. She sucked in a sob.

She was going to die in South Korea. She'd never again see the vast Alberta prairies, hear the call of Canada geese trumpeting above autumn colours, or feel the ice of a January wind.

"Allie!" Carbon's voice cut through her daze. He tugged roughly at her arms. "Allie, we're here. Get up! Now! Wake up. Stand up. Allie!"

His face was so close to hers she could feel the heat from his brilliant, mystical eyes. She blinked rapidly against the pull of his gaze and the power of the dream. "Carbon, please don't..." She pushed him away, but the flames from his eyes licked toward her. Writhing within the fire were the dream images of her death, her bones on white rocks splashed in red. There was no doubt the vision was emanating from Carbon's mind, burning its way from his soul to hers. Suddenly from nowhere a rolling dice screamed and tumbled through the chaos. It landed six up and crumbled into a mass of silent bleached skeletons. Six skulls. Death.

"NO!" Her shriek doused the fire in Carbon's eyes.

Six. How did the bones of six men get into Carbon's head? Why is he thinking about six dead men?

"Shut up and get up," he demanded.

She shook her head and struggled to her feet. *It's just a dream.* "What the hell kind of pills did you give me?"

"No questions, remember? Go!" He pushed her into the aisle and toward the exit. "Quietly."

In the terminal, as the men watched suitcases twirl by on the carousel, Allie stared out the wall of windows. It was offering a deceptive view, the tinted glass darkening and cooling the scorching heat of the midsummer sun. She glanced down at her new fleece pants and cringed.

She wondered if Carbon and Saber had cooler clothes for themselves in their bags. They looked almost respectable, having at some point sacrificed their T-shirts for pressed white cotton with collars and cuffs.

Forceful announcements in Korean started coming over the speakers. Afraid instructions were being given that ought to be obeyed, Allie swept her eyes over the throng pressing past her. No one else seemed to be listening.

The foreign chatter, dull lighting and rhythmic sweep of the carousal were hypnotic. As her eyes slid closed, vestiges of her death vision resurfaced–green mountains, shadows, a stream in a canyon. Her bones laid on white rocks. She flicked her eyes open. The graphic images vanished but the terror persisted–a roiling, dark, foreboding omen. She shuddered.

It was so very likely her death dream would come true. She was, after all, in the company of strangers who rode Harleys and sketched the symbols of their trade deep into their skin. She had no identification or money and was in a country with a language she didn't understand. She knew nothing about the justice system—other than it was to be feared. Who would help her?

After Carbon and Saber got whatever it was they wanted from her, they'd have no reason to risk smuggling her to back Canada. "Are you okay?" Carbon asked. She turned. He now had his suitcase and was eyeing her up quizzically.

"Am I okay? Seriously, how can I be okay?"

"Remember, no questions." He set down his bag and, placing a hand under her chin, tilted her face to his. "I know you don't believe me, but I wish I could've convinced you to come here on your own accord."

She swatted his hand. "Yeah, right."

"Let's get a coffee. You'll feel better once you wake up. I know you will. *Dunkin' Donuts.* I see one right over there."

"You have the money for it?"

"Don't worry. I have money."

She raised her eyebrows. "Korean money?"

"No, U.S. dollars."

"No one in Korea will take that."

"Everyone takes American."

"They won't, believe me. Wons or nothing."

Carbon looked around the terminal. "Okay. Well, I guess we'll wait for Saber and then..." He listlessly kicked at his suitcase, leading Allie to suspect he knew nothing about exchange booths.

When Saber arrived they both pulled out their wallets and poked through their green American bills. There was a quick exchange of glances and then Carbon looked to Allie. *He's going to ask me to help.* She quickly stared down at the bright floor tiles, polished to a shine.

"Allie?" Carbon asked. She thought of a cup of coffee, a doughnut, summer clothes. A shower and a bed. Being without money was not going to save her, but perhaps proving useful, would. She headed toward the shops and exchange booths. "I'll show you."

As the lineup slowly moved, Carbon edged as close as he could to the fellow in front of him, studying the transactions at the wicket ahead. His height, coupled with his scrutiny, was making others uncomfortable. However, he completely ignored the scowls, either unaware or uncaring. Allie wasn't sure.

When he reached the counter he asked her, "What do I do?"

"Give her your American money," Allie said.

"I know that, but how do I calculate the exchange rate? How will I know if she gives me the right amount in wons?"

"Don't worry, you'll get lots."

"I should keep some American?"

"It's up to you, but I suggest you exchange all of it since there aren't many currency exchanges outside the terminal. The few there are have strict hours and aren't open on weekends."

Carbon stepped to the window and passed over his cash. Allie watched the teller count it. Knowing the exchange would take a while, she walked a few feet away and leaned against the wall. Five thousand American dollars wasn't an exorbitant amount, but it wasn't a shoestring budget, either. What the hell was he intending to do here?

She heard Saber's ghostly voice rise above the foreign drone. "I told you she was a bad idea." She turned to see Carbon marching toward her.

"What's this?" he demanded in an angry whisper. He held a massive wad of Korean bills. "What the hell is this?"

She remembered her amusement and surprise the first time she'd exchanged dollars for wons. "Wons," she said with a nod. "Lots and lots of wons." She was about to giggle but stopped short when she caught the fury in Carbon's eyes. Saber walked to Carbon's side, folded his arms across his massive chest and widened his stance.

"I didn't...I'm not...It's..." Allie tapped at the bills in Carbon's hands. "Wons." Carbon glared. Allie flicked through the bills. "These orange ones are five-thousand. These are ten-thousand won. A few are—"

"I can fucking see that!"

"The ten-thousand ones are worth about ten dollars Canadian and that's the largest bill they make. Honest." Carbon scowled. "I said you'd get lots in exchange. I meant lots of wons." His features softened slightly, but she wasn't sure if he believed her.

"How the hell do they expect you to carry this?" he grumbled as he began stuffing bills into various pockets. "Do men pack purses here? I should've just used my credit card."

"Well, depending on what you want to do, I guess. However, there aren't many credit card machines. No debit machines." She looked up at his face intensely. "Honest."

CHAPTER 5

"You must have been terrified!" **Dr. Erica Freid**

"It's a bit presumptuous of you to tell me how I must have felt." **Allison Montgomery**

"Then you tell me, how were you feeling, Allie?"

"I don't believe in ESP and shit like that. Or dreams and stuff. Nothing was as it seemed. I wasn't terrified. I wasn't feeling much of anything. I was just kind of confused. If I was scared, it was just a stupid dream scaring me. Had I been more cooperative, there'd have been nothing frightening happening. As it was, Carbon had no choice but to do what he did—for my safety, as well as his."

"You were wishing you were at home, wondering if you'd ever make it back to Canada."

"Maybe, but that doesn't mean I was terrified. I was just...like...dead inside. I'd been so unhappy for so long it was like nothing bothered me much. I was confused, that's all. The drugs he gave me left me confused. Mixed up and stuff. Once I got over that..."

"You weren't entirely miserable before you met Carbon. You were wrapping up a very successful career as a business woman. You had much international travel under your belt. You had enjoyed your earlier vacation to South Korea. You said you had many pictures. You were having fun sharing them with your friends—"

"No! That was just an act in the bar. I was trying to stay sane. I was drinking too much and getting giggly and stupid. I wasn't enjoying anything about my life. It was all just a pretence to cover up my loneliness. Carbon knew that. He saw through the shit. He knew what I was really feeling. He's an expert that way. He always knows what people are really feeling, despite what they might say. Just like on my deck when he knew right away when I was lying. He knew. He always knows."

"Does he always know or is he just good at convincing you that you're feeling the way he wants you to feel?"

"You're not making sense."

"Did he tell you that you were lonely? That you needed him? That Tim was no good for you?"

"Yes, he told me all that because it was the truth. What's your point?"

Allie sipped at the creamy hot liquid which passed as coffee throughout South Korea and pondered the men's anger over the currency. Just weeks before, she and her pals had been laughing about the lack of large bills. She wondered if Saber was going to cross his arms and glare at her every time something in Korea offended him.

"Are you okay, Allie?" Carbon asked softly.

His eyes had lost their demon luster and she felt herself falling for his sympathy. She hastily looked at her coffee. "No."

"I'll get you something to eat. You've got to be hungry."

"Don't bother."

He rose and slipped behind her. "At least a donut. I'll bring us all some." Allie felt his eyes piercing her back. She expected him to leave, but he didn't.

"Okay," she finally felt compelled to answer. When he still didn't leave she turned and stared at him. "Okay. Fine. A donut."

"Chocolate? Jelly?" he asked, holding onto her gaze, just as he'd done in the bar when they'd first met.

"Fritter," she answered quickly, covering her face with her hands. She wished she could think clearer. She remembered learning in a self-defence class that people ought to fight for their lives if being forced into a vehicle because very few victims of an attack survive if removed from the scene. In Canada, she'd been drugged and wasn't given the chance to fight. Perhaps, though, now was the time to take a stance. Perhaps she ought to refuse to leave the terminal with Carbon.

Once on the streets amongst millions of people unfamiliar with the customs of international travellers, who knows what Carbon and Saber could get away with? There'd be a billion places they could take her and if she protested, no one would know what she was saying.

She looked around; there wasn't a white person in sight. Everyone was speaking Korean. Perhaps no one in the airport could help her, either. Carbon returned with six donuts, slid into his chair and tossed a handful of coins to the table. Allie motioned to the wons. "Pick them up."

Carbon pushed them into a pile. "I'll leave it for a tip."

"Don't tip, it's an insult."

"That so?" Carbon gathered the change and pocketed it. She wished she'd thought to take the coins for herself. A few wons could've bought her some internet time at one of the many public PC stations, or perhaps even a phone call.

"Find us a hotel and then I'll take you out for some of that Korean beer you like," Carbon said. He popped the last bite of his donut in his mouth and rose. Motioning Allie and Saber to join him, he headed for the exit with his luggage. As soon as they'd squeezed through the door of the restaurant, he pushed Allie into the lead. She stopped, unsure of where to go next.

"You're taking us to a hotel, remember?" he said, looking down at her quizzically. "Lead the way."

"Which hotel?"

"Any hotel that's a step above cockroaches. Find us one."

"But..." Allie raised her arms in frustration. If she'd been kidnapped to be his tour guide, he was going to be disappointed. Unlike on her last trip to Korea, she didn't have a travel dictionary, phone numbers or even a map. Most significantly, she didn't have her friend's daughter to lead her through the cultural and language barriers. He was about to discover she was useless to him, which undoubtedly meant she'd never see another sunrise. Tears began splashing down her cheeks. Saber uttered a disgusted sigh and dropped his suitcase.

"Stay with the bags, Sabe," Carbon ordered, setting his down, too. Wrapping an arm around Allie's shoulders, he ushered her to a corner and faced her to the wall. He used his massive body to conceal her from the crowd. "Calm down. It's going to be okay. You're going to be fine." A new surge of tears wet her face. "Christ, Allie. Get it together!"

Beneath Carbon's arm, she caught a brief glimpse of a uniformed officer walking past with a machine gun. On her last visit, Suzie's daughter had warned her to steer clear of the KNP, Korea's intimidating national police. This time, that advice was probably even more relevant. There were probably severe repercussions for entering the country on false documents–with men *'known to police'*. She quickly sopped her tears with her sleeve.

"That's better," Carbon encouraged, stepping back. "Good. Okay. Come on, now. You've done this before, been here before. You can do it. What hotel did you stay at last time?"

Allie glanced at the retreating officer and then peered up at Carbon. *Which man is the safest?* Carbon's eyes were deceptively soft. His dimple was almost showing. She looked at the officer. At least Carbon spoke English and didn't have a machine gun slung over his shoulder. "We travelled all over the country. I can't remember the hotel names."

"Well, tell me how to say hotel in Korean and I'll get us a cab."

"*Hotel.*" She smiled feebly. "Honest. That's how you say it, *'hotel'*."

"Great! Let's go."

She groaned. "That won't get us anywhere. Incheon has twelve and a half million people. God knows where we'd end up if we just say *hotel*."

"Incheon?"

"The city," she said, waving at the bustle outside the terminal windows.

"Isn't that Seoul?"

"No," Allie said wearily.

"We have to be in Seoul, it was on our tickets."

"Although it is sometimes called the Seoul International Airport, believe me when I say we are in Incheon. Seoul has another ten million people and is an hour from here."

"Okay," Carbon said. "Okay." He looked over his shoulder at Saber and began edging away. *Is he thinking of leaving me here? I have no money. No passport. No ID.* Another officer strolled by. He was so short that Allie could see the hair thinning on the top of his head—but he was armed to the hilt.

"I have an idea," she interceded quickly, "let's find the Tourist Information Centre. Sometimes they speak English, and if not, they'll at least be able to communicate with us in some way and help us get a ride into Seoul."

"All right." Carbon wrapped a bulky arm about her shoulders. The weight and the warmth across her back felt oddly comforting.

"Look for a scripted lowercase letter *'i'* in a circle," she said as they made their way to Saber. "That indicates the information centre."

Carbon asked Saber to carry the bags and then hugged Allie to him. She was so tired, so scared. So dizzy. She rested her head on his chest. She needed to sleep. She needed to think. She definitely needed a hotel.

"Carbon," she said drowsily. "When you flag us down a taxi, don't wave frantically. They'll just wave back. Do this." She dropped her hand to her hip. With her palm down, she opened and closed her fingers.

"That's all? They'll notice that?"

She snuggled into his embrace. "This is a gentle country, gentle movements, lots of 'thank-yous' and bowing."

Carbon nodded toward another security officer. "M16s. A gentle country?"

CHAPTER 6

"When did you lose your fear of Carbon?" **Dr. Erica Freid**

"I was never really afraid of him." **Allison Montgomery**

"You ran out of the bar to get away from him the night you met."

"I told you, I was afraid of myself because I was drunk. I wasn't scared of Carbon."

"You dreamed you were going to die in Korea. That you'd never get to come home."

"It was a dream! And it wasn't even a dream about me. I just thought it was. Later on, I'd discover what the so-called dream was really about. I was confused by the drugs. I was just confused. Don't keep telling me I was afraid of Carbon. I wasn't. Not at all."

"You were in a foreign country with no money, no identification, no phone. You were there against your will. You expect me to believe you weren't afraid?"

"Believe whatever the hell you want to believe! I know what really happened and so does Carbon. That's all that matters, all that I care about. I'm leaving now and you can scratch my next appointment. I'm not coming back. I'm getting my parole next week and I'll be a free woman. I won't have to do anymore of this lying shit just to get out from behind bars. Scratch my appointment. I am not coming back."

Allie held up three fingers to the hotel clerk. "Three rooms."

"Ah," the fellow said. He bowed his head and handed Allie three electronic key cards attached to rectangular wooden blocks.

Allie bowed her head in return. "Gamsa hamnida. Thank you." She bowed her head again.

"Two rooms, Allie," Carbon interrupted gruffly.

"You're rooming with Saber?"

"Not likely!" Carbon stripped the keys from her hand and tossed one onto the counter. "Just two rooms," he said to the clerk, raising two fingers.

There was no way she was letting that happen to her. No way. Allie slowly reached for the other key but Carbon slapped her hand to her side.

"I'm not sleeping with you!" she screamed, twisting away and clenching her teeth. "I want my own room."

"One minute," Carbon said to the clerk before spinning Allie to him. "You're not getting your own room!"

The deep furrows in his forehead pushed his thick brows down over his eyes and his teeth protruded like fangs from under his top lip. He looked like a terrifying monster but she knew she either had to stand up to him now or tonight...alone...in the bedroom. She willed her voice to remain steady and firm. "Carbon, these rooms don't come with two beds and I'm not sleeping with you. I'm not!"

"Ask for a room with two beds." His voice was rippling with anger and his eyes were ablaze. Saber stepped toward her. Together, the two of them. Towering over her, closing in.

She grabbed the clerk's pen and sketched a room with two beds. The man smiled, nodded and crossed his index fingers at his navel—that meant no. She threw the pen to the desk. "I knew it. They never have rooms with two beds." Carbon grinned. Looking about wildly, she caught sight of the exit and ran for it.

The instant she flung open the door, the fiery sun walloped her face and the grating noises of Seoul exploded about her ears. She raced down the ten steps to the street and stepped off the curb. A horn blasted through the heat and tires squealed. The smell of hot rubber against pavement wafted to her nostrils.

"Allie!" Carbon caught her shoulders and pulled her onto the sidewalk. A bizarre halo from the sun behind him framed his head and concealed his face with dark shadows. She wrenched at his arms, trying to get free of his hold.

"Don't be like this!" He grabbed her hands and entwined his fingers in hers. "I'm not about to hurt you. But you've got to realize you can't have your own room. I'm not intending to...you know."

"What are your intentions?" She tried desperately to shake loose but it may as well have been a vice grip on her fingers. "What are your intentions? What am I supposed to think your intentions are?"

"Calm the hell down, woman!"

"What are your intentions, Carbon?"

He touched a finger to her lips. "I'm not intending on hurting you. Keep this up, though, and I just might. Understand?" She glared at him but the heat was wearing at her resolve. Rivulets of perspiration began trickling under her bra, tickling at her tummy. Cascading down her legs. "I'll sleep on the floor if need be. So calm down. Come on. Let's go in there, get settled in our room and go for a cold beer. Okay?"

Slightly built, olive-skinned people scooted around them, conversing in words Allie didn't understand, avoiding eye contact, pretending she was invisible. It was the culture, polite and nonintrusive. It would appear to them that Carbon and she were holding hands, excited about something. Tourists, unbearably boisterous as usual.

She looked at the strip mall, a mile away it seemed—across and beyond six lanes of honking, incessant traffic. The shop signs were an assortment of unfamiliar icons, none were in English. A police car drove slowly by, its flashers on as they always were. Sweat burned into her eyes and dripped from her nose.

She looked to Carbon and nodded weakly. He took her hand and led her from the harsh sun to the cool hotel lobby. Saber joined them with the suitcases and two keys. They all silently stepped into the elevator.

Allie walked into the room ahead of Carbon, picked up the remote control and flopped into a chair by the window. "We'll take you shopping for some clothes tomorrow," Carbon said as he opened his suitcase. Allie punched at the buttons on the remote. If she hit the right buttons... If only she could remember. If only she knew. If only she could understand the symbols written on the damned thing. How would she be able to report an abduction in a country where she couldn't even get the air conditioner to work?

Carbon opened his luggage and searched through the clothes. "Did you hear me?"

"Take off your shoes," she replied.

He looked at his feet. "Why?"

"It's what you do in Korea. There are slippers by the door if you want footwear."

Carbon looked to the entry way and then down at his sneakers. "They take off their shoes in hotels?"

"Yes."

"Why?"

"Traditionally they eat and sleep on the floor. Foot cleanliness is important to them. That's what the bowl in the shower is for–to wash your feet."

"Well, I'm not washing my feet. But I guess I could take off my shoes." He sat on the bed and untied his laces. "What are you doing?"

What was she doing? Why was she talking about feet and shoes and Korean customs? "Trying to turn on the air conditioner."

"With the TV remote?"

"It's what you do here." She finally hit the right combination of buttons and the air conditioner on the ceiling began purring. She lifted her face in the direction of the cool breeze. "I don't feel like going out in this heat for a beer."

Carbon kicked off his shoes. "I'm with you on that." He removed his shirt, lay on the bed and closed his eyes. She watched the steady rise and fall of his breathing. Beneath the tight whorls of his chest hair, well-tanned skin stretched across taut muscles.

Allie set down the remote and scanned the room. There was a telephone on the bedside table. On her last trip, when she'd picked up the room phone there had been no dial tone and the proliferation of instructions on the keypad had all been in Korean. Even if she could get it working, she wouldn't know whom to call. All she could remember was that dialling 119 would get her an ambulance. That is, if she were lucky enough to reach someone who understood English. There was a different three-digit number for the police but that number she couldn't recall. It wasn't 911.

Last time, she'd had all those emergency numbers in her purse along with the toll free numbers and email addresses of the Canadian Embassy in Seoul and the Consulate in Busan. Today, however, she didn't even have a purse.

Carbon began softly snoring. She eyed up the complimentary basket of toiletries snuggled against the bureau mirror. The various levels in the family-sized bottles were a testament to their communal use. Beside the chest was the hot and cold water-dispenser. Beyond that, where the soft yellow carpet ended, was the front entry. A sea of dark tiles flowed through to the bathroom. There'd be no separate room for the shower—the water would simply spill onto those tiles and flow toward the drain. Wet floors were another reason to wear the slippers provided.

She looked out the window to the dark hills beyond the traffic and then to the nearby businesses. She could see several 'PC' signs, indicating cyberspace access. She knew at some cafes, internet was free and computers provided. She glanced at Carbon, wondering if she should try sneaking out to dash off an email.

She doubted anyone in Canada had even noticed she was missing. The only thing marked on her calendar this entire month was the appointment with her lawyer to discuss a restraining order against Carbon. Since she'd cancelled twice before, it wasn't likely a no-show this time would alarm anybody. If, she thought dourly, she'd not been so stubborn and had reconciled with Tim as he'd begged, there would be someone missing her.

Tim was so very far away, though. Anyone who could help her was far away, across the ocean, over the dateline.

She'd arrived with a phony passport so when her remains were found, no one would be able to identify them. She'd die here, unmissed—an unknown victim of unknown assailants. White rocks and dark shadows... Six...something about six. Six dead men, their bones laid out on white rocks.

"Allie!" Someone was slapping her shoulder. "Allie!" Surprised to discover she'd fallen asleep, she lifted her head and stared groggily up at Carbon. "You can have the bed. Come on, climb in."

He helped her up and led her to the bed. She crawled under the covers, clothes and all, and returned to dreams of green mountains, screams that turned red, canyons, white rocks, shadows and bones.

CHAPTER 7

She awoke to see Carbon and Saber silhouetted against the sun streaming through the hotel window, talking quietly at the table, taking advantage of the ability to smoke anywhere they wanted. Even with the tinted glass holding out most of the sun's glare, Saber had on his reflective shades. Today he was once again in his T-shirt–strutting his muscles and tattoos.

"Ah, Allie, you're awake finally," Carbon said. Allie wished he hadn't noticed because now that her eyes were open, his conversation with Saber had ceased.

"Come join us," Carbon invited. "I've rousted up something they say is coffee." He rose and motioned her to take his chair. She joined Saber at the small table while Carbon made her a cup of instant coffee. He set it on the table and then took a spot behind her. Allie picked up her cup and ran the steam under her nose. It didn't smell like coffee.

She wondered if she could use the friction between Saber and Carbon to help her escape. Perhaps she could cozy up to Saber and generate some jealousy. However, just the thought of making a pass at him caused an involuntary shiver.

"Cold?" Carbon asked. "I could turn down the air conditioning." He picked up the remote and scowled at the foreign script. "Or not," he mumbled, tossing it to the bed.

Allie sipped at the creamy, sweet coffee while Saber and Carbon again lit cigarettes. Her drink was half-gone before Carbon spoke again.

He reached around her to grind his cigarette out in the ashtray. "The Foreign Quarters..." He walked to the bed, straightened the blankets a bit and sat on the edge. "You mentioned it in the bar that night. Where is it?"

"Foreign Quarters?" He must have been listening in on her conversation with Missy and Fran in the bar. That was a scary thought.

"The Foreign Quarters," Carbon repeated impatiently.

"Oh, Itaewon." Her heart beat faster. American service men frequented that part of Seoul. If there was anywhere in Korea where she could make herself understood, it was Itaewon. "Yes. We could go there. I'll show you."

"Where is it?" Carbon tossed her a folded map.

Afraid that if she showed him where Itaewan was, he'd go there without her, she slowly set the map on the table. "I'll take you there. It's not far." Carbon's jaw tightened and a vein in his neck bulged. *He has no intentions of taking me there.* As the silent seconds ticked by, Allie tried desperately to think of a way to make good on this chance to escape.

"Just show me where it is on the map," Carbon finally enunciated.

Although the Itaewon streets would be busy, it would be easy to identify the Americans. They'd be a head taller than the locals. Perhaps in uniform and usually in groups. She could holler for help and then make a run for it. Surely soldiers would know how to defend against Carbon and Saber should they try to stop her.

Afraid that Carbon would be able to tell from her eyes that she was plotting, she pulled her foot to her lap and studied the gold paint on her toenails. "I thought you were taking me to buy clothes," she said. "We should go to the shopping district for that. Insadong, perhaps."

With a resounding crack, Saber slammed his fist to the table. Startled, she slid her foot to the floor and stiffened. "You're pissing me off, woman." He leaned into her and unfolded the map. "The Foreign Quarters. Where the fuck is it?"

Locking her eyes onto his, she stood. His reflective shades and monotone voice made him hard to read. She inched away, not dropping her gaze until she was on the bed beside Carbon.

Remembering how Carbon had softened to her on the roadside, she peered up at him through her lashes. "I need clothes. And a toothbrush, deodorant, a hairbrush. Woman things. You promised."

Carbon looked at Saber and sucked in his lips. It must have been a signal because instantly Saber was squeaking back his chair. Like an entranced cobra, he rose. For a moment he stood stock-still, a dark threatening silhouette between Allie and the window. Then, slowly he slithered toward her. When his toes touched hers, he raised his hands. His fingers curled. He grunted and reached for her throat.

Allie gasped and buried her face in Carbon's shoulder but Saber kept coming. Digging his nails deep into her collarbone, he stripped her from Carbon and laid her out on the bed. His face—with no passion, no anger, nothing— closed in on hers. He dropped onto her belly, ground a knee into her crotch and pressed his thumbs against her throat.

Footsteps passed in the hall. The muted noise of traffic rose from the street below. In her wide-eyed reflection in Saber's dark glasses, Allie saw desperate fear.

His fingers dug deeper.

Darkness seeped across her vision until the walls and ceiling disappeared and all she could see was Saber's face. Her heart thudded in her ears. Time slowed; she was going to die.

As the aching in her lungs increased, her skin began to burn. Rational thoughts ceased, leaving her only with instinct. She clawed at Saber's hands and slashed at his cheeks but his grip just tightened.

A warm rush moved from her belly to her brain and diffused throughout her body. Her lids slipped closed over now-sightless eyes. From afar, she felt her hands fall to her sides. Her limbs convulsed and stilled. Her heartbeat slowed, weakened. She was going somewhere special and she did not mind.

Just before she left, however, a searing pain and shallow gasp nudged her consciousness. Allie flicked open her eyes. Saber was gone. A breath tore up her windpipe—it was her own tortured breathing waking her. With a renewed compulsion to survive, she clutched her hands to her neck and rolled to the floor. Desperately seeking air, she stood on wobbly legs and headed for the door.

Carbon caught her and led her back to the bed. "Sit! Calm yourself. You'll need less oxygen if you do."

With no energy to protest, Allie closed her eyes and swallowed. *It hurts so much. Too much.* A series of short, desperate pants scratched at her throat. Carbon sank onto the mattress beside her. She leaned against his chest and listened to her surreal gasping and throttled sobbing.

"Woman," Saber called in his ghostly voice. She opened her eyes a slit. He was again in his chair, lighting a cigarette. He inhaled deeply, set the cigarette in the ashtray and exhaled a haze of blue smoke. "Next time, don't fuck with me."

CHAPTER 8

Glad to finally be able to pack away her joggers, Allie ripped the tags off her new pair of white cotton shorts and slipped them on. As she was folding the joggers she caught sight of her image in the bathroom mirror. The marks around her neck were changing to deep purple and creeping up her jaw. Threads of pink laced the whites of her eyes. She looked unfamiliar. Sallow and sad. Defeated.

She rested her hand on the doorknob, contemplating whether she'd rather stay in the bathroom with her unsettling reflection or be in the bedroom with Carbon.

'Woman, next time don't fuck with me,' Saber had said, and left. Carbon had covered her with a blanket and woke her as the sun was sinking beneath the horizon. 'Itaewon,' he'd said, pressing the map to her. She'd laid her finger on the foreign district.

'An address to get there.' She tried to speak, but only raspy, wheezing breaths came out. He tossed her a pen and she wrote instructions for the subway system. He tucked the paper in his pocket. 'Let's get your woman things.'

It had been a very quick shopping trip. She'd cared little about the fabrics and fashions, cared little about anything. She'd returned to the room and slipped on the top thing in the shopping bag—the white shorts. *Now what?*

Allie slowly opened the door. Saber was leaning against the opposite wall, tossing a roll of duct tape from hand to hand.

"Where's Carbon?" she croaked.

Saber grabbed her shoulders and wrestled her to the bed. "Take these," he ordered, shoving two pills between her teeth. He quickly rolled her to her tummy and straddled her. Grabbing her hair, he lifted her face from the pillow and began winding tape across her mouth and around her head. Just when she was sure he intended to keep wrapping until she smothered, he ripped the tape from the roll, bound her hands behind her with a zip tie and flipped her over.

She managed one quick kick to his chest before he also got her feet bound.

He said nothing, just straightened and walked out without looking back.

Allie flicked her tongue over the pills. Her hands were already going numb beneath her weight. But whenever she tried to move, the ties dug deeper. Afraid that in her panic she might wrench until her hands and feet were severed, she forced herself to concentrate on her breathing. As she'd learned to do in yoga, she exhaled and inhaled through her nose, deeply and evenly, finding comfort in the sound of her breathing.

Above her, the white ceiling was dusted with shadows and pocked with imperfections. The menacing unknown stretched outward to infinity. Her arms spasmodically twisted against the ties and her breathing quickened.

She swallowed the pills.

* * *

Allie awoke to see the soft light of the early dawn peeping between the curtains. She tentatively wiggled her fingers. Her hands were free. She kicked off the covers and stretched. She ached everywhere. Her mouth was dry and her mind was still thick from the drug.

Beside her, Carbon lay snoring softly. His chest rose and fell. With his strange eyes closed and his strong arms loose at his sides, with his lips parted and his body wrapped in the warm emanation of sleep, he looked like a gentle man.

He stopped snoring and stirred beneath her stare. His eyelids flickered. If she and he were skin to skin and she laid her head on his chest, she would hear his heart beating. He slid his arm around her waist. *If he were to love me, would he stop hurting me?*

CHAPTER 9

"Shrug said it will be a condition of my parole that I continue counselling. He said if I don't keep seeing you, I'll have to see a court-appointed psychiatrist so I might as well stay with you." **Allison Montgomery**

"Ah, I see. And Shrug is...?" **Dr. Erica Freid**

"An idiot cop, but I don't want to talk about Shrug. He's just being manipulative. He says Carbon got into my head and screwed me up. It's Shrug, though, who's fucking with me. Since when does a cop get to tell the parole board what conditions to put on a prisoner? He's screwing with the entire Canadian justice system."

"Why would he do that?"

"To get his murder convictions. Notches in his belt. Shrug can go fuck himself because no matter what he may think, Carbon is not a violent man. He was just doing what he had to do. He got caught up with the wrong crowd. Hooked in with the wrong friends. Inside, he was always a very gentle man."

"If you could have escaped him, if say Tim had shown up in Seoul to return you to Canada, would you have left Carbon?"

"Well, at that time, maybe. But I would have missed so much. I would never have known..."

"What would you have never known?"

"I would never have known Carbon's love."

Carbon was sitting at the table having a smoke the next time Allie awoke. She pressed her knuckles against her hard nipples. Below, her crotch was slick and engorged. In her dreams, Carbon had been her lover.

"You okay?" Carbon asked.

"Sure."

"You still look groggy."

"Those are potent pills Saber hands out."

"I'm sorry," he said quietly. "It wasn't supposed to go like this."

The room was hazy, wavering, tinged with a strange smokiness. She sat on the bed and stared at Carbon. He'd been so tender in her dreams, his lips soft and warm. He'd drawn her in through his eyes and she'd touched his soul. He'd loved her. She'd not been at all afraid.

"Do you need some help?" Carbon walked over and held out his hand. She accepted his help and pulled herself to standing. "Coffee?"

"Sure." Her feet were heavy—distant, as if they weren't hers. Sweat beaded her brow and her heart palpitated as she trundled the ten steps to the table. "Fuck." She flopped into a chair and laid her head on the table, trying to stifle the breaths torching up her throat. Her ankles and wrists burned where the ties had rubbed and a dull ache cramped her shoulders.

"I'm sorry," Carbon repeated, standing over her. "It won't happen again. I won't let it. I promise."

"Don't worry. I'm okay." Allie lifted her head and desperately searched his eyes for any sign of the love she'd seen there in her dream.

"I think this is coffee." Carbon handed her a plastic tube marked 'Maxim'. "It's the closest you'll get."

Carbon set a cup of hot water in front of her. "Here, I'll do it," he said, plucking the 'Maxim' from her hand. He tore off the end of the tube and shook the brown and white powder into the water. "It's not altogether gross." He stirred the drink and slid it to her. It all seemed so caring, as if her dream may have been real.

"Maxim's okay as long as it's the caffeine and not the taste one is after," Allie managed, reaching for her cup. Last night's drug had weakened her and she began trembling violently. She clutched the cup in both hands to steady herself and was finally able to take a sip. It tasted awful. She set the cup down. Canada had such good coffee. Or, maybe it was the water that made it good. Maybe.

"Shit, Allie," Carbon said quietly. He walked to the window. Through the glass and the walls, she could hear the unrelenting traffic of Seoul. Carbon jammed his hands into his front pockets. "I just saw three taxis and a bus go through a red light."

"I think maybe that's legal, as long as you honk first." He looked forlorn standing there, his shoulders sagging as if bearing a tremendous weight. He shifted and was no longer looking at the traffic but at his feet. "What's the matter?" Allie asked.

"I didn't mean for my life to turn out like this."

Carbon looked at her, expecting a reply. Although tempted to say something nasty about what he had done to her life, Allie simply wrapped her hands around her cup and stared numbly at the steam.

However, she did need the caffeine, so once again she tried lifting it to her mouth. Halfway there, the hot liquid sloshed over the brim and onto the table. Frustrated, she set the cup down and moaned.

"Pardon?" Carbon asked.

"I was just...I'm sorry about your life." Carbon's chin dropped to his chest. He closed his eyes and inhaled deeply, looking much like he needed comforting. Fighting the pull of last night's dream, Allie listlessly ran her sleeve through the spilled coffee. He looked like the man in her dream–his muscles rippling in the dazzle and shadows of the summer sun. His eyes, deep and dreamy. His rich lips lifted in a sad, soft smile. *I want to wrap my arms around him.* "I'm sorry," she murmured.

"It's not your fault."

"I'm sorry anyway. Sorry things aren't as you wish them to be."

There was a rap at the door. "Must be Sabe," Carbon said, striding past her. Allie stiffened. What was the proper greeting for someone who tried to kill her? Saber walked in and ambled toward her, his face cold, his eyes hidden behind his shades, his mouth a straight line.

She'd learned in the dog-eat-dog business world, being self-confident was sometimes the best defence. Pretending one was powerful could also help. She forced herself to speak. "Good morning."

"Morning," he answered dully, taking the chair opposite her.

She tried to peer past his dark lenses but all she could see were squares of lights from the window behind her. He lit a cigarette. He was probably staring at her. Probably admiring his prints around her neck. She lifted her coffee. Perhaps he was laughing. Her hands shook. Wave after wave of coffee scaled the side of her cup, breaking just below the rim and splashing back into itself.

"Your directions were okay, woman," Saber said. "Got us to Itaewon no problems."

"Good," she answered with a nod, setting her cup on the table.

"Yeah," Saber said. "Mighty fucking good for *your* sake."

Behind her, Carbon's breathing quickened and deepened. "Leave her alone!"

Saber clenched his fists. *They are going to fight and neither of them gives a shit that I'm here between them.* A shadow crept across her shoulder. She ducked as Carbon reached over her to jab a finger in Saber's face. Her knees caught the underside of the table and set her cup rocking. She stared in horror as it slowly toppled. A stream of coffee headed directly toward Saber. It pooled briefly at the table edge and then cascaded into his lap.

In one smooth motion, Saber was on his feet, flipping the table her way. Maps, coins and the half-full ashtray struck her chest and rolled to her lap before tumbling to the carpet. Warm coffee trickled down her legs.

"I'm sorry," she said.

"Out!" Carbon ordered Saber, pushing him toward the door. Saber stormed from the room.

Allie looked to Carbon, her breath returning in sharp pants. "I'm so sorry!"

Carbon shrugged and returned to staring out the window. Allie righted the table. There was a sopping mess that it seemed was hers to clean. She found a towel in the bath and after first wiping the table, gathered the maps and coins from the floor and patted them dry as best she could. It actually felt good to be doing something ordinary and familiar; cleaning and organizing had always been her forté. Taking to her knees, she blotted the coffee and ashes from the carpet. Finally, she stood and wiped her legs.

"Were you okay last night?" Carbon asked.

She cleared her throat. *What the hell does he want me to say? What's the right answer?* "I don't remember much."

"We'll likely do it again tonight." His eyes were still on the traffic. She studied his profile. Just moments ago, he'd promised not to let it happen again. As she slowly set the wet towel on the table, he turned to her. "You're hungry?" She shrugged. Carbon wrapped his massive arms around her shoulders and pulled her to him. "I'm so sorry."

"It's okay, really. I'll be fine." She pushed against his chest but he tightened his hold and began gently rocking.

"Carbon, let me go." Her dream seemed more distant now. Unreal. "I'll be fine."

CHAPTER 10

Allie ran her tongue over the tape covering her mouth and strained against the ties. Saber had bound her hands in front instead of behind, and given her only one pill. She wondered if these minor concessions were things Carbon had ordered. Although the drug had taken the edge off her panic, this time it hadn't knocked her out. She had no idea how long she'd been lying there but it seemed like hours.

She listened drowsily to the boisterous post-tavern laughter outside her room. A distinctive Tennessee accent mingled with Saber and Carbon's low voices. Suddenly the conversation quieted and Allie heard the soft click of the magnetic key in the door. Carbon cursed and stumbled as he entered. In the dim light rising from the street lamps below, she saw him flicking at the light switch. After several fruitless attempts, he teetered toward her in the semi-dark. Sitting on the edge of the bed, he struggled first with his shoelaces and then his buttons.

He finally lay down beside her and snuggled his chin to hers. The nauseating smell of beer and cigarettes permeated the air between them. Allie turned her head but his sour breath still brushed heavily across her nostrils. He tucked his cheek to her shoulder and began caressing her arm, gently for a minute and then more roughly. Rolling closer, he struggled for a moment with the buttons on her shirt and then thrust his hand inside her neckline. When the top button gave way, he cradled her breast, first through her bra and then skin to skin.

"Allie," he whispered, wiping her hair off her brow and moving in for a kiss. His lips hit the gag sealing her mouth and he pulled away and cursed. For a long while he struggled for balance but eventually he was astride her and working his fingers impatiently along the edges of the tape. Eventually, he freed a corner by her ear and ripped.

The tape tore her lips and scalp. "Stop it!" she cried. He dropped onto her, driving her hands into her belly and squeezing the air from her lungs. His lips and hands feverishly pried open her mouth.

She tilted her chin and pushed her head deeper into the pillow but his lips pressed tighter and his thick tongue drilled down her throat. She was suffocating, nauseous, unable to move and terrified she was about to die beneath him.

Carbon's knees drove into the soft flesh of her thighs and began prying apart her legs. The tie around her ankles cut deeper. When he finally lifted his mouth, she gulped a breath. "For Christ's sake," she gasped, "cut off these ties."

"I'm sorry," he slurred. Rolling to the side of the bed, he fumbled with his clothes on the floor.

With her breath now back, Allie began sobbing and circling her hands over her aching belly. "You said it wasn't your intentions, Carbon. You promised!"

He touched a finger to her lips. "Shush." She twisted away but he ignored her anger and began shaking his pants over the bed. "If I had a damned light I'd be able to find my knife."

"I told you, put the card key in the slot by the entrance to make the lights work." Carbon stumbled to the door, cursing as he went. When the foyer light finally came on he returned to the bed and switched on the table lamp. He found his knife in his pants pocket, flicked it open and began sawing the band around her wrists.

"You promised me," Allie moaned.

"Shush." He cut her hands and feet loose, sat on his heels and stared at her. Allie gently rubbed her swollen wrists and sore tummy as she continued sobbing. He pointed to her hands. "I'll massage for you," he said, reaching behind him for the courtesy lotion.

He lifted her hands from her stomach and pulled up her blouse. "No," she pleaded, shivering as the icy slime oozed across her belly. His fingertips touched her navel and a zing ripped through her body. "No!"

Under his massaging, the lotion slowly warmed. He squirted more on her arms and worked it around her wrists, his touch so light she could barely feel his hands even when they rubbed the raw marks left by the ties.

Interweaving his slick fingers with hers, he bent and quickly kissed her belly. "I feel badly about Saber doing this to you. I'll make it better." He slipped off her jeans, briefly massaged the welts on her ankles and then slid his palms higher—around her calves and over the bruises that just moments before his knees had left on her thighs.

Allie winced. "Carbon, no. You're raping me!"

"It's not like that. Roll over. I'll do your back."

"No!" She glanced at his knife lying open at her feet, glinting metallic against the white of the sheet. His eyes followed hers and locked onto the switchblade. She had so few choices.

Shivering, she rolled to her stomach and squeezed her eyes shut. It was a dark world behind her lids. She pretended it wasn't her lying motionless on the bed. It wasn't her bare back catching the draft as he drew up her shirt.

"Come on, Allie, don't be like this." Carbon kneaded the knot between her shoulders. "You have to admit this feels good." He nuzzled his lips to her ear. "It's not rape. It's seduction."

Her emotions were gone. Hidden. The pain was somewhere else.

"Tell me where you want me to massage. Am I rubbing too hard?" He moved his hands to her neck. "Here? Does this feel good?"

His weight shifted and Allie felt his hands at her feet and heard the click of the knife closing. Cold metal brushed her cheek as he dropped it by her pillow. He rubbed her neck. "Allie! Allie, does this feel good?"

A wrong answer from her, a wrong move and his passion could become fury. All she could think of was that with a flick of his fingers, the blade would end her life. "Yes," she said dully as his fingers dug between her shoulder blades. "It's okay."

He squirted more lotion into his hands. "How's this?" he asked, caressing her buttocks.

"No, Carbon. Please."

He tugged at her elbow. "Roll over and I'll do your front."

"I don't want to."

"It will feel good, I promise." He yanked her arm impatiently.

"I don't want to feel good."

"Yes, you do. Everybody wants to feel good. Come on! Let me make it up to you for what Saber's done." He curled his fingers between her and the knife.

She wanted to lie still. Sink deeper into the quiet. Let it be over. Die.

"Allie!" He tugged at her arm. She slowly turned over. He brushed at the strands of hair stuck to the tape remnants by her mouth. "If you want me to stop, I will."

However, before she could speak, his lips were clamped onto hers. He raised his hips, pressed her hand to his crotch and wrapped her fingers around his penis. "Like this," he said, forcing her to stroke. He again sealed his mouth to hers. In her hand, his penis swelled and moistened.

Still holding his kiss, he rolled to his back and pulled her with him. She did as he wanted until at last he released his kiss, groaned and flung his head to the side. With her hand still coiled around his penis, Allie sank against him, her cheek coming to rest on the soft hair of his chest.

"Can I come inside you?" he panted. The knife was still there, inches from her cheek. Glinting and cold.

"No."

"Please." He wrapped his arms around her middle and hugged her close.

"Please, no." He moaned in displeasure and shifted slightly, causing the knife to slide down to her hips. It stopped just shy of his fingertips. "Do you at least have a condom?" she bleakly requested.

"It's okay." He pushed her off him, rolled on top and began pumping briskly against her belly. Allie counted four thrusts and one quick kiss before the warm trickle of semen ran across her stomach and under the small of her back. "You're very good," he said, dropping onto her with a sigh. "You do that so well."

Allie jimmied her hands between their bellies and then up between their chests. "Please, move," she gasped. His breathing slowed and his shoulders relaxed onto hers. "Carbon!"

She frantically scratched at his ribs until he finally rolled off her. She lay very still, listening to the traffic outside the window, the muted steps in the hallway, his breathing slowing to the rhythm of sleep. When she heard a small snore, she grabbed her pants and headed for the shower.

Running the water as hot as she could, she scrubbed at her body with the small, abrasive Korean towel. She wanted to remove the semen, the lotion, his scent, her skin. Silent tears joined the water pounding down around her.

When she could take no more, she reluctantly switched off the shower and stepped from behind the curtain. Her clothes had been soaked by the water on its way to the drain so she tossed them into the garbage and wrapped herself in a towel. She'd washed it all away. It was gone. It hadn't happened.

She opened the bathroom door and looked around. She was simply in a room with a bed and it was night; time to sleep. Time to turn off the light and forget. As she stepped over Carbon's clothes to reach the lamp switch, her toe hit something hard. She looked down. The butt of a handgun was protruding from under his jeans.

Keeping her ears on Carbon's snoring, she very slowly knelt and pulled the revolver into the open. Gingerly laying it on her palm, she touched it with one finger. It was much heavier than she expected and much colder—colder than the knife. It was power. She walked to the table and, keeping her fingers far from the trigger, examined it.

She had no idea how to tell if it was loaded. She glanced at Carbon. He was on his back, sprawled across the width of the bed, still snoring. Here was her chance to escape.

She sucked in a deep breath. Whether it was loaded or not, she could pull the trigger and take the chance. It was worth it. She had no choice. Using both hands, she raised the gun and aimed at Carbon's heart. Slowly, slowly she slid her finger toward the trigger. Her heart pounded and her thoughts raced. Nearer to the trigger. Nearer. The metal was smooth and cold. Sweat dripped from her brow and stung her eyes.

She'd never used a handgun; didn't know how loud the shot would be. Would the noise bring Saber running? Would he knock down the door or perhaps shoot his way in? If he did, would she be able to get off a second shot to stop him? Was the gun even loaded? With only a single bullet or more?

Her hands started trembling violently. What if it wasn't loaded and Carbon heard the click of the trigger and woke?

She exhaled and set the gun on the table. She remembered Saber had cocked the hammer when he'd threatened her in the car. Did she have to do that before firing? She ran a nervous finger over the etching on the metal grip. Was there a safety switch somewhere she had to release? Saber's gun hadn't looked like this one, perhaps it hadn't even been a revolver. She couldn't remember, didn't know. But this was her chance; she had to try.

Other worries, though, kept her hands off the weapon. She couldn't begin to guess what would happen to her if she killed Carbon. Would anyone speak English well enough to understand her story? Maybe there wasn't such a thing as justified homicide in Korea. Maybe the law favoured men over women.

Her shower had washed away the evidence of rape and faded the red marks on her wrists and ankles. Would the bruises on her thighs and the tape and ties on the floor be enough to convince authorities the murder of a sleeping man was justified?

She finally got enough courage to again pick up the gun. She flipped it carefully from one palm to the other as she listened to Carbon snore. She needed it to feel more familiar, less frightening, so when she raised it, her shot would be steady and sure. The last thing she needed to do was merely wound the man. If she was going to shoot, it had to be for the kill. She hesitated.

Was life with Carbon and Saber a better fate than the life of a convicted killer in Korea? What was the Korean penalty for murder? A whipping? Capital punishment?

She set the gun on the table. It couldn't fire if she didn't pull the trigger—that much she knew. She also knew it was called a revolver because the cylinder holding the bullets revolved. If there were no bullets, she was wasting her worries. But if it was loaded, she needed to know how many shots would be hers to fire.

There was a tiny lever on the side. She wasn't sure if it was a safety lock or perhaps the latch needed to open the cylinder. With her eyes darting between her fingers and the trigger, she slowly slid the lever the way the arrow pointed. Nothing happened. She picked up the gun with her left hand and pushed against the cylinder. It moved slightly. She pushed harder and the cylinder swung open. Nestled in the chambers were two bullets.

Only two when there is room for six? It was as if Carbon knew whoever the bullets were for, wouldn't be returning fire. Perhaps that meant her and Saber were the intended victims. He'd catch them both by surprise when the mission was accomplished. When it was time for Carbon to return to Canada. Perhaps, at night, when they were both asleep.

She slowly rolled the cylinder closed and again eyed up Carbon, who was still snoring gently. Even if one of those bullets was meant for her, could she really kill someone? A siren wailed in the distance, the elevator dinged, someone rapped at the door across the hall. If she shot Carbon, would she be forfeiting a chance at an escape with far less serious consequences? Could she just leave instead? Put on some clothes and walk out into the Korean night?

Carbon quit snoring and rolled to face her, his eyelids fluttering as if he were struggling to wake—as if he knew she were there. She rose, slipped the revolver into her new purse and slid it under the bed. She gently moved Carbon's leg and arm and lay beside him. Would he remember in the morning where he'd left his gun in his drunken stupor? Would he ask her for it? Would she reach in her purse and pull it out and shoot him? If she shot Carbon, how would she deal with Saber? How would she deal with the police?

Wrapping herself tightly in the duvet, she shivered. Her teeth chattered. Silent tears fell.

"Allie, he raped you!" **Dr. Erica Freid**

"No. No, he didn't. He was drunk. It was just his clumsy attempt at seduction. He apologized later when he sobered up. It wasn't really rape. There was no...penetration."

"Honey, listen to me. Carbon sexually assaulted you. He had a weapon—"

"The knife wasn't a weapon. He'd used it to cut the ties. It was just there. It wasn't rape. I didn't like it, but it wasn't rape. He loved me so much and I was being an idiot about it and he was just trying to convince me and he was drunk. It wasn't an assault, okay? The next day, he let me keep the gun. A rapist wouldn't have done that. Only somebody who loves you would do that."

CHAPTER 11

Allie stopped to regain her breath and nervously looked behind her. Taking advantage of Carbon and Saber's reluctance to admit they couldn't keep up, she'd slowly pulled ahead of them on the steep mountain trail. They'd realized their mistake too late and now, with the gun in her purse and a switchback hiding her from their view, she was the freest she'd been in a long time.

She was well aware, though, that her freedom was fragile. There was no guarantee Carbon didn't have another gun and it was a certainty, Saber did. Although she might be able to outrun the men, she couldn't outrun bullets.

However, before she could outrun anything, she needed to catch her breath. She leaned against the metal balustrade and looked over the lush green countryside. She was above the neighbouring mountaintops and could see for miles. Gurgling water in the distance compelled her to peer through the bushes. At the bottom of a steep gully, she caught sight of a stream rushing over white rocks. She froze. It was the brook that had cradled her bones in her vision on the airplane.

She stared at the water, horrified. Images from her dream intertwined with the scene; shadows and bones writhed through the white rocks and stained the river red. It was here she would die. Today. Saber would come around the bend, shoot her and push her over the railing.

She quickly stepped away and felt for the revolver in her purse. Perhaps the gun was the talisman that would alter destiny and take her safely into tomorrow. She had to get much farther away from the men, though, and past the white rocks. She scurried up the trail, her feet pumping and her thoughts racing as she tried to plan her escape.

On her last visit to Korea she'd learned there was a fork in the trail ahead. One path led to their intended destination—the Hwanseondonggul limestone cave of Samcheok—while a second, less travelled path wound down the opposite side of the mountain. She was tempted to take that second trail—it seemed more secretive and safe. However, its grassiness suggested little wear and she was terrified she'd end up all alone in the Korean wilderness.

The alternative was to stick with the familiar and popular. She could keep her distance from the men and continue to the cave. Lights were strung inside to mark the walkways but she remembered there were plenty of dark corners. If she could avoid the notice of security officials and slip under the ropes into the shadows, she could watch for Carbon and Saber to pass and then retrace her steps and take off down the mountain. It would give her a good hour's lead on the men.

Or, she thought, moving aside to let a noisy group of school kids pass, she could chance the other path and...

The trail became steeper and her thoughts heavier. Allie paused at the fork and blinked away tears as she studied the map. With either of her escape plans, even if successful she'd end up at the foot of the mountain with a handgun the only thing of value in her purse—an item more likely to net her trouble than make her friends. The cave was remote and she had no money to buy a bus ticket to a city, hail a cab or make a phone call. With her Korean vocabulary limited to food items and etiquette phrases, she couldn't fathom what she'd do.

She reluctantly conceded that escaping in the Korean mountains was not viable. However, she at least wanted to be alive tomorrow. She squared her shoulders and continued her hike. Today, she would work at getting safely past the river with the white rocks.

* * *

"You might say I fucked her last night," Carbon said to Saber between pants. Both men leaned heavily against the railing and looked across at the green mountaintops, washed in blue by the distance.

"You either did or you didn't," Saber suggested dryly.

"She did me with her hand."

"This was something she wanted?"

"Perhaps." Carbon was still struggling to breathe. "If circumstances were different, I think me and her, you know..."

"Oh, I know, all right, but it ain't happening. I won't let it."

"I think she likes me. That night we first met, she stayed and had a drink. Rumour has it, she twice dropped restraining orders against me. She says she feels sorry my life didn't turn out the way I wanted it." Carbon inhaled deeply. "I think she likes me."

"If I had my way..." Saber pointed at the creek tumbling over white rocks at the bottom of the canyon. "That's where the bitch would be."

It was a long few minutes before their laboured breathing eased and the sound of the rushing water reached them. "She *is* going to end up dead," Saber continued. "I don't give a shit whether you fall for her or not. That cunt's dead meat before our three weeks here are up."

After another long silence, Carbon again started up the trail. "Yeah, I know."

"Does this goddamned mountain climbing have anything to do with last night's fuck?" Saber asked, chasing after him.

Carbon cast his eyes up the trail. It was switchback after switchback as far as he could see. He wondered how much higher he could climb. Although his gym workouts had given him muscle, his lungs and heart were struggling with the altitude and heat. After ten minutes, he stopped in front of a posted map of the trail. It was clear from the English translation the Hwanseondonggul limestone cave of Samcheok was still a kilometre climb. "Damn!"

"How much farther?" Saber panted behind him. "Still a long way to go?"

"Not just that, the trail splits here. Goes over the mountain and down the other side."

"What?" Saber roughly shoved Carbon away to get a better look at the map. "Which damned path did the cunt take?"

Carbon looked up both trails. The one to the cave was obviously the most travelled, the best maintained, with handrails and steps. The one to the left was nothing but a narrow line of dirt that reminded Carbon of a cow path. He cast a nervous glance behind him. As much as he hated to, he had no choice but to tell Saber. "She has my six-shooter," he admitted sheepishly.

"She what?" Saber removed his sunshades and stared at Carbon. Carbon shrugged and gave him half a grin. "This has something to do with the fuck, too," Saber guessed, putting his glasses back on.

"I'm pretty sure she doesn't know how to use it. Besides, I don't think she has it in her to shoot someone."

"You kidnap a woman, force her to hand fuck and don't think she has it in her to shoot you?"

Carbon ran his eyes up both inclines and then scanned the path behind them. A white woman alone here would stick out like a neon sign, a sign that would surely draw the attention of authorities, especially if she were to appear frantic. Unfortunately, attention on Allie meant attention on him and Saber. That would not bode well for their mission.

"You're not thinking she'll take that other trail around and come up and shoot us from behind?" Saber asked. Carbon shrugged. "She's in that good of shape? She could hike all that way and then up here again?"

"She's out there somewhere," Carbon said.

"I think today's her last day on this planet. You stupid son of a bitch. This might be *your* last fucking day, too."

Carbon threw his arms in the air. "Go ahead, shoot me. But guess what, pal? I got your passport. Think you might need it? Think you want to take a chance on reporting it stolen?"

Saber stared over Carbon's shoulder at the distant hills. "When I kill you, I'll get my passport."

"I'd rethink that if I were you. I don't have the passports on me. They're hidden and I ain't telling you where."

"That so?"

"Yup."

"I guess today's not my day then, is it? No passport and a goddamned bitch on the loose with a gun."

"Don't worry, she'll give it to me as soon as it scares her more than I do."

"Don't worry? Did you fucking say, 'Don't worry'?"

"You've been terrorizing her since day one and we're going to need her big time in Busan. I was trying to do right by her."

"Trying to do right by her? You think your dick in her hand is right for her?"

"It wasn't like that."

"Is the gun your payment for the hand job? A high-priced whore she's turnin' out to be!"

"You ever wonder why you can't get a woman, Sabe? Let me tell you. It's because you know shit-all about them. So shut up. Just shut the hell up!"

"I'll shut up when she's dead."

"That's not today. We need her. You take the trail to the left and I'll continue up to the cave. We'll both watch our backs. Meet you at the bottom."

"If I see her," Saber warned as he started up the path, "I'm shooting."

"The gun's not loaded," Carbon called. Saber stopped. "She thinks it is, but it's not." Saber turned and quickly strode toward Carbon, forcing him to step back. "Take it easy, buddy," Carbon said. "I removed the bullets when she wasn't looking. I'm testing her."

"Testing her or testing me?"

"I need to know what she'll do. Will she try shooting me or will she hand me the damned gun when I tell her to? I need to know that for Busan. I need to know if we can trust her."

"I don't care about your damned test. Don't care if the damned gun's not loaded. If she aims it at me, she's dead." He turned on his heel and headed up the trail.

"We'll need her in Busan," Carbon called.

* * *

Allie passed the entry gate to the cave and after a five-minute walk, slipped under the rope off the lit path and into the pitch black. The roar of the cavern river, wild from last month's monsoon, masked all footsteps and voices. She shivered as the cool musty air touched her skin. The revolver seemed a flimsy weapon against the immensity and gloom pressing against her.

Her fear of the darkness deepened and the river roared louder. Should someone grab her, no one would hear her screams. Just as her nerves were about to force her to the light, she spotted Carbon passing through the gate alone.

She steadied herself and when he finally walked by, she scurried toward the entrance and into the sunshine. She was now out of the cave but where the hell was Saber? Her heart quickened. She took a few hesitant steps down the path, afraid because the lush vegetation blocked her view of what lay around the next corner. Clutching her purse tighter, she fingered the clasp. Despite being armed, she was very vulnerable—to Saber, to the police, to the white rocks.

She squared her shoulders. She had a gun and was out of sight of the men. *I ought to be feeling powerful.* She started down the path, intent on getting safely past the white rocks and to the parking lot where the tourist busses stopped. Behind her, or beside her in the bushes she wasn't sure, a dog growled menacingly. A few feet ahead, around the bend and behind the trees, laboured footfalls steadily approached; they sounded like those of a large man—someone the size of Saber. Branches cracked.

Allie looked about frantically, there seemed to be danger everywhere. She raced to the cave and stood nervously outside the entrance. Without Carbon beside her, she could be just moments from possible death.

Whether or not I have a gun, I need the man. She spotted a bench against the granite wall of the mountain and took a seat in the shade...and waited.

CHAPTER 12

"If I'd known at the time what was going on in Carbon's head, I would've been totally unafraid." **Allison Montgomery**

"What do you think was going on in Carbon's head?" **Dr. Erica Freid**

"Oh, I can't say. It's all covert gang business, stuff he told me in confidence. That man totally trusted me. I am NOT going to betray him by telling his secrets."

As soon as he emerged from the cave, Carbon spotted her and casually walked over. He pointed to her purse, snapped his fingers and held out his hand. Allie passed him his revolver and followed him down the mountain. They waited a long, silent hour in the parking lot for Saber.

"You fucking bitch," he greeted coolly when he finally arrived.

Carbon draped an arm about Allie's shoulders and wordlessly herded them onto the bus. She was so disappointed in herself, at her cowardice, at her lack of ability to formulate an escape plan. She hated the fact Carbon had simply snapped his fingers and she'd passed him the gun. She was angry she'd let him wrap his arm around her and that she was now, on her own accord, resting her head on his shoulder.

The exertion and humidity had exhausted her and left her wringing wet. The whir of the air-conditioner was comforting and its coolness, a gift. During the one-hour return trip to their new hotel in Samcheok, she thought of little, dozed a bit and felt utterly defeated. Once in her room, she fell onto the bed.

"Tomorrow, Busan," Carbon said, stripping off his shorts and shirt. He left his boxers on and flopped beside her.

When she turned to look at him, he'd already closed his eyes and slowed his breathing. He'd soon be asleep and she'd be alone. What would she think about? There were no plans to be made. No goals to reach. There was nothing in her future. Nothing.

"First, Sinnam," she said loudly. She could at least plan that. He'd seemed interested in the Penis Park in the bar in Canada. Perhaps a green hillside sprouting phallic carvings would take the rough edges off him and Saber.

"No! Straight to Busan."

"Sinnam. You can't tell me you came all the way to South Korea and you're not going to visit the Penis Park."

"I can tell you that," Carbon replied, his voice drifting. "After today's cave adventure, I'm not taking any more of your travel advice."

"You didn't like the cave?"

"The cave was fine, nice and cool. It was the climb that was the problem." He turned on his side to face her. "And you, taking off like you did. Don't ever fucking do that again."

"Okay," she said quickly. He yawned and stretched. His jaw relaxed and his eyes again slid closed. "Why Busan?" she asked.

"Fourth largest cargo port in the world." He drew her to him, wrapping his heavy arm around her middle. "About last night, I wanted to make you feel better. It was okay for you, wasn't it?"

"It didn't make me feel better."

"If I hadn't been so drunk—"

Allie pushed his arm off her and sidled away. "Not bloody likely."

"Stay close to me tomorrow. If Saber had found you today, you would've been dead." Carbon lightly brushed her cheek but Allie batted his hand away.

"I know," Allie said. "I'd have been dead on the white rocks in the canyon."

Carbon's eyes opened wide and he quickly lifted himself onto his elbow. "How the hell would you know what Saber said about the white rocks? Were you spying on us?"

"I just know. Like I know you killed six men."

"You bitch!" Carbon whacked his palm across her cheek and rose to his knees, fully prepared to strike her again.

She covered her face with her arms. "What the hell are you doing?" He was off the bed and flinging her to the floor before she could protest further.

"Are you in with the Shadow Riders?" he roared. "Is that what the hell this is about?"

She tried to stand but he kicked at her knees. "What are you talking about?" she cried.

"Are you pals with Jacobs? Reporting to him what we're doing here?"

Allie scrambled away from his feet. "I don't know any Jacobs or any Shadow Riders!"

"I'll tell you what I'm talking about!" He grabbed her arms and hauled her up to face him. "Nobody besides Riders and Jackals know what the hell went down, so how can you tell me *you* know? I'm damned certain it wasn't a Jackal who told you."

"A Jackal?" His fingers dug into her shoulders and his thumbs inched toward her windpipe. As she stared into his fiery eyes, the images in her vision clicked with his words. Splashes of red blood. Shadows. White Rock. "The Shadow Riders biker massacre near White Rock, B.C.," she gasped. "I remember following it on the news." His expression was cold—no guilt, no fear. "You're the mass murderer they never caught?"

"How the hell would you know that?"

She pried at his fingers. "I don't know how I know." He didn't loosen his grip. "Carbon, I really don't know. No one's told me anything. It's just...on the plane. When I was drugged–I had this vision—"

"On the plane?" His features softened and he released his hold. Allie nodded.

"I thought you were passed out on the plane," he said. "Were you just pretending?"

"I wasn't pretending. I was out of it, Carbon. I had this vivid dream. There were white rocks and rolling dice and—"

"Roland Eisman? What about him? What the fuck did you dream about him?"

"Not Roland Eisman! Rolling dice and a canyon..." The name sounded familiar, perhaps Roland was one of the murder victims. Although the police had never released much information about the massacre, she thought she recalled the victims' names being in the headlines. Rollie Eisman...and perhaps, a Rod or Robert Canyon. It had been years ago, though.

"You heard Saber and I talking, didn't you?"

"No. I told you, I had this dr—did I? Were you talking about the murders on the plane while I was sleeping?" Carbon tilted his head. The red, the bones, the shadows. The white rocks...Roland Eisman. Six skeletons. It had not been a dream foreshadowing her death; her drugged subconscious had simply been matching images to the men's words about the massacre.

The terrifying reality struck her. "You killed six men." Allie covered her mouth. She thought the news had said there were five victims but Carbon didn't argue. He just heaved a sigh of relief.

"Fuck, woman, don't make me think the Riders set me up to have you spy on me." He stepped around her and reached for his cigarettes on the table. "Don't scare me like that." He lit one and inhaled deeply.

"You're a member of the Jackals biker gang?" Allie asked numbly. "What the hell does a Jackal want in Korea?"

He took a seat at the table and motioned her to join him. "You want to know? You really want to know?"

"Yes, I want to know." She slid into the chair opposite him.

He pushed his pack of cigarettes to her. "Want one?"

"I don't smoke."

"You should." Carbon inhaled. "It's true what they say; it kills the pain. Better than cocaine."

Allie shoved the cigarettes back at him. "I prefer Tylenol for pain."

"Other kind of pain." He blew a smoke ring and watched it float between them. When it dissipated, he cranked open the window and looked to the lights lining the shore of the East Bada. The sleepy sound of the night surf washed over them. "Other kind of pain."

Allie became acutely aware she was in a room with a mass murderer, listening to the sea. Watching smoke rings. She slid her quaking hands under her thighs. "What does a Jackal want in South Korea?" she asked again.

"Do you want to be a Jackal?" He took another drag on the cigarette and exhaled. "I'm thinking you do. I think you're looking for something in your life, something besides a group of giggly bitter women who once a week drink too many *Bacardi Breezers*."

He killed six men. He was studying her; waiting for her answer. "Maybe," Allie said.

"Maybe?" He inhaled, set his cigarette in the ashtray and blew another smoke ring. It floated slowly inward on the warm ocean breeze.

"What does it mean to be a Jackal?" she asked. "If it means killing people..." He cocked his head and looked at her. "I have no idea how to ride a motorbike," she said.

He grinned. "As a woman, you'd just sit on it. Think you could handle that?"

He was doing it again—flashing his brilliant, satanic eyes at her, inviting her into his soul. Providing she gave up hers first. Perhaps, offering her survival. *What the hell ARE his eyes saying?* Allie shrugged and quickly looked down at the table.

"As far as the killing part," he continued, "I'm done with that, man. Done with that. It's what I got Saber for now."

"Ah, that's what Saber's for."

"He doesn't mind. He's the right kind of guy for that shit." Carbon stopped talking. Stopped smoking. Just sat there, staring out the window at a night time ocean that couldn't be seen.

"You aren't, are you? Never were the right kind of guy to kill."

"I didn't say that."

"Your mama didn't raise you a killer, did she?"

"Don't talk about my mama!"

"Don't worry, I didn't listen to my mama, either." Allie reached for his cigarettes. She plucked one out and rolled it between her fingers. "'Don't marry that boy!' she told me. But, I did. 'Don't open the door to strangers!' and I did. Tell me..." She poked at the filter end of the cigarette. "If I hadn't opened the door to you and Saber that day, would you have busted it down and come in and got me?"

"Maybe," Carbon answered quietly, staring into her eyes. "You have no idea how much I wanted you, from the first moment I saw you in the tavern. Remember that night? It was magical for you, too, wasn't it?"

His deep, even voice is magical. His smile. "I don't... Maybe."

"Ah, come on. You liked me, more than your girlfriends. They left and you stayed for another drink."

A cold gust of wind whipped the curtain around Allie's head. She pulled it off her face and when she looked at him, the enchantment was gone. "Seems to me, you forced me to stay with you for another drink."

"Forced you?" Carbon raised his eyebrows as if amused. "Is that the way it always is for you? I forced you? I raped you? Do you ever do anything consensual with a man?"

"You're twisting things!"

"Think about what I'm offering," Carbon continued lightly. "You and I, in Canada straddling a Harley this fall. The rhythm of the road, the power of the pistons."

She slouched in her chair and scowled. "And guns and murder. I've heard about bikers—the drugs, the money, the bribes."

"Something like that." A grin creased his face. "You know a lot. Are you sure you don't have any connection to the Shadow Riders?"

"Don't keep saying that! I was born and raised a farm girl and spent the last thirty years typing and answering phones. I can't tell a Harley from a moped."

"Would you like to learn?" He picked up his lighter and motioned her to put the cigarette in her mouth.

She hesitated. *I need something. Anything. He killed six men.* The filter felt cottony between her lips. He clicked his lighter and she inhaled deeply as she had watched him do, and waited for the pain to disappear.

CHAPTER 13

"Allie, did you think about what I asked you last night?" Carbon inquired as they packed for the trip to Busan.

She rummaged in the suitcase, looking for something although she didn't know what. "What did you ask me?" She didn't want to think about last night, didn't want to go to Busan, and nothing fit right in the suitcase. She took out the clothes she'd just packed and spread them on the bed. The cigarette had not eased the pain last night; it had made her lightheaded and nauseous. Carbon had laughed at her and carried her to the bed.

"What the hell are you doing?" Carbon's rough voice cut into the memories. "You're supposed to be packing, not making a God damned mess!"

"I'm trying to pack. Nothing fits right. I need my own suitcase."

'I feel your hurt,' Carbon had said last night, stroking her arm. 'Your husband leaving you, tore your heart right out, didn't it? I can't believe he'd crawl in bed with another woman when he had you.' Allie had pushed his hand off her and told him that was none of his business.

'No, it's not my business.' He'd touched his lips lightly to her forehead. 'Perhaps if we do something consensual, it might work better than the cigarette to ease the pain. What do you think?' The world had begun spinning.

'Just a massage,' he'd said, 'to relax you. No sex.'

'Let's just sleep. It's a very long bus ride tomorrow.'

'All the more reason to relax and get a good night's sleep. You just lie there and you can fall asleep while I massage you. Think how good it will feel.' He'd rubbed her shoulders. 'You can lay on your stomach if you want.'

He'd massaged her neck, ran his fingers along the band of her panties. At some point his hands slid up her hips, around the curve of her waist—his fingertips brushed the sides of her breasts.

She'd rolled over, reached her arms around his neck and pulled him to her for a kiss. He'd pried at her lips with his tongue and she'd opened for him.

She'd been ill from the cigarette, fatigued—hurting. Later, sometime in the future, when she was safer, she'd think about it. Reconsider, perhaps.

They'd done it, gently. Slowly. He'd even paused to put on a condom. She'd fallen asleep in his arms.

"Answer me!" Carbon slammed the suitcase closed and grabbed both her wrists.

This morning, it had all seemed different; she'd betrayed herself for reasons that were vague and surreal. She'd stood in the hot, hot shower for almost an hour, scrubbing. When she finally dried off and wiped the steam from the mirror, she saw the marks across her cheek. He'd thrown her off the bed, slapped her, kicked her knees...and she'd made love to him. What kind of woman did that? Perhaps the pain from her bruises was well-deserved.

Carbon tightened his grip on her wrists. "Last night I asked you if you wanted to become a Jackal." She looked over her shoulder at the wall mirror. The redness from the slap had ebbed but the swelling hadn't. Faint blue outlined where each finger had hit.

"Oh," Allie said. "Yes. That question."

He dropped her hands and stepped away. "Well?"

She unfolded a skirt, shook it and held it between her and the window. It was much too short for a woman her age. However, Korean women were tiny and she hadn't yet found a shop that carried Western sizes. She folded the skirt and opened the suitcase. Carbon said he liked short skirts. Said she had great legs. She should not have made love to him.

"Do you want to get home alive or not?" Carbon reached into the suitcase and fumbled through his shirt pockets until he found his knife. *He's threatening me.*

He flicked it open and casually ran his finger along the blade then pretended to clean under his thumbnail. "Well?"

"I could just say yes and I'd automatically become a Jackal? I thought you had to do more than that."

"You'd be with me."

"You're sure the Jackals want me?"

"You lied to me last night." Carbon held the knife point-outward, between them—just inches from her gut—casually, as a writer might hold a pen when pausing for conversation. "You haven't been typing and answering telephones for the past thirty years. You've been running the office of the biggest importer/exporter west of Toronto."

"That's an exaggeration. Could you please put your knife away, it's making me nervous."

"No one tells me to put my knife away." His hand moved ever so slightly toward her.

"Fuck, Carbon! What is it you want?" She threw her skirt into the suitcase.

"You had a large Asian clientele, you know the ropes. Know the paper work. Bet you know a hell of a lot about getting things into and out of Korea."

"I was a glorified secretary. That's all." *He needs me! Thank God, he needs me.* Allie rapidly re-packed her clothes. "It was my husband's company. I could give myself whatever job title I wanted. I wasn't, in truth, managing much of anything. I made sure we always had coffee for the staff room and paper for the copier."

"Fuck, I hate it when I'm lied to." His arm muscles were taut and quivering. *He's angry that he needs me.*

She made a dismissive motion with her hand. "Please, put that thing away. Yeah, yeah. Put my name down to become a damned Jackal."

"Yeah, yeah?" Carbon clicked the knife closed and shoved it into his pocket. "I was hoping it would mean a bit more to you than that."

"How the hell did you get that thing past airport security, anyway?"

"You think you get to know all my secrets the moment you say, 'Yeah, yeah'?"

"You seem to know all my secrets."

"It's my job to know your secrets." He swept up the suitcase and stormed out.

CHAPTER 14

"What happened in the noraebang, Allie?" **Dr. Erica Freid**
"It was just a noraebang. I sang." **Allison Montgomery**
"What happened that night?"
"I just sang. The sun was setting on the ocean. Korea is almost entirely surrounded by the ocean. Miles of shoreline. It was kind of obvious if Carbon wanted to smuggle stuff into Korea, with the right planning, it wouldn't be hard."
"What did you sing?"
"I sang..."
"Yes?"
"I sang a song."

"Careful!" Allie warned, pushing against Carbon. An electric scooter puttered past them on the sidewalk.

"Christ," Carbon complained. "Those damned things are everywhere."

It was a soft summer evening and he was walking close to her, his arm brushing hers with each stride. "Actually, those 'damned things' are only in the cities. They're not allowed out of town." The conversation—so casual. His body—so close. As his arm swung toward her, she caught his hand in hers. *If I give him everything he wants...*

Carbon squeezed her fingers. "I can understand why they're restricted. Damned nuisance is what they are."

"Nothing with two wheels is allowed outside the urban centres. Not motorbikes, either."

"Why not?"

"Damned if I know." *Can a biker gang function without bikes?*

Carbon dropped Allie's hand and wrapped his arm about her shoulder. "So, this is Busan."

It had been a very long ride down the coast to get here. They'd eaten a quick supper and when twilight had brought a semblance of coolness, the three of them had decided to stroll along the sea. A refreshing evening breeze blew in over the water. *If he falls in love with me…*

"It's so peaceful." Allie tugged at his sleeve to stop. The coolness had brought hordes of city dwellers down to the sand. Old and young alike, families, seniors, and lovers mingled unperturbed. Flashing through the falling darkness were the displays of the vendors selling light-sticks and sparklers.

She pointed to a bridge in the distance. "Look, Carbon. Koreans like lights." Small bulbs lit the entire structure; their dazzling colours glinted off the water below. "Entire walls of some of the downtown buildings are lit up and I'll have to show you the street decorations. There are so many lights it puts Canada's Christmas efforts to shame."

"It's pretty," Carbon agreed, rubbing her neck.

"It's so clean. No broken bottles. No rowdy drunks. No garbage lying around. A city of three point eight million and you feel safe walking at night."

"Safe except for these damned scooters." Carbon pulled Allie out of the path of another moped. "They're allowed to drive on sidewalks?"

Allie pointed to a car parked on the sidewalk, snuggled against a storefront. "Vehicles do, too." She pulled at Carbon's elbow and stepped into the crosswalk. "We're going to go to a noraebang."

"What the hell is a noraebang?" He looked at Saber, ten feet behind them. Despite the deepening dusk, he was still wearing his dark glasses.

"A noraebang is a singing room," Allie said. "A private karaoke session."

"Singing? I don't think so." Carbon yanked her back onto the sidewalk.

"You'll enjoy it—beer, cigarettes, a little English music."

"It's a no, Allie."

She looked up at him through her lashes. "There's more to it," she said. "I can promise you'll enjoy the scenery."

"Scenery?" A grin was teasing at his lips. "What kind of scenery, beautiful Korean women?"

"Better than that."

"What's better than that?"

"You'll see." She again tugged at his arm. He sighed and reluctantly followed her across the street.

She ordered two beers for each of them and an English songbook and then followed the host to their noraebang. The twelve by seven foot room offered comfortable bench seats, a table with ashtrays, overhead monitors at each end of the room and two microphones. The entire south wall was a window overlooking the sea.

The host bowed his head and left and Allie opened the songbook. "Who's going first?"

"Like fuck." Saber reached for a beer with one hand and his cigarettes with the other.

"What's your poison?" Allie continued. "Country? Folk? Rock? The Blues?"

"If you sing, woman," Saber droned, "you better damned-well sing good."

Carbon stared at the bada where the remnants of daylight silhouetted the boats lingering in its water. He nudged Saber.

"Told you that you'd like the scenery," Allie said.

"Big ship out there," Carbon commented.

"Yeah, and little boats coming in to shore."

If Carbon was looking to establish trade with Southeast Asia, Korea was ideal. Allie had learned through her time with Mahogany Imports that having options always gives one power, and South Korea had options, with a coastline on three sides, a culture in turmoil, one of the world's largest ports under massive expansion, and possible mob influence down on the docks...options.

One of those options was out the window. In the international water of the open seas, a ship could offload illicit cargo to a hundred little fishing boats like those now lazily returning to shore. One could unobtrusively pimp those fishing boats with powerful motors, high tech guidance systems, state of the art communicators. Plus, she knew what Carbon could offer to make even the most honest and upright fisherman become an ocean runner for him.

"It's such a quiet beach," she said. He turned to her and she stared into his face, looking for answers. Is this what he wanted?

"Hmmm," Carbon said noncommittally.

There was also a way to bypass customs and inspections at the docks—if one were powerful enough. Persuasive enough. If one were to play one's cards right. "The main reason the beach is clean and safe," Allie said, leaning toward the men, "is there's not much of a drug problem here." She paused and licked her lips. "Just wondering what is it the Jackals want to import to Korea."

Saber slammed his beer to the table and, facing Carbon, slowly rose. "You told the bitch?" His monotone voice hit the acoustic tiles and vanished.

"Allie!" Carbon scolded, glaring at her as if she'd revealed a secret.

Her breath left her. Without the approval of the Jackals' assassin, Carbon's promise to get her back to Canada was likely a very empty one.

Saber slowly slid his hand under his jacket. The faint sound of Korean voices singing two rooms over touched the thickening quiet.

"Allie," Carbon instructed, rising. He reached over and flicked at Saber's wrist. His hand reappeared empty. "Practise singing your favourite song so when we return you can do it up good for our buddy, here." He drove his fist into Saber's chest and pushed him roughly toward the exit. "Let's you and I talk."

Allie kept her eyes on the men until they disappeared. She closed the songbook, rested her chin on her hands and stared out at the ocean, now masked in black.

"What happened in the noraebang, Allie?" **Dr. Erica Freid**

"I think...that was the night..." **Allison Montgomery**

"Were things different after that night?"

"I think...maybe it was the night we learned to love each other."

"Did you learn to love or did you give up, Allie?"

"Give up? What do you mean, 'give up?' There was nothing to 'give up'. We learned to trust each other that night. I had nothing to 'give up'."

"Carbon made you feel you had nothing left to fight for? That without him, you were nothing?"

"You're making things up. That's not at all what happened. That night in the noraebang, we learned how to love. Don't make it sound dirty. It wasn't dirty. It was beautiful."

CHAPTER 15

"Don't you fucking ruin this for me!" Carbon threw Saber against the wall and wrapped his hands around his neck. "I'm an inch from having her at my beck and call and you come up with shit like that."

"Your beck and call?" Saber scoffed. "She ain't nowhere near your beck and call."

"Wanna make a bet?" Carbon tightened his grip.

"She's feigning it. First chance she gets, she bolts. She talks. I don't think you want her knowing anything you don't want repeated to the cops."

"She's breaking fast, pal," Carbon answered evenly. "She wouldn't have brought us here to look at the boats if I hadn't told her what it is I'm after. She's aiming to please...and I like it."

"You like it?" Saber wrenched Carbon's hands off his neck. "You're liking it a bit too much. You're falling for her, Carb."

"That's not the problem, here. Never has been. Love 'em and leave 'em, I've done it all many times."

"This one's different, Carb. She's making problems for you. I can smell it. I'm warning you...she ain't coming back with us and if you don't watch your step, you won't be either."

Carbon grabbed Saber's shoulder. "Go ahead and tell me all you want that she's ending up dead and I don't give a shit, but once more...just threaten *me* one more fucking time and we'll see who ends up dead."

Saber broke Carbon's grasp and stepped aside. "You haven't got it in you. You burned yourself out with the Shadow Riders. I know what happened to you after that hit." He lowered his voice to a touch above a whisper. "Why the hell do you think they sent me here with you?"

"You little shit! You're here so *I* can keep an eye on *you*!" He stabbed his finger at Saber's face. "If you return without me, you're dead before you say your last amen. I took out the Riders for the Jackals; they wouldn't look kindly on some upstart taking me out. I have friends in low places and high places. You've got no friends in any fucking place."

When she heard the men at the door, Allie quickly dried her tears and straightened. "The Russian mob," she said lightly, "has headquarters down by the docks. An entire Little Russia set up there. Even Russian signs in neon on their storefronts."

"Interesting," Carbon said. He motioned Saber onto the bench ahead of him. "You'll have to take us there tomorrow." He gazed at Allie across the table. "Do you have your song ready?"

"Yes," she said, hastily plugging numbers into the computer. "A little something for you, done up good."

She stood and wound her fingers around the microphone cord. As the intro music began, she widened her stance and slowly raised the microphone to her lips. The lyrics for '*I don't know how to love you*' from the movie *Dispassionate Lies* began rolling on the screen. She raised her chin and clasped the mike with both hands.

"*I don't know how to love you, it's tearing me apart...*" Carbon lit a cigarette, relaxed in his chair and zeroed his eyes in on hers. "*Should I love you with my being? Should I love you with my heart? My soul? Love you out loud, let the whole world know?*"

CHAPTER 16

"There's lots of construction going on," Carbon noted to Allie as they sat in the morning sunshine at their hotel room table. A map of red veins embroidered the whites of his eyes and he still smelled of beer.

"Yes," she answered. He'd come home very drunk last night and hadn't made it off the floor and into the bed until the sun was up.

"Office towers or apartments?" he asked.

She'd seen him cry last night. She'd heard him talk about the Shadow Riders massacre—six dead men and his troubled soul. This morning it was easier to answer his questions; he was no longer just a biker, a gangster, a murderer. He was a hurting human being.

"Many new buildings are a combination workplace and living space," she said. "There's a lot of shit happening to this culture right now." He'd personally known one of his victims.

"How so?"

"If you're looking to bribe someone, Carbon, don't offer American dollars. Offer them a western education for their kids. That's the strongest currency. Fathers are putting in eighty-hour workweeks to earn enough to send their kids to Canada or the States for education. Thus, the combination towers. Living quarters attached to the offices–so they can catch their catnaps, before hitting their desks again."

"Yeah?" Carbon said, eyeing her up. "What else?"

She'd been right that his mama hadn't raised him a murderer. His babble last night proved he was too gentle for what the Jackals had called upon him to do. He was a broken man. She now knew beneath the tattoos, beyond the slap of his hands and the glare in his eyes—inside his heart, Carbon was not an evil man. "What else? Hmmm..."

Though she didn't know the Korean language, on her last visit here her friend's daughter, a keen sociologist, had taught her a lot about the culture.

"Then the kids come home and don't show their parents any respect. You know, return with a Western attitude. Dad's exhausted, peeved his efforts appear unappreciated and the beatings set in. Adding to the misery is the tradition of the eldest son looking after the parents–and sometimes the in-laws, too."

"Lots of people in all generations hurting," Carbon mused.

"Yeah, hurting." *Hurting like you.*

"Younger generation," Carbon asked, "mesmerized by the West?"

"Ambivalent. They want to be like us, but it's a bit different than in other developing nations, perhaps. It's not so much they envy us, respect us, or feel inferior to us. It's as if they feel they deserve everything we have and are fully capable of getting it. If you listen closely to their music, the first two lines of almost every song you hear are in English–the rest is in Korean. That's symbolic of the entire cultural shift."

"Forty-seven-point-six million unhappy people," Carbon said, catching Allie's eyes and holding them.

"Yeah, and the Russian mob controlling the docks." Carbon continued to stare at her as if he wanted to say something but didn't know if he should. She boldly met his gaze. "You want to import some feel-good medication for those unhappy throngs?"

"I never said that."

"No, you didn't. You never say much of anything. Seems I do most of the talking. What am I talking myself into, Carbon? Isn't it time there was a bit of a two-way thing happening here?"

"The less you know, the safer you are." Carbon watched his smoke ring waft toward the ceiling. "And the more I know, the safer you are."

"I see."

"What do they do now to ease the pain, besides beat on the kids?"

Allie shrugged. "I didn't see much happening. Mind you, I didn't make a point of going to places which might reveal that side of life here. There seems to be a lot of Soju and duplex barber poles."

Carbon squinted at her. "What do you mean?"

"If you see two barber poles in close proximity, it indicates a whorehouse. At least that's what I was told. You never seem to see the girls on the street, though, except perhaps in Little Russian quarters. Soju is what you see the men drinking out of the green bottles. It's their favourite liquor. Someone told me it's made from rice. Foreigners call it Korean saké or Korean vodka. It's pretty strong stuff." Carbon held out a cigarette. She shook her head. He was watching her intently. "This is all pretty irrelevant," she said.

"Not really."

"Probably the same stuff you learned in Seoul from the American soldiers."

Carbon chuckled. "But you tell it better."

"What have you been doing on your nightly sojourns?"

"Just scouting. I was told it was a tough market, but you make it sound easy."

"Have you checked into the penalty for drug trafficking? It's not easy, Carbon."

"Desperate people are always easy." His words hung in the air, thick and heavy. She shifted uncomfortably. "If the Russians can do it," he added, "no reason the Jackals can't."

"I didn't mean to make it sound easy. You can't just look at the desperation. You have to consider the pride of these people. Their independence. Their family values."

"The Americans are a proud, independent nation," Carbon argued. "Most of our best customers reside south of the forty-ninth."

"This is different. You know the American culture inside and out. You don't even know the language here."

"Neither do you, yet you did business here. The south east Asian market was a going concern for Mahogany Imports."

"But not until we'd spent a lot of time establishing contacts. It didn't just happen."

"Are you saying Jackals can't establish contacts?"

"I can't see it being easy for a biker gang."

"Don't fret, it's been in the works for a while now."

"What do you mean, 'in the works'?"

"It's not like I'm walking into this cold. I know what I'm doing." Carbon inhaled deeply, cast his eyes to the ceiling and puffed a stream of blue rings.

"You have Asian contacts here?"

Carbon shrugged.

"At home?"

"I have contacts everywhere."

"Are the Jackals in with the Asian gangs in Canada?"

"I didn't say that."

"You didn't have to say it."

"Perhaps I just meant I have you to help me. Besides, there are drugs here. It's not like I'm going where no one has gone before."

"Just because anabolic steroids are available over the counter, it doesn't mean other street drugs are easy to come by."

"Steroids are available over the counter?" Carbon snickered. "Do Korean's not buy them or do they just not work well for them? I've yet to see a man with arms thicker than broomsticks."

"Don't judge ferocity by size."

"Survival of the fittest." Carbon grinned at her. "Want another coffee?"

Allie drained her cup and passed it to him. "Can I come with you?" she asked.

He walked to the hot water dispenser. "Come with me where?"

"To the Russian docks. I know some Russian."

He filled her cup and set it before her. "Do you know enough Russian to be my interpreter?"

"What would I be interpreting?"

"Things like 'Good day' and 'How are you?'"

"Carbon, they're not going to want to share their sea port with you."

"How do you know until you ask?"

"It would be like asking a pit-bull to share his bone! And you're very likely to get the same kind of response."

"If you ask before you touch, it isn't likely you'll get eaten."

"You're going to touch, though, Carbon. They'll know that. Asking their permission first will just give them time to sharpen their teeth."

"I'll drop some names. Some dollars. Let them know I'm a friend."

"You're friends with the Russian mob?"

Carbon shrugged. "Either way, a kennel of pit-bulls ain't no match for a pack of Jackals. Do you know how to say that in Russian?"

"You're taking me with you?"

"I don't see why not."

Allie struggled to conceal her surprise, she didn't want to give him any reason to think he ought to reconsider. The more he needed her, the safer she was. His offer to include her confirmed he realized something had transpired in the noraebang.

He'd pasted his sinister, dazzling eyes on her as she'd serenaded him. When the song had ended, she'd lowered the microphone. In the silence, with the wall of black windows behind him, with his lips gentle and his dimple showing, dark magic had fused their souls.

"Tomorrow, after visiting the docks, what would you like to do?" he suddenly asked.

"How about we go to the Busan Aquarium? It's awesome! And then, if you don't mind, could we buy some swimwear? The beach is right there and last trip I wanted so badly to go for a dip, but it was raining."

Carbon grinned. "Yeah, we'll do that." He prepared two cups of instant coffee and passed one to her.

"Just the two of us?" Allie asked.

He took a swig from his cup and peered over the brim. "Would you like that?" he asked quietly.

"I would."

"I'll see what I can do."

CHAPTER 17

Allie was relieved to see Carbon enjoying the aquarium. He was finally rising above the dour mood he'd been in since yesterday's tense visit to the Russian docks. She laid her head on his shoulder and reached for his hand.

He pointed to the feeding frenzy in the piranha tank. "Look, Allie! Watch. Look at them!" In seconds, the food was gone and peace returned to the tank. Carbon kept his eyes on the fish. "I didn't know piranhas were so small. They're scarcely bigger than guppies."

"I told you not to judge ferocity by size." Allie tugged at Carbon's hand and nodded to the glass roof. "On the other hand, do you see what's above us?" Two full-sized hammerheads were circling them.

Carbon wrapped a protective arm over her shoulder. "Don't worry. I'll keep you safe."

The crowd around the piranha tank parted for an elderly Korean couple. They hobbled, hand in hand, directly toward Allie and Carbon, their eyes fixed on the fish. Allie tugged at Carbon's hand. "Move!" she whispered.

"Why?"

"If you don't move, they'll walk right into you."

"Oh." Carbon retreated quickly and the couple planted themselves where he had been.

"As a privilege of aging, they get to watch whatever they want when they want," Allie explained.

"I want to grow old in Korea," Carbon said.

Having been distracted from the fish by the couple, Carbon now seemed restless. His eyes roved the walls ahead, as if seeking an exit. "Have you seen enough?" Allie asked.

Carbon nodded. "Are you anxious to try on your bikini?" he asked.

"It's not a bikini. It's a two-piece bathing suit."

"You didn't answer my question," he chided.

"You didn't answer mine, either."

Carbon chuckled. "I've forgotten your question, so, I'll answer mine. Yes, I'm anxious to see you in your bikini."

"Carbon!"

He laughed again and reached for her hand. Allie pointed to a sign above the doorway. "See the little green stick man running? That's the symbol for 'exit'. If you ever need to find a quick way out, follow the little green men."

"I'll remember that."

* * *

Allie stood before the mirror in the beach bathroom sizing up her revealing two-piece. A discomforting feeling of shyness swept over her. She sucked in her stomach and once again viewed herself from all angles. If she could ensure Carbon stayed smitten with her...

As soon as she entered the sunshine, his eyes were on her. Heat soared up her torso and reddened her cheeks. "Wow," he said. "Turn around."

Allie ran the six steps to him and buried her face in his chest. "I shouldn't have bought it."

He pushed her away, his eyes dreamily caressing her cleavage and then skimming down the bold yellow piping outlining the curves of her hips. "Why not?" he asked.

Very few of the locals on the beach were in swimwear, making Allie feel even more naked. She hugged her clothes to her heart and hung her head. "It's too skimpy. It's not me!"

Carbon gave an appreciative sigh. "It's you." He tugged her to him and slipped his fingertips beneath her waistband. Pressing his lips to her ear he whispered, "All of you."

Allie desperately surveyed the canopy of colourful umbrellas smothering the beach. "It's so crowded."

"We can find room. Should I rent an umbrella?"

"No," Allie said quickly, tossing her clothes to the sand. "I'm not into sunbathing. I just want to go for a quick dip to cool down and then get dressed."

Carbon pulled her tight to him. "I don't think I'll let you get dressed."

She broke free and splashed into the East Bada. As soon as she was deep enough, she ducked beneath the cover of the water and crept out deeper. When Carbon caught up, he dove under and grabbed her ankles. She sucked in a quick breath before he pulled her beneath the water toward him. His eyes were open and his lips parted. He let go of her legs and took her in his arms and floated her to the surface. His lips lingered on hers in the hot gold of the afternoon sun. Carrying her, he moved out deeper.

His steps became more buoyant, the water cooler, his lips more demanding. When he stopped moving, she tried to stand. However, her feet didn't reach the bottom. Panicked, she tightened her arms about his neck. He appeared not to notice and slid his hands down the curves of her waist.

"Carbon!" she protested, helplessly eyeing up the public beach in the distance. It was too far to save her and too close for privacy.

In response to her fear and the cool water, her nipples unexpectedly erupted, intensifying the feel of Carbon's chest undulating with the waves against her breasts. His hands tickled up her back then cradled her head. He again drew her lips to his. His skin was warm against hers. His body, firm and tight. His mouth, hungry.

He abruptly let go of her. "Don't!" she squealed, thrashing her legs and clinging to his neck. Down below, she felt him strip off her bottom piece, then he had her in his arms again. A flutter of water chased his hands down her spine. He hugged her crotch to his, circling his palms over her rump as he carried her to shallower water.

His cock, hard and pulsating behind the thin slick of his trunks, was tantalizingly close to her vagina. When she was finally able to touch bottom with her feet, she slid her hand under his waistband and wrapped her fingers around his penis.

In the cool of the water beneath the heat of the sun, her fear was eased by the sound of waves and the taste of salt. Hands and water moving–around, and over and under. Floating, submerging, breaking into the sunshine. Eyes closed and eyes opened.

He again tugged her under, killing her breath and muting her world. She slid his penis inside her.

CHAPTER 18

"It wasn't just about sex." **Allison Montgomery**

"What else was it about, Allie?" **Dr. Erica Freid**

"About love, of course."

"No, it wasn't love. Maybe it was about surviving?"

"That's a shitty comment. You promised you weren't going to judge me. I'm not saying anything more."

"Tell me about that love, convince me. Don't leave me thinking it was about surviving."

"I believe our session is over."

"Okay. I guess I'll see you next week."

"Not unless I'm forced to come here. I intend to be on parole."

Allie hummed as she stepped out of the shower. She'd arrived at the hotel wearing only her bathing suit and a towel because when they'd finished their swim, Carbon had stuffed her clothes under his arm and refused to give them up.

As she reached for her brush, she caught her reflection in the mirror and her humming ceased. The woman staring back at her looked like a stranger. Allie ran her fingers over the bruising on her cheek. Although the mark was fading to yellow, it still hurt to the touch. She frowned.

It was surreal that she'd just made love to the same man who'd struck her. A man who rode with a biker gang, led a high-risk lifestyle with drugs and weapons, maybe strippers and paid ladies. A murderer. She ran her palms down her sides, skin against skin, hoping to make herself feel real. It didn't work.

She wrapped a towel about her waist and closed her eyes. If Carbon didn't continue liking her, she'd end up dead. Of that, she was sure. That's all this afternoon had been—insurance against certain death.

She glanced again at her reflection. There was an unsettling truth in her eyes. Her humming had nothing to do with surviving. It had been her heart, not her head that had led her into Carbon's arms in the ocean.

The sex shouldn't have happened. She'd not wanted it to happen. Carbon was dangerous. He was...

Suddenly the whole day seemed like a silent, black nightmare–the piranhas' feeding, her bikini, the ocean. The walk home, when Carbon asked if she still owned shares in Mahogany Imports.

"Yes," she'd replied, although as part of her divorce settlement she'd given up all financial interest in the company. "I could do it for you, Carbon. I know how."

"Do what?"

"Build a cover for you to run your drugs under."

"Did Mahogany Imports ever do illicit business?"

"No, we made our fortune honestly. However, there was a shift or perhaps more accurately, an expansion, going on just when I left. We were doing a lot of consulting on export issues with the government and other businesses. Some of those receiving our advice were perhaps a little shadier than most. In fact–" A look of intrigue brightened Carbon's eyes. "Yeah," she quickly ended.

"You think your ex would let you back into the office?"

She snuggled against him. "I own half. He wouldn't have a choice."

More than once on their walk home he'd pulled her into the shadows and kissed her, said how beautiful she was and how everything was going to be okay. She was convinced if the walk had been ten minutes longer, he'd have said he loved her.

Allie pulled her eyes from the mirror and looked at her wet bathing suit on the floor. She'd not even used a condom. A sudden rage ripped through her. She was being seduced by the devil and was too weak to resist. She grabbed her suit, scrunched both pieces tightly in her hands and hurled them into the wastebasket.

She was alone, guilty, angry and terrified. She squeezed shut her eyes. She was falling in love.

The rhythmic sounds of her breathing and heartbeat drummed strong against the drone of the air conditioning. She was all that, but she was also still alive. She slowly opened her eyes, lifted her two-piece out of the garbage and hung it over the shower rod to dry.

She could do this. She had to do this. She had to get home. She wrapped the towel tighter around her and opened the bathroom door. Saber was there with his ties and roll of tape.

"No!" Allie gasped, pulling the towel up over her breasts. "Not tonight, Saber. Where's Carbon? Go get Carbon! He said not tonight."

"Listen, lady." Saber tossed the tape from one hand to the other. "I don't do anything without Carbon telling me to. You know that. Hell, I don't even sip my beer until he's sipped his. You remember."

"Carbon didn't tell you to do this. No way! What have you done with him? Where's Carbon?"

"You know the routine. Go, lie down on the bed like a good girl."

"I don't believe you!" Allie lunged toward the exit.

With one quick step Saber had her. He dug his fingers into her shoulders and whipped her around. "Believe me."

Allie twisted violently. "Don't do this! Carbon was taking me for supper. He told me to put on the dress he bought this morning. That's what he said."

Saber grabbed her wrists and shoved her against the wall. He slowly walked his fingers up her arms, leaving a trail of pressure marks. "There's no supper," he said, sliding his thumbs to her throat. "The bed."

"No!" It had all been for naught—the bikini, the kisses, the unprotected sex, the spilling of importing information. Carbon had used her. Her brain, her body, her heart.

Saber's thumbs pressed tighter. She couldn't breathe. "If I have to put you on the bed, it's going to hurt." Her world was going black. She was giving up, giving in, getting it over with. Her legs gave way and her towel slipped to the floor. As she began her fall, however, a primeval need to survive took hold.

She writhed against Saber's grip, driving her nails into his fingers and her knee into his groin. He cursed, grabbed her shoulders and wrestled her toward the bed. His boots mangled her bare toes and his head walloped her chin. However, her anger masked all pain. Not until he had her naked beneath him on the bed did she cease struggling.

"Open your mouth, you fucking cunt," he said, his hand on her cheek, ready to shove in the pills.

Emboldened by the sight of blood oozing from the scratches across the back of his hand, she turned her head aside. "Just put the fucking things in my hand!"

"Not likely, bitch." He pinned her to the bed with his elbow and pried at her mouth. "Open!" When she refused, he sealed her nose with one hand and drilled his other thumb into the soft spot below her chin.

Allie gasped. The moment her teeth parted, his fingers were in her mouth, gouging her gums and cheeks. A handful of bitter pills began melting and sliding down her throat. Frantic, she twisted her fingers through Saber's hair and yanked. Saber loosened his hold just enough for her to turn her head. She spat out the pills and began screaming.

"Cunt…"

She rammed her knee into his groin. The instant he cringed, she rolled from under him and hit the floor still screaming. Behind her, the door slammed.

She twirled toward the noise. Carbon was stalking toward her, rage etched on his face. He pressed his hand over her mouth to silence her. "For Christ's sake quit screaming."

She collapsed into his arms, sobbing. "Saber tried..." She struggled to breathe, struggled to talk. "Saber...Saber... He was trying to kill me!"

Carbon released Allie and strode to the bed. He grabbed a handful of Saber's hair and yanked him to sitting. "You're bound and determined to fuck things up, aren't you?"

"I heard you're the fucker," Saber replied.

Carbon released Saber's hair and pumped three quick fists into his side. "You piece of shit, you're pissing me off!"

Saber groaned and rolled over. "You gotta believe me, buddy–" He groaned again and set his feet on the floor. "The cunt's trouble, Carb." He coddled his belly in his hands and staggered to the chair by the window.

"Allie," Carbon asked. "Are you okay?"

"No." She ducked past him to the closet, grabbed one of his T-shirts and slipped it over her head. "We were supposed to go for supper." She was sobbing now.

He wrapped his arms around her shoulders and planted a kiss on her curls. "Tomorrow, I promise."

"You said—"

"Saber," Carbon growled. "Get the hell out of here." Allie felt Saber brush past and then heard the door slam. Carbon glanced to the dozen green pills strewn across the duvet. "Did you swallow any?"

"No." She ducked past him, grabbed her white shorts that were laying on the chair and tugged them on.

He sat on the edge of the bed and motioned to her. "Come here."

She took his hand and he drew her to his lap. The smoky, rustic, raw edge of his now-familiar scent mixed with the warm salt of her tears. "Today meant nothing, did it?"

"Don't say that." He gently laid her on the bed and curled beside her. "It's just too dangerous out there for you. I can't risk it, Allie. You're safer here, tonight." He wiped at her tears with his thumb.

"Safer?"

"I'll keep Saber away, I promise." He cupped her chin and forced her to look at him. "You'll be safe." Hot tears streamed down her cheeks. "Hey," he soothed. "Hey." He wrapped his arms about her and began gently rocking. "It'll be okay, Allie. I promise."

"I...I...I want to...go home."

"I know. I know."

"Now, Carbon. I want to go home now!"

"Shh. We have lots to do here yet, Allie. You know that. I need you. I need your help. You're doing good, girl. You're doing good. Then I'll take you home. And we'll go for a bike ride together, like I promised. You and I. It will seem so right."

His comforting words ended abruptly and he rolled off the bed. "Stay here. I'll be right back."

Allie buried herself beneath the quilt, curling her knees to her chin. Seeking comfort in any way she could, she stuck her thumb in her mouth. It seemed it was only a minute before she heard him at the door again. She tightened the blanket about her.

"Allie!" Carbon shook her shoulder. "Allie!"

She snuggled deeper under the cover, hiding her fear, muffling her voice. "I know that I'm not going home. You're going to kill me. I know."

Carbon yanked the blanket off her face. "You just take this and curl up for a little sleep. Sabe and I won't be gone long." He tossed Saber's tape and ties onto the dresser. "There's no need for those. Here." He held out a pill.

Allie tugged at the cover.

"Come on, Allie," he encouraged impatiently. She reluctantly sat, took the tablet and swallowed. He motioned her to make room for him on the bed. "I'll stay here with you until you fall asleep."

"You're going to kill me," she moaned, crawling deeper under the blanket.

"Shh." He draped a heavy arm around her and the quilt. "Sleep."

CHAPTER 19

It was pitch black in the room when Allie woke. Carbon was in bed beside her, snoring.

She ran her tongue across the tickle on her lips and was surprised to taste the vaporous remnants of tape. She flicked on the lamp. Cut ties and a strip of torn adhesive were on the floor. *He gagged and bound me despite his promises!* Feeling betrayed and doomed, Allie sank back onto her pillow. Carbon exhaled and the smell of beer wafted through the room.

I'm a fool to be surprised. Stickiness itched at her crotch and she squeezed her eyes tight, wondering if Carbon had at least freed her hands and feet before raping her.

She slipped from bed and tiptoed to the washroom. In the darkness behind the closed door, she could hear her breaths scratching at the night. Her heart pounded so loudly it was as if it were beating outside her chest. The sounds terrified her. She groped for the switch and flicked on the light.

At first she could see nothing, but slowly the room appeared—misshapen and foggy, wavering and teetering. The floor moved like gelatine beneath her feet. She pressed herself against the wall and slowly slid to the floor. The drugs were too much. Carbon's putrid breath, his touch. His eyes. His lies. Everything was too much. She wondered how much longer she could survive. Drawing her knees to her chest, she lay her head between them and inhaled deeply. Exhaled. Steadily. Evenly. She kept her eyes closed and her mind focussed on the soothing sound of her breath. Eventually, the room quit spinning.

She crept across the tiles to the toilet and hauled herself onto the seat. As she prepared to cradle her head in her hands, she spotted a familiar pink tinge in the water beneath her. She pulled at the crotch of her shorts. It was soaked in red. A warm gush of blood swept down her vagina and splashed into the bowl. She hadn't had a period for four months and had believed menopause had set in to stay. She whipped off her shorts, tossed them behind the shower curtain and staggered in after them.

She turned on the tap and sank cross-legged to the tiles, the water blasting at her back. She'd hoped to keep herself safe by making Carbon fall in love with her. That plan now puddled red and poured down the drain. There was no way she could seduce him when she was menstruating so heavily. He'd have no patience with her cycle, would find the mess and the odour distracting. Perhaps, repulsive. She reached for her shorts and scrubbed at the crotch. Pink trickled over the pockets and around the waistband. If this period was anything like her last one, it would be fourteen days of gushing, clots and cramps.

She tossed the shorts into the corner and rose. For a long time she stood motionless beneath the thunder of the water, swaddled in the steam and heat. When she finally turned off the shower, she still felt dazed and dirty. Warm rivulets of red snaked down her thighs. She grabbed a towel, stuffed it between her legs and leaned against the shower wall. She was dizzy. She was bleeding. She needed to lie down. She needed to sleep. She took two more deep breaths and slid the curtain open. Carbon was in the doorway staring at her.

"What's the matter?" he asked.

Allie wrapped the shower curtain around her. "My period started." She searched his face. "I'm sorry. I wasn't expecting it. I have no tampons. Nothing." Carbon shrugged. The lump in her throat swelled. Heat flushed her cheeks. She swallowed a sob. "I'm so sorry."

"It's not the end of the world." Carbon stepped closer.

"Easy for you to say." She wrenched the curtain closed.

"Allie, we'll get you what you need. I'm sure Korean women have periods, too. Hey." He drew open the curtain and hugged her to him. "Don't cry! It's okay. It's fine. I'll send Saber to get you some–"

"Don't!" Allie struggled. "No. Not Saber."

"Why not?" Carbon chuckled.

"I'll go myself." She grabbed a second towel and wrapped it around her. "I'll figure something out. Don't say anything to Saber. Don't let him near me, Carbon. I never want to see that man's face again! Not after last night—"

"Okay. Okay. Okay," Carbon consoled. "Get yourself dressed and I'll come with you."

"We won't find anything in the middle of the night."

"We're downtown. This city doesn't sleep. Besides, the sun's on its way. Get dressed."

Carbon's willingness to help and his calm acceptance of her problem was deeply comforting. Once out on the street, Allie wrapped an arm around his waist and synchronized her step with his. *Perhaps I still have a chance to make my plan work.*

"Can we get rid of Saber again, today?" she asked.

The moist morning air hung heavy over the city, veiling the distant hills and swallowing the noise of the traffic. She could hardly hear her own footfalls. Quietly, as if in a dream, people appeared out of the fog, scurried around them and vanished.

Allie groggily watched her sneakers thread their way through the dips and bumps carved by centuries of rushing feet. Her belly was as heavy and thick as the fog. "Just the two of us. We could do the supper thing you promised. We could talk about...things."

She was wrapped in air so warm and still, she could scarcely feel it against her skin. She was dizzy and sleepy, soaked in hormonal emotions and burdened by the surging wetness between her legs. She was oppressed and suffocated–like the faint morning sun.

"Why? Do you have plans?" Carbon stopped and pulled away. He drew his cigarette package from an inside pocket and peeled off the cellophane. Allie stared at his profile.

In the strange half-light of the early morning, Carbon's features became ugly. His crooked smile became a sneer and his teeth, transformed to fangs. His haunting eyes narrowed and darted. He looked like a jackal; she felt like his prey.

She shivered. The sun burst through the fog and laid a square of gold at her feet. Carbon put a cigarette in his mouth, clicked his lighter and inhaled. He slowly turned. His eyebrows were raised, his chin tilted. He looked pleased—as a cat looks toying with a mouse. He'd smelled her terror and found it arousing. Satisfying.

She stepped toward him. "Carbon, don't you dare let Saber near me—not ever! Don't send him in to me before you go out."

"It's okay. Don't worry." Carbon reached for her hand.

Allie laced her fingers behind her back and stepped away. "He would've killed me last night!" Chuckling, Carbon moved toward her and she retreated until her back hit a light standard. "He'll try again. I know it! All he'd have to do is wrap the tape around my nose as well as my mouth. What if he shoots me?"

Carbon grinned and grabbed her hand. "Come on, don't worry. He'll be okay. I've talked to him." He kissed her curls and tugged her closer.

"Talked to him? About what?"

He flicked his ashes, wrapped his arm over her shoulders and resumed his stroll. "Allie, Saber is just paranoid. He thinks you're going to rat us out. I've told him what you can do for us. I told him about you wanting to join. I've told him you have connections...done some stuff. He understands, now. He's okay with it."

"Done some stuff?"

"Yeah, you know, the Mahogany Imports stuff. I know what you were talking about. I know it's true what you said about consulting with...you know."

"Oh." She wondered if Carbon meant his gang had been one of her shady customers. Was it a Jackal who'd flashed cash under Tim's nose before even telling him what it was he wanted?

It must have been, or how could Carbon have known about the visit? She shivered. Although Tim's meeting with the Jackals seemed to please Carbon, if he knew what Tim did after that meeting...

A convenience store emerged from the gloom and Allie struggled free of Carbon. "I can get what I need here. I'll be right back."

"What's this?" Carbon asked suspiciously when she rejoined him and offered him a small brown can.

"Careful," she warned. "It's hot."

He made a tentative grab for it. "Hot what?"

"Not *that* hot! It's a coffee."

"Hot coffee in a can?" He clicked off the tab and sniffed at the brew. "Does it taste any better than the powdered stuff in the room?"

"Not really. However, the powdered stuff is in the room and this is here."

"Where'd you find it?"

"It's in all these little stores, in beer-fridge-like things. There are usually two cabinets– one with iced tea and cold drinks, and the other with hot coffee."

"I like it," Carbon decided. "Not bad. They didn't have any black stuff?"

"No. Sweet and creamy–that's the only choice."

There was a moment of silence as they slurped their coffee, then Carbon spoke. "I thought about your suggestion we ditch Saber. A day alone with you is a prime idea. I'll talk to Saber and meanwhile you can think up something for the two of us to do."

"You didn't trust him. He lied to you—about not tying you up." **Dr. Erica Freid**

"No. It wasn't me who was distrusting, it was Carbon. He didn't trust me. He loved me but he didn't trust me." **Allison Montgomery**

"You asked him if he was going to kill you and he wouldn't say 'no'."

"He couldn't! Don't you understand? Until he knew for sure I was on his side, he couldn't promise anything. He couldn't tell me anything. If I'd just trusted him at the very beginning... He was keeping me safe. He was. Really. It was my fault he had to be rough with me. And even then, he made Saber do it because he couldn't hurt me. He loved me... I know that he did—he does. He always will."

CHAPTER 20

Allie booked her and Carbon a one-hour ferry tour of the Islets of Oryukdo. It was a tourist thing that didn't involve much walking–something she had to consider due to her heavy bleeding. As the boat slipped out to sea, Carbon drew her to him. She snuggled in and rested her head on his shoulder.

"I know I've told you this before," he said quietly, "but I'm telling you again. You're very beautiful." He tilted her face to his and moved in for a kiss.

"Carbon, let's not."

"Why not?"

"Because...you know."

"I know what?"

"Carbon!" Allie protested. "You're going to go get yourself all horny and then I won't be able to do anything about it."

"Why not?"

"You know why not," she snapped. "My period. It's not just a little bit, you know. It's...not pleasant."

"That's the best time to make love. It forces you to find delicious new ways to seek pleasure."

"Carbon!" A blush raced across her cheeks.

"Your husband never taught you that? Give me a kiss. Make me horny and I'll show you what I mean in bed tonight."

"Public displays of affection are frowned upon in Korea."

He gave her a quick peck on the cheek and wrapped his arms around her middle. "Allie, I lied to you a bit this morning. Saber's biggest fear isn't that you'll report us to the cops. He says you've bedazzled me." Allie choked on her breath. *Saber noticed? Does that mean it's true?*

"I've bedazzled you?" she managed. "Why would that bother Saber?" *Is he afraid that Carbon won't be able to kill me when the mission here is over?*

"In my world one has to earn trust. He doesn't think you have. Love without trust is a dangerous thing. I tried to prove there is no bedazzlement by treating you roughly. He's right, though. I can't deny it any longer. I'm hopelessly in love with you."

Allie struggled free of his grip and peered into his eyes. They were a deep, empty, magnetic blue. "Although I might love you," he continued, "I'm not sure I trust you. But I want to. How about you? Do you trust me or have I screwed it all up too badly? " His eyes were inviting, demanding. "Do you love me?" *He knows I don't love him.*

She quickly hid her face in his jacket. "I want to love you. I do. Yesterday, in the ocean..." It had been deliciously salty, hot and cold, dark and light.

"Do you trust me?" Carbon asked.

There was no use lying. He knew the answers to all his questions before he asked them. He knew her thoughts and her heart. It was like their souls had merged. It was like love. "No."

"Were you serious about wanting to join me in this venture? Allie, look at me when you answer."

She pulled away and stared over the ocean. She'd not forgotten that sunny Alberta afternoon on her deck when he'd so easily detected her lie about Koreans speaking English. She snuck a peek at his face. He was not yet angry.

"When you asked if I'd join the Jackals..." She struggled to find safe words. He was holding steady eyes on her. She licked her lips. "I should've stuck with my maybe instead of yeah, yeah."

"I know," he said softly. "What else have you lied about?"

"I lied to please you, Carbon. I want to make you happy." *I want to survive and get back to Canada.* "I don't own any interest in Mahogany Imports. I gave it up in the divorce settlement."

"It's okay. It changes things, but I can work with that. What else have you lied about?"

Allie sighed. "You already know, don't you? You know everything about me."

"What do I know, Allie? What do I know that you haven't told me?"

The ferry lurched over the wake of a freighter and Carbon reached to steady a senior who had toppled toward him. Allie rose and strolled to the rear deck. The fog had lifted and the sun, hot and high, sparked off the water like diamonds. She leaned over the rail.

Beneath her, the motor churned up a blast of foam and spray. A few feet out, the roiling water settled into a smooth wake, slicing a wide trail through the sea. Eventually, the wake lost to the power of the waves and folded itself back into the ocean. Beyond that, there was no trace of the path they had taken, nothing to show where they'd once been.

She'd serenaded Carbon, swam with him, slept with him. She'd admired his smoke rings and accepted his kisses. However, there was a part of her she'd not intended on sharing with him. Now, he was asking for that part. He wanted all of her. She looked across the water to where the sky met the bada. Out there, somewhere, miles and hours and a dateline away, was Canada.

Whether she told Carbon her secrets or not, he somehow knew them all. Yet he wanted to hear her share them–as if that gave him permission to love her. To keep her. To save her.

She glanced at Carbon. His legs were stretched across the aisle, his arms folded and his eyes closed. His face was tipped toward heaven. He was waiting for her.

"I wasn't a mere secretary," she said. Carbon straightened and opened his eyes. He patted the bench beside him. She sat and stared at her shoes. "It was sort of a lie, too, when I let you think I was involved in the Southeast Asia market. I wasn't. Tim took care of that. I was trying to break into the Russian market."

"Russian? I didn't know that! I wondered where you learned to speak it."

"Actually, I heard Russian as a kid. My Grandfather spoke only Russian. I found it easy to pick up."

"So, how did your Russian business experience pan out?"

"It didn't go so well. I had to drop it after six months. Things were too corrupt over there. At first I considered the kickbacks and bribes the cost of doing business—a cultural thing I could work with. I imaged the tradition to be somewhat like the ancient traders' practice of bringing gifts to the king. But when the demands started to be accompanied by threats and it became apparent that there was no effective legal process in place to counteract the danger, I decided to pull out."

"Tell me more."

"Russia has great potential but the internal disparity, dishonesty and fear keeps it from flourishing. If they could get their act together..." She paused, lost in memories from a lifetime ago when she'd been suave and savvy and unafraid to take on the world. She was a different person now, very much afraid. Carbon coughed. She had to keep talking, keep sharing her secrets. She had to make him think she was sharing her heart. "I've come to believe Canada would be no better off than Third World nations were it not for our underlying culture of honesty and integrity. Perhaps there's a lot to be said for the value of bringing Christian morals into the business climate."

"So, how do your Christian values fit in with, say, the drug trade?"

Allie shifted uneasily. "You won't like my answer."

"You have to be honest. It won't work otherwise. If we can't get some trust going between us, Saber will slaughter us both."

"Don't bring drugs here, Carbon. You're going to destroy a gentle people."

"They're not gentle."

"It's not right to take advantage of the cracks caused by the societal shift, by the younger generation's fascination with the West."

"It's not my society."

"It doesn't matter that it's not your country. You can't just destroy it!"

"You ever play *Risk*, the board game where you try to take over the world?"

"You want to take over the world?"

Carbon shrugged. "Just want to win. That's all."

"Win what? A few extra million in your wallet? To do what, Carbon? Think it will make you happier to have a gazillion instead of a million?"

Carbon chuckled. "Forget the dollars; it's all about believing in yourself and succeeding. About playing the game better than the other guy." The ferry rocked gently. "My turn to be honest," Carbon finally said. "About Saber—he understands even less than you do. I've tried telling him what you can do for us, but he just doesn't get it. He thinks to be a Jackal you have to be able to throttle up a Harley. That's old school, though, Allie. It's all about business, now. High tech. Computers. Networking. Power. Saber's like the enforcer on a hockey team. Yeah, you still need someone like him around to take out those wanting to play dirty against you, but that's not the real power. Saber just doesn't get it, though. Just doesn't get it."

"How about we switch things up?" Allie asked. "Would you consider joining me in a legitimate venture? I know enough about the business and it wouldn't bother me to set up competition against my ex."

"I'll think about it. We're not all illicit, you know. You asked what I'd do with the millions. A hell of a lot of it gets invested in legitimate businesses."

"You missed my point. I'm not asking for an investment. I'm asking you to give up your business for a legitimate one."

"That won't happen. It's not who I am. Not what I'm about. You'll have to accept that." He wiped a curl off her cheek. "Not that I want to give it up, but if I ever were to try to walk away from the Jackals, I'd be dead the next day."

"Why?"

"People with dirty hands don't trust those with clean ones. It was a big concern Saber had about you. If you're clean, there's nothing stopping you from ratting. If you're as guilty as the rest of them, you're not going to be turning on them. That's why, more than anything else I said, telling him you'd had dealings with the Jackals in the past settled him down the most."

Dealings with the Jackals? Is he lying to see if I'm honest enough to correct him or does he think that's the way it really was? She struggled to find a safe response. "I told you about the brothels and the Soju," she finally said, deciding to change the subject to one she knew would still interest him. "Did I tell you about the escalating problem with online betting?"

CHAPTER 21

After the ferry ride, Carbon insisted Allie take him to a PC room. There were several within a few blocks. Allie chose one which displayed a sign in English. After Carbon paid a few wons at the front, a small Korean man escorted them down the aisles of desks. A curtain of cigarette smoke hung blue and heavy between the ceiling and floor.

Carbon trailed behind, scanning the monitors of the other patrons. The host seated Allie and scurried after Carbon, motioning intensely for him to take the seat beside her. Carbon strolled down yet one more aisle before joining Allie. The Korean man set their computers to English and stepped behind them.

"It's hard to tell what they're doing online," Carbon complained to Allie. He pulled out his cigarettes. "It's all in Korean."

Allie glanced over her shoulder. "Carbon, do something on your computer to get this guy off our tail. Go to your email or something."

"Let the idiot stand and watch." He tapped his lighter on the desk. "Is this," he said, waving about the room, "all online betting?" He tucked his cigarette between his lips and again tapped his lighter.

"Carbon!" Allie started typing. "We attract enough attention just by being white. We don't need to make trouble."

"I'm used to making trouble." Carbon lit his cigarette and inhaled.

Allie plugged in the web address for Canadian news. As the CBC site loaded, she turned to watch Carbon. He rocked back, tilted his head to the ceiling and blew a smoke ring. He kept his eyes on it until it disappeared into the thick haze. Setting his cigarette into the ashtray, he rolled up his sleeves and finally began tapping at the keyboard. A tattoo of the bloody claw of a jackal rippled over his forearm muscles as if alive.

"You wouldn't be thinking of emailing home or anything?" Carbon asked. Allie grabbed her mouse and stared at her monitor. He became motionless beside her.

"I'm checking the news," she answered testily.

"Looking to see if your kidnapping has made the headlines? It hasn't." Allie's fingers froze. That he'd read her mind was bizarre; that he knew she hadn't made the news was terrifying.

In her monitor, Allie saw the reflection of their Korean host. She swivelled and stared directly at him. Although he was obviously suspicious of Carbon, she doubted she could rely on him to help her escape—he looked more like he wanted to have them both locked up. If he was involved in online gambling, it wasn't likely he'd call the cops for any reason, good or bad. However, if she frightened him enough, he might call a friend and she could end up with a Korean enforcer on her tail. Perhaps intimidated by her stare, he eventually bowed deeply and sauntered away. She turned to her computer and folded her hands in her lap.

Carbon resumed pecking at his keyboard. "You're thinking no one has even noticed you're missing."

"It's kind of sad no one misses me."

"Your whole life is sad." Carbon looked across at her. "It shouldn't be that way, Allie. You're so beautiful. You should have a whole bunch of people looking out for you, caring about you. Why did you let yourself become so alone in the world?"

"It's not being alone. It's like...I feel...free."

"Is that what you have told yourself?" he asked softly, reaching for her hand.

"I—" There was something in his eyes, perhaps a promise. Perhaps, the truth. She blinked rapidly. "Maybe I was lonely."

"Allie, Allie, Allie." He dropped her hand and began rubbing her shoulder. "It would be different if you were with me. You'd have the whole gang there for you. The Jackals don't cut people loose and forget about them. You'd be well looked after."

"Looked after?" she murmured, afraid to tell him being looked after by a biker gang held little appeal.

He rolled his chair closer. "It's a kinship, a brotherhood," he said. "Family."

"I have a family."

"Where is it, Allie? You've been missing for two weeks. Where's your family?"

"They're...they are around."

"Hmmm." He pulled away and began to type. "Do you know much about computers?"

"A little." She remembered the dazzle in his eyes which had frightened her so much in the bar the first time she met him, and again on her front step when he'd hunted her down. Lately, his eyes were much different—the dazzle gone, replaced with...something. It was as if the romancing was now over and the next step underway—whether she wished that to be or not.

Carbon motioned to his monitor. "Do you know how to check the history on computers? Find which web sites the previous customer visited?"

"Maybe." She placed her hands on the keyboard. "I'll try."

"I'm thinking you actually have been reported missing but the cops pretty well feel you've left on your own accord. That's what I'm thinking."

Allie looked at him sharply. "Why would you say that?"

"You've been in their radar for a while now."

"You're lying!"

"Who's lying, Allie?" He kept his eyes on hers until she could stand it no longer and dropped her gaze. Her heart thudded painfully against her rib cage. "What will you do if I take you with me back to Canada? Is Saber right? Are you going to go running to the cops the first chance you get?"

Scared to lie and scared honesty would attract a bullet, she simply shrugged.

"I'm giving you one last chance to come clean with me. If you love me, I'm expecting you'll be honest. Tell me again about your dealings with Mahogany Imports. Tell me what really went down."

"I haven't lied to you about anything regarding the company." Allie ran her dry tongue over her lips.

He again tugged at her hand. "Allie, look at me. Tell me."

"I didn't lie." She forced herself to look at him. "You're the one who said I dealt with the Jackals. I lied about nothing." She pulled her hand free and slouched into her chair. "My husband...had some contact."

The air conditioner roared and a cold wind whipped around her bare shoulders. She wrapped herself in her arms. "I didn't know who it was he was dealing with. He..." Would she survive the truth? Would he, could he, did he love her?

"Look at me!" Carbon insisted.

She straightened. Coughed. Found his eyes and fixed her stare. "Tim reported certain things to the police. And the cops came. They talked to Tim and to me. Then, we didn't hear any more from either them or the...Jackals, I guess."

Carbon grabbed his cigarette, inhaled and relaxed. "I knew all that. But I needed to hear you say it. Now I'll tell you something you don't know." He exhaled, flopped forward and butted his cigarette. A wisp of smoke danced around the rim of the ashtray. "The Jackals weren't happy with Tim siccing the cops on them." Her world was dark and rapidly getting darker. There was hardly any smoke now rising.

"They played tit for tat," Carbon continued, grinding the last life out of the butt and lighting another. "Certain things were said and done to sully your reputation and get the cops looking your way. You've been under police surveillance. Think now what it looks like to law enforcement that you took to meeting with me. Reneged twice on a restraining order. Left the country on a phoney passport. Gave bribes to the Russian mob. Tell me again, Allie, when we get to Canada, are you going to go running to the cops?"

There was only one answer that would get her home. "No."

"You're already in with us as far the cops are concerned. I'm thinking you'll be a lot safer on my side of the law than theirs. Do you understand?"

Safer on his side of the law... He was right—she'd need a hell of a lot of protection if she turned against the Jackals and would get little from a police force that viewed her as a criminal. She covered her face with her hands. He had her trapped. She was his, now and forever.

"There were only two ways for the Jackals to deal with your betrayal," Carbon said. "Setting the cops against you was one, and killing you and Tim was the other. Of course, the second option is still available." He said nothing more and Allie sat in the darkness behind closed eyes listening to the clicking around her.

"Let's get the hell out of here," he finally said and she was very happy to follow.

CHAPTER 22

"I'm sorry to have scared you," Carbon said once they were at the hotel. He was standing at the window, his hands deep in his pockets, gazing over the cranes and cargo of the seaport. Neither of them had spoken on the cab ride, nor dared to look at the other.

Allie stayed just inside the door. She'd not moved since letting Carbon pass. She could think of nothing to say.

"Allie, I didn't tell you all that just to be mean," Carbon continued. "I had to let you know how things are." He turned to her, his eyes soft again. He held out his hand. "Come here." She walked as if in a dream toward him and took his hand. He put his thumb under her chin and tilted it up. "Believe me when I say I don't want you dead. Believe me. I love you, girl. I do." He gently cradled her chin in both palms. "I'm scared, though. Scared for you. I'm scared what Saber says is true. That you've bedazzled me and I don't see you for what you really are. I had to know, Allie. I had to warn you. If you're not really on my side, as Saber says... I had to let you know how it might pan out for you."

Allie swatted his hands off her face. "That feels like blackmail. How odd, because I haven't done a damned thing wrong for you to blackmail me with."

"Technically, no. However, an electronic and paper trail has been created saying otherwise." Allie stared at the traffic. "It wasn't me who set you up," Carbon continued, laying a hand on her shoulder. "Believe me, I'd be shot if anyone knew I told you about it. I'm not blackmailing you, love. I'm trying to keep you safe." He forcibly spun her to him. "Please, believe me."

"I want you to get me out of this. If you love me like you say you do, get me out of this!"

"That wasn't what I was hoping you'd say."

"What did you hope I'd say?"

"I hoped it wouldn't matter to you that you can't rat me out. That it would be okay with you, that it had been your intention all along to stay with me."

She sucked in a deep breath and held it. *What are my intentions?* She breathed out and crumpled, cradling her head in her arms on the table. "I'm sorry," she finally managed. "I'm so confused, Carbon. I'm so fucking confused!"

Carbon took a chair opposite her. She heard him pull out his cigarettes and light up. Heard him exhale. She imagined the smoke ring which was undoubtedly wending its way to the ceiling.

"I don't know about you," Carbon finally said, "but it felt good today to come clean with each other. It felt special when you confided in me, let me in on your secrets. I thought it meant you were comfortable and trusted me. That you love me." He inhaled again. "That wasn't it, was it? You were talking because you were scared of me, not—"

"Stop it!" Allie interrupted, keeping her face hidden. "I don't know why I talked, Carbon. I...I don't know anything anymore."

"The Jackals wanted you in on Korea. I told them I could get it done for them. I really hoped I could convince you to come here with me willingly. I had no choice when you refused. You realize that, don't you? I was under orders." He tousled her curls. "I didn't want them to kill you in retribution for reporting them to the cops but I knew if I couldn't make this plan work for them, your life would be in danger. I hadn't planned on falling for you, Allie. Hadn't planned on that happening."

The silence between them gradually filled with the incessant traffic noise from the street below. The whir of the air conditioner joined the squealing and tooting. The soft buzz of the water dispenser kicked in. Allie could hear Carbon's breaths, her own breathing, the beating of her heart.

"Christ, Allie," Carbon cut in loudly. "If you knew anything about biker gangs, you'd know I was telling the truth. A Jackal simply wouldn't let a woman in on gang secrets unless he was feeling something pretty damned strong toward her."

Allie slowly raised her head and stared into his eyes. *Does he really love me?*

"You have to believe me," he pleaded.

Everything he said made sense. It explained everything. "I believe you love me," she said. A look of pleasure and relief washed over him. She squirmed uncomfortably, afraid she'd committed to something. "I'm not so sure, though, about my own feelings."

"That scares me." He walked to the window and jammed his hands in his pockets. "That fucking scares me."

His fear is likely no match for mine. "I'm sorry." Allie lifted his cigarette from the ashtray. She inhaled, tilted her face up and tried for a smoke ring. She almost had one.

"What do I have to do?" Carbon asked. "Is there someone else in your life? Are you in love with someone else?"

"No, there's no one else. Just like you said, there's no one at all anywhere in my life."

"So then, why not? Why not me, Allie? I'm not attractive to you?"

"No, it's not that. I'm attracted to you. It's just...you scare me. And Saber scares me."

"I'm not asking you to fall in love with Saber."

"No, but falling in love with someone who has scary friends is scary."

"If I got rid of him, would I be less scary to you?"

"Carbon…" She returned the cigarette to the ashtray and once more laid her head on the table. Smoking made her dizzy. This whole conversation made her dizzy.

"Hey." He walked over and pulled her to her feet. "Don't cry." He tilted her chin and mopped at her tears with his thumb. "Tell you what, how does this sound? I'm going to work at making you love me. I'm going to..." He picked her up and walked to the bed. "I'm going to unleash all my passionate powers. I'm going to..." He laid her on the bed, straddled her and bent for a quick kiss. "If that's okay with you?" Carbon wiped once more at her tears. He gazed into her eyes. "Is it okay if I seduce you? Show you my charm?"

She nodded weakly.

"Seems to me, I promised to show you how to make wild passionate love during that time of the month. I always keep my promises." He touched his lips to hers, gently.

It felt good. She didn't need to think; didn't need to have answers. Whatever else was happening, whatever pain she felt, whatever the future held or didn't hold. Whatever... For a few minutes, he could make her feel good. She pressed in for more passion.

"Easy, easy." He flicked his tongue over her lips. "It's my turn. You do nothing. Just relax and enjoy."

Allie ran her fingertips over the taught skin of his muscular shoulders and stared up at him. "Carbon—"

"No!" he admonished. He placed her arms on the bed at her sides. "Do nothing."

He caressed her arms before gently and slowly stripping off her clothes. When she was naked except for her panties he touched his lips to her forehead, licked at her cheeks and nuzzled her ears. Gazing into her eyes, he began circling his palms around her breasts. "Is it working? Do you love me yet?"

"Not quite yet."

"Hmmm, not yet." He began to work her nipples with his tongue and his lips. He was tantalizingly gentle–unbearably so. She moaned and wriggled beneath the intense sensation. He kept licking and kissing and sucking–too quickly. Too gently. For too long. He was promising much but delivering only tease. As her body heated she ached to have his whole body close, skin to skin. She wrapped her legs and arms around him but he quickly brushed her off him and pinned her hands above her head.

"You must do nothing. Just relax. Relax and fall in love."

Her crotch was swollen and aching for pressure, anticipating climax, seeking release. She wiggled her hips. "Carbon!"

"What's the matter?" he badgered, finally leaving her breasts to nibble at her ear. He swirled his tongue around the creases. She thrust her pelvis toward him but he tightened his grip on her wrists and lifted himself out of reach.

"Relax," he whispered, his lips again slipping to her nipples.

"But, I want—" He pressed his mouth to hers. He begged with his tongue and she sucked it in, farther and deeper until it filled her. Deliciously and slowly he tickled his tongue free and flicked at the fleshy insides of her cheeks. When he pulled away, she felt bereft. Alone. Empty.

He gazed down at her. "What do you want? What is it Allie wants?"

"I can't have what I want. I want you inside me."

"Ah." He released her hands and sat on his heels. "Allie can't have what she wants." He ran his fingers down the curves of her hips.

"Carbon," she groaned. The bulge in his pants was tantalizingly close to her hand. She inched her fingers toward it. To feel his love...to touch his love. To arouse his love. To forget all the bad stuff.

He caught her wrists, though, and brought her hands to his lips and licked her fingertips. "Later, Allie. For now, this is all for you." He kissed her ears and breathed fire behind them. His tongue tickled down her neck to her nipples, to her navel. Down her thighs. He caught her toes in his mouth and rubbed his tongue between them.

"Don't, Carbon," she moaned. "No more. Please?"

He curled beside her and began massaging her though her panties. "Is this what Allie wants?" he asked, removing his hand from her crotch as he spoke.

"Yes, that's what I want." She grabbed his wrist and thrust his fingers toward her genitals. He placed his palm just shy of her navel and wiggled his little finger a decimetre from her swollen clitoris.

"But are you in love yet? I wouldn't want to do this to someone who doesn't love me."

"Carbon!" He knew she didn't love him. He always knew her heart, could always spot her lies. She pressed her own fingers to her crotch.

"Ah, that's no good." He caught her hand and curled it tightly in his. "We can't have Allie doing that!"

He rolled on top of her, pinned her hands above her head and lowered his hips. She ground against his hardness. A flush heated her face. She stopped breathing, clenched her jaw and heaved her hips upward, anticipating climax. He pulled away once more. "Is Allie in love with me yet?

"Carbon, don't!" She reached for her own crotch with one hand and his with her other. All she had to do was say it. Say it and mean it. Believe it. Let it be. '*I don't know how to love you...*'

"Nope." He caught both her wrists. "I don't think she is. I don't think I've made her love me yet."

I don't know if you love me, in what manner, in what way... He kept his eyes on hers and slowly lowered himself onto her, touching first with his thighs, then his penis, his belly...

There was no one else. Nothing else. "I love you," Allie surrendered as his lips approached. She closed her eyes. "I love you."

Keeping his kiss soft and gentle, he rocked against her faster and faster, harder and harder. She ground fiercely, aching for an orgasm. However, her pad and the clothing between them kept climax tantalisingly out of reach.

Carbon lifted off her and she writhed against his hold on her wrists. "I love you, I love you. Please?" she begged, flipping a leg over him and levering herself closer. She did love him. Because...

"Are you sure?" he asked. "Is Allie sure she loves me?"

"I'm sure. Please! I love you."

He lay beside her and ran his fingers across her forehead and down to her pubic bone. He slipped his hand under the band of her panties, pressed firmly with his fingers and rubbed.

Allie tensed. Her breathing ceased. The heat built. She lifted her hips and her vagina clamped closed. There was a nanosecond of unbearable intensity before her passion exploded.

Her vagina opened and sucked—searching, demanding. She pressed tighter against Carbon's hand and shifted her hips. She wiggled and moaned as his fingers slid to the opening. He pressed his palm to her clitoris and sunk his fingers deep inside her. Spasms ripped through her body—spontaneously arching her back and pinning her head to her pillow. Tense. Tenser. Rhythmically, more tense. Moment after moment. Forever. Unstoppable.

She struggled for a breath. Gradually the spasms slowed and her vagina winked softer. Exhausted, she opened her eyes and looked at Carbon. He smiled and once again drove his palm against her clitoris and his fingers deep inside her.

"No," she moaned, as her body again began convulsing. "No, no more!" She tugged at Carbon's arm.

He rolled onto her and pressed his crotch against hers. Her vagina continued its search, opening, closing, sucking—caressing his penis through her panties.

As the sensation ebbed, Carbon lowered his lips to hers and this time let her kiss him back. She worked her hand between their bellies, slipped her fingers under his waistband and grasped the head of his cock.

"Lie on your back. It's your turn now."

"Doctor, do you understand?" **Allison Montgomery**
"Understand?" **Dr. Erica Freid**
"You must understand!"
"What must I understand?"
"You must understand that he loved me, despite appearances. He had valid reasons for everything he did. He had to keep me safe. He couldn't tell me anything until he knew he could trust me. You must understand that. Somebody besides me in this fucking world has to understand that!"

CHAPTER 23

There was no time to do anything between the moment Allie heard a rustle in the hall and the door burst open. She still had her lips around Carbon's penis when someone called in halting English, "Police. Police."

"Fuck!" Carbon cursed.

She heard the unmistakable click of firearms and the fall of combat boots behind her. Allie slowly lifted her head and peeked over her shoulder.

"Told you to kill that bitch!" Saber shouted as someone hauled him past the open door. For the first time ever, Allie heard emotion in his voice. "I fucking told you!"

"Canada! Canada! English!" Allie said desperately. She slid off the foot of the bed and raised her hands to her shoulders. "Embassy. Canada. Canadian Consulate."

There were four officers with weapons in her room and she could see two more in the hall. Through the open door came the receding sounds of stomping boots, the clatter of guns and Saber's continuing protests. "That cunt is going to get us killed!"

In the room, the men began yelling and flicking the butts of their long guns at her.

"Wrap the blanket around you," Carbon suggested, setting his feet on the floor and pulling on his pants. "You're making them nervous standing there half-naked."

She slowly reached down and tugged at the duvet. The chattering ceased once she was covered, but the action began. In moments, they had Carbon handcuffed and against the wall. One officer had his rifle pointed at Carbon while another aimed his at her. Two others searched the room. Clothes flew as they rummaged through the closet, the suitcases and the nightstands.

"Don't say anything, Allie," Carbon warned. The officer guarding him yelled and waved his gun menacingly. "Don't say—" The guard cut him short by viciously hammering his head into the wall.

She couldn't understand what the officers were saying to each other as they ripped off the bed sheets and sliced open the pillows. Their voices were loud and staccato, urgent. Next, the mattress was flipped and thrown to the floor. The chatter rose ten decibels when an officer pulled Carbon's revolver and knife from somewhere beneath the bed.

"What's happening, Carbon?" Allie sobbed. "What's going to happen to us?"

"Shut up!" Carbon ordered. His words netted him another hit to the head. She stifled her shouts but couldn't stop sobbing. She wrapped the blanket around her tighter and watched for what seemed like hours as toiletries, clothes and bedding flew. When an officer finally pulled three passports from somewhere in Carbon's luggage, the activity slowed. The guard with his weapon trained on Allie, motioned to her clothes on the floor and spat some words at her.

"Get dressed?" she asked tentatively. She slowly knelt and picked up her bra, shirt and shorts. "I can get dressed?"

"Ne, Ne," he said, nodding and pointing.

"Yes?" Allie confirmed. With the blanket still about her, she sat on the edge of the bed and, keeping her eyes on him, fumbled with her bra. She was terrified her slowness would antagonize him, but he held steady in his gaze and stance. When she was finally clothed, she dropped the blanket and glanced nervously around. Carbon was gone.

Panic-stricken she rose and pointed to where he'd been held against the wall. "What did you do with him?" she screamed. "Where is he? Where did you take him?" The officer answered by motioning her to lead the way from the room.

"Canada," she tried once more as she obediently moved past him in. "I'm Canadian. I want to talk to someone from the Consulate. Please," she begged. "English? Someone who speaks English?"

CHAPTER 24

Allie looked about the small room. Other than a second wooden chair opposite the tiny table in front of her, there was nothing of note—no window, no clock and no sound other than the distant drone of an air conditioner.

She shifted in her chair and wrenched at her handcuffs. Although she'd resolved to obey Carbon's order not to talk, an intense uneasiness was twisting inside her, as if something forgotten was begging to be remembered.

She was so wrapped in her thoughts that when the door swung open, she jumped. A Korean man walked in. He was not in uniform but portrayed the aura of someone in command. He glanced at her briefly before striding to the table and throwing down a sheaf of papers. As he pulled out the chair opposite her, the legs screeched against the floor tiles. He stiffly sat and picked up the papers.

"English," Allie began again as she took her seat. "Please. Canada. Canada—"

"I speak English," the fellow interrupted harshly without a trace of an accent. Startled, she searched what she could see of his face for a clue but she could read nothing. "And I'm advising you to shut up."

She'd been alone with her thoughts for far too long to be able to obey. After an unbearable moment of silence she asked, "What have I been charged with?"

"Nothing yet." He kept his eyes on his papers. "But you will be if you don't shut up."

"The man I was with—?" she began. The fellow looked up at her sharply and she knew she had no choice but to fall silent.

It seemed to take him forever to read the file. He finally shuffled the papers into a neat pile, tilted his chair and gazed across at her. "You're in a lot of trouble," he announced.

"But—"

"Don't say anything."

"But—" She fell silent under his stern gaze. The man leaned forward and, while clicking his pen on the table, began reading the papers again. "Who are you?" Allie asked.

"That's not for you to know."

"Is there anything I can know?"

"Quit asking questions if you want to get back to Canada." He finished reading the papers for the second time, shuffled them together and stared across at her. "I'll send you someone from the Consulate—if that's what you want."

"Is that what I should want?"

He shrugged and kept his eyes on her. "I'm not promising it will do you any good."

"What will do me good?"

He cast his eyes about the holding cell as if suspicious of being watched and then leaned into her. "Talking as little as possible." Picking up his papers, he stood and strode to the door. "I'll send someone to take off your handcuffs," he called over his shoulder. "And someone from the Consulate to speak with you."

CHAPTER 25

"You're Allison Montgomery?" She'd been in the same holding cell for hours and knew the intimate details of every stained tile that the fellow was walking across.

Allie rose as he approached and held out her hand. "Yes."

"Gregory Sands, Canadian Consulate." He shook her hand and settled in across from her. "I've been told you wish to speak to me."

"I've been told it might not do me any good." Gregory was tall, mid-forties, greying hair and receding hairline. He sported an expensive suit and a nametag identifying him as being from the Canadian Consulate.

"Well?" he asked impatiently. "Which is it?"

She sank into her chair. "I'm hoping you can help me, but I've been led to believe you can't."

Gregory leaned toward her. "It's this way. I can't interfere in the legal processes of this country. What I can do is provide you with contact information for English-speaking lawyers and put you in touch with a translator if you require one."

"I need more than that." Allie squeezed her eyes shut in an attempt to stem her tears.

"I can't offer much more than that." His voice was harsh and abrupt. Tears seeped through her lashes and wet her cheeks. His voice softened. "I can contact someone in Canada for you if you wish."

His mention of Canada and the thought of Tim stirred the restlessness inside her. Snippets of a subconscious idea bubbled to the surface. "Do you have a pen and paper?" Her own voice sounded strange and faraway, as if it wasn't her who had spoken. Sands passed her his pen and a business card.

She flipped it over. '*I was…*' she wrote and then stopped to re-read the words, wondering if they were leading to somewhere she shouldn't go—to a place she didn't want to be. She clicked the pen against the desk.

"Well?" Sands asked, reaching for the card.

Her restlessness surged and she again started writing. '...*kidnapped. My passport is in my safe in Canada.*' She stared at the words. Before she could rethink them, however, Sands snatched the card. She followed it with her fingers, certain she wanted it back. But he curled his palm around it and drew it beyond her reach.

"I see," he said, furrowing his brow as he read. He crumpled the card and looked up at her sharply. "That's not the information I was given."

"No," Allie whispered. "I didn't think it would be."

He pursed his lips. "This would change things." He kept looking at her until Allie felt forced to drop her eyes. She wasn't at all sure she'd done the right thing. Wasn't sure why she'd done it. That hot summer day on her deck was so long ago. So much had changed. She had changed. She knew things now she didn't know then—things that made that afternoon very different.

"If a crime against you has taken place..." Sands began. Allie looked up at him. "If that's what happened, I would be able to help." His eyes bored into her as if accusing her of something.

"I've been told I haven't yet been charged with anything," Allie offered.

"I'm under the impression it's only a matter of time. It's very bad company you've been keeping."

"I—"

"I have no patience for people, Canadian or otherwise, who bring drug trafficking into foreign countries." Allie's heart dropped. *They know what I've done.* "I'll get you a lawyer for your legal problems here." He rose. "And look into the other matter for you."

"Thank you."

"Say nothing to anyone, including the lawyer, about any other specific matters." He waved his crumpled card at her. "Other than..." He trailed off and she nodded. "Are they treating you okay?" he asked.

"I guess so." He kept his eyes on her for the longest time before turning to leave.

The moment he was gone, Allie began pacing. Betraying Carbon as she'd done made no sense at all, yet mingled in with the guilt was an intense feeling of relief.

A female in uniform arrived, escorted her to the washroom and after some frantic signalling by Allie, brought her a clean pad. When she returned to her cell, the officer handed her a bottle of water and a cellophaned gimbap. Allie's mouth was so dry that for every bite of the rice roll, she had to take a swig of water to wash it down, vaguely reminiscent of swallowing Carbon's pills on the trip to the airport. This troubling memory lay heavy on her soul and the rice, heavy in her stomach.

She finished eating, scrunched the cellophane into a tight ball and wondered what time it was. What if she were to be locked up here forever? She resumed pacing, folding and unfolding her arms and at times crying. She'd heard stories about foreign nationals being imprisoned without even a trial, sometimes for years. She sat and then rose to pace again, acutely aware she was not innocent and terrified of what that might mean. She'd been on the Russian docks with Carbon. She'd done things, said things, set up things. She knew things.

Her pacing and her thinking and her sobs tired her and she returned to her chair, exhausted. Laying her head on the table, she dozed off.

"Allison Montgomery?" a loud voice startled her. She sleepily sat up and blinked. "Today's your lucky day!" Standing in front of her was the Korean man who'd earlier spoken to her.

"Next flight out of here to Canada," he said raising his brows, "you're on it."

"Really? I'm going to Canada?"

"An agreement has been reached. You'll face the charges at home."

"Charges?"

"It will take a few minutes; do you want me to read them all to you?"

"Charges?"

"Mostly to do with conspiring to bring drugs into the country. I wouldn't object if I were you. Save your arguments for a Canadian courtroom." He motioned her toward the exit. "You don't know how lucky you are to have been given that chance."

"What about Carbon and Saber?" she asked nervously as he handed her a passport.

"Same deal," he said. She opened the passport. It looked exactly like the one in her safe, except for a few less stamps. She hurriedly flipped it closed. "A quick stop for fingerprints and to say cheese, and then you're out of here." He directed her down the hall. "Under guard, first class, I've been told." He held open a door for her and waved her to the seat for her photo. "Have a great flight." He disappeared, leaving her to struggle with Korean instructions being fired at her by a small man behind a giant camera.

She wondered if Carbon would be pleased if he were to find out about the note she'd written that had bought them a flight home.

"What happened, Allie? When you met Sands, why was Carbon suddenly your kidnapper and not your lover?" **Dr. Erica Freid**

"It was just an idea that struck me of how we could get home. I wouldn't have wanted Carbon to spend time in a Korean jail. Foreign jails, you've heard about them. He might never have gotten out." **Allison Montgomery**

"What about you?"

"Oh, me, too. There was absolutely no guarantee any of us would get a fair trial. I was desperate to make sure we avoided all that."

"Or were you desperate to get free of Carbon's control?"

"Why would you say that?"

CHAPTER 26

They arrived in Vancouver six hours before they left Korea. However, Allie could tell by the ache in her bones and the fog in her head, only a trick of the dateline had nullified the ten-hour flight.

She waited in what she assumed to be the Vancouver RCMP detachment. Before they'd asked her one question, she'd demanded a lawyer and had been left alone in one of the bare rooms designed to drive people insane. With nothing at all to look at, she had little to do but fret.

It hadn't been a pleasant flight; starting with being escorted onto the plane in handcuffs, after all the other passengers were seated. Allie could've died from embarrassment. She'd curled up as small and as quiet as she could in her window seat, refused all offers of food and drink and hadn't once asked to use the loo.

Besides all that, she'd fought a raging torrent of emotions throughout the journey. Although she'd been up for eighteen hours before the flight even began, sleep hadn't come. She remembered a time when she'd desperately wanted to get safely home. It seemed so long ago, though, and so much had changed since then.

She hadn't been allowed one word with Carbon since he'd been taken from her hotel room in Busan. Carbon confounded her confusion by refusing to look at her throughout the hurried preparations to get them out of the country.

She'd have done anything just to have him acknowledge her; a smile of support would've been nice. Even one more warning not to talk would've offered some comfort. She was terrified his coolness meant he'd learned that she'd reported being kidnapped.

She tried to think of something pleasant about arriving home to Canada but being locked in a room was a stark reminder that the police had been after her long before she'd met Carbon and were likely unsympathetic toward her. Perhaps she ought to have stayed in Korea.

"You can make arrangements for legal counsel now," a female officer interrupted her thoughts. Constable Dorin was a big woman, bosomy with stocky legs and thick around the middle so although fairly young, she came across as matronly. After handcuffing Allie, she led her through a maze of halls, un-cuffed her and left her alone in a room with a phone.

Allie dialled Tim and prayed her ex would answer. When she heard his familiar voice, tears welled. "Tim," she sobbed. "I need you to get me a lawyer."

"Allie? Allie, where the hell are you? I've been trying to reach you for over two weeks."

"I'm in Vancouver and I need a lawyer."

"Vancouver?"

"Yes. I know you have contacts here through your business. I'm thinking maybe Parker—"

"Parker? You need a criminal lawyer?"

"Perhaps one familiar with international law."

"Allie, what the hell's going on? Why do you need a criminal lawyer?" The worry in his voice resonated with the pain in her soul.

"I don't know what's going on," she finally managed.

"It's okay, Allie. It's okay. I'll get you a lawyer. Don't worry. Don't worry, darling. It'll be okay."

When Constable Dorin returned for her, Allie was loath to disconnect from Tim's soothing voice. But the officer's increasing impatience forced a final goodbye and she gently placed the receiver in the cradle.

After being led to a cell with a cot, she curled into the fetal position and cried herself to sleep.

CHAPTER 27

"Allison Montgomery? Jason Tudor," her lawyer introduced before sitting down opposite her.

Allie's five-hour nap had done little to refresh her. Though she couldn't remember the dreams that had visited her, she knew they'd been there— confused visions, tumbling in her head like the greens, whites and reds in a kaleidoscope.

"How are you doing?" Tudor asked kindly. Allie was familiar with the Tudor name but had never met the man. He was probably in his early fifties but his smooth skin and full head of hair marked him as someone much younger. A set of soft blue eyes contrasted with the bronze of his face. Allie saw in him a very handsome, gentle man.

She nodded.

"You want me to represent you?" he confirmed. Again, Allie nodded.

"Have you talked to anyone yet?"

"Only Tim."

"Okay. That's good." He scanned his notes. "You've got yourself into a heap of trouble here."

"So they say." She wiped her eyes and stifled a yawn. Everything felt very dreamlike.

"What can you tell me about it?" Tudor picked up his pen.

"Nothing."

"The last few hours have been pretty rough?"

"The last few weeks, actually."

"Tell me about the last few weeks."

"I can't."

"There's a note here saying you're claiming you were kidnapped. What's that about?"

Allie shifted in her chair and gazed down at her nails. "I don't think that's what really happened."

"You told the authorities in Busan you were kidnapped."

"I was hoping that lie would get me home and it did."

"You said you were in Korea on a phony passport."

"But that was before I saw the passport. I think it might be the right one after all. Once I saw it, I realized it looks pretty much the same."

Tudor cleared his throat, looked down at his notes and then up at Allie. "Allison," he said sternly. "You have serious charges against you. If you were in anyway coerced into participating in these activities, we can certainly mount a good defence. So, did you or did you not willingly go to Korea?"

"At first it seemed like I was being kidnapped," Allie began, remembering that afternoon on her deck. Although she hadn't wanted to go, she hadn't known Carbon was in love with her. Hadn't known if she didn't go with him, the Jackals would kill her. "I learned later that's not how it was. That's not really what happened."

"I see." Tudor shuffled his papers. The mixture of disbelief and understanding on his face reminded her of Tim's expression when his mother had pronounced herself cured of cancer just days before the disease claimed her life. *Does he think I'm being dishonest with myself?*

"These two men you were with," Tudor finally continued, his eyes still on his notes. "You knew them before you went to Korea?"

"Yes. Well, I sort of knew them, I'd met them before. Yes."

"They were friends of yours?"

"No, not really friends. They were okay, though. Carbon was okay. Saber I never liked much."

Tudor leaned in to her and looked deeply into her eyes. "Are they your friends now?" he asked softly.

For some reason her heart began pounding. "Why are you asking?" She rose and paced to the wall. Her chest was so tight, she could hardly breathe. Leaning her forehead against the cool of the bricks, she concentrated on drawing in air.

"Sometimes good friends can get us into trouble. Is that what happened here, perhaps?"

"Yes." Allie squeezed her eyes shut. "That's what happened."

"Can you remember your first day in Seoul? The day you landed there, what was it like?"

"It was hot. We took the shuttle to Seoul and booked into our hotel. Carbon slept on the floor in my room and Saber had his own room."

"Was the whole trip like that? Carbon sleeping on the floor?"

Allie whirled around. "That's a bit personal!"

"Was it?" Tudor whispered, drilling his blue eyes into her again. "When did it start getting personal? How many days into the trip?"

Allie tried to match his gaze but found she couldn't. "I don't remember." She faced the wall. "This isn't working. I want a different lawyer."

"The second day. What do you remember about your second day? How friendly were things that day?" Tudor persisted.

Allie clenched her teeth. "I said, I want a different lawyer!" She ran to the table, flung her chair aside and leaned into Tudor. "Leave! I want a different lawyer!"

"Allie—" he started. The cool, accusing look in his eyes told her what she didn't want to hear.

"Out!" She swiped his papers off the table. "Get out!" The door opened and an officer called her name. "Take me to my cell," Allie demanded, striding over and holding out her hands for the cuffs. "And don't let this guy in to see me again, ever. He's no longer my lawyer."

CHAPTER 28

"You have a bail hearing in two days," Constable Dorin advised. "You need a lawyer for that."

"I don't want a lawyer and I don't want a bail hearing." Allie pulled her blanket over her face. Her cell was safe and comfortable. No one was demanding anything. There was nothing that needed doing, no decisions to be made.

"So, your buddies are going to be free and you're going to be stuck in here?" Dorin persisted.

Allie thought of Carbon— his bright eyes, gentle touch, the tears he'd cried. She pushed the blanket to the floor. He'd make bail. Be out there somewhere. She could find him. "Okay." She swung her feet to the floor. "I'll get a lawyer."

After calling Tim and reaching his answering machine, Allie returned to her cell and flopped onto the cot. She could hardly wait to hear Carbon's voice again, his chuckle. Feel his heavy arm about her shoulders. She hoped she'd be able to finish what she'd started in Busan before the police barged in. It was as though their profession of love for each other had been left unconsummated.

She must have spent an hour reminiscing—the noraebang, the Busan Aquarium, her swim in the Bada—before a female guard unlocked her cell. "Your husband's here to see you," she said.

"I don't have a husband."

"Your ex-husband, Tim? He says you left a message to find you a lawyer. He's here to talk to you about that. I'll take you to him."

Tim rose and rushed to her. "What did they do to you, Allie?" he moaned, wrapping his arms around her middle and laying his head on her shoulder.

Allie didn't know if he meant what the cops had done to her or what Carbon and Saber had. Neither made sense. However, before she could ask, she burst into tears and began sobbing uncontrollably.

Tim rocked her gently, swaying to the rhythm of both their sobs. "Allie," he kept whispering. "Allie."

Finally, he pulled away and taking a hanky from his pocket, wiped at her tears first and then at his own. "Come." Tim pulled two chairs together and motioned to one. "Sit with me and talk."

"I've been told not to talk." After she was seated, he took the other chair and drew her to him. She stiffened under his touch.

"Who told you not to talk?"

"Some guy in Korea."

He wiped the hair from her brow and gave her forehead a quick peck. "That was in Korea. It's okay to talk now, darling. You can talk to me. They've told me I can stay for as long as I like, provided you don't freak out like you did with Tudor."

"I don't think I should talk." Allie tried to wiggle free. "But I'll ask Carbon when I see him."

"Who's Carbon?"

"A man I love." She wrenched his arm off her shoulder.

"Allie," Tim protested quietly. He folded his hands in his lap and sighed.

"He's better in bed than you are."

"Allie—"

"You're not the only one who can have a lover. I have someone now, too."

"Okay."

"Besides, I thought you were here to discuss getting me a lawyer."

"I got you a lawyer. Tudor is your lawyer."

"I don't like him. He's a pervert or something. He kept asking about my bedroom activities. I need a new lawyer, someone who can get me bail. I have to get out to see Carbon. I haven't been able to talk to him since Korea and I need to."

"Allie, darling." Tim sighed. "Keep Tudor as your lawyer. He's had experience with cases like yours. He's not perverted. Don't think that way. He has reasons for asking those questions. Give him a chance."

"What reason does he have for asking me if I slept with Carbon? What the hell kind of reason, Tim?"

"If you were coerced—"

"I'm not a fricken teenaged girl. It's not as if some guy looks at me and I melt into an idiot. We are both adults. What happened between us is nobody's business."

"But the criminal part of what you did together is. A lawyer has to know how that all fits together."

"That's bullshit. I can understand the prosecuting attorney yammering away about such things, but not my attorney, not my OWN attorney. I need to get out of here and see Carbon. He'll tell me it's all bullshit, I know he will!"

"If you make bail, I don't think they'll let you see Carbon."

"Who won't let me?"

"It's just a thought. They might make it a condition of your bail that you steer clear of him."

"Why would they do that?"

"Because... Maybe because he got you in trouble." Tim was choosing his words carefully, as if trying not to hurt her. "And he might get you in more trouble if you get together with him again."

They're not going to let me see Carbon! Allie's ribs would not rise to let her lungs fill. "Then, I don't want bail."

"I'll let Tudor know," Tim said quietly.

The air was heavy and dark and pressing against her chest. Everything about today was threatening to steal the past and when she tried to see the future, there was nothing there, either. "What the hell do I have to live for? I might as well just die."

"Don't say that, Allie. Please, don't say that!" Tim wrapped her hand in his.

"It's what I feel."

"I want you to meet with Tudor again and talk to him. Please. It's okay to talk. You can talk to your lawyer and no one will ever find out. He's not allowed to tell anyone what you say to him. You need someone you can talk to about things."

"I only want to talk to Carbon. I can ask him if it's okay to talk to my lawyer."

"If you want bail, you're going to have to talk to a lawyer."

"If I can't be with Carbon, I don't want bail. Remember?"

Tim stared at the floor, absently running his thumb across her fingernails. "Okay. Talk to me, then."

"About what?"

"You've just got back from a trip to Korea. Tell me something about it. Just talk. What was the weather like?"

"It was much different than when I was there in July. We had sun and we had heat."

"What did you do over there?"

"Some of the same stuff I did with the girls. Some different stuff. We went up to the Samcheok cave. That was the day Carbon let me have his revolver."

"You had a guy's revolver?"

"Yes, and it was loaded. Two bullets. I had it for most of the day."

"What were you doing with a revolver?"

"I wasn't doing anything with it. I just carried it in my purse for Carbon. When he asked for it, I gave it to him."

"What else did you do?"

"Why the hell am I'm talking to you?" She quickly rose and walked behind him. At her feet, the polished tiles sparked back the white and blue of the overhead lights. Above her, behind the banks of fluorescents, was a strange, almost artistic collection of painted piping, flat surfaces and webbed trusses.

"You're talking to me because you just got home from a vacation in Korea and there's no one else around to talk to. I'm sure there are things you want to say."

"You're tricking me. You're tricking me like Tudor did!"

Tim quickly stood, marched over to her and grabbed her shoulders. "Allie! Look at me, for Christ's sake. You were brutally kidnapped, forced out of the country, and God knows what else those guys did to you. Now you have to admit to that. You have to talk about it or you're going to be in so much shit for such a long time, you'll never be free to walk in the sunshine again. Give Carbon up, Allie! Give him up! The time to talk is now."

"Who told you all that bullshit? Who told you I was kidnapped?"

"Well, it sure as hell wasn't you! You won't tell me a damned thing."

"Whoever told you that was lying. It might have seemed like I was kidnapped, but I wasn't. Someone has lied to you."

"Okay." Tim raised his arms in defeat. "If that's the way it was. Should I just leave? Do you want me to leave?"

"I thought you were here to talk about getting me a lawyer."

"I told you, Allie. This time listen to me—Tudor is your lawyer. Have you got that? Tudor is your lawyer!" He inhaled deeply and exhaled. "Now," he finally continued. "Do you want me to leave?"

The thought about being alone again in her cell panicked her. "I wouldn't mind you staying if we didn't talk, if we just sat together."

"Okay." Tim motioned her to her chair. "I don't mind." Allie folded her hands in her lap and bowed her head. She was feeling very tired. Lost, perhaps.

"I don't think Carbon would mind if I put my arm around your shoulder," Tim said, not waiting for a response. "And you could put your head on mine. I know Carbon wouldn't mind."

"I don't suppose he would." Allie leaned into Tim and closed her eyes. "I'll ask him the next time I see him."

"Tim has been very supportive of you, Allie." **Dr. Erica Freid**

"Like fuck! He's been taking advantage of me since the moment I landed back in Canada."

"What do you mean?"

"I was exhausted when I arrived from Korea. Confused. I hadn't eaten or slept for two days. Handcuffed. Locked up. I needed Tim. He was the one person I could call for help and he knew it. He was there for me all right. Touching me..."

"You don't think he was there because he loves you?"

"He was there to manipulate me!"

"Manipulate you into what?"

"Manipulate me into reconciling. He always wanted to reconcile. He thought if he caught me when I was weak...when I needed him...he'd get what he wanted."

"Maybe he wants to reconcile because he loves you?"

"I don't know and I don't care. I don't want to reconcile. I never did and he knows that and he isn't respecting those feelings. Not at all. He's acting as if because he helped me, got me a lawyer, talked to me, I owe him something in return. He thinks I ought to live with him again ...or something."

CHAPTER 29

"Allie, I want you to see a psychiatrist," Tudor said.

Two weeks ago, he'd surprised her by not objecting to her choice to waive the right to a bail hearing. *'It's something we can do later if you change your mind,'* he'd said.

Since then she'd been transferred to the new remand facility in her home province of Alberta, as spaces for women in pretrial custody were scarce. The move had put her closer to Tim, but five mountain ranges away from her lawyer.

On his own accord, though, Tudor had travelled all the way to the Edmonton Remand Centre. "I know a good psychiatrist," he said. "A woman. She—"

"I don't—"

"We have lots of possibilities for your defence," he continued quickly. "But until you talk about what happened, I'm not able to do anything for you. I think a psychiatrist could help you deal with things and speed up the process."

"I know what you're thinking."

"What am I thinking?"

"You believe I was forced into all this."

"And you don't?"

"Not in the way you do. Although to those on the outside it might seem like I was coerced, when you know the whole story, it's different."

"I must know what happened, Allie. There are some offers on the table but until you start talking, I can't begin to look at them."

"Offers?"

"The cops believe you have information of value to them and the Crown attorney may be willing to cut a deal with you."

"Don't you understand? There's no deal! Nothing!"

"I don't understand. However, if you were to tell me what happened I might be able to."

Allie straightened, struggling to regain a sense of control. Talk of a deal made her head spin and her heart, ache. Even her own lawyer was trying to get her to turn against Carbon, trying to wrench him away from her. She took a deep breath. Sometimes working with a situation was better than fighting it. "Tim and you may be right," she conceded. "Maybe Carbon doesn't love me. Maybe even, I don't love him."

Much to her angst, Tudor's eyes brightened. She hastily continued. "Let's forget about all that shit for now because when it comes to making legal decisions, our love or lack thereof, is irrelevant. Totally, absolutely, irrelevant."

"Not true, Allie. The nature of your relationship with Carbon might be useful in your defence. If you committed crimes because Carbon was threatening you, the law won't hold you accountable."

"The law might not." She leaned forward and lowered her voice. "I believe, though, a biker gang would."

"What are you saying?"

"Whether or not Carbon and I love each other, if I use kidnapping and coercion as a defence, it's likely to lead to more charges against Carbon and Saber, isn't it?"

"Yes," Tudor agreed.

"And that will not make the Jackals gang at all happy, will it?"

"I hear what you're saying."

"Pissing off a biker gang is not something I want to add to my résumé…or to my obituary as would be more likely the case."

Tudor sat silent for a moment, looking into her eyes. She thought she detected some new-found respect there. "I may be able arrange police protection for you," he finally said. "Especially if you were to agree to work with them."

"There are problems with working for the cops. For one thing, Carbon told me the Jackals set me up over some dealings Mahogany Imports had with the gang when I was still with the company. He said the cops were tailing me long before I went to Korea. And secondly, I know you don't want to hear this. I know it sounds crazy to you and I'm sorry but I just can't give up on Carbon. I can't rat on him. I want to get together with him again, Tudor."

"I see. I can do some sleuthing to find out if what Carbon told you about the police is true. It could be all lies, Allie. You realize that, don't you?"

"It could be, but I don't think so. That's not the kind of relationship Carbon and I had. He was very honest with me and forced me to be honest, too. We…" Allie paused, remembering the afternoon on the boat tour. Rocking with the waves. The PC room afterwards. That day when all her lies had crumbled and Carbon had revealed that everything he'd done, he'd done to keep her safe from the Jackals. Because...he'd fallen in love with her the night when they'd met in the tavern. "We grew very close."

"Very close," Tudor repeated, as if trying to memorize a fact. "I need more information on that when you're ready to talk. Perhaps in the meantime you can tell me a bit about your ex. I understand you've been talking to Tim quite a bit?"

"Yes. He's been good to me. I think he'd like us to get back together."

"What are your feelings about that?"

"I don't have feelings about that. I have feelings about Carbon."

"Do you want to deal with those feelings alone, or with some help?"

"Alone," Allie said. "Definitely alone."

"Okay, I have to respect that. Since you won't talk, I will. I haven't seen all the evidence yet, but I can tell you some of what the prosecution is going to hold against you. They'll present evidence that you knew Carbon and Saber before you went with them to South Korea. I've seen some bank records that might link you to drug transactions and electronic messages that implicate you in the conspiracy to export drugs to Korea. Mahogany Exports figures in there, too. You were allowed to return to Canada to face the charges under rarely-used general extraterritorial jurisdiction because both the crimes and investigation crossed several borders and fraudulent Canadian passports were used to facilitate the crime— but Korea will be watching closely. If they don't think you are prosecuted and sentenced to their liking, they could ask for you to be extradited to be tried for crimes committed on their soil. We don't want that to happen."

"I suppose not."

"You're very lucky Canada swung a deal this way. When it comes to international drug offences, this nation tends to be quite willing to let others with stiffer penalties do the prosecuting. International investigations involving our police have often led to Canadian citizens being arrested on foreign soil."

"Canada swung my deal?"

"It's why you're back here."

"I thought it was my note to the ambassador that got me to Canada. Are you saying I'd have been brought here anyway? I betrayed Carbon for no reason?"

"Carbon is in deep trouble, with or without your note, Allie. You are, too. The prosecution will bring up your twice-dropped restraining orders against Carbon. Your previous trip to Korea. Your experience with importing and exporting. They have evidence you and Carbon were lovers. Your presence down on the Russian docks–"

"I was just interpreting. It was a touristy visit. I know some Russian."

"I suggest if you didn't lie to Carbon, you shouldn't lie to me, either."

"Lie?"

"I doubt you were under surveillance in Canada before you left, but I'm damned sure you were in Korea. Lies aren't the way to go. If you contradict in court what surveillance captured, it will only hurt your defence."

"I see." She remembered her unease down on the Russian docks. She'd told Carbon afterwards she was sure they were being double-crossed. There'd been too many people within earshot for the type of conversation they were having. There'd been too much forthrightness, not enough double talk—not enough slang. No demands for money, no sealing of the deal with a toast of vodka. Carbon had brushed off her concerns, saying she shouldn't compare the business culture in Korea with the one she knew in Russia.

She wondered who'd been the betrayer on that musty wharf. Perhaps the investigators had primed the entire mob beforehand to turn against Carbon and his gang. The Russians would likely have been willing co-conspirators in a police operation that would keep the Jackals from moving into their turf. Maybe the Asian gangs in Canada, which Carbon had befriended, were actually in on the takedown, too. They may have hoped the Korean police operation would weaken the Jackals at home and allow their gangs to take over the Canadian drug trade. The Jackals expansion into Southeast Asia may have been doomed from the start.

Allie sighed. Knowing how Carbon's gang had been thwarted might be helpful to the Jackals in the future but it did nothing to help her present legal situation. She struggled to remember what emails she'd written and what money had changed hands. It had all been done under Carbon's watchful gaze. He'd dictated, she'd translated and typed. She'd sent messages home to Canada. Much of the terminology he'd used she hadn't understood. If pressed, though, she'd have to admit that she knew the emails were about arranging the shipment of drugs. She'd also helped him jump the hoops to access online banking from Korean computers. Had he put her name on one of his offshore accounts?

"If you can't be honest with me," Tudor continued, "perhaps you should get yourself another lawyer."

"I want to be honest but things are so confusing. I don't understand where all this is leading. What chance do we have of successfully fighting this without a coercion defence? I didn't do anything illegal in Canada. Can we argue our police have no jurisdiction over what I did in Korea?"

"I'm not beyond trying for that. However, it's exceptionally rare for you to be given the chance to face trial in your home country and I'm concerned if we follow that line of defence, it could lead to you being extradited to Korea to face charges. We wouldn't want that—their justice is a lot tougher than ours, their prisons, hell holes. All that aside, my point is, it isn't the court that needs your honesty, it's me. I have to know what really happened or I can't be of any help."

"I'm not talking about it to you or anyone else," Allie said. Tudor's kind eyes clouded. "I'm sorry."

Time played tricks on Allie. Sometimes it passed so slow it felt like she existed in an eternal 'now'. Sometimes she believed time started the night she'd met Carbon and ceased the moment he'd looked up at her singing in the noraebang.

At some point, Tudor returned to see her. He stepped into the room and she could immediately tell there was trouble. He sat opposite her and rolled his pen in his hand. "I feel obligated to tell you this," he began.

"Has something come up to make things worse for me? Did you find some information about the cops investigating me before I went to Korea?"

"It doesn't seem there's much truth to Carbon's allegations. There was an investigation because Tim had reported his suspicions. It wasn't like you, personally, were suspected of having done anything wrong. That's what I know for now, anyway. There might be more but I'm not all that worried it's going to have any bearing on these charges you're facing."

"Carbon said the police were investigating me for bribing the Russians. It wasn't like that, Tudor. I was just trying to work with the system over there. I wasn't intending on going into business with the mob. But things like that look bad in this context. Fuck! How does innocent stuff end up looking so corrupt?"

"The Jackals are powerful, Allie. They're clever. However, the cops are, too. You know that. They realize what they're up against here. I'm sure they'll deal fairly with you. We can talk about the Russian stuff some more, but I really don't think it's important. We can worry about it if and when it results in any new charges or if it appears the Crown intends to use it against you at trial."

"If it's not the Russian thing bothering you, what is?"

"I'm not sure if you've been told, but Saber and Carbon made bail. They're out on the street. I want to point out that if you had used their lawyers, you'd likely be out, too. The reason I'm mentioning all this is their lawyers have approached me to roll the cases into one. In other words, they want to be your lawyers, too."

"Why would they want that?"

"Oh, boy. Boy, oh boy, oh boy." Tudor exhaled and closed his eyes. He drummed his pen on the desk. "Look, Allie," he finally continued. "The only reason I'm telling you this is because you've suggested you might want to reconnect with Carbon—that's what this would entail. If you want to break with the gang, then you don't want this. Believe me."

"I have to decide now?"

"No, you don't have to decide anything now. But..." With his thumb and forefinger, he squeezed his brows together and looked intently at her. "You do have to start talking to me now. I'm working blind here! I'm trying to make decisions. Trying to get something together for you. If you want me for your lawyer, you have to talk to me. If I'm not going to be your lawyer... Let me fill you in. You might have a better chance of getting off if you take their lawyers—"

"Why? Are their lawyers that much better than you?"

"No, but they have more to work with. You've told me you won't deal, told me you won't testify against the boys, told me you don't want to use a coercion defence. It doesn't leave me much, does it? Carbon and Saber's lawyers don't have any of that. They'll do whatever they damned well please. They don't have to worry about anyone's safety, worry about who loves whom, worry about testifying against you. They'll do it all– whatever it takes. They don't even care if it ruins their reputations. Carbon and Saber are gunning to walk out of that courtroom free men and they just might. If you agree to take their lawyers, you might, too. However, it ties you in with them. The cost to you for their representation will go way beyond any set fee. It will be a lifetime commitment to the gang they'll undoubtedly want. So?"

"Wow," Allie said.

"There are other things to consider. If you don't accept their offer to represent you, they're going to be pretty damned sure you're aiming to squeal on the Jackals and use a coercion defence. And you know what that might mean—retaliation. On the other hand, I'm not guaranteeing you the Jackals' lawyers will get you off, either. It might be a ruse. Saber and Carbon might get much better legal advice than you get. The gang's best interests might override yours. They might intend on setting you up to keep the heat off the boys. I just can't say for sure."

"You make it sound like the lawyers are Jackals!" Allie protested.

"In this case, pretty damned close. Pretty goddamned close."

Allie shifted in her chair. Although it bothered her little to know Carbon was a Jackal, for some reason it upset her immensely to hear that his attorneys were. Considering she was almost a Jackal herself, it ought to have felt like good news. She ought to be jumping at the chance to hire Carbon's legal team but Tudor's reservations about the offer made her uneasy.

She was learning to trust this man with the gentle eyes, partly because of his openness and honesty but mostly because of his respect for her relationship with Carbon, despite his obvious misgivings. "Tudor," she finally said. "I'm really happy you told me all this. You respected that this was a decision that had to be mine to make."

Tudor shrugged. "It was a battle with my conscience. I didn't know if you were able to understand what would be in your best interest, especially since you haven't let me in on what happened. I was scared I'd be offering you an option that should you choose unwisely could hurt you badly—in so many ways. I have so little on which to base my decisions."

"I know."

"I want to help you make these choices, Allie. I want to give you good advice. I promise I'll listen to your entire story. You've noted things about this predicament I wouldn't have considered. Given a chance, I can do the same for you. We can work on it together and look at all the tangled threads of this mess."

"You're right, Tudor. It's time I talked. But you have to promise not to laugh at me or dismiss my feelings. You must promise you'll work for *me* and not for Tim."

"It's a deal."

Allie squeezed her eyes shut. "Where should I start?"

"I know so little, I can't say. Where do you think it started?"

"It all started..." Allie put her elbows on the table and cradled her chin in her hands. She offered up a sly grin. "Back in Penis Park."

CHAPTER 30

Allie's harsh reality of cell blocks, small cots, prison food and scheduled and rescheduled trial dates made reuniting with Carbon seem a far off fantasy. As she waited for Tudor to show for his appointment, she became increasingly edgy. With only two weeks until her trial, she expected it would be today that he'd insist she admit being kidnapped.

She wondered if refusing would mean she'd end up in front of the trial judge without a lawyer at her side.

Tudor walked into the room and immediately began talking. "I get the feeling it isn't information about your Korean trip the police are interested in." Springs creaked as he nestled into the chair opposite her.

"No, probably not."

"Am I safe in assuming there may have been some pillow talk between you and Carbon? Did he spill the beans to you about some other aspect of gang activity?"

Allie stared at her hands in her lap. Her knuckles were rough and red. Her palms sweaty. Her nails, broken and dull. She looked up into Tudor's kindly eyes. "He did," she said.

"Of course, the police can't know for sure so they're not willing to put anything on the table. Is there something I can give them to keep their interest alive?"

White rocks, shadows, and bones. *It wasn't like I was mad at them,* Carbon had moaned. *If I'd been angry, if they'd pissed me off...* He wasn't an evil man, just a man caught up in evilness. He'd buried his buddy in a sacred place that had never been discovered. *I don't know how to love you...*

"White Rock," Allie said. "If I ever decide to talk, you can tell the cops I know all about White Rock."

"What was White Rock?"

"Murder."

"Murder?" Tudor's face blanched. "You have information about a murder?"

"I might."

"Please tell me it's not the White Rock biker massacre."

Allie shrugged.

"What kind of information?" Tudor persisted. "The kind that would solve the case?"

"Maybe."

"You know who did it? Carbon?"

Allie shrugged.

"Do you want me to tell the police you know who killed the Shadow Riders at White Rock?"

"Tell them nothing. Let them keep guessing what I know."

"At least talk to *me* about it."

"I'm not ready to talk about it."

"Are you scared of gang reprisal? Is that why you won't talk?"

Allie stared past the blue of his eyes to his kindness and honesty. Her thoughts whirled. Her heart beat painfully against her ribs. "No, it's not that."

"We can keep you safe, I promise. You have a chance here to avoid a criminal record. That's got to be worth something to you."

"It's not because I'm scared. It's Carbon. I'd be betraying Carbon."

"He's not worth it, Allie."

"He opened up to me one night, told me things in his heart. He cried like a baby. A big huge biker dude with tattoos of the devil on both arms, crying to me. He's a broken man, not a wicked one."

"Okay, Allie. But at some point you must tell."

"No, there'll never be that point."

"You realize this man you think you are in love with is a mass murderer? You've thought about that side of things, right? You think he's the kind of guy you want to be with?"

"I don't know what I'm thinking. I only know what I'm feeling."

"Where do we go from here?" Tudor asked.

Allie sucked in her breath and gazed up at the ceiling. He was going to object, argue, yell at her. Forfeit her retainer and walk away. "Perhaps the best thing for me to do...I want to plead guilty."

"Why?" His gentle voice surprised her and she looked across at him. His blue eyes were shining with something more than mere respect for her decision; what it was, though, she didn't know.

"It keeps my options open," she said. "I won't get Carbon into worse trouble, meaning if I want to get together with him when this is all over, I can."

"These are criminal charges. Are you sure you're willing to live with a criminal record?"

Allie nodded.

"It won't be easy to plead guilty," Tudor warned.

"What do you mean?"

"It's not legal to plead guilty when you're innocent."

"You're kidding me, right? It's legal to plead innocent when you're guilty, but not vice versa?"

"Justice is sometimes strange." Tudor chuckled and rose. "I'll see what I can do for you." He gave her a warm smile and patted her on the shoulder. At the door he stopped, and keeping his eyes on his notes, spoke. "Perhaps if you were to talk to the cops about White Rock down the road, they could do something about that criminal record." He left without looking up.

Allie stared at the exit. She knew now what his eyes had been saying—it was his plan all along that she plead guilty.

"You were willing to go to jail, have a criminal record, just to protect Carbon?" **Dr. Erica Freid**

"It's more complicated than that." **Allison Montgomery**

"How so?"

"Although I wanted to plead guilty so I wouldn't have to betray Carbon, it made sense for many other reasons. Tudor wanted it so I'd be safe from gang retaliation. Carbon wanted it so he wouldn't face kidnapping charges. Shrug wanted it…Yeah, it wouldn't have happened if Shrug hadn't wanted it."

"Shrug? The cop? Why did he want you to plead guilty?"

"Take a guess why Shrug wanted me locked up. Guess. We all get to guess why Shrug wants what he wants. We all get to guess how it is Shrug always gets exactly what he wants."

CHAPTER 31

Although Tudor had warned her that pleading guilty wouldn't be easy, she hadn't believed him. However, just a day into the proceedings and she knew what he meant.

"Are you sure you're getting proper legal counsel?" the judge hollered across to her at one point. Tudor had twice interrupted the Crown's reading of the Agreed Statement of Facts to ask for a publication ban on the evidence and had twice been refused. He'd first argued if the evidence was made public it would affect the trials of the others involved in the Korean operation. Next, he'd argued releasing sensitive facts about the case could endanger Allie.

Both times the judge asked for proof that making the evidence public would have such dire effects. When Tudor conceded he had none, the judge ruled justice, as always, would best be served in an open court.

Now with the Crown having just finished reading the agreed facts of the case, Tudor was again on his feet. "Your honour, my client has very honourably agreed to plead guilty to all charges against her and has accepted full responsibility for her actions. As you can see by the facts, she was involved with very powerful men and for this court to further endanger her, and endanger justice, by publishing the facts of the case while the others are still free and before they have been tried, might be construed as misaligned justice."

"Are you saying there's a problem with the Statement of Facts?"

"My client has no objections to the facts as outlined by the Crown, however—"

"Well, I have some objections," the judge bellowed. "How is it everyone in the country, including the CBC, seems to have evidence your client was kidnapped and coerced, yet the Crown doesn't?" A gasp went up in the court room. Tudor stared at the judge, his mouth gaping.

Allie looked about nervously. Obviously the judge's comment was out of the ordinary but what it meant to her, she didn't know. She was about to ask

Tudor but he'd regained his composure and was again speaking.

"Sir, I don't believe kidnapping is listed in any of the charges against my client and, as such, any supposed evidence regarding an abduction is irrelevant to these proceedings. Also, sir, media reports are not generally accepted as evidence in our Canadian courtrooms."

When the judge's red face deepened to burgundy, Tudor quickly added, "With all due respect, sir. Your honor." Then, in an apparent act of contrite submission, he sat.

The judge looked to Allie. "Allison Lisa Montgomery, are you aware your guilty plea will result in a criminal record and jail time?"

"Yes—"

Tudor jumped to his feet, again. "Sir, I cannot have statements about a supposed abduction left unchallenged and become part of these proceedings. It unnecessarily endangers—"

"I'm aware of your objections, and your reasons," the judge roared. "However, it is within the mandate of this court to assure the facts of the case are presented truthfully and unabridged and your client receives justice. I must be satisfied she truly is guilty of the offences she's charged with and that the court has received all the necessary information to reach the proper conclusion in that regard. Do you not agree?"

"I apologize for my outburst. You are right, of course." Tudor sank into his chair, defeated. Frustration still plying his brows.

"Allison Lisa Montgomery, are you pleading guilty on your own accord, with no pressure from your lawyer, friends, or co-accused? Or anybody else?"

"Yes."

"Are you pleading guilty because you fear for your safety should you enter a not guilty plea and proceed to trial?"

"No."

"Did you participate in the crimes you are charged with on your own free will, free of coercion?"

"Yes."

"Before or during the commission of the offences to which you have pleaded guilty, were you fearful for your life, health or safety should you refuse to participate?"

"No."

"Do you understand that should you have been acting out of fear, you could be found not guilty of the charges, even though you did engage in illegal activities?"

"Yes."

"Do you understand it is a crime to lie to me? That you can be charged with contempt of court should your answers to the foregoing questions not be truthful?"

"I understand."

"Do you understand that I do not have to accept your guilty plea? That if I have any doubts about your guilt, I can order this matter to go to trial?"

Allie looked at Tudor. They had come all this way and were going to lose the battle.

"She understands," Tudor said, rising. "She admirably wishes to accept responsibility for her actions, accept the consequences and make reparation as far as is possible." The judge glared at him, silently. "She must do this, sir," Tudor added quietly. "She must."

The judge and Tudor exchanged a long, long stare, the judge being the first to drop his gaze. "I hereby accept the defendant's guilty plea. A sentencing hearing will be scheduled in the near future. A publication ban is hereby ordered on all evidence presented and all court proceedings other than the court's acceptance of the defendant's guilty plea. This ban will be lifted following the trials of the co-accused. Court is adjourned."

"All rise!" the court clerk called as the judge stood and strode out of the courtroom.

"Oh, thank God," Tudor said, pallor replacing his flush. "Now let's hope the judge's misgivings result in a light sentence and not the other way around."

"What evidence does the CBC have that I was kidnapped?" Allie asked, a bit bewildered by what had happened.

"Apparently there's an airport security tape showing you quite drugged during check in." Tudor was gathering his papers and stuffing them into his briefcase. An officer of the court was standing not too far from them, obviously waiting to lead her to prison.

"But Carbon told the Air Canada clerk I'd taken *Gravol*. How would anyone know otherwise?"

"*Gravol* doesn't generally knock a person out for fourteen hours straight and there are flight attendants who remember. And..." Tudor paused to wave the waiting officer out of ear shot and then sucked in a breath. His words were reluctant and hurried. "There's the small matter of the hypodermic needle found on your deck."

"Shit!"

"And," he added even quicker and quieter, "your jeans on the road and the passport in your safe."

"You knew about all that?"

Tudor nodded.

"The police know? The Crown knows?"

"Yes."

"Why wasn't it in the Statement of Facts?"

Tudor looked at her steady for a full minute. "That's not my department," he finally said, as the officer of the court once more began approaching.

"What's going to happen now?" Allie asked, besieged by panic.

Tudor motioned the officer to halt. "Next will be the sentencing. I'm hoping the judge's reluctance to accept your guilty plea might result in a lighter sentence. However, it might work in reverse. If he feels he's being manipulated and justice is being maligned, he might want revenge. It's delicate."

"Shit!"

"The other worry is your plea will influence Carbon and Saber's trials. The publication ban will help, but it's hard to keep secrets in today's age of technology. Besides, I believe I saw some of Carbon's legal team in attendance today. They'll glean what they can from the proceedings to benefit their clients. That's why things like we're doing are frowned upon. It can spiral, Allie. Justice can get lost. We're taking the chance, though. Okay? "

Allie nodded.

"The hope is, if what we're doing today does adversely affect the Crown's case against Carbon and Saber on their drug trafficking charges, it will at least keep you safe until the police can get them for White Rock."

"Who's hoping that?"

Tudor again looked at her in silence for a long time. "That's not my department," he said once more.

CHAPTER 32

Allie was trying to control her nervousness by surfing the news pages of the Web. Her parole hearing was tomorrow. Unlike when she'd been arrested over a year ago, she was now quite ready to give up the comforts of confinement. Tudor's gentle blue eyes must have curbed the judge's misgivings about the shenanigans in his courtroom, because it was merely four months since he'd handed down her sentence. With time already served, her stint behind bars was hopefully going to be brief—if she managed to convince the board she was ready for release.

Once again, there was to be no mention of her kidnapping, no excuses made. She was going to admit to being very remorseful about her role in things and very convincing about her desire to return to her life on the straight and narrow.

She'd be in and out of jail before Saber's and Carbon's trials even started. Their lawyers were working their magic, with delay after delay in the proceedings. Playing on the judge's objections to Allie's plea, they'd tried to argue the investigation into the whole matter was tainted. However, since there were no kidnapping charges on the table, their arguments about the missing information were eventually dismissed. The attempt, however, had successfully created another three months of freedom for the boys—and a lot of stress for Tudor.

Allie zeroed in on a headline about South Korea. An international environmental group was upping pressure to legalize the use of two-wheeled vehicles outside of the Korean cities. It was arguing the benefits of energy efficiency and pollution reduction. *Are biker gangs financing that lobbying effort?*

In Montreal, two men with Russian names were found shot outside a pub. Victims of a gang war, the police said. *Russian gangs...Carbon and the Jackals. Was this revenge for being betrayed on the Busan docks?*

In central Alberta, a generous gift to a charitable foundation by an anonymous donor was making it possible to set up a private school to cater to Asian students. The school's speciality was its curriculum which would contain a heavy dose of Asian cultural training to enable its students to reintegrate when they returned to their native lands. *Damned if he didn't listen to my advice on how to disguise a bribe.*

Allie tapped her fingers on the desk. It was obvious the arrests of Saber and Carbon had done little to thwart the Jackals' plan to take over the drug trade in Korea.

"Allison!" a voice thundered behind her. She turned to see a giant of a man. He was at least six-and-half-feet tall and bulked up with three hundred pounds of pure muscle. A tapestry of tattoos snaked along the curves and dips of his arms. He was looking at her with warm grey eyes and an amused grin.

Allie swiveled her chair. "Did no one tell you this is a *women's* prison?" she asked.

He chuckled. "What better place for a man to be?" Reaching over her shoulder, he tapped through her computer history, stopping to scan the same three stories which had caught her eye. He stepped back, smiled down at her appreciatively and then took a chair at the desk across the aisle. He looked comically out of place, sprawled on the steno chair, his legs so long his toes almost reached hers.

"So," he said in his reverberating voice, "obviously you're good at makin' connections."

Allie was wondering if it was at all possible that Carbon had sent him. "Who the hell are you?" she asked.

"Shrug."

She blinked. He reached in his pocket and handed her a business card. His name was Shrug and his card sported the distinctive Northern Alberta Police logo.

"How the hell do you get a name like 'Shrug'?"

He lifted his massive shoulders and dropped them. "I dunno," he said, grinning even broader.

"So what does Shrug want?"

"You bloody well know what I want," he growled, all niceties abruptly replaced with a piercing glare. *He wants me to talk about the White Rock murders.* Allie involuntarily shuddered. He cast his eyes to his loafers.

"What if I don't have what you want?" she asked, tensing in anticipation of another hit by his eyes. However, he kept his gaze focussed on his feet. "Fuck," Allie muttered, turning to her computer. She rested her chin in her hands. A small part of her knew she should talk about the massacre. Her heart, however, told her she loved Carbon and could not betray him. Upward of five minutes of silence ensued. Allie was about to sneak a peek behind her to confirm the man was still there, when he spoke again. "Nervous?"

"About what?" she asked over her shoulder.

"Your parole hearin's tomorrow."

"Yeah, I'm nervous."

"Don't be."

She slowly swivelled to face him. "Why not?"

He lifted his eyes. There was warmth once more behind the grey. "You'll do okay," he said softly. He crossed his arms and pulled his long legs under the chair. "You know what you have to do. Your husband will be there for you, to provide a place for you to go home to."

"I don't have a husband."

"Allison!"

"I've been divorced for almost two years. Like hell they can make me live with my ex. He left me for a sex pot secretary. Why would I want to go home with him?"

"Your choice, I guess." Shrug rose.

"What does that mean?"

"The parole board is gonna want to see some good influence in your life. They're gonna want to see you makin' a move to get your legitimate lifestyle back."

"What the hell does any of this have to do with you?"

Shrug looked first to her and then cast his eyes to the ceiling. "You might say it's my department." Three of his giant strides had him through the door and out of sight.

It took Allie a moment to make the connection between Shrug's words and Tudor's. *His department?* She rose and raced down the hall. "Shrug, stop!"

He was held up at the glass door, waiting for it to be unlocked.

"Shrug," she said between pants. "I didn't know it was you who pulled strings so I wouldn't have to admit that I was kidnapped. I owe you a thanks." He looked at her impassively. "In fact," she said, "I think I owe you a bit more than that."

"Allison, if the only reason you have for doin' good with your life is to repay a debt to me, I ain't interested."

The door clicked and the glass panels moved apart. Shrug stepped through and turned to her. "It's okay. I understand." He gave a quick nod. The doors began their slow slide together. "I wish you well. God bless." On the freedom side of the cellblock, he walked away. Allie leaned her forehead against the door and closed her eyes.

She hadn't meant for her thank you to be an insult or a disappointment, but he'd made it clear it was both. Perhaps he was right; she was living her life for all the wrong reasons. Six men had come to a brutal end one hot August afternoon and no one was paying for that crime.

She strolled down the hall to the window overlooking the parking lot. There was no mistaking Shrug, even when viewing him from four floors up. His stature and stride would be identifiable at any distance. He stopped beside a motorbike, threw on a leather jacket and donned a helmet.

He even has a Harley to match his thunder and tattoos. She watched until his bike passed through the gates and out of sight. She looked at the business card she had clutched in her hand. "Shrug," she murmured, wiping at her eyes.

"What's the matter?" one of her fellow inmates asked. "Have you been given bad news about your parole hearing?"

"No," Allie answered dully. "I guess you might say I've been given bad news about myself."

CHAPTER 33

"Jeppard!" Shrug's voice rang through the room as he strolled to the desk of a co-worker at the detachment. "I need a safe house for her. A brand new one. A place we've never used before."

"It's not in the budget," Jeppard said, his hands flying across the keyboard.

"I want a cabin." Jeppard paused his typing and looked up at Shrug, whose eyes were glazed as if observing a fantasy in the empty space between them. "Isolated, but fully serviced—a flush toilet and a satellite TV. On a lake, preferably one with perch. And loons. Perhaps, a sandy beach. And a sheltered cove for moorin' the fishing boat. Northern Alberta."

"Sure." Jeppard looked to his monitor.

"This afternoon!" Shrug bellowed so loudly, Jeppard jumped and placed his hand over his heart.

"Shrug, for Christ's sake, don't scream like that, man! God, you're crazy."

"This afternoon," Shrug repeated, thumping his fist on the desk.

Jeppard clenched his teeth. "A fishing cabin for you is not in the budget."

"Have I got the wrong man?" Shrug said, looking around the room. "Have I got the Auditor General instead of Property Acquisitions?"

"Oh, I imagine you'd get the Auditor General real fast-like if you start buying yourself fishing lodges with company money."

Shrug grinned down at him. "You're no fun. It's obvious I'm losin' my touch. I can't seem to get any cooperation around here these days." He pulled a chair to Jeppard's desk and lowered his voice. "I'm serious. I need somethin' ultra-safe. Allison Montgomery's gonna turn for us."

"Wow! When did that happen?"

"Tomorrow. Or perhaps the day after. Sometime before the week's up, anyway."

"She told you this?" Jeppard asked sceptically.

"Hmm, not exactly. Come on," he urged, pointing at the monitor. "Pull up the real estate page, buddy."

"She's not in love with that Carbon guy anymore?"

"Perhaps." Shrug pointed again to the computer screen.

"What the hell did you say to change her mind?" Jeppard positioned his hands over the keys.

"I blessed her." Shrug nodded quickly a few times.

"You blessed her? And who granted you the authority to bless people?"

"God." Shrug tapped at the keyboard just once before Jeppard swatted his fingers.

"Shrug was a minister before he was a cop," a female voice behind the office divider called.

Jeppard pushed back his chair and walked over to peer around the divider at Constable Wray. "You expect me to believe that?" He looked to her and then Shrug. Both nodded vigorously.

"Shrug? A minister? This Shrug? This man before me with tattoos from his eyebrows to his dick? Who rides a Harley? Whose every second word is 'fuck' and every second sentence is a lie? *This* man was a minister?"

They both nodded again.

"And you can prove this? Beyond a reasonable doubt?"

"Yup."

"Don't bother with the evidence," Jeppard mumbled, returning to his seat. "Knowing Shrug, he'd probably come up with a certificate of priesthood signed by Jesus Christ himself."

"Ultra-safe," Shrug said, wiggling a finger as close to the keyboard as he dared. "Immediate possession..."

"I'm serious. There's no money for that and by the sounds of it, no time to find the money."

Shrug sighed and stared at his shoes. "You're sure?" he finally asked.

"I'm sure. I'll show you what we do have—"

"No, it has to be new. Not new, like built yesterday new, but, well, you know. Somethin' absolutely no one but you and I will know about."

"I know what you mean. It doesn't change anything, though."

"All right," Shrug said, rising. "You find it, put an offer on it and I'll take care of the money end of things." He walked away.

"Sure. Whatever you say, Shrug." Jeppard reluctantly pulled up the real estate website. "Hey!" he called. "You weren't serious about this isolated, in-the-neck-of-the-woods cabin thing, were you?"

Shrug stopped to grin at him. "The usual. You know what to look for. We'll get the cabin next time."

"Just so you know I'm not a totally trusting idiot, I'm putting a *'subject to finding financing'* clause in any offer to purchase that I end up signing."

CHAPTER 34

"Hi," Shrug greeted with mock enthusiasm when Chad opened the door to him.

"Shrug," Chad replied, not bothering to conceal his disdain.

From Chad's police uniform and the car keys he was juggling, Shrug surmised he was on his way to work. "Don't let me hold you up." He motioned Chad to pass. "I'm here to see your wife, not you."

"See my wife about what?" Chad took a firm stance to bar his entrance.

"An investment opportunity."

"Oh, no you don't! Have you no morals at all, for Christ's sake? You've used her for all else, and now you're after her money?" Shrug raised his eyebrows.

"That you, Shrug?" he heard Katrina's voice coming down the hall.

"Hey, 'trina!" Shrug called. "Wanna ride?" It was the phrase he'd used a decade ago to invite her into The Traz biker gang. He knew it was a phrase that riled Chad every time he heard it, mostly because Katrina had been only thirteen at the time and Chad wasn't a very forgiving man.

"Shrug!" Chad warned. "Every time you say, 'Wanna ride?' it means you're after her for something. That's stopping. Now!"

"Buddy, can I help it if the girl likes me?"

Chad lowered his voice to a harsh whisper. "You've had enough counselling, enough advice to know goddamned well why she likes you. And it's high time you quit taking advantage of her misplaced feelings for you."

"Shrug!" Katrina greeted with a smile as she arrived at the door. She looked from him to her husband. "What's the matter here?"

Shrug left it to Chad to answer and eyed up the couple in front of him. Chad's dark eyes were swirling with a fury directed straight at him. Shrug admired the man's courage. More than once, Chad and he had come to fist-a-cuffs and Chad, being a good six inches shorter than him, always came up the loser. However, that never deterred him from taking a stand.

Especially when it came to defending his blue-eyed bride. Katrina was fifteen years Chad's junior, had amber locks which put the sun to shame, and a feistiness that rivalled that of a cornered wildcat. Shrug figured since the woman was less than five feet tall and hovered around one hundred pounds, she'd developed a sharp edge to survive the traumas life had thrown at her.

"He's after your money now, Katrina," Chad said, keeping his eyes on Shrug's. "Your inheritance."

"I'll deal with it, hon," Katrina said quietly. "Don't worry." She stood on her tiptoes and gave Chad a quick peck on the cheek. "I'll see you when you get home."

"Katrina..." Chad finally dropped his eyes to look at his wife. "Katrina—"

"I've been dealing with my millions since I was thirteen and I've done okay with it. It'll be fine. Shrug's just badgering you; don't let him get you so riled."

"You've been dealing with Shrug since you've been thirteen, too, and I don't think you've done so 'okay' with that part."

"Chad," Katrina scolded, closing her eyes. "Come on! You're going to be late for work. I'm not a kid anymore. Go. I'll be fine."

Chad brushed angrily past. Katrina and Shrug watched him get in his car and squeal away.

"Girl," Shrug said, turning to Katrina. "You've gotta do more for your man in bed. Mellow him out a bit." He watched a blush creep across her cheeks.

"Fuck off!" She marched down the hall to the kitchen.

"You still like him?" Shrug teased, following her in. He knew Katrina worshipped Chad, perhaps because he was one of maybe three people in the entire world who liked her. Shrug found Katrina spunky but most who knew her preferred the adjective 'abrasive'.

Shrug also knew he was to blame for her coming up short in the social skills department. Many besides Chad were ever ready to remind him of that. By the time Shrug had swung out a chair and sat, his thoughts had put a damper on his humour. He was half-way thinking Chad had very valid reasons for not welcoming him into his house.

"So what's really up?" Katrina asked. "Can I get you a beer?"

Engrossed in bittersweet memories of the girl, Shrug leaned his elbows on his knees and stared at his feet. "No, I'm on duty."

"You're here on business?"

"Yeah."

Katrina hammered her fist on the table. "For fuck's sake, Shrug. Quit looking at your cheap lace-up loafers and talk!"

"Chad's right about things," he started.

"What things is he 'right' about? I haven't been noticing many lately."

"He's right about me usin' you. He's right about... Do you know why you like me?"

"I haven't got a fucking clue."

"I'm serious." Shrug laid his grey eyes on her. "Why do you like me?"

Her father had been a prominent police officer, killed along with his wife in a car crash, leaving Katrina an orphaned only child. A wild child with street smarts and dollars and guardians unable to control her. Shrug had decided if guardians couldn't keep her off the streets and out of the alleys, it wasn't likely foster parents could either. He'd been pretty sure that she'd be safer with him than those with whom she was mingling. At least that's what he'd told himself when he'd asked her to ride with him. Others said he was after her parents' life insurance payout.

"I know what you're getting at." Katrina walked to the sink and stared out the window. "And I'm fucking tired of hearing about it. Tired of hearing about my fucking 'fascination' with you."

"Katrina, I swear like the best of them, but not four times in the same sentence. For Christ's sake, find a new word!"

"I'm fucking tired about hearing about my fucking swearing all the time, too"

"Aren't you scared Shasta's gonna hear you?"

"The kid's at playschool. I don't swear when she's around."

"How fucking considerate of you." Katrina's foray into the gang with him probably wouldn't have done her much harm—except for one cold October night in an isolated metal shed. He'd been outplayed and out-witted in a culmination of the power struggle within the Traz biker gang. The night had ended with a shed full of blood, Katrina's friend mutilated and dead, and the girl bent and twisted for life.

"What are you here for?" Katrina asked.

"I was tryin' for a conversation, to start things off."

"Go for it." Katrina rejoined him at the table.

"There's a reason I was askin' about your feelin's toward me. You were thirteen, an orphan. I recruited you into the biker gang. Got you involved in all kinds of drug deals and stuff. Set you up to see your best friend slaughtered. Yet you depended on me for survival. Fell in love or fascination or whatever with me and have liked me ever since. Even though you don't have much reason to."

"That's what they say." Katrina wasn't hiding her disagreement.

"I'm thinkin' it's true, girl. You knew you needed me to survive with that bunch of hoodlums and knew you had to keep me likin' you or you'd be dead. I'm thinkin' that's pretty much what happened."

"You're a psychiatrist now, too?"

"If it had turned out that I was in fact a biker like you thought and not an undercover cop, would you still be likin' me? If I'd truly been evil, would that have mattered to your heart once you were free of the gang? Would you have felt compelled to keep likin' me?"

"You said you're on duty, when do we get to talk business?"

"You're avoidin' the question, Katrina. Why the hell can't you answer?"

"I can answer your question. Don't insinuate there are reasons I wouldn't." She dropped her eyes. "Shrug, I don't know the answer."

"I want to tell you about Allie. First, I'm lookin' for your advice, because you've been where she's been. And then, yeah, I'm lookin' for some money."

CHAPTER 35

"No, Katrina. No," Shrug said, attempting to give her back the cheque. "I wasn't lookin' for a donation. The house would be in your name. I'd get you a long-term lease. The equity would be yours. An investment, girl. No, not this."

"Shrug, it's not breaking me. The entire two million from my parents' life insurance policies are secure. I'm only playing with the interest from—it's fine. Really."

"No. I can't." Shrug waved the cheque at her. "You're makin' me feel bad for askin'."

"I know you weren't expecting a donation, but I have my reasons. Considering my history with biker gangs and the fact I testified against the lot of them, having my name on the title of a safe house doesn't make it very safe. Even though my identity is hidden under witness protection, we both know the power of the gangs. It's safer this way. Please, keep my name well away from the property."

"We could use a numbered company. There's ways we could do it."

Katrina shook her head no. "It's best this way. You and I know this money should be returned to the world and do some good to make up for it coming from such evil."

"I take it you're meanin' this ain't interest from your inheritance. More like a return on the investments you made for The Traz gang?"

"Don't play innocent," Katrina chided. "It was your investment advice I followed."

"That's the way you remember it?"

"That's the way it was. My bucks financed the mega cocaine deals that got you into the bikers' inner circle."

"So, now I get to share the illicit rewards?" Shrug waved the cheque.

"Only because I decided to let you."

Shrug looked once more at the cheque in his hand. "I'm thinkin' you're gonna have to do Chad up real good in bed tonight and I'm gonna have to sleep with my eyes open."

"Chad's not going to find out about my donation. No one finds out about safe houses."

"Okay, girl." Shrug slipped the cheque into his breast pocket and flicked his eyes to his motorbike at the curb. "Wanna ride?"

* * *

Shrug handed Jeppard the cheque and without a word, strode off. "I'm sure glad I wasn't around *before* you lost your touch," Jeppard hollered, watching the giant of a man leave the room and disappear down the hall. "Constable Wray," Jeppard called through the office divider. "How does Shrug get away with what he does?"

"He told me once he has no qualms about overriding man's laws if it serves the greater universal system of justice."

"Don't those around him, above him, or below him, have qualms?"

"He has his ways."

"Has he ever had his way with you?"

"There's been the odd time a dozen yellow roses and a box of chocolates has appeared on my desk."

Jeppard stood and walked around the divider. "You can be bribed with a dozen roses and a box of chocolates?"

"Thanked," Wray answered without looking up. "I can be thanked with roses and chocolates. He always obeys the intent of the law. I've never heard him ask anybody to do anything that contravened the spirit of justice."

"So what was it you did for him?"

"It's not likely you'll ever find out." Wray laid down her pen and got to her feet. "Because the roses," she said, avoiding Jeppard's eyes as she headed for the door, "were thanking me for my silence."

CHAPTER 36

"Shrug says if I see you a couple more times, he'll try to do something about my conditions of parole." **Allison Montgomery**

"What conditions of parole?" **Dr. Erica Freid**

"As it stands, I'm supposed to live with Tim. It's bizarre the justice system would force me to live with my ex. Don't you think?"

"Perhaps."

"Tim is…he's like an ambulance chaser. I get in trouble and zap. He's there trying to save me. Trying to force me to reconcile, to convince me Carbon is manipulative. That's like the pot calling the kettle black."

"You don't want to reconcile?"

"No!"

"Why not?"

"Because…"

"Told you, you'd do okay," Shrug said, resting a hand on Allie's shoulder as she walked out of her parole hearing a free woman—with conditions.

"Twenty minutes of lies to gain my liberty. The biggest lie being I was looking forward to living with my ex."

Shrug nodded towards Tim. "He's there by the door waiting for you."

Allie didn't even glance at Tim as she skipped down the six steps out of prison. "It isn't him I want."

"Why not?"

"I can't deny he's been very good to me since I returned from Korea. He set up my legal help. Visited or phoned every day. I'd have gone insane if he hadn't been there for me, talking, listening. But…"

"But?"

"He divorced me. I don't have a place in my heart for him."

"Carbon's still in your heart?"

"Perhaps, but I've only heard from him once. He sent a message through my lawyer that he was keeping his distance to make sure he didn't make things worse for me legally."

"You think he's ignorin' you because he still cares about you?"

"Maybe," Allie said wistfully.

"Wanna ride?" Shrug asked, pointing to his bike.

Allie returned his mischievous grin. "I've never been on one of these. I won't tip it over if I lean wrong or something?"

"Nah." Shrug handed her a helmet. "Just sit."

"Just sit?" *That's exactly what Carbon said to me in Korea!* She juggled her helmet as Shrug ran his eyes and hands over the chrome and leather of the bike.

It was more than just Shrug's words and tattoos which reminded her of Carbon; there was something mysterious about the two men's eyes—the way they sparkled, captured everything. If she looked in either man's eyes, she couldn't see anything of their souls, just a flattering reflection of herself.

"Allie!" Tim hollered from behind them. Allie quickly slipped on the helmet and clambered onto the bike. "She can't do that," Tim protested to a guard at the door. "She was to have left with me. Just two minutes ago she was ordered to stay away from all bikers!" Shrug slid into the saddle, revved the engine and whisked onto the street.

She remembered Carbon's poetic musings about the rhythm of the road and the wind in her hair. As Shrug sped down the freeway, she agreed there was something exhilarating about being on a bike. The engine roar, the tight turns, the speed—freedom and power. So close to the pavement, so open to the world. Powerful and vulnerable all at the same time.

She caught the sound of sirens and looked behind to see a police car, its flashers blazing. Shrug crossed a bridge and went three more blocks before pulling to a stop on a side street. "How adventurous are you feelin'?" he asked as he removed his helmet. "After a rousin' six months in prison, are you up for some fun?" He kicked out the centre stand and dismounted.

Allie looked nervously behind her at the cop car. "I guess I could do with some fun," she answered hesitantly.

The officer had his hand on his holster as he approached, anger lighting his eyes and sharpening his words. He obviously hadn't liked the three-block slow speed chase. "Show me your licence and registration." Shrug reached under his jacket. "Keep your hands in view!"

"I can't do both," Shrug complained lazily. "One or the other."

"I want the woman off the bike."

"Is she under arrest?"

"Not yet."

"Then she stays on the bike," Shrug said decisively, slowly pulling his papers from an inside pocket and even more slowly passing them to the officer.

"You stay off the bike until you're checked out," the officer ordered. He kept his eyes on Shrug as he returned to his cruiser.

"Are you a bettin' woman?" Shrug asked Allie.

"Not really."

"Well then, just for fun not money, after learnin' I'm a cop, what will he say to me when he brings me back my papers?"

"He won't be as amused as you are."

Shrug chuckled. "That, in itself, is amusin'."

"You're not scared he'll get angry? Maybe at me, just so he'll have something to justify his existence?"

"You're a good predictor of human behaviour," Shrug said with an appreciative grin. "I'm bettin' you're right. Here he comes now."

The officer slapped Shrug's papers into his hand. "You could've said something!"

"Would've, if you'd asked."

"We still have a problem here." The officer nodded to Allie. "She's breaching parole by not having left with her husband."

"I left with a cop, idiot," Allie said. "I think that kind of makes everything okay."

"Allison!" Shrug scolded. "Just because you're with me, doesn't mean you can talk like me. Buddy," Shrug laid a giant hand on the officer's shoulder. "Let's have a chat."

Allie watched the men retreat to the police car. Shrug's voice became a distant rumble, sprinkled with the odd chuckle. In less than a minute, he had the officer grinning. Allie kept her eyes on the two until the officer climbed into his car, pulled around her and sped down the street.

"Shucks, Allison," Shrug said, returning to the bike and picking up his helmet. "It ain't going to work. He says I've gotta take you to Tim."

"He did not."

"How the hell can you tell I'm lyin'? Even my wife was never able to figure that one out." An amused grin tickled at the corners of his mouth.

"I know darn well it's you, not the officer, who wants me to live with Tim. Why?"

"Because," Shrug said slowly, eyeing her up, "you have somethin' I want and I intend on gettin' it. This is the best way to go about that."

"I have something you want?"

"You know what it is."

"What's your plan? Make me live with Tim so my life becomes so unbearably miserable I'll talk to you about White Rock just to end the torture?"

"Perhaps." He mounted the bike and slipped on his helmet.

"Are you making me a deal? If I agree to give you what you want, I don't have to live with my ex?"

"No deals. Not yet, Allison." He throttled up the bike, whipped a U-turn and took her to Tim.

CHAPTER 37

Allie felt like a visitor when she followed Tim into the place they'd both once called home. He kicked off his shoes and disappeared into the kitchen, leaving her standing uncomfortably in the foyer. She looked through to the living room and was startled to see some of her own things there. She tentatively stepped in. On the coffee table in front of her sat a marble angel which had caught her eye at a garage sale a few months before...before she'd met Carbon. She picked it up and hugged it to her chest.

"Coffee?" Tim called.

"Something stronger would be nice." The Mexican throw cushion which once decorated her rocker, was leaning against the arm of Tim's sofa.

"Wine?" Tim asked quietly from the kitchen doorway.

With the angel in her hand, Allie motioned to the cushion. "How did you get my stuff?"

"When I reported you missing, I was allowed into your house with the cops to confirm you weren't there. To look for clues." He pointed at the angel. "You're not mad about that are you? I just thought you might like to have some of your stuff here. There's more." He led her into the bedroom and slid open the closet. "I brought over some of your clothes."

"You reported me missing? You knew I was missing?"

"Yeah. I was trying to get a hold of you. I sold the company for significantly more than it was valued at in our divorce settlement. I wanted to give you a cheque, to top up your share. When I couldn't find you and none of your friends had heard from you..." He stopped dead. "Allie, what's the matter?"

"You sold Mahogany Imports?"

"Yes," Tim answered slowly. "Is there something wrong with that?"

"Who did you sell it to?"

"Some numbered company. A lawyer-to-lawyer deal. I never actually met

the purchaser. Why? What difference does it make? I got an excellent price."
Allie stared at him.

'It changes things,' Carbon had said lightly when she'd confessed she no
longer had shares in Mahogany Imports. *'But I can work with that.'* She had no
doubt Carbon and his Jackals had bought the company. Perhaps he was
planning to have her run it for him. She now knew what the Mahogany Imports
evidence was that Tudor said the Crown might hold against her. She tried to
remember if anything about Mahogany Imports and its sale had been mentioned
in the Agreed Statement of Facts. It would certainly have looked suspicious if
the company she once owned had been sold for big bucks to the gang she'd run
off with to South Korea.

"Allie?" Tim asked. "What's the matter?"

"Nothing." She shook her head. "That's great. So what are you going to do
with your time now that the company is sold?"

"I haven't got any plans yet." Tim pulled her close. "I thought maybe you
and I could use some time to get to know each other again. I missed you."

"Tim!" Allie protested, struggling free of his arms. "I only agreed to live
here to get my parole approved. In reality, I don't want to get together with you.
I told you that."

"I know, I know." There was the same strange look in his eyes that
Tudor's had held the day she'd arrived home from Korea, as if saying it was sad
but okay that she wasn't being honest with herself. "I've been told you may
change your mind once you're out from under Carbon's influence. I intend to
let you have this room to yourself for as long as you like. I've moved all my
stuff to the other bedroom. I'm not going to pressure you into anything." He
gave her one last long lingering look of sadness and strode past her.

She chased after him. "Tim! I appreciate all you've done for me. I do. I felt
close to you when we talked. It was nice to have someone to confide in. But..."
She caught up with him at the bar where he was rummaging in the drawer,
probably looking for a corkscrew. She tugged at his sleeve. "Tim!" When he
turned to her, she was distressed to see he was crying. "You left me for another
woman. I'm not ready to forget that."

"Allie, it was never that way and you know it." He tossed a broken wine
opener into the drawer and noisily searched for another. "Connie and I were not
sleeping together."

"Do you think I'm stupid enough to believe that?"

"Whether you believe it or not, it's the truth." Tim gave up on his hunt and
looked her right in the eye. "You used to believe it, remember? Did that son of a
bitch Carbon tell you otherwise? Is that why you don't believe it anymore?"

"Don't be knocking Carbon! It wasn't him who walked out on me after
twenty years of marriage to take up with some tart."

"It wasn't me, either. Get real! You had as much a hand in the divorce as I did. You were the one who refused marriage counselling, saying you didn't want to get together. That you just wanted your half of the take and to disappear."

They glared at each other for a while, before Tim blinked and dropped his eyes. "I'm sorry," he said softly.

"Sorry about what?"

He gave her a small sad smile and resumed his quest for a corkscrew. "I'm sorry. I'm just sorry."

"Tim, don't look at me like that. Why are you looking at me as if my pet cat died or something?"

"Ah," he said. "Here it is. Red wine or white?"

CHAPTER 38

"Who was on the phone?" Tim asked Allie.

"None of your business." Hearing Carbon's voice again was exhilarating. He'd told her he missed her, needed her and was waiting for her on his bike in the alley three blocks over.

Tim grabbed her arm. "It *is* my business."

"Get your hands off me!"

"Where are you going?"

"I said, get your hands off me!"

"Was it Carbon on the phone? Because if it was and you're heading out to meet him, that's very much my business. You are prohibited from contacting him and I signed papers saying I'd—"

"Like hell it's your business!"

Tim grabbed her shoulders and pushed her backwards into the living room. "Don't, Allie," he said, shaking his head in short sweeps. "Don't screw things up for yourself. You're breeching parole by doing this. It'll get you in so much trouble."

Allie tugged at his hands. "You're abusing me! What kind of justice system forces you to live with an abusive ex-husband? Get your hands off of me."

Tim tightened his grip. "Allie, I'm not abusing you. Settle down. Settle down and listen to me."

"I'm not listening to you. I do not have to listen to you. Get your fucking hands off me!"

"Allie, I listened to you, spent hours listening to you. I'm asking you to return the favour. Please. Just listen to me for five minutes."

"It's different to listen to someone because they're sad than to listen to them because they're trying to control your life. It's two entirely different kinds of listening. I don't want to hear what you're going to say, because I've already heard it a million times. You're going to tell me evil things about Carbon and look at me with sad puppy eyes. I don't want that."

Tim dropped his hands. "Allie, for Christ's sake! When are you going to get real about this? That man drugged you, kidnapped you, raped you, used you. Held you prisoner. He's a drug dealer and a con man. He's no good for you, Allie. He's fucking slime!"

"He didn't walk out on me after twenty years of marriage!" Allie ran from the house.

* * *

As soon as Carbon caught sight of her at the end of the lane, he left his bike and strolled toward her, holding out his arms. She melted into them and resting her head on his shoulder, started crying.

"Hey, hey," Carbon soothed, nuzzling at her ear. "What's this with the tears? You ought to be happy—you're a free woman."

"It's so good to see you," Allie sobbed. People had been telling her for so long that what she had with Carbon wasn't love, she'd begun to doubt her feelings. However, immersed in his familiar scent and snuggled into his strong arms, her uncertainty disappeared. "It's good to hear your voice. I love you." She tried to muffle her sobs but they tore from her lungs uncontrolled. "I missed you so much."

"I know. I know." Carbon gazed into her eyes. "You got my message, though, right? You know why I stayed away?"

Allie nodded. "It helped a lot at the parole board hearing that I'd had no contact with you."

Carbon wrapped an arm around her waist and led her to the bike. "I've got to thank you, Allie."

"Thank me for what?"

"For taking the hit and keeping quiet. It didn't go unnoticed. You've paid your dues and the Jackals are ready for you."

"Oh. Okay, I guess," Allie murmured.

"Now," Carbon said, sitting on the bike and pulling out his cigarettes, "if I can do as well as you in the courtroom..."

Allie watched him pluck his lighter from an inside pocket of his jacket. She'd seen that move so many times. He lit his cigarette, inhaled deeply and blew a smoke ring. Both he and Allie watched it rise, tightening its shape, tightening, until it merged into itself and floated off as a simple puff.

"Will you talk to my lawyers?" Carbon asked. "Now that you're done with your own stuff?"

"Talk about what?"

Carbon shrugged. "Don't know." He flicked his ashes into the gravel. "They think you might be able to help."

Allie's heart dropped. "I suppose I could. It won't get me in worse trouble?"

"It's okay if you don't want to do it." Carbon inhaled and kept his eyes on the sky.

"I didn't say I didn't want to."

Carbon stood, dropped his cigarette and ground it into the dirt with his heel. "I told you the Jackals are happy about what you did. They'll be there for you. They'll look after you."

"What does that mean?"

"You'll be well taken care of."

"You make it sound like they'll put a few thousand in a bank account for me when I get out of jail."

"I didn't say that. You're making things up. I told you that you don't have to do it if you don't want to."

"I don't want to spend any more time in jail!"

"Just forget it. Forget I asked." He lit another cigarette and in moments a ring of smoke was rising over his head. This time it stretched out, thinned, snapped apart. "Come here." He threw down his cigarette and leaned against his bike. Allie took his outstretched hand and he pulled her to him. "Let me say hello to you properly."

Her disappointment melted as he gently plied at her lips. His hands massaged her shoulders, circled down her spine and rested on her buttocks. He half-rose and fit his crotch tightly against hers.

"You bedazzle me, woman," he said softly. He wiped the hair off her forehead and stared deeply into her eyes. "You bedazzle me."

"Take me with you." Allie rubbed her thigh against him and ran a finger up his fly. "I want to finish this."

"Oh, woman," Carbon groaned. He leaned on his bike.

She straddled his legs and raked her fingers through his hair. "Take me."

"You wouldn't believe how much I want to do that." He gave her a quick peck. "I can't, though. Not tonight. It's my wife's fucking birthday. I said I'd be there."

Startled, Allie drew away. "Your wife? You didn't tell me you were married!"

"You didn't ask," Carbon chided with a grin.

"Carbon, no!"

"Ah, come now," he soothed. He tugged at Allie's arms. "If you saw her, you wouldn't be jealous. Believe me. She's nine hundred pounds and has a face like a horse."

"I didn't know you were married." Allie pried at his fingers. "Don't you think it's something you should've told me?"

"Gees, Allie. Don't let some overweight ugly ruin what we have, for Christ's sake. It's you I love. You understand me. You love me, too. If you want, I'll take you to meet her. Hop on. I'll introduce you."

"You'll introduce me to your wife?"

"Why not? She won't care. I know she won't."

"How do you know she won't care? How many women have you introduced to your wife?"

"Come on, Allie. You know you're special to me. Don't hold me to sins committed long before I knew you!"

"I'm not going to meet your fucking wife!" Allie spun from him and crossed her arms. Behind her, Carbon cussed and then the growl of the Harley filled the evening. *He probably has kids, too!*

"I know about Shrug," Carbon said, his words barely audible over the bike engine. "I'm sorry if I told you anything I shouldn't have that night, things which bother your Christian conscience."

"I...I...don't know what you're talking about." Allie looked over her shoulder. Carbon's deep, demon eyes were on her.

"I hope the hell Saber wasn't right about you."

"No," Allie said, shaking her head.

"He was right about you, wasn't he? He was fucking right about you. You bedazzle me, get me to tell you things. You run to the cops. Is that how it's going to be, Allie? It wasn't fucking love at all with you, was it?"

"No, Carbon, you're wrong," Allie pleaded, stepping up to him. "You're so wrong! I love you, I do. I'll talk to your lawyer—I'll do anything for you. Anything for the Jackals."

"I don't know." Carbon reached in his breast pocket for his lighter. "Just don't know anymore. I'm thinking you don't love me. The only woman I ever learned to love and she don't love me."

"Carbon, I do!" Allie grabbed at his shoulder. "Don't say that! I'm just ticked you didn't tell me you had a wife. You can't blame me for that, can you?" He lit a cigarette, put the lighter in his pocket and pulled out his knife. He snapped it open and ran his thumb down the blade. He folded it together, stuffed it somewhere under his jacket and revved the bike. When the noise subsided, he turned to her. "I'll see you here tomorrow. Same time. Come without Shrug."

CHAPTER 39

It was a long, long three-block trek home for Allie, a journey with nothing at either end. When she walked into the house, Tim was sitting on the sofa in the living room, her Mexican cushion on his lap and an empty red wine bottle in front of him.

His expression changed to worry when he looked up at her. He tossed the pillow aside and stood. "What's the matter, Allie? What the hell did he do to you now?"

"He's married. He's fucking married, Tim."

"And?" Tim frantically searched her face. "What else? You can't tell me it didn't bother you that he kidnapped you, but you can't handle the fact he's married?"

"I guess that's the reality, isn't it?" She wondered what Tim would think if he knew what else Carbon had done.

"The reality," Tim quietly confirmed. "Can you see it, now?"

"I see it. Carbon's everything you told me he was. I should have listened instead of screwing you around."

"It's okay, darling." Tim rushed to her and swept her up in a hug. "No one is blaming you for anything. I don't blame you for not listening. I don't blame you for loving him. Allie, it's okay. It's okay. It's going to be okay now. It's okay, sweetheart," he said as he rocked her.

"He's going to have me killed. He's going to get Saber to kill me!"

"He told you that?"

"Not in words, but he mentioned Saber while pulling out his knife. It's no secret to me what that means."

"Why does he want you dead? Because you learned he's married?"

"When I got upset about his wife, he...he doesn't trust me anymore."

"Shh," Tim soothed, leading her to the sofa and wrapping her in his lap. "We won't let him kill you. It'll be okay. Perhaps I should call the cops."

"I'll be in trouble if they know I was with him." For months, Carbon had been her life; reuniting with him, her dream. *I can't believe it wasn't the same for him.*

"Aren't you scared?"

"It's an empty feeling. I look inside me, and there's nothing there."

"Let me be there."

"The entire last two years have disappeared. Nothing was real. It's all gone." Allie began to sob.

"What you and I have, it's still here. Remember our first house? The apple tree in the yard?"

"Those years are gone, too!"

"But we're not gone. The memories aren't. Allie, my love for you is still here. The emptiness can be good, a place to fill with things much better than Carbon."

"But if Carbon's not there—"

"*If* he's not there? *If?* Allie, he's married and he threatened you. There's no 'if' about it. He's not in your life." Tim handed her the cordless phone. "You know what you have to do. It's time to call Shrug."

"You know about Shrug?"

"I didn't meet the man until your parole hearing, but I knew about him. I was making such a noise after your trial, they had to tell me."

"A noise?"

"When I threatened to go to the media about you being unjustly convicted, they asked me not to, because you were being kept safe until you were ready to cooperate with another gang investigation. I was told they'd work a deal for you. Perhaps get rid of your criminal record and change your identity."

Allie tossed the phone from one hand to the other. "I don't feel ready."

"What is it you know? What kind of investigation is it, more drug deals?" She shook her head. "Weapons?"

"The White Rock massacre," she whispered, not daring to look at him.

"That biker slaughter five years ago?" Tim grabbed her shoulders and shook her. "You know who killed the bikers? Was it Carbon?" She hesitantly looked up at him. Terror was etched on his face. "It was Carbon, wasn't it?" He dropped her shoulders and stepped away. "Carbon killed them, now he's threatening to kill you, too." He raced to the windows and scanned the street before sliding the blinds closed and pulling the drapes.

He pointed to the phone in her hand. "You have to talk to Shrug, Allie. You have to get that thug off the streets. You have no choice."

The reality seemed so stark and sinister here in her living room. She'd been unafraid until now, having lived with the knowledge for so long and known Carbon so well. *But maybe that's why I didn't turn Carbon in. Maybe by not talking to the cops I'm keeping both Tim and me safe.*

"Go ahead," Tim encouraged, pulling the phone out of her right hand and placing it in her left. "This is reality. You've known all along this is something you must do."

Allie set the phone down and rummaged in her purse to find the business card Shrug had given her in prison. She was so nervous, it took several deep breaths and five attempts before she got his number completely dialled. She raised the receiver to her ear. "Shrug?" Tim gave her an encouraging nod and then slipped into the kitchen.

"Allison," Shrug answered.

Allie reached for a tissue and wiped her nose. "I'm ready to talk."

"You're sure?"

"Yes," she whispered. "I'm sure."

"Okay. We'll meet tomorrow. Do you have a pen and paper? I'm gonna give you an address where to meet."

"Shrug?"

"Yeah?"

"Carbon knows about you."

"I see. That's okay. Don't worry. I'll have my boys patrol your area and watch your house. Tomorrow mornin' at nine o'clock. I'll come get you."

She ended the call and stared vacantly in front of her.

"Allie?" Tim called. He joined her on the sofa and wrapped an arm around her shoulders. "Are you all right?"

"Shrug will be here in the morning. He's sending cops to watch the house until then. Tim, can you ever forgive me?"

"Forgive you for what?"

"For not turning Carbon in. For being so mean to you."

"I definitely forgive you," he said, giving her a quick kiss on the forehead. She snuggled into him, looking for warmth, for a heartbeat—for anything to fill the vacuum. His chest was rising and falling beneath her cheek. It was such a comfortable feeling, one she remembered from an eternity ago. Long before that hot summer day when Carbon had rang her doorbell.

"I didn't want to fall in love with him," she said, remembering Carbon and Saber on her front step. "I hated him. I was so scared. I was so fucking scared!"

"I know."

Allie tensed. *He doesn't know. He knows nothing. Absolutely nothing.* He didn't know... She struggled with the melange of memories which no longer made sense. If Carbon didn't love her, had never loved her, had lied to her. If it had all been a lie...

"I know," Tim repeated. "It's okay. I understand."

"What do you know, Tim? What the fuck do you know? What do you understand?"

"Just let it go," he said quietly. "It's over. Forget it."

"Forget it?" Allie pushed away. "How can I forget it? I remember..." The memories were dizzying, faltering, fading, discoloured, distorted. There was a museum, a beach, a noraebang...cigarettes and smoke rings. Duct tape and green pills. "I can't remember when I started loving him!" She rose, frantic. "I can't remember why I did."

"You loved him to survive. And it worked. Got you back alive to Canada. You did okay."

"He loved me, too."

"Perhaps, that's how it was."

"He let me carry his revolver. Told me gang secrets."

"Perhaps that's a gangster's definition of love," Tim said quietly.

She remembered pain and making love with a switchblade on her pillow. "He wants to kill me!" Allie burst into tears. "Wants me to do more jail time for him. He's married. He's fucking married!" She fell into Tim's lap and pushed her face against his chest.

"It's okay, darling. It's over now. It's over." Tim's familiar voice took her to a time before Carbon. *'Darling,'* he'd often said. Perhaps in the kitchen, over their morning coffee. Perhaps, at night when the lights went out.

"Tim." She ran a finger over his thumb. The scar beside his nail was still there, a thin hard strip of white. "I'm sorry I said you weren't good in bed. That's not true."

Tim chuckled. "Don't worry, I survived the insult fine." He tilted her head and stared into her eyes. "I love you."

"Tim, I'm clean. I was tested for HIV and stuff. I'm clean."

Tim nodded. "Good. That's good."

She ran her fingers down the buttons on his shirt. "I want to make love to you. I'm scared you won't want to. I feel so violated—"

"Not violated. You were hurt, Allie. Hurt badly, but not violated. Don't think of it that way." He gently slid her off his lap, stood and scooped her into his arms. "I can think of nothing I would rather do than make love to you."

He hugged her close, gently placed his lips on hers and walked down the hall. He didn't drop the kiss until they were in the master suite. He placed her on the familiar duvet and curled beside her. "Let me know," he murmured, "if anything doesn't feel right."

Button by button he worked his fingers down her shirt. He touched the snap on her jeans. "Just let me know, darling."

CHAPTER 40

Allie didn't hear the doorbell ring, didn't hear anything until Tim shook her shoulder. "Allie! Allie! Someone's at the door to see you." He offered his navy bathrobe.

"That's not mine," Allie complained drowsily. "It won't fit."

"It's dark and it's warm. It's what you need." She squinted at him, not comprehending. "Stand up." He wrapped the robe about her shoulders, clicked off the light and hustled her through the darkness. A uniformed officer stood in the shadowy entrance. Outside the open door, she thought she saw movement and shadows.

"They're Shrug's men," Tim said softly. "Go with them. It's time to do what you have to do."

Allie numbly walked toward the officer. His lips were taut and his toes pointed toward the open door. With his eyes flicking back and forth between her and the street, he grabbed her arm and began moving. The darkness. The haste. The tension. This wasn't the way it was supposed to happen.

Allie dug in her heels and turned. "Tim? I'm never going to see you again, am I?"

"Shh. Go, Allie. You have to go quickly."

There'd been a time just like this. On her deck in the summer. *'You're coming with us,'* Carbon had said and then everything had turned evil.

"I don't feel safe, Tim!" she cried.

"You will be safe. Go!" Tim looked past her and nodded to the officer.

"I don't want this. You set me up. Shrug set me up. You've taken advantage of an emotional moment I had with Carbon."

"No, Allie," Tim said firmly. "This isn't a set up. It's your decision; you said you're ready to talk. Go and do what you have to do."

"We'll make sure you get to see Tim," the officer said, grasping her arm tighter.

She suspected his gruff promise was hollow and empty, unenforceable once she left with him. She opened her mouth to protest.

"Shh," Tim cautioned again. "Go. You must leave. To be safe, you must!"

Carbon had said she had to go with him to be safe. Allie closed her eyes. A strong arm wrapped around her waist, hugged her close, half carried her. The cool night air whipped at her legs. A hand pinned her head against a rough fabric jacket. Cold concrete grated at her soles. This was a strange way to be doing something that supposedly was her choice.

She was having a lot of trouble lately claiming ownership of her behaviour. In prison, Shrug had said, *"If the only reason you have for doin' good with your life is to repay a debt to me, I ain't interested."* What were her reasons for betraying Carbon? To please Shrug? To make Tim happy? To get even with Carbon for being married? Were any of those valid reasons?

Before she'd met Carbon, she'd never questioned her morals and motives. Her conscience had always spoken clearly. Decisions had been made with confidence. Right and wrong were obvious and there had been no doubt that her behaviour arose from her own choices.

A car door slammed, ending her rumination. Her feet were no longer cold and there was no longer an arm around her shoulders. She opened her eyes. She was in the backseat of a police car and an officer was at the steering wheel. Keys jingled, the motor purred and the heater roared. Vehicle headlamps blitzed through the rear window and cast her shadow onto the seat before her. Down the street, a stream of red taillights blinked on. Beside her, another vehicle kicked to life.

She could barely discern Tim's form in the shadows of the covered entry. A muted voice rattled over a radio and a cell phone rang. A signal light began softly clicking. She leaned back and closed her eyes. Tires grated against the pavement. Whose decision was this?

As the squad car carried her into the dark, cold, Alberta night, Allie searched her memories for that moment in time when she'd lost the part of her that held it all together.

PART II

In the Shadow of the Cross

CHAPTER 1

Tim looked around the barren kitchen and again sniffed the stale air. This house was certainly a lot less than the one to which he was accustomed. Although he'd said that considering the circumstances, he wasn't fussy–this was about as low as one could go. He opened the fridge. No light came on. The rusted shelves were bare.

"Damn!" he muttered, slamming the door. The police said they had information that his life, too, was in danger from the gang and that for now, he'd be safer in one of their houses. He'd also been told everything he needed would be here and assumed that would include food. He ran his eyes over the walls. Peeling paint revealed at least three layers of different colours, none of them matching the mauve Venetian blind tilting crazily across the one small window.

As he pulled out a tattered kitchen chair, the squeak of metal legs against worn lino echoed eerily up at him. He shivered. He'd been in the house an entire fifteen minutes and was already feeling claustrophobic. Breathing deeply, he settled into the chair and tilted his head to the ceiling. A strange collage of brown watermarks rippled across the yellowed stipple.

He inhaled again. Compared to what Allie had been through, this was nothing. This was comfort. This, he could put up with, for her sake.

He heard a tentative rap on the front door and warily walked through to the living room. Standing to the side to avoid being seen from the street, he pinched at the gaudy floral drape and peeked out at his front step. He sighed in relief. Although Shrug, with his tapestry of tattoos and voice of thunder was intimidating, he was on the right side of the law and exactly the person to whom Tim should complain.

"Doorbell don't work," Shrug announced with a grin as Tim motioned him in.

"That isn't all that doesn't work." Tim shoved the door closed and watched in disgust as it creaked open. He slammed it again. "For Christ's sake!" He leaned his shoulder into the door and wiggled the latch. Reassured by the soft click, he locked the deadbolt and turned to his guest. "Try to make yourself at home, Shrug. If you're successful, let me in on how you did it."

"This ain't all that bad," Shrug argued in his booming voice as he bent under the misshapen foyer chandelier and strode into the living room.

"Depends on what you're comparing it to."

"It's clean, ain't it?" Shrug looked first to the spindly-legged Victorian side chair and then to the only other piece of furniture in the room—a faded orange sofa with springs showing through.

"It's clean," Tim agreed. "So clean, I can see every empty shelf in the fridge. Or, rather, I would be able to see them if the damned thing were plugged in and the light came on."

"No food," Shrug confirmed. He tested the sofa cushions with his hand. "Think this will hold me?"

"I could get you a kitchen chair."

"This'll do." Shrug gently lowered his bulk.

"I'd offer you a beer or a coffee except—"

"There ain't any," Shrug finished for him. "Sit. I'm here to talk to you about Allison, not to imbibe."

"How's she doing?" Tim brushed at what he thought was dust on the side chair. Nothing came off with his hand and he gingerly sat facing Shrug. "I hope her safe house is a step above mine."

"She won't talk," Shrug said.

"What do you mean, she won't talk?"

"She won't tell me what Carbon revealed to her about the murders."

"That slime Carbon and his Jackal pack of biker buddies has her so petrified—"

"Ain't that. If it were fear of the bikers, I could work with it."

"What is it then?"

"She's thinkin' me and you screwed her around. She ain't in a cooperatin' mood no more."

Tim scrunched his brow. "We screwed her around?"

"Said we knew she didn't want to rat on Carbon and we set her up to betray him. Says we've been manipulatin' her as much as Carbon did. Usin' her."

"Ah, for Christ's sake! I thought she was over him." Tim stared into Shrug's strange grey eyes for a moment then put his elbows on his knees and buried his face in his hands. "I really thought she saw Carbon for what he was—a no-good, drug-dealing, conniving son-of-a-bitch murderer."

"I didn't say she was still in love with him," Shrug drawled. "I said she wasn't in love with us."

"Same difference."

"No, different difference."

"He kidnaps her, rapes her, abuses her in ways we can't even imagine. She takes the hit for him on the drug charges, gets herself a criminal record and then finds it's not enough for the man. He wants her to testify in his defence, do more time for him. Threatens her with a switchblade. Has the gall to brag to her he's married. Yet, *we're* the ones screwing her?"

"Trouble is," Shrug said as quietly as his baritone voice allowed, "she's right. We used her."

"I did not!" Tim straightened and glowered at Shrug. "I gave her the space and time she needed to get free of Carbon's influence. I took great pains not to bad mouth that bastard. Slept in the spare room, didn't touch her until she asked. I love that woman. Stood by her. Visited her damned near every day in prison. How the hell can she say I used her?"

"You knew she didn't want to live with you, yet you connived with me to make it a condition of her parole."

"I wasn't doing it for my sake! Carbon was still on bail when her sentence was up. Something had to be done to keep her away from him—for her sake."

"She asked me what kind of justice system forces a woman to live with her ex," Shrug said. "No matter what your intentions were, buddy, we can't argue with the fact we set her up for somethin' she didn't want. She'd likely have gotten parole without that condition. It's not as if you're still married to her, you know."

Tim gritted his teeth. "If she hadn't come home with me, she'd have been in so deep with that gang of thieves by now, she'd either be dead or behind bars forever. Why can't she see that?"

"Dunno," Shrug said. "Thinkin' it has somethin' to do with her havin' to learn to trust people again."

"It's like accusing your track coach of controlling your life because he makes you do practice laps. Can't she see everything we did was for her benefit? Can't she see that?"

"Guess not."

"Why not?"

"You tell me."

"She knows it was your doing that she was able to enter the goddamned guilty plea like she wanted, doesn't she?"

"Yup," Shrug replied. "She knows she couldn't have claimed to be guilty if it was obvious she'd been coerced and she knows I helped keep the kidnapping evidence out of the judge's sight."

"And she doesn't feel she owes you something for doing that?"

"She also knows I didn't do it for her benefit. I was hopin' in the long run it would get me my murder convictions. She ain't stupid. She also ain't impressed. We were all wantin' a guilty plea, just for different reasons. She was hopin' it would please Carbon and he'd welcome her back into his arms. Her attorney was hopin' it would keep her safe from retaliation from Carbon and his Jackals gang. I was hopin' to swing her to my side and get her talkin'. Don't know what you were hopin'." Shrug sighed. "I hope it weren't all false hope."

"That's not the entire truth, Shrug. You had other reasons for what you did, not the least of which was keeping her safe. Your tactics bought her time to get her head on straight. You kept her from riling the Jackals with testimony about a kidnapping. Kept her in prison and on strict parole, away from the love-of-her-life slime-ball Carbon. That's why you did it."

"Sounds good," Shrug said with a quick nod. "Angelic. I wouldn't have done it, though, if I weren't after murder convictions. She knows that."

"But she should want murder convictions, too!" Tim paused to study Shrug's expression. "What the hell? Have I lost her forever? Did Carbon brutalize the conscience right out of her?" Shrug silently stared at his shoes. "He's still free on bail, isn't he?" Tim demanded fiercely. "He uses her to set up an overseas illicit drug network. She pleads guilty, does time for it and he's still a free man?"

Shrug nodded. "His lawyers have finally run out of delay tactics. Trial's underway on his international drug smuggling charges. We'll have him behind bars in a couple of weeks."

Tim looked out the window through the space where the thin tattered drapes refused to meet. The house across the street needed a paint job. The trees were overgrown. Garbage littered the front lawn.

Shrug cut into the silence. "You need to try again."

"Try what?"

"Try to get her to come around to reality. She bonded with her captor, that ain't unusual. She needed to survive. He took her against her will to a country with a foreign language and a justice system about which she knew nothing. She had no money. No ID. Fourteen flight hours from home. He didn't let her out of his sight. Brutalized her into submission. What choice did she have? Bonds built on the need to survive are deep ones. They change you forever."

"I understand all that."

"Work with her a bit more. Get her to trust you. Love you. I'd try to get her to love me– but that might make my bosses a little wild again...still."

Tim rose, jammed his hands into his pockets and cast his eyes once more to the aged ceiling. "I thought I had got her to love me. I thought we were there, her and I." He paced to the window. Most of the bright autumn colours were gone. There were just a few minor sparkles left in a world dusted with grey.

"She asked me to make love to her," Tim said. "Apologized for treating me like shit. Said she felt Carbon had violated her. I was gentle with her. Slow. I thought it was good. She said she loved me—"

"And then my guys show up and whisk her away from you."

"She's the one who said she was ready to talk."

"I'm thinkin' you need to see her again, Tim. You know what to do. Don't scold her for her feelin's. Just listen and love. Don't say nothin' nasty about Carbon. Keep it positive. You can do it."

"Yeah, right," Tim muttered, slumping into his chair.

Shrug drew his long legs under him and stood. "You do that for me, buddy, and you might find food in your fridge when you return. Perhaps a cold *Corona.*"

Tim tossed Shrug a half-grin. "I think I'm beginning to understand Allie's point about you being a manipulator. You're saying if I do what you want, you'll feed me."

"Put it this way, all Allison is right now is a convicted criminal who's refusin' to share info with the cops about a murder. I don't think our wonderful Canadian tax-payers will want to keep footin' the bill to keep her safe from a bunch of criminal associates. We have to get her to talk or she's out of the safe house. And you, too."

Tim rose. "What if she keeps refusing? Would you still be able to bring kidnapping charges against Carbon so at least it's on record that she's a victim here and that the only reason she ever loved the guy, the only reason she cooperated with him, was to help her survive? You could still do that for her, couldn't you? At least partially clear her name?"

Shrug stared down at him. He didn't blink, didn't move his lips.

"Why not?" Tim asked.

Shrug rubbed his shoe along a seam in the worn, gold carpet. "Not likely she'd testify against him on kidnappin' charges if she won't on murder. We could try it without her testimony. The evidence is there but the defence would likely call her as a witness to refute that evidence." Shrug sighed. "Buddy, justice was maligned and twisted by keepin' that evidence out of the court durin' her trial on drug traffickin'. That was only allowed to happen on the premise down the road, I was gonna get the bastards for murder. Someone will be in deep shit if that don't happen."

"Someone like you?"

"Perhaps." Shrug tilted his head. "But I'd try for the kidnappin' conviction, regardless. I've never been shy about puttin' my career on the line for somethin' that felt right. I'd try for you. For her." Shrug looked up and moved his lips, as if whipping off a quick prayer. "However…" He looked at Tim. "I want the homicide convictions."

Tim nodded.

"You'll do it?" Shrug asked.

"I'll try."

"Won't be easy." Shrug moved toward the door. "She'll know what you're up to."

"Don't get me wrong, I want the murder convictions too, but it's Allie I really want. I want her whole again. I want the clever, happy, independent, morally-upright woman she was before Carbon—"

"I know," Shrug interrupted. He unlocked the deadbolt and tugged on the door. "Your mission is to convince her of that." He gave the door another yank.

"When am I supposed to start?"

"I'll let you know." Shrug wrenched until the door finally swung open and he stepped into the cold October afternoon. "You really oughta do some maintenance on this place," he added, walking off with a whistle.

CHAPTER 2

"Allison," Shrug greeted as he walked in. She was curled around a laptop on the couch, emanating a self-confidence that made it easy for him to imagine her the successful businesswoman she'd been before Carbon got to her.

She glanced up and ran her fingers through her short blonde curls. Her green eyes dazzled in sync with the metallic shade on her lids. Shrug wouldn't have guessed her to be fifty-plus. Despite all she'd been through, she looked good.

She'd been co-owner with Tim of one of Canada's biggest importing/exporting firms, well-travelled, politically connected, wealthy. She had a talent for working with foreign cultures. In fact, she'd had everything Carbon wanted to gain a foothold for his Jackals in South East Asia's illicit drug trade. And he'd beaten her body, twisted her mind and stolen her soul to get it.

Allie closed her computer and uncoiled. "What do you want now?" She set her feet on the hardwood floor, cradled her chin in her hands and stared at the candle on the glass-top coffee table before her.

"Allison, I can't keep you here if you don't talk."

"Who says I want to be here?"

"Last time you saw Carbon he threatened to have you killed. He knows you're thinkin' of turnin'."

"I have lots of money. I'll fly off and live in Tahiti or something."

"Someone like you with a criminal record can't travel much, makin' it mighty hard to hide from those on either side of the law."

"Nice try." She pulled her feet up and sat cross-legged. "I don't need you around to feel safe. I'm sure I can survive quite well on my own. Did it before."

"It cost you," Shrug said quietly. She squirmed beneath his steady gaze and folded her hands in her lap. Shrug sank into the loveseat. As he ran his hand over the arm, the imitation suede darkened to a chocolate brown. The furniture, although new and undoubtedly expensive, looked worn—chosen, he surmised, to match the rough and rustic hand-hewn look of the wide-planked oak flooring and the fake kerosene table lamps. He smoothed the fabric and squinted across at Allie. "Tim's comin' over to visit."

"Who the hell made that decision?"

Shrug stretched his long legs. "He needs to visit. He's holed up in a 1940s shack—"

"Why's that? Something you planned? Put him up in a dive to make sure he'll want to escape and come see me?"

"It was *not* planned," Shrug replied evenly. "It's all we had available on such short notice. He was willin' to take it, for your sake."

"I need a goddamned manicure," she muttered, chewing at her pinkie. "That's the second nail today I've broken."

"Tim's comin' over." Shrug tipped his foot and studied the worn underside of his sock. It got him thinking of the saying about not judging people until you've walked a mile in their shoes. Hell, to judge Allison he'd have to run a marathon in her heels.

"Whether or not I agree?" she asked.

"Yeah."

"My ex-husband, whom I legally divorced, has a right to visit me? Against my wishes? I didn't know those in witness protection were prisoners at your mercy. Thought this would be kind of like, *my* house."

"You have one week to make it come together for me, Allison, or you won't be needin' to worry about the pros and cons of witness protection. You'll be free. Totally. To do whatever it is you wanna do…until you're murdered, that is."

"I see." Allie scowled at her nails. "If I don't submit to Tim's persuasive powers within seven days, you'll deliver me to the Jackals. God, you're a generous man, Shrug. I'm so glad our paths crossed!"

"Allison, should you choose to fend off Tim's persuasive powers and refuse to cooperate, there'll be no reason for police protection for you…or Tim."

Allie looked up quickly. "Whether or not I rat out Carbon, Tim's in danger and you damned well know that. His safety shouldn't depend on me stooping to your demands."

"How can I 'damned well know' anything when you refuse to make an official statement about those threats? Until I get some information from you enablin' us to lay charges, neither you nor Tim qualifies for witness protection."

"Screw off!" Allie rose and paced to the window. It faced west, where the last remnants of a sunset were dissipating. Twilight came early this time of the year, descending as a grey veil over a landscape void of colour—an ominous prelude to a cold, dark Alberta winter.

"Allison," Shrug said, "this isn't just a threat I made up to force you to cooperate. I'm simply tellin' it like it is. There's just no way I can convince my bosses to pay mega bucks to protect someone like Tim when all we've got to go on are hints from a convicted criminal like you that he's in danger from your criminal cohorts. The reality is, there are consequences to your decisions—"

"That's what this is all about, isn't it? Consequences." Allie glowered. "*Your* consequences. Your bosses, your career. If I don't talk, your ass is on the line for omitting the kidnapping evidence from the Agreed Statement of Facts at my drug trial. The reality is, you care about your ass and don't give sweet shit about the murders of a bunch of drug-dealing, low-life, rival gang members that happened years ago."

Shrug pulled in his legs and straightened. "You listen to me, woman! My ass means nothin' to me. I wouldn't have jeopardized justice in the first place if it did. Have I made myself clear? Do you understand?"

"Fuck, you sound exactly like Carbon."

"I sound like Carbon?"

"Yeah. The day he kidnapped me. I'm in the backseat, on the way to the airport. I asked him if he was really taking me to South Korea and he said he didn't like questions unless he was the one doing the asking. But I asked him another one anyway. He flipped out, started yelling at me. '*Which part of my last sentence don't you understand, woman? Do I have to come back there and make myself clear? Do you understand, woman? Do you understand...*'?"

"Sorry, Allison," Shrug said softly. "I didn't mean to sound like Carbon."

"You don't just sound like him, you look like him!" Allie shouted. "Tattoos all over the place. Steroid-fed muscles straining at your shirtsleeves. Glassy eyes which lie all the time. Shit, Shrug, that day after my parole hearing and you want to take me for a ride on your Harley..." Her voice trailed off and she turned to the window again. Across the alley, a street light flickered on. "I told you I didn't know how to ride a bike and you told me all I had to do was sit. Exactly the same words Carbon used when he was trying to convince me to join his Jackals. He was talking about riding together, him and me, amidst the autumn colours, the wind in our faces. I declined, saying I didn't know how to ride a bike. '*All you have to do is sit. As a woman, all you'd have to do is sit.*'"

The furnace kicked in, the clock chimed five and somewhere, way in the distance, a siren squealed. Allison turned back to the window. The neighbour across the alley had arrived home. As he always did at this time, he parked on the concrete apron outside his detached garage and wandered toward his house and out of view.

"Allison," Shrug said. "I'll let you in on somethin'. I was undercover with a gang of bikers for four years. Picked up the lingo. Picked up the tattoos.

Picked up a love for big bikes and the smell of leather. Didn't pick up the attitude, though, girl. Didn't become mean. Christ, woman, you gotta know I ain't nothin' like Carbon. You gotta at least believe that much." She continued gazing at the sunset, her slender silhouette dissipating into the thickening dusk. "You do believe that much?" Shrug queried hopefully.

"I don't know what to believe anymore."

"Don't cut yourself short. You've got me pegged pretty good, girl. You're readin' us all pretty damned good. You're right I wouldn't risk sweet shit to solve the murders of a handful of low-life Shadow Riders. Wouldn't even have thought of withholdin' evidence just to track their killer. Fact is, though, Allison, one of those dead Riders was an informant. One of mine, doin' what I'd done for four years. Riskin' his life, hell—riskin' his soul to enforce the laws of my country. Never a doubt that I'll risk all I've got to get the bastard who ended it for him. Will you, Allison? Will you risk anythin'?"

"One of the victims was a cop?" Allie quickly bent to snap on the table lamp. In the soft glow Shrug could see the panic in her eyes.

"An informant," Shrug said with a nod. "I considered him one of us."

Allie moved in closer. "You're just saying that to make me feel bad. To force me into talking."

"Thought maybe it was somethin' you already knew. Somethin' Carbon had mentioned to you."

"No. No, he didn't. I don't think he knew. He would've told me, I'm sure... He just said—fuck, Shrug! You're doing it to me again, manipulating me into telling you shit."

"Have it your way, Allison." Shrug heaved himself out of his chair. "Have it your fuckin' way!" He strolled to the door. "You decide." He paused with his hand on the knob. "And if you decide to opt out of this, you can rest assured that as you shovel coal into the fiery furnaces of hell, I'll be puttin' just as much effort into solvin' yours and Tim's murders as I'm puttin' into the Shadow Rider slayin's. Because, woman—" He opened the door, stepped out, and turned to her. "That's just the fuckin' kinda guy I am."

CHAPTER 3

"I have the feeling Shrug is a very wise man." **Dr. Erica Freid**

"He's not fucking wise, he's a manipulator! He's more psychopathic than Carbon ever was. You look in that man's eyes and you see the soul of the devil, for sure." **Allison Montgomery**

"I see."

"I hate Shrug. And I hate Tim. They are using me. They're just using me. And I fell for it!"

"How so?"

"I'm here, aren't I? Or were you flattering yourself by thinking I'm here by choice?"

"Are you saying you hate me, too?"

"Sometimes I think so. Sometimes it's as if there is no one to love."

"No one to love, or no one loving you?"

"It's kind of the same thing."

"You're not sure any more about Carbon's love, are you?"

"If they'd just let me meet with the man…talk to him. I could look in his eyes… I'm not sleeping well. Strange house. I jump every time the furnace kicks in. I'm not sleeping…"

"Sarge," Shrug said, stretching his long legs under his boss' desk. "How patient a man are you?"

"I've known you for almost half a century," Sergeant Kindle replied. "As your friend, I put up with you all through high school. As your boss, through all your suspensions, reprimands and misdemeanours. Yet, I still talk to you. I think that pretty well sums up how patient a man I am."

Shrug grinned across at the Sarge, whose ample girth was pressing at the edge of his oak desk and whose laugh-lines framed a set of kindly blue eyes. "We're gonna need every ounce of that patience because we got a fuck of a long way to go to make this thing with Allison Montgomery work."

"The language, Shrug," Kindle half-heartedly scolded.

"That should be, we *have* a fuck of a long way to go to make this thing work," Shrug corrected.

"I was referring to your choice of words, not the grammar."

Shrug figured Kindle ought to forgive his language since it was the years undercover in the Sarge's biker operation that had fouled his tongue. He tapped his toes on the underside of Kindle's desk, a habit he knew his boss considered disrespectful. Getting no reaction, Shrug was about to tap again but decided against it. Although the chastising about his swearing stung, it was just such high expectations from Kindle that had made many an ordinary man under the Sarge's command an extraordinary officer. *Perhaps he's right that I should relearn the manners of the man I once was.*

The Sergeant sighed. "What is it you want to tell me, Shrug?"

"The woman's warped. Even if I do get her talkin', I'd be scared as hell to put her on the witness stand. She's bound and determined it's against her will to hand over Carbon. One inklin' of that by the defence and they'll have her spoutin' off that the only reason she's testifyin' is 'cause we threatened if she didn't, we wouldn't protect hubby."

Kindle looked up sharply. "You didn't tell her we wouldn't protect Tim if she didn't talk?"

"I was tryin' to tell it like it is, Sarge. She twists it all. Twists everythin' I say. Unless somethin' changes, she'll be useless to us. A jury don't like hearin' about witnesses makin' deals with the Crown so I doubt they'd want to hear shit about the Crown threatenin' a witness. She gets 'em thinkin' there's reasons other than honesty behind her testimony and there goes her credibility."

"Is she still working with her psychiatrist to get over this Brussels Syndrome or whatever the hell it's called?"

"Stockholm syndrome—the tendency for captives to bond with those controllin' them. Nah, she's refusin' counsellin'. If I nag her into it, she'll undoubtedly start rantin' about how the doctor's coercin' her, too. If she throws that into her testimony, the defence will call it brainwashin' and we're fucked."

"The language," Kindle muttered.

"Screwed. Fucked. Shit out of luck. Take your pick."

"Are you saying we should've given her more time with her ex to straighten herself out?"

"Ideally, yeah. However, with Carbon threatenin' to kill her, I figured we had the choice of either a reluctant witness or a dead one. Bin' my experience it's a tad difficult to get corpses to say much in a court of law. They're shy in front of a jury. Don't stand up well under cross-examination and the smell—"

"I get the picture."

"I almost tricked her into talkin'. She caught on, though, before she'd said much. Got enough, though, to reinforce my suspicions that Carbon told her a hell of a lot about the murders."

"We don't need her to say much. There was very little information about those murders released to the public. If she'd tell us just a bit more than nothing, we'd be able to prove she was privy to stuff only the killer would've known. That would sure as hell make Carbon look guilty."

"Yeah," Shrug sighed. "I managed to learn what Carbon didn't tell her. She didn't know one of the vics was ours. Would make me feel good to prove the Jackals didn't know he was ours, either. I don't like thinking Cory got killed because of what he was doin' for us."

"Suppose it'd ease our conscience a bit. Either way, however, if he'd been on his way to a Canadian Tire desk job and not straddling a bike getting us info, he wouldn't have been slaughtered in White Rock, B.C."

"Yeah, I know." Shrug sighed. "But I also know he did stuff outside of what we asked for, stuff that would've been well-worth a fifty-cent bullet to a rival gang. Not that I blame him for dabblin' along with the rest of them in the weapons and drug trades. I mean, you can't be a Born-Again Christian and expect a biker gang to open up to you. There's no doubt he was in hot and heavy with the big boys in the Shadow Riders gang, helpin' them expand into the Jackals' territory. If that's what got him killed, I could live with it. Not the other. Not because he got labelled a traitor."

"It's not likely he was killed because he was an informant. He was giving us information on the gang he was with, not Carbon's Jackals. If anyone were to have killed him because of betrayal, it would've been his own gang."

"Oh, he was quite forthcoming about his rivals, too. I had to watch him. Make sure he wasn't just feedin' me shit on Carbon's boys to make it easier for his Shadow Riders to storm the West. It's in my investigation report."

"Ah, yes. That's the problem with handing cold case files to old-faced officers—we've forgotten half the stuff. I remember now. Do you think Allison has information about the motive for the murders?"

"I'm hopin'. Doubly hopin' she'll eventually share it with me, if she does."

"Where do we go with her?"

"Can you buy me some more time?" Shrug asked quietly, tilting his head.

"Shrug!"

"I know the brass has bin' houndin' you, sir, ever since you went to bat for me about withholdin' the kidnappin' evidence. But if I don't get more time, all those burns branded on your ass by the fire they've bin' breathin', will be for naught. I ain't askin' for more money or staff. Just time. Time to get it done right. Right, so the charges stick. Don't want Carbon and his boys weasellin' out of this one just 'cause my witness weren't quite ready."

"Brands on my ass? Is that the Saskatchewan farm boy in you talking?"

Shrug grinned. "Lookin' forward to soon retirin' to the land. Either that, or I s'pose I could revisit the ministry." He rose and walked to the door. "Of course," he said, turning to the Sergeant, "I'd have to first find a church that don't mind the f-word. Could be difficult. Might have no choice but to take up with the fuckin' prairie gophers again."

CHAPTER 4

"She's really screwed up, Tim," Shrug offered as he chauffeured him to Allie's. "I mean, really screwed up. And she's dead set against you visitin' her. So much so, I'm scared she'll accuse you of rape or assault or somethin'. I'm gonna stay there with the two of you."

"Oh, that'll make it easy, romance her with you in the room."

"I'll be discreet. Just ignore me. It's for your own protection."

"Yeah, sure it is."

"It is!"

"Allie's right. Shrug, you're one big thug of a manipulator. You want to be there so if she drops any tidbits to me about the murders, you can write it down. Why don't you just say that? What's with this, 'for your own protection' shit?"

"I'm goin' nuts." Shrug checked his side mirror, his rear-view mirror, turned down the heater fan and clicked off the radio. "I'd expect somethin' like that from Allison, not you, Tim. I thought we had trust happenin' between us."

Tim slumped into his seat. "Sorry. Really I am."

Shrug exhaled noisily. "But you're right. I need to be there for lots of reasons. I only gave you one."

"That's your right as an investigating officer. I know that. You probably didn't even have to give me one reason."

"It was a real one, though. It wasn't like I was makin' it up or somethin'."

"I do trust you, Shrug. I believe you know what you're doing. I'll try to mellow out. I'm just upset Allie doesn't want to see me. When your boys came and got her that night, she was all teary because she had to leave me. Was frantic she'd have to go into Witness Protection and never get to see me again. Now, just a couple of weeks later, she doesn't want me to visit? That hurts. It really hurts."

"Sorry, buddy. It's not easy, I know."

"How am I supposed to do this? After everything I've already done, what else can I do to convince her to trust me? What the hell can I do?"

"I took her away too soon. She was bondin', comin' around. I kinda screwed it up but I had to. Maybe it'll be easier this time. She's over her hots for Carbon, so it can be more positive this time around. More focussin' on gettin' her to love you, not tryin' in the same breath to get her to hate Carbon. Just positive shit. Just, well, romancin' her. Rememberin' the good times, or somethin'. Hell, if I know. Haven't done so good with my own marriages. You're probably way better at that shit than I am."

"I'm not allowed to yell at her, right? I have to be gentle. Let her walk all over me. Just smile and listen."

"Didn't say that." Shrug pulled to the curb and cut the engine. "You do whatever it damned-well takes to get her back. If you think shoutin' at her will work, go for it. Maybe she needs that. Needs to quit milkin' everyone's sympathy. A dose of reality. I dunno. Just no physical stuff, I mean like hittin' or shit. The kissin' kind of physical stuff, that's okay."

"I've never hit a woman in my life," Tim protested, unbuckling his seatbelt. "I don't intend to start now!" He got out and slammed the car door.

Shrug joined him on the sidewalk. "Just stay cool," Shrug warned. "Even if you're screamin' at her, keep the brain and heart workin'. She's gonna accuse you of manipulatin' her. You have to be on your toes to defend against that."

Shrug rang the doorbell but didn't wait for an answer. He immediately plugged in the security code and opened the door. "Allison? Tim's here!" He stepped into the house.

Tim followed and closed the door behind him. He could see Allie lying on the sofa, scowling at her laptop monitor, making no move to greet them. He walked past Shrug and stood before her. "Want me to leave?" She shrugged and began to type. "Would you at least look at me?"

"Why? I know what I'll see. Sad eyes—gazing at me as if I've just been diagnosed with Alzheimer's."

"Maybe the sadness is for me and not for you. Maybe you're not the only one hurting here."

"I know you're hurting, Tim." She sighed, closed her computer and looked up at him. "I know that and it's not what I want for you. I don't want you being sad for either yourself or for me. I don't want you having to live with images of me being with Carbon. Of Carbon raping me. Of me making love to the man. I don't want any of that. However, it just is, isn't it? It's a reality neither of us can escape."

"But we don't have to be stuck in that reality. We can accept all that and move on. Create something new."

"Yes," Allie said with a vigorous nod. "You do that, Tim. Please. Move on. Create something good for yourself."

"I want that something good to include you."

"It can't." Allie set her computer on the coffee table and rose. For a brief moment she caught Tim's eyes, then brushed past him to the kitchen.

"Why not?" Tim persisted, following her.

She cranked on the tap. "If I'm with you, all the bad stuff is with you, too. It's permanently entwined in my being, forever writhing in my brain and smothering my soul. Screaming out at night and obscuring the sun, itself." She grabbed a tumbler from behind the sink and held it under the tap. "It's dark where I am." Turning off the water, she took a gulp and set the half-empty glass on the counter. "You don't want to be here with me in this place where the sun doesn't shine, birds don't sing and roses have no smell." She hunched over and glued her eyes to the glass.

"Believe it or not, being with you in that dark place sounds better than being anywhere else without you."

She grabbed the glass and smashed it to the floor. "Don't say that!" Shards scuttled across the marble tiles. She took a step toward Tim. "Don't screw me around with shit like that!"

"It's not shit," Tim said, dancing out of the way of the approaching water.

"I know I'm not loveable anymore. How can anyone love a person who won't rat out a mass murderer? And that's the person I am."

"No, Allie—"

"The same fucking-ass, drug-dealing, son of a bitch who kidnapped and raped me also happened to kill six men and I won't lift a finger to put him behind bars! How do you think you can 'move on' and create something different with a person like that?"

"Six?" Shrug's voice thundered from the doorway.

"And because I'm like that, Tim, you'll be victim number seven. I'll be number eight and then none of us will have to worry about it anymore."

"Six?" Shrug bellowed again.

"And one of them worked for the cops. How does that sit with you? Go, now, before it's too late!" She wrenched at Tim's shoulder and motioned him to the exit. "You have the money. No criminal record. Flee! Go somewhere warm and sunny and find a bronzed beauty who can give you the nice, comfortable reality you're dreaming of creating."

"You haven't been listening to me," Tim said quietly, tugging her hand off his shoulder and clasping it in his. "That's not my dream reality."

"Six?" Shrug thundered a third time, moving in on them.

"Allie, I'd rather be in hell with you than in paradise with Barbie."

Allie's eyes filled with tears. "I guess if you want hell, your wish came true." Tim hugged her to him and rested his head on her curls. "Damn you, Tim," she sobbed. "Damn you!"

"Shit," Shrug muttered, walking out. "When I said to ignore me, I didn't expect you actually would."

"Allison Lisa Montgomery, I love you. It doesn't matter whether or not you tell Shrug about the murders. I don't care. I love the part of you beyond that. The sweet part of you that Carbon didn't touch. The tender part, the strong part."

Allie pulled free and wiped at her tears. "You're just saying that. There's no way you want to be with me if I don't rat on Carbon. Don't pretend otherwise."

"There'll come a day when you'll turn on him. Until then, no worries, darling. I'll be there for you."

"I'm never talking about the murders," Allie said fiercely. "Accept that, Tim!"

"Don't make a 'forever' decision; they never work. Circumstances change; you change. You told me there was a time in your younger years when you vowed you'd never get married. Right?" He smiled and stepped toward her.

She crossed her arms. "That's different."

"It wasn't all that difficult for me to get you to change your mind, as I recall."

Allie scowled. "I was young and foolish. Didn't understand a damned thing about being an adult."

"You don't understand a thing about being sixty, either. What's it going to be like to be seventy? What will you be like? What will you want? What will life hand you?"

"You'd really stay with me even if I walk away from this investigation?" Allie studied Tim's eyes.

"Yes, I would."

"You're not just saying that to get me to talk?"

"No, Allie, I'm not. I told Shrug the same thing. I'd love it if you talked, but it's your heart I'm after, not murder convictions. I admit I don't understand your reasons for not talking and I'll probably keep trying to change your mind. Successful, or not, however, I'll never have misgivings about being there for you."

"I'll think about it." Allie placed both hands on the countertop and bowed her head.

"What do you need to think about?"

"I can't tell if you're being honest. I want to believe you, but I don't. You and Shrug have both screwed me around so much."

"No, Allie, we haven't!" Tim walked over and gently tilted her face toward him. "We haven't."

"You have! Admit it, or this conversation's ending now."

Tim sighed. "Think of it this way. If you throw the ball for Fido and he brings it back, are you saying you've manipulated him?"

"That's what I am to you, isn't it? A dog. A trained dog."

"No, Allie, that's not at all what I meant. Don't do this. Don't..." Tim trailed off, his thoughts lost behind the beat of his pounding heart and the wave of heat flushing his face. He wasn't sure what it was he was feeling. Something dark, heavy and forceful. Bitterness, perhaps. Emptiness. Anger, raging against this woman Allie had become and the circumstances which had changed her. He wiped his sweaty palms on his jeans and opened his eyes.

"Don't do what?" Allie asked.

"Allie, the damned dog wants you to throw the ball. He brings it back to manipulate you into throwing it again! It's cooperation. It's communication. It's a consensual give and take. There's nothing evil about it. There's no domination, submission. You're both getting what you want. That's all I was doing, Allie—helping you get what you want. I kept you away from Carbon and you got free of him. It's what you wanted, isn't it?" She slowly ran a finger over the patterned stone countertop. "Allie, Shrug threw the ball for you when he let you plead guilty. It's your turn now. Bring it back for him. Give him his convictions. I know it's what you want as much as what he wants. Why paint the process dirty?"

"You just don't get it, do you?"

"Get what?"

"How many times do I have to say it? I'm not talking to Shrug. I don't want murder convictions."

"Why wouldn't you? I want it. Shrug wants it. The whole damned nation wants it! And you don't, because...?"

"I'm not sure."

"What *do* you want?"

"I was ticked at Carbon when he told me he was married. That's a piss-poor reason to go after him for murder, though, isn't it? It was like a sacred husband-wife conversation when he confided his secrets. He trusted me. Cried to me. Don't get me wrong, Tim, I don't approve of the murders, but it wouldn't be right to betray his confidence. He talked to me about that day because he was emotionally distraught about it. It ripped his soul out. He got no pleasure from the murders. He got nothing, gained nothing. He just...followed orders. Did it to survive. Now, he's paying with his guilt. And, if anyone can understand the price of guilt, I can. I've been there, done that. Still doing it."

"You're still feeling something for Carbon? You're kidding me, right?"

"I feel for Carbon, Tim. I feel lots for Carbon."

"What are you saying? You're reuniting with him? Is that it? Is that what you'll do next to survive? Reject the safety Shrug's offering and run to Carbon for protection?"

"I might," Allie whispered.

"What does he have to offer you? What kind of life do you foresee with Carbon?"

"He has Mahogany Imports," Allie said. "That lawyer-to-lawyer deal which netted you the big bucks when you sold Mahogany to a numbered company? It was Carbon, bought it thinking I'd run it for him. I know he did."

"Allie," Tim protested quietly. "Allie, no."

"He threw me the ball."

CHAPTER 5

Shrug lounged in the dark upholstered chair across the desk from his boss. "Sarge, Allison says there were six victims, not five." He popped a *Nicorette* in his mouth and ran his feet across the chipped corners of the floor tiles. There was a push on for a new building for the detachment. However, he quite liked the comfort of the old and familiar. It reminded him of the importance of the past; lessons learned, friendships made, cases not solved.

Kindle set down his pen and leaned across his desk. "She's talking to you?"

"No. She was talkin' to Tim. But, it's still talkin', sir. Said Tim would be Carbon's seventh victim and her, his eighth."

"Kind of suspected we were missing one, didn't we? The unmatched DNA at the crime scene—we may have been right that it belonged to another victim, not the perpetrator." Kindle picked up his pen and clicked it gently on the single thin strip of oak visible between the papers strewn across his desk.

"Yeah," Shrug agreed. "Number six would work with the evidence and the rumours."

"Does she know where the sixth body is? It wasn't laid out under the trees with the others."

"My guess would be she does. I heard her sayin' to Tim that Carbon spilled his guts to her, like a 'husband-wife sacred conversation.'"

Kindle glued his eyes to Shrug's. "Get it from her! Now!"

"Bin thinkin' we might not want her knowin' we were in the dark about the sixth victim. Especially since she's threatenin' to get together with Carbon. Perhaps it's best if she doesn't slip that kind of info to him."

"She's talking about going back to Carbon? We can't let that happen!"

"Mentioned she might run his international drug traffickin' business through the importin' and exportin' company her and Tim once owned."

"Darn it, Shrug. If Allie were to know where the sixth body is hidden, we'd have him. We'd nail Carbon for sure because no one but the killer or killers would have that information."

"Sarge, she has to not only know, she has to tell."

"Don't give her any more time to think about joining up with Carbon. Do anything it takes to get the woman talking."

"Anythin'? I've played dirty before in my career with your approval and once...or maybe, twice...without. Not this time. With Allison, I won't be usin' any strong-arm tactics."

"Why not? We have an unsolved mass slaying with one of our own among the dead. That ought to be enough to ease your tiny conscience."

"She's hurtin' enough as it is with what she's been through. If usin' honey don't convince her to talk, I won't be convincin' her."

Kindle rose. "Then I will," he said decisively.

"I'm off the case?" Shrug chuckled.

"Yeah." Kindle dismissed Shrug with a wave of his hand. "You're off the case."

"Whoa!" Shrug pulled his feet under him and rose. "Take it easy. I'll get her for you, I will. If she's got gently, she'll be much better for us. I'm just needin' time. Promise I won't let her turn. I'll up the heat. I'll do that for you. But, gently, sir. One little notch at a time. No firebrands on her ass."

"I think your emotional connection to this woman is clouding your judgement. It's unlike you to object to pressure tactics, especially when it comes to biker gangs."

"I'm a gentle man."

"That's an outright lie!"

"I admit I've got myself into a passel of trouble over the years, but my techniques to elicit cooperation never involved hurtin' anyone."

"Never? What about Katrina? She was a thirteen-year-old orphan when you recruited her into The Traz biker gang to help you with your undercover work. Are you saying she's not hurting because of that?"

"There's a big difference between that girl and Allison, Sarge. Katrina was well on her way to hell before I ever met up with her. Workin' the drug scene, manipulatin' dealers and undercover cops alike. She might be hurtin', but it weren't me who did the stabbin'. Allison, now she was an angel before Carbon got his claws into her. You can't deal with angels the same way you deal with she-devils."

"Alright then," Kindle conceded, dropping into his chair. "You've got one week to make it come together with your honey and gentle manner. One week, Shrug. Then, I'm taking over."

CHAPTER 6

"Someone special here to see you, Allison," Shrug announced, motioning an older couple ahead of him. Allie was sitting stiffly in one of the four wooden chairs around the tiny round table, looking exceptionally vulnerable. He wished he could have arranged a more comfortable meeting space than this cramped interview room at the detachment but the need for security trumped comfort when it came to plans involving Allison.

She was staring at her hands laced tightly in her lap, and did not look up. Shrug closed the door and strolled to the table. "Mr. and Mrs. Ash, Cory's parents, are here to see you."

"Who's Cory?" Allie cast a disinterested glance at the woman hesitantly approaching her. Mrs. Ash was an older woman with greying hair and soft blue eyes. She lifted a hand off the two large photo albums she was hugging and wiped her brow. Mr. Ash stepped to her side and together the two of them approached.

"Cory was one of your lover's murder victims." Allie looked up sharply. Ignoring her reaction, Shrug pulled out the chair opposite her, motioned the Ash's to take the other chairs, and settled in. Allie stiffened and kept her eyes on Shrug as the couple took their seats.

"Allison, Cory was the Shadow Rider workin' for me," Shrug explained. "Thought you might like to hear a bit about him, put a face to the victim. Go ahead, Mrs. Ash." Shrug nodded to the albums.

Mrs. Ash slowly set the books on the table and splayed her hands protectively over the top volume. Tears welled in her eyes as she gazed at her husband. The pain between them was obvious and undeniable. Mr. Ash wrapped a comforting arm about her shoulders and she finally slid her hands to her lap, allowing him to open the album.

"He was our first and only child," she began tearfully. She cast a quick sidelong glance to Allie before running a finger around the edges of the studio portrait filling the first page. "His was a difficult pregnancy and I was told not to have any more children."

Allie stole a look at the picture of a golden-haired toddler in a sailor suit. Tucking in her lips, she lowered her chin and glowered at Shrug.

"He won The Bay's Beautiful Baby Contest with this photo." A sob caught Mrs. Ash's words.

Allison rose and in two quick steps was around the table at Shrug's side. With her voice a low rumble, she bent to confront him. "It's this way, Shrug. Carbon was somebody's beautiful baby once, too."

Shrug turned slightly. "Yeah," he agreed calmly, "and Carbon's mama can still go visit him, touch his cheek, give him a kiss. Mrs. Ash gets to visit Cory's grave."

Allie clenched her teeth and, leaning in closer, dug her nails into Shrug's shoulders. "How dare you do this to me? You claim you're not manipulating me, but this—" She straightened and poked a finger toward the Ash's. "This is the ultimate in coercion!" She stalked out, her heels clicking on the tiles as she retreated down the hallway.

Mrs. Ash slowly closed the album. "I'm so very sorry," Shrug said over her sobs. "I know how difficult this is for you. If you can remain strong for me and help get justice for your son, this pain will be worth it."

"How dare she compare my son to his murderer." Mrs. Ash buried her face in her husband's shoulder. He closed his eyes and nuzzled her silver curls.

"I warned you it wouldn't be easy," Shrug said softly. "But I think Allison will come around for us. If I can't get her in here again, I promise I'll listen to your story myself. I'll look at every one of the photos in those books. It'd be an honour to get to know your son."

Mrs. Ash's weeping grew louder. Shrug rose and put a hand on her shoulder. "You don't have to do this. I'll take you home right now, if that's what you want."

"No, I'm okay." Mrs. Ash straightened and wiped at her eyes. "I promised I'd do it for you, and I will. Whatever it takes to bring Cory's murderer to justice."

"Perhaps it would help if you were to understand..." Sticking his hands in his pockets, Shrug gazed at the ceiling and sighed. "Or, maybe not."

"If there's something you can tell us, Corporal Hayes. Anything," Mr. Ash pleaded. "So very little has been shared with us."

Shrug looked down at him. "I was just gonna tell you, Allison is one of Carbon's victims, too. Dunno if that's much comfort to you, though, seein's how she's still walkin' and talkin'. But that man stole from her 'bout everything except her breath. This ain't easy for her, either. I was wantin' to give her more time to heal, but I imagine you'd be sidin' with my boss' opinion we gotta move on it right now."

Mrs. Ash nodded and wiped her nose with a tissue. "It's been way too long, years, without answers. If there's anything we can do to speed things up we will, Corporal Hayes. You just ask us and we will."

"I'll go talk to Allison. Why don't you two use the time to bask in some warm memories?" He nodded at the albums. "Better times."

Shrug found Allison pacing the small foyer in front of the locked exit doors, a feral look in her eyes. "Allison," he said gently. "I know what you're sayin'. I understand what you're feelin'."

"Like hell you do!" She hammered on the glass door. "Let me out of here."

"You're sayin' good people sometimes do bad things. Get caught up with evil friends. I know that."

"Let me out. You have no right to keep me here."

"From the law's perspective you might be a free woman, but you're not free of the gang and that means danger. We need to keep you safe."

"Quit insinuating Carbon's evil." Her voice was strong between intermittent sobs. "He was ordered to murder those guys. If he hadn't obeyed, he'd have been killed himself."

"That may be true," Shrug continued quietly. "And he'll have a chance to argue that in court."

"He won't argue that." Allie stopped pacing and glowered at him. "If you know as much about biker gangs as you pretend you do, you know he won't."

"Why wouldn't he?"

"Because he'd be dead if he did. He can't rat out the gang—they'll kill him. Those with dirty hands don't like those with clean ones."

"He told you that?"

"Don't you try telling me it isn't true, Shrug. Don't even try."

"I'm not arguin' with you."

Allie wiped her eyes. "It's also why he had to kidnap me. He'd been ordered to."

"Was he ordered to rape you? To beat you? Drug you?"

"He had to get me to South Korea and cooperate or I would've been dead and he would've been, too. I was a marked woman because when the Jackals came fishing for information on exporting to Asia, Tim and I reported them to the cops. Carbon fell in love with me the day we met and the only way to keep me from getting killed in retaliation for ratting out the gang, was to convince me to help him and the Jackals."

Shrug inhaled deeply. "Allison, I ran with a herd of bikers. And yes, several of the boys were good at heart. It tore me up to testify against some of the lads I'd ate and slept and played with for four years. For the depraved ones, though, I was tempted to lie on the stand to make things worse for 'em."

He took a step toward her and lowered his gaze to meet her eyes. "The good thing about our justice system is it wasn't left up to me to decide just how evil each man was. The charges were laid, I gave my evidence and the accused defended against it, then the jury decided. It's not up to you to judge Carbon. I'm not askin' you to do that. I'm just askin' for the evidence, girl. Mr. and Mrs. Ash are just askin' for the evidence."

"Carbon's a good man. Really, he is. He talked to me about growing up, being a football star in high school. Winning trophies and making his mama proud."

Shrug gave a few quick nods. "That may have all been true. His entire life ain't on trial, though, is it?"

"But..." Allie hammered her fist against the door and then, resting her forehead against the glass, concealed her face with her hands.

"Just the evidence, girl. That's all I'm wantin'."

"But he can't defend against it."

"Yeah, he can. And he will. Don't you doubt he'll have a pack of the best lawyers money can buy. He'll defend."

"He loves me. That's the only reason he told me anything about White Rock. He didn't have to, shouldn't have. But he did. He was crying, I mean really crying. He trusted me with his darkest secrets. I'm the only person he ever loved enough to do that. And I'm going to betray his confidence?" She peeked up at Shrug.

"Allison, come off it. He didn't love you. You know that. If someone I loved was being threatened by a biker gang, I wouldn't be drugging her and packin' her off to Korea. I wouldn't be beatin' and rapin' her. What the hell kind of love is that?"

"I see," Allie said stonily.

"I have two very distraught parents waitin' for you in the other room. I want you to go in there and listen to their story. Listen to the kind of love they had for their son. Just listen. Then decide which type of love you wanna side with, Carbon's kind or theirs."

Allie squared her shoulders. "What Carbon told me won't be of any use to you, anyway, so just lay off. He was so damned drunk that night, it was probably all lies. Inadmissible evidence."

"His insobriety may have loosened his lips but I happen to know it wasn't lies he told. I can prove it, although, in a court of law Carbon will be free to argue otherwise."

"I need to talk to him. Let me see him again, just for five minutes."

"Why do you need to see him?"

"Because I'm not sure who to believe. You're telling me things are different than how I remember. If I could talk to Carbon, I'd be able to tell if he was lying about his feelings toward me."

"Allison, damned near everything he told you was a lie."

"How do I know you're not telling me lies?"

"I don't give a fuck whether or not you think I'm lyin', you're not seein' him. Not talkin' to him. Not goin' into business with him."

"I wasn't planning on going into business with him."

"That's what you told Tim."

"If you're talking about Mahogany Imports, when I said I'd run it for him I meant as a legitimate business. We could make just as much money legally as he does drug running without the hassle and danger. I've talked to him about that—him giving up the bad life."

"He agreed to that?"

Allie looked to the floor. "I know I could convince him. It would be a chance for him to break free of the gang once he does his time for the drug charges. An opportunity to do something good with the rest of his life. I could do that for him."

"He'd have clean hands. Thought you said that was dangerous for a Jackal?"

Allie stomped her foot. "I don't know what to think anymore or who to believe."

"It's okay," Shrug said, quietly. "It's okay." He placed a giant hand on her trembling shoulder. "You're doin' good, girl. You're doin' okay. You'll work it through. I know you will. Come," he invited, gathering her to him.

Allie leaned her head on his massive chest and reached for his hand.

"Let's go listen to a mama's story about one of those good boys caught up in bad decisions and bad friends. Because she needs to tell it. She's not askin' you to talk to her, just wants someone to listen. You don't have to say a word, Allison."

CHAPTER 7

"You might as well go home now," Allie said, keying in the security code and opening the front door. "Because I'm heading off to bed." The squad car Shrug had used to ferry her from the detachment to the safe house sat at the curb. He'd killed the engine and followed her up the steps.

"Not likely." He steered her into the foyer ahead of him, closed the door and locked it. "We're gonna talk."

"You said I didn't have to talk. Just listen."

"I said Mrs. Ash didn't want you to talk. You bloody well know, I do."

"Well, I'm not going to talk to you, either." Allie tried ducking around him but he shifted his bulk to bar her from heading toward her bedroom.

"Yes, you are."

"We'll talk tomorrow. I want some time and space alone to think about everything."

"No. We're talkin' now. My very wise boss once told me when it comes to tellin' the truth, one doesn't need time to ponder word choice." Shrug laid his hands on her shoulders and guided her toward the sofa.

"Shrug, stop it!" He leaned his weight into her and she had no choice but to step into the living room. "Even if I were to say anything tonight, it would get thrown out of court," she said. "Think about it. Making me talk after a day like I've had would be like coercing evidence from a prisoner after hours of questioning under a bright light."

Shrug chuckled and nudged her onto the sofa. She sat where she fell, half on and half off. "You watch too much TV," he said. "And you don't even watch it good. I ain't after a confession, Allison. I know you weren't anywhere near the Jackals five years ago when the murders happened. I'm only after information."

"You're not getting it." Allie rolled to the floor, hugged her knees to her chin and stared at the hardwood.

"How about we don't talk about Carbon, then. Let's talk about Cory. You didn't say a damned thing the entire time the Ash's were there. I'd like to know what you think of their son."

"I think he was as rotten as Carbon. If the dice had rolled differently, Carbon would be the one dead and Cory would be the asshole behind bars with blood on his hands. The fucking gangs were at war."

"You could be right."

"Bad guys kill bad guys and the good guys have to stick their noses into the pile of stinking shit, thinking they're somehow making it better. Why does it have to be that way?"

"Taxpayers complain about it all the time. Complain about it myself. Sometimes it seems more sensible to just leave it up to God to deliver justice."

"That's my point. In God's world things always work out even in the end. Life will get Carbon for what he did—if his conscience doesn't get him first. We don't need a roomful of proficient-looking mere mortals passing judgement and sentence."

"Good point."

"Why not just drop it? Just leave it?"

"God's law only works well in theory. The universe has an eternity to even things out; man has one lifetime. Since evil breeds quicker than rabbits, if we did nothin', it wouldn't be long before good guys existed only in history books."

"Hmm. Perhaps." Allie buried her head in her knees.

"There's a preventative side to justice, too. If we'd been able to capture Carbon right after the murders, he wouldn't have been free to hurt you."

"That's a moot point because murder charges or not, once the jury comes in on his drug-trafficking charges, he won't be free to hurt anyone for a long time."

"Cory's parents need more than a drug conviction."

"They'll be happy if he gets locked up."

"No, Allie. They need a murder conviction. I've been around the system long enough to see how it works. A murder trial's too late to do the victim any good but those who loved him get somethin'. Society gets somethin'."

"I don't think revenge is necessary; an eye for an eye is a perpetuation of violence."

"You wanna empty our prisons of guys like Carbon and leave it up to God to keep you safe?"

"I didn't say that."

"You might as well have. It'd be awfully hard to lock up the bad guys if we skip the part about chargin' them and tryin' them."

Allie hugged her knees tighter, distressed at how sensible Shrug's arguments were beginning to sound.

"Our justice system," Shrug continued, "might not take eyes, but it takes criminals off our streets. It's compelled to, whether or not that suits you. You can either work with it or against it and if you don't talk, Allison, you're gonna learn what happens if you choose to work against it."

"What will happen?"

"Don't talk to me and you'll learn more about our justice system than you ever wanted to."

Allie crawled up on the sofa and stretched out. "I don't have to talk. It's my right."

"There's such a thing as setting you and Tim loose on the street for the Jackals to stalk. There's also obstructin' a police investigation." Allie reached for a pill bottle on the end table, shook some tablets into her hand and threw them in her mouth. Shrug jumped up and grabbed the bottle. "Allison! What are these?"

"You might as well go home because in five minutes I'm going to be passed out. There will be no more talking tonight." Allie pulled the throw cushion under her head and drew the afghan off the sofa back. "Sleeping pills." Her eyes slid closed.

Shrug scowled at the label. "How many did you take?"

"Three. I know it's one more than the instructions say but it won't kill me."

"*Dr. Erica Freid*," Shrug read. "You've been seeing your psychiatrist?"

"Yes."

"When?"

"This morning."

"You snuck out of here?"

"Don't worry, I didn't put myself in any danger. I took the bus and didn't inform the doctor of my address change."

"We've gone to great lengths to conceal your location and you agreed to stay put—" Shrug rattled the bottle. "What games are you playin' with me, woman?"

"If you're scared I'm going to kill myself, don't be. I'll be damned if I'll survive what Carbon put me through only to take my own life." She yawned and rubbed her knuckles over her eyes. "I'm a survivor, Shrug."

"That you are." Shrug watched the rise and fall of her chest until the movement became imperceptible. He lifted her wrist and held it tightly until he finally detected a pulse, strong and steady. Satisfied she was okay, he slipped the pills into his pocket and looked around.

"Allison!" he called loudly. She didn't stir. "I'm gonna look at your computer." He flipped open her laptop and tapped at the keys. "You don't mind, do you?" He scrolled through the history. She'd joined an online chat room for victims of violence. Googled Carbon's name at least a dozen times.

"Shit." He rapidly scanned her emails. The internet security for the home had been designed to keep people from monitoring her activity and finding her—not the opposite. That would have to change. He quietly closed the computer and gazed down at Allie. He'd have to ensure the phone was under close surveillance, too.

"I'm leavin' now," he said, shaking her shoulder. She uttered a soft moan and turned her head. "Takin' your pills with me." He unplugged her laptop and tucked it under his arm. "And your computer, if you don't mind."

"I don't care what Shrug might've told you, Doctor. I'm not suicidal." **Allison Montgomery**

"You are feeling strong?" **Dr. Erica Freid**

"No, I'm not feeling fucking strong. Doesn't mean I want to off myself, though."

"They're trying to rip Carbon from you, Allie. You have been obsessing about him for almost two years, what will happen to you when you see him for what he is? Who or what will replace him in your life?"

"Don't say that."

"You are going to let him go. We all know that's going to happen. You know that is going to happen."

"No, I don't know that."

"You do know that. Are you strong enough, Allie, to let him go?"

CHAPTER 8

Shrug tossed Allie's laptop onto Kindle's desk, walked to the window and gazed down into the parking lot. Kindle rolled his chair forward and gingerly ran a finger over the laptop lid. "What's this?"

"Allison's computer."

"She gave you her computer?"

"Not exactly. I told her I was takin' it and she didn't object."

"Why did you take it?"

"I think she's bin' tryin' to connect with Carbon over the internet. Not only would that compromise our case, it might compromise her life. I have no doubt if she were to arrange any kind of meetin' with him, we'd be investigatin' another murder—hers."

"Was she able to contact him?"

"She didn't confess to that."

"I didn't ask if she confessed."

"My guess is she didn't connect with him."

"Should I get our computer techs to take a look?"

"Probably shouldn't."

"I see." Kindle tightened his lips. "I'm assuming they shouldn't because you don't have Allie's permission." He pushed aside the laptop and rose. "What good is any of this without—"

"I took these, too." Shrug reached into his shirt pocket and tossed Kindle the bottle of Allie's pills.

Kindle squinted at the label. "What are they?"

"Sleeping pills from her psychiatrist."

"Why do you have them?"

"We've been over this before—I prefer live witnesses." Shrug approached Kindle. "Sir, I give up. You have a go at her. She says my tattoos remind her of Carbon. Maybe someone without the body art can shake her up and get her talkin'. I was sure hearin' Cory's parents, puttin' a face to the victim, would do it. And it probably would've, if she hadn't knocked back a mittful of those." Shrug nodded to the pills. "Successfully extricated herself from the hot seat."

"I have no problem with stepping in." Kindle hesitantly set the pills beside the laptop and quickly pulled away his hand.

"They ain't hot." Shrug chuckled and settled in opposite Kindle.

"Temperature-wise, no. But they aren't legal, either. I don't remember applying for a search warrant."

"Didn't know you need a warrant to search your own house."

"It's not your house."

"It's a safe house—it belongs to us."

"It doesn't matter whose name is on the title. If you're not living in a house, you can't just go and search and seize."

"A mere technicality."

"A technicality that will render null and void any evidence that might be on that computer."

"I didn't confiscate the pills and laptop for evidence. I took 'em to keep the witness safe. I believe I'm allowed to do that."

"You're going to argue in court her laptop and prescription medicine were an immediate danger to her?"

"I ain't worried about my arguin' skills. Besides, I won't have to argue nothin' unless she sues to get it back from us and she ain't gonna do that."

"What if we find there *is* evidence on there?" Kindle said, jabbing his finger at the computer. "And we can't use it because we're illegally in possession of it?"

"If we ever need to search it, we can get a warrant."

Kindle glared at Shrug. "And how easy do you suppose it is to get a warrant to search stolen property? Property stolen by us?"

"If you don't like 'em here, return 'em to her," Shrug said. "She's your case now, remember?"

Kindle sighed and sank into his chair. "If I'm taking over that part of things, you've got to take over some of this crap." He flipped through the folders and loose papers covering his desk. "Our experts are saying if there's a body missing from the massacre site, it likely belongs to someone Carbon was close to. Perhaps, in his mind, giving his buddy a decent burial would make up for killing him. I want you to research Carbon. Have any of his close friends or relatives been missing for about five years? Do any of them match anything in our biker gang database?"

"Sure."

"The other possibility is the missing body held some sort of incriminating evidence the killer wanted to get rid of. That scenario, however, doesn't give us any leads. So, for now, we'll go with the first one."

"I'll see what I can come up with."

"Check previous cell mates, high school buddies. Cousins, siblings—"

"What are you gonna try with Allison that I haven't already?"

"I'm considering using Katrina on her."

"Are you fuckin' nuts?"

"I knew you wouldn't like the idea."

"Wherever that she-devil is, there's chaos. 'Trina's trouble, Sarge. You know that."

"She's not as evil as you make her out to be. She's female and was trained as a police officer. Considering Allison's recent experiences with men, a woman's touch may be what's needed. Besides, Katrina's been through a similar—"

"Don't, Sarge! Don't be sayin' nothin' more."

"Why not?"

"You're gonna tell me the girl has Stockholm Syndrome because of her time with me in The Traz. There's no fuckin' justification for that. That little siren was ridin' with the bikers 'cause she wanted to. Usin' her wiles and millions, more than any of the rest of us, to work her drug deals. She wasn't no victim, Sarge, and I saw to it she wasn't."

"She was a victim of Lukas' murder. She watched her best friend tortured and slaughtered. Make no mistake about it, she was victimized."

"Not by me! I didn't kill Lukas, wasn't even there for the murder."

"In her mind you were. You took her to the Quonset and left her there with Gator's boys to watch the bloodletting. She trusted you to protect her and you didn't."

"That's bullshit."

"Yet, to this day, she's mesmerized by you. You have nothing good to say about her, yet she adores you. Why? I'll tell you why, because she knew she needed you to protect her. She built a bond with you. She'll understand what Allison went through with Carbon. It's worth a shot."

"It's a big mistake involvin' Katrina in this, for whatever reason. Don't do it. You'll regret it, I swear. She's not even a member of the police force anymore. You shouldn't be draggin' a civilian in to work such a sensitive case."

"You involved the Ash's."

"Only in a minor way and under my direct control. I didn't have 'em out and about alone with my witness."

"I'm not getting into another argument with you about Katrina. I don't have a problem involving her, and neither do my bosses. She's meeting with Allison. It's happening. If it doesn't work, we'll be serving Allison the legal papers to make her talk."

"There's nothin' in our laws compellin' witnesses to tell us about crimes. It's her right not to and she knows that."

"If she lies to police investigators, it's all we need for an obstruction of justice charge. I'm sure one of us can get her to lie."

"Sarge, I threatened her with arrest. Didn't seem to scare her. Even if we do get her to lie, arrest warrants may be pretty, but they can't make someone talk who doesn't want to. I got the feelin' Allison's so stressed a jail cell might be lookin' good to her. I can see her curlin' up in a ball and silently wilin' away eternity."

"I guess time will tell. However, if you do your job real good and get an ID on our missing victim, maybe we won't need to rely on Allison's help."

"Sure. I'll do that."

"What am I supposed to do with these?" Kindle waved the pill bottle and motioned to the laptop.

"Put 'em in a safe place. There may come a time when we'll want to know for sure if she contacted Carbon and if she did, what was said."

"We don't want to know for sure, right now?"

"Fine. I'll leave it to you to get the papers needed to make that happen."

CHAPTER 9

"Nice place, Allie," Katrina said, circling her eyes over the smooth maple cabinets and stone countertop. "Sort of neat to see what my fucking money bought."

"What do you mean?" Allie guessed Katrina to be barely five feet tall, however she exuded beauty. Long amber curls rippled over her shoulders like a slow moving river in a sunset. Allie was drawn to her brilliant blue eyes, dazzling almost violet against her porcelain skin.

"The bureaucracy was too slow for Shrug's liking." Katrina giggled. "He wanted a new safe house for Allison– *fuckin' now!'* So, I donated the funds. Nice." She ran a stockinged toe along the vein in a marble tile before casting her bright eyes to Allie.

"Thank you, I guess."

"So…" Katrina smacked her lips. "Are you ready?"

"Ready?"

"Shrug said you're in dire need of a manicure so I made you an appointment. Can get you a massage, too, if you like. We could do a whole fucking afternoon of woman things. What do you say?"

"You're sure it's all right? I was told not to leave the house. Got in trouble last time I snuck out. Do you know how loud Shrug can bellow?"

"I know all about Shrug's bellow. However, our day on the town has been approved by Sergeant Kindle, himself. No worries." Katrina tapped her hip. "I've got my sidearm with me. You'll be safe. I'm a sharp shooter. Been firing off fucking revolvers since I was six-years-old."

"Katrina, what…who…? Are you—?"

"You mean why the fuck am I here?"

"Something like that, yeah."

"The Sarge thinks I can make you talk about the Shadow Rider murders because I sort of went through something like you did. I agreed to try, mostly because I just wanted to see the fucking house my dollars bought. Will you talk to me about the murders?"

"No," Allie answered quickly.

"There, I tried. Now, let's go have fun. I've been stuck at home all fucking week with the kid. I'm into some freedom."

Allie tucked her fingers under the heat lamps to set her gel nails and looked over her shoulder at Katrina lounging alone in the waiting area. "Katrina, Sergeant Kindle told me you're a friend of Shrug's."

"The Sarge has a warped sense of reality." Katrina set down her magazine.

"Keep your fingers under the lamps," the manicurist said, pushing her chair back and rising. "I'll return when the timer goes off." She grabbed her coffee mug and disappeared.

"I take it you're *not* friends with Shrug?" Allie asked.

Katrina scowled. "We have a history together. He's known me since I was thirteen. But I don't think our relationship qualifies as friendship. The man hates me."

"Shrug hates you? I didn't think he hated anyone."

"He hates me. Calls me evil. A 'she-devil'. I don't believe in God and that drives him fucking wild."

"He hates you because you're an atheist?"

"Oh, he thinks he has lots of reasons to hate me. Says I'm 'connivin'. A bit like the pot calling the kettle black, if you ask me."

Allie giggled. "Are you 'connivin'?"

"Yeah," Katrina admitted slowly. "But I don't think that's an evil thing. I know what I want and I go after it. That's all. A car crash killed my parents when I was twelve and I was left with no living relatives, forcing me to make it on my own. Shrug thinks it's bizarre I was able to get along quite fine without anyone watching out for me. He says I must have had the devil's help. But being an only child, I was an expert on grownups. And with my IQ of two hundred, I can get what I want without any supernatural intervention."

"There must be more to that story." Allie wiggled her fingers in response to the heat, careful not to hit the edges of the lamp. She'd opted for decals, at Katrina's suggestion. The white doves seemed to have sealed in nicely. "Sergeant Kindle told me you have personal knowledge of what it's like to grow attached to someone who has control over you. Where does that part come in?"

"That's all fucking bullshit. He's talking about Shrug and I, but Shrug never had control over me. I was running wild after my parents' deaths and I ended up in a biker gang with Shrug. I didn't know he was working undercover. I just thought he was a big fucking biker dude trying to take over leadership of the gang. I did stuff to help him out. He's twisted it all around in his head. He got everyone believing he was somehow able to control me, he was using and manipulating me. Then, to top it all off, my fucking psychiatrist decides I must have needed Shrug to survive in the gang. No one seems to think a thirteen-year-old girl could have run with bikers for a year and come out unscathed unless she had some big macho man protecting her. It's all bullshit."

"But are you attached to Shrug? Do you like him even though he hates you?"

"Yeah, I guess I like him."

"I don't think I would like him if he called me a she-devil." *Or if he stole my computer and sleeping pills....*

A timer beeped and the manicurist returned. She checked each nail carefully and then massaged Allie's hands with rose oil. "All done," she said with a smile. Allie reached for her purse.

"No, I'll get it." Katrina jumped up and laid some twenties on the table. "My treat." She waved off the offer of a receipt and motioned Allie to follow her into the mall. "To be honest," she said, continuing their conversation, "my feelings for Shrug *are* somewhat suspect."

She stopped walking and tilted her head to stare up at a fashion mannequin in a shop window. "Shrug was there for me when I had no one else. He did a lot for me, dried many tears. Rocked me to sleep when I had nightmares after the murder..." She wrapped her hand around her chin. "I wish I was taller. I so want to wear short dresses but they make me look like a kid. I need long, flowing lines—and very high heels."

"There was a murder?"

"Yeah. Saw my friend fucking slaughtered. Wasn't pleasant."

"I'm sorry."

Katrina looked over at Allie. "It wasn't Shrug's fault but he blames himself. When he came to my place to ask for money to buy the safe house, he asked me why I still liked him despite not having any good reasons to."

"What did you say?"

"Told him I didn't know. Then he asked if I'd have kept liking him if it had happened that he was a real biker and not a cop." Katrina abruptly took up stride and Allie scurried to catch up.

"And you said?"

"It was a stupid fucking question. *If*—how the fuck would I know *what if*? He probably asked it just to get my money. The massage is right here." Katrina opened a door and waved Allie in ahead of her. "I booked us both a session. Side by side, so we can talk."

"I told you I'm not going to talk." The receptionist greeted them and pointed to two massage tables. Allie set her purse down on one of the side chairs and closed the circle of privacy drapes.

From behind the curtain, Katrina laughed. "You're pretty good at keeping your word about not talking; I'm the one doing all the yapping. I've always been chatty. Shrug says that's what he liked about me in the gang. He could carry on hour-long conversations with me without having to say a fucking word. That man says little. Listens lots."

Allie stripped to her underwear and crawled, belly-down, under the cool cotton sheet. It had been a long time, a lifetime, since she'd been pampered. She remembered the heat of Korea. The chronically damp sheets of the coastal nation, the narrow hotel beds. Carbon beside her.

She inhaled the clean smell of fresh linens and massage lotions. Carbon had often smelled of beer, always of cigarettes.

"Which kind of massage would you like?" a soft female voice asked.

"Deep," Allie answered. "Very deep." The woman set a heavy warm towel across the small of her back and gently rolled the sheet off her legs.

South Korea was painted blue and green in her mind. Oceans and dark mountains. Painfully spicy food, sweet coffee—thick with cream. The pervasive odour of seafood... White rocks. Allie flashed her eyes open. *I mustn't go there. Not White Rock.*

"Katrina," she said loudly. "This is good. I really needed to get out. Thank you."

"Are you happy with your nails?" Katrina asked.

"I'm glad I went with the pearl finish like you suggested. It looks very rich." Dark shadows, splashes of red, deep green. Screams— "Katrina!" Her heart was racing, she was in so much fricken danger…from Carbon, from the gang, from the legal system. From Shrug. She wanted someone to protect her, to save her. Was the tiny lady behind the curtain the one who could get her out from under it all? "What are we going to do after this?"

"What do you want to do?"

White rocks...White rocks. "Do you know much about computers? I'm stuck in that house all day with nothing to do. I thought if I had a computer I could play some games on it or something. Right? *On the floor at Carbon's feet, my cheek stinging. Purple marks on my thighs, red welts around my wrists. His feet inches from my face. The Busan Aquarium and making love to him in the ocean—*

"Allie, I know more about computers than anyone in the world. And that's not a fucking lie. When I worked for Kindle, I solved computer crimes."

"Could we go shopping for a laptop for me?" *With Carbon in the noraebang, a wall of windows overlooking the sea. A fleet of small fishing boats in the East Bada, silhouetted against a setting sun, making their way to shore.*

She'd arranged a private Karaoke session as a hint there were ways around port security—a safe hint she was on his side. *'Don't bribe with American dollars, Carbon. The strongest currency here is a western education for the children'.*

The microphone in her hand, words rolling up the monitor. Soft music playing. Her voice– strong, mellow, sultry. *'I don't know how to love you...'* Carbon leaning back, a cigarette in one hand, appreciative eyes fixed on her...' *It's tearing me apart. Should I love you with my being? Should I love you with my heart—'* She was glad when Katrina's voice cut into her reverie.

"No need to buy a computer. I have a laptop I don't use anymore. I'll give it to you. Show you how to use the fucking thing."

"Would I be able to go online with it?" Katrina was instructing the masseuse and during the lull in their conversation, Carbon's deep dark eyes filled Allie's mind. *'Let me show you how to make love during your time of the month...'* His tender touch, tantalizing, teasing. Lips and fingers...

"Sure, I'll set it up for you," Katrina finally responded. "What do you want to do online?"

"My doctor mentioned there are chat rooms or forums or something—for victims of violence. Does that make sense to you?" *That night Carbon talked. The tears, the pain. His wounded soul, open to me...*

"I'm sure there are," Katrina said.

"Can people tell what you're doing online? I mean, if I wanted to talk about personal stuff, would everybody in the whole world be able to read it?"

"Depends."

The masseuse laid a heavy heated beanbag across her lower back and a smaller one on her neck. "I'll leave you now for five minutes to let the heat soak in," she whispered. "Is there anything you need?"

"No," Allie answered. "Everything's fine. That feels good." The curtains rustled and Allie heard both masseuses' footsteps whisper down the hall.

Dead men..."Did Sergeant Kindle tell you anything about the Shadow Riders murders?"

"Nope."

"Do you think I should talk to the cops about it? Shrug says it's not up to me to pass judgement. Just share what I know. The killer gets to defend against the evidence and the judge or the jury will decide on the guilt."

"I had to testify about my friend's murder. I was an eye witness. I didn't want to talk about it. I had decided it hadn't happened. It was just a bad dream or something. I was scared talking about it would make it real."

"What convinced you to talk?"

"Chad came down hard on me. He was one of the investigating officers, now he's my husband. He said that with or without words, the murder was real, that *'there was real fucking blood all over the real fucking place. I can show you the crime scene photos.'* Actually, it felt good when I finally talked. Putting words to the violent images that were haunting me made the memories easier to deal with. It was good for me. Felt real good."

"It's different for me, though. I wasn't a witness. I don't have any memories. I'll just get someone in a hell of a lot of trouble. Someone who loved me enough to confide in me."

"It's up to you. Totally. But I sure as fuck wouldn't let someone who murdered a bunch of people ruin the rest of my life. If you lie about what you know, you'll be facing obstruction charges. Don't ever think Shrug won't carry out his threats, because I know he will. He gave me a licking once. Pulled down my jeans in front of the whole gang and laid me over his knee. I can't believe to this day, he actually did that. I was thirteen, for fuck's sake. Idiot!"

The curtain swished open and Allie felt the cool of the sheet as the bean bag was lifted from her back. The masseuse folded down the cover and a brush of air raced across Allie's bare shoulders. *Hands that had caressed her. Hands that had hit her. Hands that had killed. Hands that had buried...* She tried to focus on the thick, strong fingers kneading her neck. She was glad when Katrina began to talk again.

"Allie," she said forcefully, "if this guy really loves you, he wouldn't want you to get in trouble because of him. He'd want to take responsibility for what he did and leave you out of it. At least, that's how I'd define love."

The masseuse hit a tender spot below Allie's shoulder blades. Her fingers stayed there and circled. Allie moaned. "I wish I could talk to Carbon. See if he feels that way and if he doesn't, why not."

"Chad would do anything for me. He loves me so much. Despite everything I ever did over the years, he sees the good in me. He encourages me. He believes in me. God, Allie, I love that fucking man to bits."

CHAPTER 10

"Just a minute!" Allie called as the doorbell interrupted her online conversation. "I have to get decent." She hastily slapped her laptop closed, unplugged it and raced to her room. She shoved the computer under the bed, making sure it and the cord were well hidden by the dust ruffle. She tousled her hair and with her heart still pounding ran back to answer the door. She plastered on a smile and flung it open. "Shrug," she greeted.

"Allison."

She searched the slate grey eyes gazing down on her for any hint of suspicion, but could tell nothing of what Shrug was feeling. "Come in."

"Today's the day," Shrug's deep voice rumbled. "The time is now." She followed him through to the living room. He sank into the recliner and said no more.

Full of trepidation, Allie slouched opposite him on the sofa. The one thing scarier than Shrug's voice was his silence. She fought desperately not to blurt out what it was he wanted to hear. *'Carbon killed six men...he buried his friend.'* Shrug was hunched over, staring at his feet—his hands clasped above his knees.

"What's your decision?" he finally thundered before looking up at her.

"Decision?" He pulled a paper from his pocket and tapped it against his hand. Allie could see a seal above the signature, a crest on the letterhead. "Are you saying I have to talk now or...?"

"Yup. Or..."

"I need more time. Just one more day."

"Nope."

"It's coming together for me, honest. I just want to be sure that if I decide to talk, it's truly my decision and not yours. I need to feel I'm not just being manipulated again."

"I've given you lots of time, more than was appropriate. Given you lots of tools to help you along."

"I know, but you've also put lots of pressure on me." *Are those eviction papers? Notice of withdrawal of Witness Protection? Are Tim and I on our own?*

His eyes were on her. He tapped the papers quicker and harder against his hand and straightened, obviously anxious to finish what he'd come to do. "Got your nails done?" he said.

Allie realized her right hand was pasted over her mouth. "Yes," she said, spreading her fingers toward him, relieved that although he might not be willing to give her another day he was offering her at least another minute or two. *I can't betray Carbon. I just can't.* "See the decals?"

Shrug leaned forward and squinted.

"Doves," Allie explained. "Symbolizing hope. Or as Katrina said, perhaps they're just fucking pigeons and I'm a fucking marble statue and they're going to fucking shit on my fucking head." Shrug rolled his eyes. "I had an entire fun-filled fucking day with Katrina."

"And you didn't talk."

"But Katrina did."

"No doubt," Shrug said, a small grin creasing his stony face.

"She likes you. Even though you don't like her."

"Talked about me, did she?"

"Yeah. And about her husband and about how much they love each other. What they'd do for each other."

"I see." Shrug closed his eyes.

"Katrina told me what Carbon should be doing if he loved me."

"Good," Shrug said, with a quick nod.

"I just want one more day. A little bit of time to sort through it and feel good about my decision."

Shrug peeked out at her from under raised brows. "I'll make you a deal."

"A deal?"

"I let you do your sortin' thing for one more day and you let my techs look through that laptop I took down to the detachment."

"No," Allie objected quickly.

"Do you want your lawyer here? Shall I call Tudor?"

"No, I don't want any lawyer here. I just want some more time."

"This massacre happened five years ago, I don't have more time. I need to know what you know, Allison. Did Carbon tell you how many guys were murdered at White Rock?"

"No."

"Did he tell you there were six?"

"He might have—you overheard me talking to Tim. You're not being fair."

"You've lied to me, Allison. We know Carbon told you there were six men murdered. What else do you know? Did Carbon tell you he buried one of the bodies?"

"Who the hell's telling you this shit? How the hell would you know what Carbon told me? There's no way you can prove I'm lying."

"All the media reports said there were five bodies—you told Tim there were six victims."

"Maybe I lied to Tim—there are no laws against lying to your ex."

"Maybe we found the sixth body, Allison."

"Now *you're* lying. How fair is it I'm not allowed to lie to you but you can lie to me? Where's the justice in that? There's no way anyone would've found the body."

"How do you know that? Did Carbon tell you he buried it where no one could find it?"

"No!"

"He told you where he buried it, didn't he?"

"No!"

"Allison Lisa Montgomery," Shrug recited, slowly rising. "You're under arrest—"

"I need more time, please?" Allie frantically interrupted. "Go ahead and look at the damned computer. Just give me another day."

"Too late." Shrug beckoned her to stand. "If you don't think handcuffs are the right jewellery to go with your new nails, come quietly."

"I have no choice?" Allie slowly rose.

"Nope, and, neither do I." Shrug steered her toward the foyer.

"If I were to talk—I still have that option, don't I?"

"You've lied to me. This is now an entirely separate matter." Shrug opened the door and motioned her ahead of him.

As the door shut behind them, Allie heard the tinkle of breaking glass. Before she could turn to the sound, the crack of a rifle boomed from the street. Instantly, Shrug was on her, his weight taking her down hard to the concrete steps. A volley of gunfire rang out. He rolled between her and the street, roughly shoving her against the sharp brick wall. An engine revved and tires squealed. Shrug's elbow dug into her ribs as he reached for his sidearm. She hurt everywhere. Then all was quiet.

"What was that?" she cried.

Shrug shifted his weight and scanned the street, his pistol drawn. "Christ, Allison," he muttered, dropping his gun and grappling at her arm. He pressed his palm against her shoulder. Blood covered his hand and oozed between his fingers.

"You've been shot!" she sobbed.

"It's okay." He pressed his palm tighter and rose to his knees. "It's you, not me but you'll be okay." He quickly ran his free hand over her head and neck and patted down her chest and abdomen. "Can you sit?"

"Sure." She reached for his hand but as she lifted her head and shoulders, a rush of pain stole her breath. Shrug blurred and everything went black.

"Fuck." She slumped to the concrete and closed her eyes. "Does that ever hurt."

"Damn!" Shrug pulled out his radio with his free hand and struggled to work the buttons. "Get an ambulance here!" he shouted. "Drive-by shooting. We've got a woman down. An officer on the scene..."

"I'm alright," Allie moaned, unsettled by his panic.

"And as many units as we have, plus ten," he roared. "Heading east on Fifty-Third Street, a dark sedan."

"You're hurting me," Allie quietly protested, clawing at his fingers curled around her shoulder.

"Ain't me hurtin' you. Thinkin' it's likely the bullet." He returned to his radio. "I got a partial marker. Alberta plate. Yankee Juliette Alpha..."

CHAPTER 11

"She in surgery, yet?" Shrug inquired at the hospital desk.

"An operating room has just become available. As soon as it's scrubbed, she'll be going in," the nurse replied.

"It's been almost two hours," Sergeant Kindle protested.

"We've got the bleeding stemmed and we've dosed her up so she's not in any pain. In fact..." The nurse winked. "She's feeling so good if you were looking to elicit a confession, now would be the time."

Shrug and Kindle exchanged glances. "I was joking," the nurse quickly cut in. "It's something we kid about because our sedated patients often lose their inhibitions and get chatty. But you definitely can't go in there."

Shrug puffed out his chest. "Why not?"

"Hospital rules."

"You need a better reason than that! She's a victim of an attempted murder. The quicker I get any information she has, the safer our streets will be."

"Hospital rules," the nurse repeated, picking up the ringing phone.

"Can we?" Shrug asked the Sergeant.

"Not illegal."

"Just hospital rules, right? And we can break those without gettin' sent to prison."

"If she's drugged, Shrug, we can't use anything she says in a court of law."

"But if she were to tell us where the missin' body is and who it belongs to, we could use that info in our investigation?"

"Can't think of a reason why not."

"You stay here and keep pestering the angels of mercy." Shrug strode down the hall and through the door marked '*Restricted Area*'.

"Allison?" he asked, looking down at her on the gurney. She was deathly white. A swathe of bandages, edged in red, cradled her shoulder. A bag hung above her, its clear liquid lazily dripping into a tube running to her wrist.

"Hmmm."

"The doctor will be gettin' to you soon."

"Yeah."

"How're you feelin'?"

"Fine." Her tongue was thick and she was struggling to open her eyes.

"That buddy of Carbon's he buried, what was his name again?"

"Green," she answered slowly. "Jed Green."

"Yeah, that's it. Jed Green. And Carbon buried him not too far from where he killed him, right?"

"I didn't... You're not... Stop it, Shrug!" Allie thrashed her hand free of the white sheet.

"Carbon told you that, right?"

"Carbon told me... No, not that. I had a vision. On the plane."

"Oh, good. That means you don't have to tattle on Carbon. You can just tell me the vision."

"I saw white rocks," Allie said dreamily, flicking her eyelids. "Shadows. Green mountains."

"White rocks, like White Rock, B.C.?"

"White rocks... Along a river. White rocks..."

"Shadows as in the Shadow Riders?"

"No! Just shadows."

"Green, like Jed Green?"

"It was green. I thought it was a vision, but it wasn't." Allie ran her tongue over her lips and looked up at Shrug through half-closed eyes. "Carbon had me so drugged. He was talking to his buddy, Saber, on the plane to Korea. I just thought it was all a vision. A dream." She closed her eyes and moaned. "I thought Roland Eisman was a rolling dice and...."

"Roland Eisman, one of the victims? What did Carbon tell you about him?"

"That he wasn't a rolling dice."

"Did they talk about where they buried Jed?"

"It wasn't in the vision. It was after. When I knew I loved him. In the hotel room. Carbon got drunk..." Her voice became fainter and trailed off.

"He told you it really ripped him up killing his buddy? Seeing Jed dead?" Shrug guessed, calling on what the forensic experts had surmised.

"Yeah." A small sob caught Allie's voice. "He wanted to at least bury him. Didn't want the bears ripping him apart or something. He went down by the river. Covered the grave with rocks. If you look at it when the sun's rising, the stones cast a shadow in the shape of a cross."

"Down by the river," Shrug confirmed.

Allie nodded. "I saw bones by the river in my vision. I thought they were mine. I thought the vision meant Carbon was going to kill me and leave me to rot in Korea."

"The bones by the river," Shrug persisted. "What else did you see? If I go there, Allie, how can I find them?"

"Don't go there," Allie said, shaking her head slowly. "They're not in Korea."

"They're in White Rock, Allison. If I go to White Rock—"

"A clearing above the waterline. Where the soil was soft and he could dig a grave. When he was done, he walked to the river and sat on a big black rock. Had a cigarette. Looked across the water at a cell phone tower which looked like a giant altar and felt he was in a sacred place. He waited until the blinking lights at the top of the tower disappeared with the rising sun. Went to the grave and added one more rock—the top of the cross."

"Sir, who are you?" a strong male voice demanded from the doorway.

"Oh, no!" Allie tried sitting, as if startled awake by the new voice. "I can't believe I told you all that. I've betrayed him."

"You had to tell me, you know that. It's over now, Allie. It's finally over."

"I can't believe…" She settled into her pillow and her breathing slowed.

"Which is the hardest to believe, that you betrayed him or that he shot you?"

"No...no. Don't say that."

"You'll do okay, Allie."

"I can't believe any of this. I can't believe today happened. What the hell, he tried…to…kill me? He shot me? Did Carbon shoot me?"

"You have no reason to regret talking. You are strong. You'll do fine."

"No. I won't. I'm alone." She groaned and her eyelids fluttered. *Without Carbon, I'm so fucking alone.*

"Sir! I'm calling Security. What's your name?" The orderly pulled out a pager, as if to make good his threat.

Shrug lifted and dropped his massive shoulders, cast the man a quick grin and walked past him into the hallway.

CHAPTER 12

Shrug stepped into his boss' office and glowered at the Sergeant. "We need more people on this!"

Kindle sighed. "Believe me, I'm trying."

"I'm researchin' this Jed Green fella, tryin' to find a body by a big black rock, looking into Allison's hard drive, investigatin' a drive-by shooting and...tryin' to remain pleasant."

"You took her computer to the techs?" Kindle asked, nervously looking about his office. "I didn't get any warrants or..."

"Don't have to," Shrug interrupted. "I got her permission."

"That won't work. You can't get legal permission from someone who's doped up in a hospital bed."

"Don't worry, Sarge. Before all this happened, I talked to her about it and she distinctly said our techs were free to look through it. Betcha she was talkin' to Carbon online, tipped him off as to her whereabouts. How else would someone know to gun her down on her own front step? I've never had a more covert safe house."

"Well," Kindle said, settling into his chair. "The shooting certainly has complicated things. Let's try prioritising. A day-old attempted murder probably beats out the cold case murders—"

"Not when the two cases are linked," Shrug objected. "If we follow up on the White Rock clues and get good old Carb behind bars for those murders, it'll give us the breathin' room we need to find the evidence linkin' him to Allie's shooting."

"Okay, let's chase down White Rock," Kindle conceded. He chewed on his pen for a moment. "I can get someone else to research Green. That I can do for you. And I already have a team chasing leads on the sedan at the scene of the shooting. So, that's more or less covered. I'll liaise with everyone, the investigating team, the techs, the researcher, you. Organize the info and keep everybody informed. That leaves you with locating the body."

"Sarge..." Shrug walked over to Kindle's desk. "The statement Allison gave in emergency will be enough to arrest Carbon, provided it leads to us findin' the grave. It's not likely to make it into evidence at a trial, though, considerin' she was doped up and said she saw it in a vision. She's gonna have to testify she came by the knowledge through a conversation with Carbon."

"Right."

"Which means someone's gonna have to keep up the pressure on her."

"We'll deal with that later. Let her recover from her surgery. It'll become a hot issue if and when the body's located."

"Just don't be siccing Katrina on her again," Shrug warned. "I wouldn't doubt the girl had somethin' to do with Carbon getting to Allison."

"Why would you even think such a thing?"

"You know the girl. You shouldn't have to ask."

"The *'woman'*."

"If I were you, I'd have the investigatin' team that's lookin' for a dark sedan, talk to the girl with the golden curls." Shrug strode toward the door.

"Shrug!" Kindle rose and marched after him. "If you're insinuating Katrina purposely set Allison up, you are way out of line!"

"Didn't say *'purposely'*. But, I bet my bottom-ass dollar, she had somethin' to do with it."

"I neither need nor want your advice on how to run this investigation and I don't need to hear your biased opinions about Katrina."

"Gotcha." Shrug opened the door and stepped into the hallway.

"One more thing, since you're going to be in White Rock, instruct all your people including the computer techs to forward any and all information directly to me. Understand?"

CHAPTER 13

Shrug noticed his boss looked uncharacteristically harried; the papers in front of Sergeant Kindle were piled twice as high as usual, his hair was uncombed and his tie, askew. "Sir," he said, tapping on the open office door. "My flight's this evenin'."

Kindle motioned Shrug to come in and sit. "I need to talk to you before you leave for White Rock. I'll bring you up to speed. I'm trying to keep everybody in the loop. Sometimes it takes many minds to fit the pieces together. How long until you're out of here?"

"I was on my way home to pack," Shrug said, slipping into the chair opposite Kindle's desk. "I need to be at the airport in three hours."

"Okay, I'll make it quick. Let's start with the good news. The techs found nothing suspicious on Allison's laptop. They say unless she's a computer genius or has access to some super-technology to hide her activity, we can safely assume no online contact was made with Carbon. We've had the safe house phone tapped since day one and there's nothing untoward showing up there, either."

"Carbon found her somehow. Has Katrina been questioned yet?" Shrug tilted his head.

Sergeant Kindle slammed his fist to his desk, his eyes spitting fire. *I ought to apologize,* Shrug thought, slumping deeper into his chair. The Sergeant had been like a father to Katrina during The Traz investigation and trials. She was the orphaned daughter of one of their own; he had a valid reason for feeling protective toward her.

Kindle, as if his anger had become too much to bear, leaned back, clasped his hands on his belly and closed his eyes. Shrug stared at his shoes, as he always did when he could think of nothing intelligent to say. It seemed a long time before Kindle squeaked his chair forward and exhaled loudly. Shrug peeked up.

Kindle was now looking out the window. Three stories below, the grey of autumn was disappearing, flake by flake, beneath the white of winter. He gave a quick nod before turning to Shrug. "Carbon found Allison somehow, which means our security was severely breached, another thing to add to our agenda. Who compromised our safe house?"

"Agreed."

"I haven't ruled out Katrina," Kindle added softly. "The investigators have been told to speak with her but I haven't got their report yet."

"Look at it thoroughly when you get it."

"Don't tell me how to do my job—" Kindle quickly swallowed and lowered his voice. "I've asked them to note anything indicating Allison and Katrina were being followed or watched, any evidence a dark sedan was in their vicinity. Anything out of the ordinary Katrina might have noticed that day they were together."

Shrug pulled in his legs and straightened. "Sorry, Sarge, for the disrespect."

"Likewise. The stress is getting to all of us. I'm supposed to hear tomorrow if I get the extra manpower I requested."

"I got my team together to search the river at White Rock. I'm makin' use of the volunteer Search and Rescue people. Findin' graves ain't exactly within their mandate but I sweet-talked them into callin' it an evidence search and doin' it as a training exercise."

"Bonus. That will help with the budget."

"Any word on Allison?" Shrug asked.

"She's under guard at the hospital. Haven't heard otherwise, so I'm assuming for now, everything went okay with her surgery yesterday."

"Think the fact her lover shot her will end her fascination with him, once and for all?"

"I'm hoping it works in our favour. However, I won't be confronting her for a couple of days yet."

Kindle's phone rang and Shrug stood. "I'm off! Likely out of radio and cell phone range in the mountains. I'll let you know as soon as I can if we find anythin'."

Kindle waited until Shrug left before hitting the talk button. "Hello."

"We talked to Katrina Buckhold as you suggested." The officer's youthful voice ruefully reminded Kindle that he hadn't had a seasoned officer available to deal with Katrina. "She noticed nothing suspicious during their outing. No one was seen following them and Ms. Buckhold had specifically been watching for that."

"All right." Kindle sighed. "Do you have an itinerary of their day out?"

"Yes, I did that for you. Approximate times and locations. Mostly just to the mall and back."

"Mostly?"

"Other than Katrina made a quick stop at home after the mall visit. She reports she parked inside her attached garage, with all doors closed and locked. Allison remained in the vehicle. No other vehicles or pedestrians were in the vicinity."

"Okay," Kindle sighed. "Check if there's any surveillance cameras along the route. I don't like thinking about where we're next going to have to cast suspicious eyes."

"Is it starting to look to you as if the suspect had insider information?"

"Well, we're the only ones who knew anything about the safe house."

"I guess I'll have to ask you for a list of those who know, us or otherwise," the fellow suggested quietly.

"Will do," Kindle grimly agreed, jotting down names as they came to mind. Shrug, himself, Katrina, Tim, the IT officer who'd set up the secure internet. The officer in Property Acquisitions.... "And you'll get me that itinerary of the ladies' outing, ASAP?"

"Later today, sir."

"What was the stop at Katrina's house about?"

"Likely a bathroom break or something."

"Likely?"

"I didn't pry, but I'll certainly look into it if you think it might be important."

"Probably not. But ask and let me know as soon as you find out," Kindle ordered, hanging up.

CHAPTER 14

"Allison, how're you doing?" Sergeant Kindle said, gently patting her bandaged arm. Allie moved restlessly beneath the white hospital sheets. "They say you'll be released soon." He spoke a little louder, hoping to rouse her. "My apologies for not protecting you."

Allie's eyes fluttered open. "It's okay." She briefly focussed on him. "It wasn't your fault."

"I have another safe house lined up for you once you get released. We'll double the security." Allie nodded and closed her eyes.

"You did good for us. Shrug's at White Rock as we speak, trying to locate the body."

Allie grimaced and tossed her head. "I told him all that, didn't I?"

"It was important you did. Thank you."

"I had no choice, did I?" She caressed her bandage with her free hand.

"If it leads us to the body, we'll need your testimony."

"I know." Allie opened her eyes and stared at Kindle. "Don't worry, I'll testify."

"Good for you." Kindle patted her hand. "Good for you."

"It's not like I'm being heroic. I had the choice to obey Carbon and not talk or do what Shrug wanted. And since Shrug didn't use a bullet to get me to agree..." She sighed and faced the wall. "I'm so screwed up inside, Sergeant Kindle. So fucking screwed up. I can't decide anything for myself, anymore."

"You just told me otherwise."

"What do you mean?"

"You just told me you decided to go with Shrug's wish rather than Carbon's. That's a decision."

"I suppose it is, isn't it?"

"It is. A difficult decision, but the right one."

"It'll be so hard to testify against Carbon. He'll be there. Watching me.

Listening..."

"You'll do fine. I know you will." Allie fidgeted, her eyes unfocussed and pained. "There's something else we have to talk about," Kindle continued. "How did Carbon locate the safe house?" Kindle's cell phone rang and he looked apologetically to Allie. "I guess I'm not supposed to have this damned thing on in here, am I?" He hit the talk button and walked from the room. "Hello?"

"Sergeant Kindle," the young officer greeted. "You wanted to know what the stop at Katrina's was for during their girls' day out. Katrina was picking up a laptop."

"Why?"

"It was an old one she was lending to Allison."

"She lent Allison a laptop?"

"I guess it was one she didn't use anymore and Allison had complained about being bored and wanting to play games on it or something."

"Play games?"

"Yeah, and there's a chat group for victims of violence she wanted to join. Katrina apparently set it all up for her."

"I believe that's an encrypted internet connection into and out of that house."

"Well, you know Katrina," the officer said with a laugh. "Simple encryption won't stop that gal."

"You'd need a password plus special software to hook up a new device."

"Maybe she went 3G."

"3G?"

"Mobile internet connection—new technology which would bypass all security we had installed."

"Get that computer!" Kindle flicked off his phone and stormed into Allie's room. "Allison! You got a computer from Katrina?"

"Yes."

"Were you talking online to Carbon?"

Allie nodded.

"You told him where you were?"

"I just wanted to see him."

"Why?"

"He begged me to believe he loved me and that everything he's ever done was to keep me safe. He pleaded with me to keep my mouth shut about the murders because he knew the Jackals would kill me if I talked, maybe kill him, too. I wanted to see him. Look in his eyes. Listen to his voice. See if he was lying."

"You told him where you were living?"

"No! We talked about meeting up but I didn't give him my address, I swear. Sir, please understand. I needed to talk to him. I knew the phone was tapped. And I knew that after revealing I'd snuck out to see my doctor, there'd be no way I'd make it past your security a second time. I told Carbon he wouldn't get past it either but he said he'd figure out some way to get together with me."

"Do you know anything about 3G?"

"No. What's that?"

"The computer you used, what did Katrina do to get it working for you?"

"Not much. I didn't watch closely but she had it working in less than five minutes."

"It wasn't a secure machine," Kindle said.

"I know nothing about stuff like that."

"Maybe not, but you were clearly told not to contact Carbon. Told it was very dangerous to do so."

"I know. I'm sorry. I didn't believe you. I didn't dream Carbon...I didn't think he'd...I'm sorry. I wasn't thinking straight, obviously. It's my fault."

"You should have—" Kindle abruptly stopped shouting and sighed. "I guess that solves that mystery," he ended quietly.

"You can say 'I told you so,' anytime you want."

"I'm just sorry it took a bullet for you to realize where your trust should lie."

"I know. I know."

"It's important we get him locked up so he can't hurt anyone else. Do you have anything more you can tell us which might help?"

"Maybe later." Her voice was barely a whisper. "I'm so tired right now."

"I understand. Thank you for helping us, Allison. But before I leave you to rest, the nurse asked me to tell you Tim wants to see you. I told her I have no objections but she said as you two are divorced, she's shared no information with him and it's up to you if you want to see him."

"I'll think about it."

"He's in the waiting room as we speak."

"I wouldn't know what to say to him. I feel so damned bad about everything."

"I don't think he's looking for an apology."

"He should be."

"Tim understands better than any of us what you've been through and what it's done to you."

Allie nodded. "Perhaps he'll be happy I'm finally cooperating with you."

"I'm sure he will be. He'll be happy he's getting back the woman he married."

"No, I'm not that woman; it wouldn't have taken a bullet to get her to talk. She'd have done it because it was the right thing to do, not because... Shit!" Her voice grew weak and shaky. "Carbon killed six people yet I might never have turned him in if Shrug hadn't hit me up when I was drugged..."

"It was your decision to talk to us, a very brave and ethical decision during trying circumstances." Kindle patted her arm. "There'll come a day when it will feel that way to you."

"Perhaps." Allie sighed and reached for Kindle's hand. "Please let Tim know he's safe. I didn't tell Carbon anything about him."

"Another good decision, made for all the right reasons. I'll let Tim know."

Tears trickled down her cheeks. "I'm going to make another good decision. Tim must be sick with worry. Send him in, sir."

"Allie," Tim greeted, stopping just inside the door. Hearing of her decision to talk to the cops had him expecting to see some spunk in her eyes, but she looked pale, drawn and vulnerable.

"Come in, Tim," she invited.

Tim took a tentative step toward her. "I've been so worried. But they say you're doing great."

"I'm doing okay. I'm only on regular Tylenol now for the pain."

"Sergeant Kindle suggested there's another type of healing happening as well."

"He's giving me too much credit." Allie patted the bed beside her. "Come here. I need to touch you." Tim slowly approached, uncomfortable with the look of defeat washing over her. "Sergeant Kindle said you're not after an apology but I have to give you one. Sit."

Tim gingerly took a spot beside her. He wanted to hush her, tell her to conserve her energy but she quickly continued. "I'm so sorry about the way I've treated you. So very, very sorry about the things I said."

Tim took her hand and brushed her knuckles across his lips. "You're one strong woman," he offered with a smile.

"I don't feel strong at all right now. I feel battered and beaten and ready to give up—perhaps I already have, maybe betraying Carbon simply became the easiest road to follow."

"None of this is easy but I have no doubts you're going to win the battle."

"Which battle am I going to win?"

"All of them. The battles in your heart, your soul, your mind." He nodded to her shoulder and her IV drip. "Your battle to survive."

"I'm going to win them all?"

"Why not?"

"I feel so tired. Dead inside, as if I'm a marble statue with pigeons shitting on my head. Hurting in places even morphine doesn't touch."

"You'll survive. You'll heal. You'll win."

Allie gripped his hand. "Sergeant Kindle said since we're divorced, you have no legal rights to see me."

"Apparently I don't need legal rights."

"Would you like to have them, though?"

"Are you proposing?"

"It's the new millennium. Women get to do that."

"I'd love to say yes, but it's something you need more time to think about."

"No, Tim. I shouldn't have to think about it, not after everything you've done for me."

"I'm not looking for repayment. You're hurting and drugged, darling. Give yourself time to decide what you want."

"It's not a rash decision, we've know each other for how long? Decades? And we've been through so much together these past two years. Unless of course, you don't want to marry me."

"Allie—"

"There are so many things right now which are confusing but this I know for sure—I want to spend the rest of my life with you. It's not a difficult concept."

"In that case, I accept." Tim leaned in for a quick kiss. She threw her good arm around his neck and sealed her mouth to his. Her tongue frantically scoured his teeth. Tim closed his eyes and opened his mouth.

She thrust her tongue deep—sucking, twirling, and searching. Tim tentatively played the tip of his tongue over the smooth underside of hers; they'd never kissed like this before. *Is this something Carbon taught her?* At last she released her hold and sank into her pillow. He kissed her quickly on the lips. When he drew back, her eyes darted over his face.

"I accept your proposal on one condition," Tim said when her eyes finally settled on his. "You have the right to change your mind at any time, no questions asked."

"Tim, this isn't a half-assed commitment I'm making."

"It was just a few short days ago you told me you still had feelings for Carbon."

"But look what's happened since!"

"I want to be sure those feelings are now all for me—and will be forever. Take the time you need to sort it all out."

She pulled her hand away. "You don't want me anymore, do you? You've finally convinced me to abandon Carbon and now you're going to abandon me?"

"Shh." Tim put a finger to her lips. "I accepted your proposal, remember? I'll buy you an engagement ring. We'll announce our intentions to the world. We'll get there, slowly, okay?"

"Slowly? I thought you'd be rushing out to find the hospital chaplain."

"I know beyond a doubt I love you, but whether or not we can live together...let's make sure. We weren't doing good even before Carbon appeared in our lives."

"But it was the business that tore us apart. We both got so involved in the company, we lost each other. You've sold Mahogany Imports. That problem's gone."

"I hope so much you're right."

"You're having second thoughts," Allie's eyes filled with tears. "I've left it too long, screwed you around too much. You're never going to trust me again. You're always going to be wondering if Carbon's still in my heart somewhere."

"Allie, your proposal made it quite clear what you want and that's so very special to me. Let's just take the time to prove to ourselves and to each other that we can get our lives in line with our hearts."

Allie wiped a stray lock of greying hair off Tim's temple. "What are you saying?"

"You proposed," Tim soothed. "I accepted. We're engaged and that makes me very happy. The rest will make sense when you're feeling better. Trust me, Allie. Please, learn to trust me."

CHAPTER 15

"You lent Allison a computer?" Kindle asked, eyeing up Katrina. She'd been waiting for him in his office, sitting in the chair opposite his desk. She was so short her feet swung above the floor much as they did a decade ago when she was a kid and he was questioning her about her year with The Traz. He closed the door and walked to his desk.

"Yes. Why?"

"The security of the safe house was breached and we're trying to determine how. We think it might have something to do with your computer."

"Why would you think that?"

"Because we're not sure the laptop you lent Allison was secure."

"You're talking to the master of internet security, you know that. Anything I gave her would've been a hundred times more secure than what your pale techies could've come up—"

"I don't like cockiness," Sergeant Kindle interjected. "It is always the bear expert who gets mauled to death by the grizzly." Kindle took his seat behind his desk and picked up the phone. "Send in Constable Josh Anderson." Replacing the phone in the cradle, he leaned back in his chair.

Josh was indeed one of his pale techies and with his red hair and freckles he looked even paler. Katrina and he nodded at each other in recognition. They'd trained together in Depot and then competed for top spot in the computer centre under his command. The rivalry had been friendly but intense.

"There's no way my computer can be blamed for any security breech," Katrina insisted. "I of course can't control what Allie did online. If she told someone the location of the safe house, that's hardly my fault."

"She insists she didn't," Sergeant Kindle said. "Constable Anderson's crew will be looking to prove that as soon they get the computer. We need to know what else to look for."

"Did that computer of yours have any tracking software? GPS?" Josh asked.

"No, of course not."

"The router in that house was encrypted and password protected, how did you—"

"I didn't use your damned system. My Dell has a built-in mobile internet connection—"

"Somebody could've traced the IP of that mobile internet connection," Josh said.

"No! It is set up to run through a virtual network. It also uses alternating IPs which are registered to a numbered company with a box number. Not even my internet service provider itself would be able to trace the location of the computer—even with a search warrant."

Kindle looked to Josh and he nodded in confirmation. "How do we catch paedophiles who live stream child rape?" he asked. "Don't most of them conceal the IP number of their computers?"

"Some not as cleverly as Katrina," Josh said. "Others we track down through clues in the photos—wait. Your computer has a built-in web cam, doesn't it?"

"Yes. But like I said before, I can't be responsible for—"

"I'm on it!" Josh rose and walked out, quietly closing the door behind him. The silence was heavy.

"Is that a grizzly I hear approaching?" Katrina finally asked.

Sergeant Kindle coughed. "As part of our internet security protocol, we disabled the cam on the original computer."

"Nobody told me that. I'll feel terrible it if proves my computer was responsible for getting Allie shot."

"Don't."

"Don't?"

"Don't feel terrible. Allison was warned not to contact Carbon, but she did. She was dishonest with you about needing a computer, didn't tell you the one we provided had been confiscated due to her questionable activities. Your job was to bond with her and get her to talk; our job was to protect her—but without her help, neither of us could reasonably expect success."

"I had no idea her computer use was a problem. I understood the danger of someone tracking her through computer signals and made sure I maximized the firewalls, virus sweeps, etc. Made sure her IP was hidden..."

"She's a grown woman, a free woman. She served her time for her crime and we can no longer tell her what she must do, only what she should do."

"I know but..." Katrina paused, remembering when she was fourteen. "After I was rescued from the gang, I was warned time and again not to contact Shrug, but I did. Of everyone involved in protecting Allie, I ought to have been the one to best understand her compulsion to reach out to Carbon. I should have fucking thought of that."

"Leave it," Sergeant Kindle said, rising and motioning Katrina toward the door. "It's time for Allison Montgomery to take responsibility for her life."

CHAPTER 16

"Does this look like a sacred spot to you?" Shrug asked his lead volunteer as officers scurried to string yellow police tape about the site.

The man ran his hand through his thick dark hair. "Yup. That's what drew my eyes to it."

"You have good eyes."

"Perhaps I've just spent too much of my life in a pew." The fellow chuckled. "Who's buried here? Someone important?"

"We'll find out soon." Shrug kicked at a stone.

"Not just another one of those bikers slaughtered near here a few years ago?"

"My guess is, it's some poor mother's son."

"You're probably right because every man has a poor mama."

Shrug inhaled deeply and looked across the water to the communication tower. "Yeah," he finally said, exhaling noisily. "And some are lucky enough to be loved by her. You never know."

"Anything else we can do for you, Shrug?"

"That about wraps it up for your end of things. Thanks, and tell your crew thanks, too."

"Our pleasure. If anything comes up and you need us again..." The fellow waved his guys in.

"I have you on speed dial," Shrug said, watching the sea of bright vests congregate and head up the bank through the bushes. The sound of the volunteers' steps echoed through the dead fallow of a dry winter. Dusk was coming and the rest would have to wait until tomorrow.

Shrug looked at the pile of rocks marking Jed Green's grave. A rising sun, he decided, would very likely create a shadowy cross. He tapped one of his officers on the shoulder. "I want a picture of this site at sunrise. From all angles."

With the perimeter sealed and the darkness deepening, Shrug sent his own crew home. In the hush that followed, he felt the sacredness that Allie had mentioned—the rush of the river in the near distance muted by the boulders along its shore, the spongy soil beneath feet accustomed to miles of unforgiving rocks. Across the water, the red lights of a communication tower were beginning to spark in the deepening dusk. If he'd ever had need to bury a friend, this was a spot he might have chosen.

He wandered to the river's edge, sat upon the boulder that Carbon must have sat on and pulled out a *Nicorette*.

It's funny, he thought, how a man can kill a friend.

CHAPTER 17

Josh tapped on Sergeant Kindle's door and tentatively stepped in. "I finally have some news about Katrina's computer."

Kindle looked up from his keyboard. It had been days since they'd confiscated the computer. Paperwork, staff vacations and another murder had slowed the investigation. Because of Katrina's cyberspace security expertise, and Allie's statement denying she'd revealed her location, Kindle wasn't expecting much. "Good news or bad?" he asked.

"There was only one web cam photo taken—of a sunset."

"That means Allie didn't reveal her location via the computer?"

"Actually, it appears she may have, inadvertently. She emailed that photo to Carbon."

"And it contained identifying address information?"

"She took it out her living room window. At the bottom of the photo there's a car parked in the drive outside the neighbour's garage across the alley. With a bit of manipulation we were able to read the plate number."

"Don't keep me guessing, just tell me where this is leading."

"We ran the marker and confirmed the car is registered to the owner of the home across the alley from the safe house. If someone else were to have done what we did..."

"It didn't require any special equipment or computer skills to decipher the plate number?"

"Nope. Just enlarging the image and lightening the exposure, something everybody these days can easily do. However, not everybody can get personal information about the registered owner of a plate number, especially with our new privacy laws."

"A plate number would be pretty useless without a name and address, wouldn't it?"

"Alberta has over two hundred and fifty vehicle registration offices across the province, with umpteen number of employees able to easily access that information. We're looking now for a connection between the Jackals and a Registry agent."

Kindle sighed. "Does it look like this was planned? Did Carbon ask for the photo?"

"No. The conversation was all about her not knowing whom she should trust and Carbon saying to trust him. While both expressed an interest in getting together, they also seemed resigned to the fact that doing so would be dangerous for them both. The 'gorgeous sunset' just kind of happened and Allie said something about how digitally sharing that moment was about as close as they could get and stay safe. Little did she know."

"Okay. Keep me posted."

Shrug tapped on the open door. "Have you got a moment, Sarge?" he asked.

Kindle set down his pen. "Josh is just leaving. Come in." Once Shrug and he were alone, Kindle relaxed back into his chair and ran his hands over his weary eyes. "Congratulations on a job well done in White Rock, Shrug."

"I can't say enough about the volunteers. They were great."

"You got us what we needed. As of now, Carbon's behind bars."

"About fuckin' time." Shrug stretched his legs under Kindle's desk.

"Although he hasn't been handed his drug trafficking conviction yet, he lost bail last night following the laying of his murder, attempted murder and kidnapping charges."

"Kidnappin' charges?" Shrug looked up sharply.

Kindle nodded. "Looks like Allison will finally get her day in court."

"Kidnappin'?" Shrug straightened. "Whose fuckin' poor decision was it to put the kidnappin' charges on the table?"

"It wasn't mine but I don't think either of us should be surprised."

Shrug smacked his fist into his palm. "God damn it!"

"Something had to be done with the kidnapping evidence. It couldn't lay there in limbo forever."

"Couldn't it have waited? Remember how Carbon's lawyers tried claimin' the international drug trafficking investigation was tainted because the Crown didn't bring that evidence forward? The only thing savin' us was the ruling that because there were no kidnappin' charges, the Crown was right—that evidence was irrelevant. Why the hell would we decide now to open the door for them to claim the murder charges are tainted?"

"The lawyers have studied the situation and feel because the murders and kidnapping are vastly separate in both time and place, kidnapping charges won't affect the current charges. It could possibly net Carbon and Saber an appeal on their trafficking convictions, but the rest—"

"It's a can of worms. The defence will milk it to the fullest; find a way to cast doubt on the integrity of all the investigations. Couldn't it have waited?"

"We're prepared to fiercely argue that without Allison's cooperation at the time of the drug trials, the kidnapping investigation was stymied and incomplete and the evidence, therefore, useless. I really can't see how Carbon's lawyers can claim the lack of kidnapping evidence at his drug trials will now hurt his defence against murder charges."

"They'll undoubtedly find a way," Shrug muttered. "They'll say Allison's testimony is simply revenge; she wasn't truthful at her own drug trial and isn't being truthful now."

Kindle clenched his jaw. "We knew delaying the kidnapping charges was risky but we decided if it got us the info needed to lay murder charges, it would be worth it. Right? You were in on that decision. Right, Shrug? Right?"

"Shit."

"And it did get us what we needed, so let's focus on that and get to work. I'll bring you up to snuff on all that's happened." Kindle flipped open a file. "For starters, Allison has agreed to cooperate and testify, although she's not at all happy about the kidnapping charges, either."

"Because?"

"Testifying at a kidnapping trial means her feelings toward Carbon will be under public scrutiny."

"We'll need to provide some good expert witnesses to explain how the mind works when under duress."

"It'll be tough on her, no doubt. She's cooperating because she wants to clear away her criminal record. However, she asked us to drop the kidnapping charges, believing if she testifies at the murder trial and gets a new identity under the Witness Protection Program her problems will be solved."

"It doesn't work that way. You can't hide a criminal record behind a new identity. However, we could—hmmm."

"What are you up to? I know that look, Shrug!"

"Never mind."

"I told her it's not up to the victim of a crime to decide whether or not it gets prosecuted and it's not up to me, either. I also told her it was unlikely any of us can convince the Crown Prosecutor's office to drop the charges. If the evidence is there, they are compelled by law to proceed."

"There may be other ways out, but for now," Shrug nodded at the file in Kindle's hands, "just tell me the rest of what you've got there."

"Carbon and Jed Green's relationship dates way back. They were in a couple of the same foster homes as pre-teens in Ontario."

"Carbon was a foster child? Thought he told Allison he had a mama."

"Yeah, there was a mama in there somewhere, single parent. Had some problems with alcohol and drugs. Apparently, cleaned herself up when Carbon hit high school and he went back with her."

"Did Jed and Carbon like each other as foster-brothers? Maybe get in trouble together?"

"We're still investigating that part. Accessing juvenile records isn't easy, especially this long after the fact. We know there was some trouble, but it's not clear exactly what…or why. There may have been some abuse happening at one of the foster homes. No charges were ever laid, but the suspicion is the two boys banded together to defend themselves against it in some way. If it proves to be true, I can see that creating quite a bond. Jed, being the older one by a couple of years, may have emerged a hero in Carbon's mind."

"A hero he'd kill forty years later." Shrug shivered. He'd learned all about the dark side of gangs during his time undercover with The Traz. He'd never forget watching Gator wring a puppy's neck in front of Katrina to introduce her to the idea that gang life was violent, the cost of membership, steep. Then there was that cold October night in the metal shed. To prove one's loyalty, one had to be willing to kill.

Kindle's voice shattered his thoughts. "We don't know how Carbon and Jed ended up on opposite sides. After high school Carbon moseyed out west to dip into the lucrative Alberta oil sands economy. Spent time up in Fort McMurray mingling with the itinerant crowd—single men, miles from home, with lots of cash. He likely saw the looming potential of the drug trade. Must've had something the Jackals thought they could use. Jed stayed down east. Not sure how he got tangled in with the Shadow Riders." Sergeant Kindle leaned back in his chair and stared out the window, deep in thought or perhaps deep in regret.

He'd never said so, but Shrug suspected if Kindle had known what he now knew about gangs, he wouldn't have recruited Shrug, his high school buddy, to infiltrate The Traz. In fact, there likely wouldn't have been an undercover biker operation.

Shrug stared at his feet. The Traz operation had left scars on both their souls. Perhaps it had been worth it, though. Shrug knew his legacy wasn't simply the two hundred and fifty convictions the operation netted. It was the intel he'd gathered for law enforcement. It's why both he and Kindle and been called in to help the Homicide Unit with this case.

"It's not always money that's the lure of gang life," Kindle said. Shrug looked up to see Kindle roll his chair forward. He put his elbows on his desk and stared at Shrug. "It's the excitement, the power, the bikes. The call of the wild, perhaps. The boys obviously had rough upbringings, maybe it was simply the brotherhood they were after. A chance to belong, be respected, be needed."

"Motives ain't ever easy to decipher. I s'pose belongin' makes sense to the vulnerable." Shrug drew his feet in and straightened. "Has Allison talked about the motive for the murders?"

"She says the Jackals wanted the Shadow Riders to tuck tail and head home East, get out of their territory."

"And Carbon was the one to make that happen?"

Kindle again stared out the window, his brow creased, looking as if his thoughts were out there somewhere and he was desperately trying to gather them in. Perhaps he was wishing he was back at his desk fighting computer crimes, a role they'd both been assigned as part of their healing process after the biker convictions came in.

It was obvious the gang murders were wearing on him. Both he and Shrug were getting too old to believe they could make a difference and that was making this tough job damned near impossible.

Kindle finally drew his eyes from the window. "Allison says Carbon hinted that the massacre was his initiation into the gang, a chance to prove his loyalty and worth. He was told if he killed these bastards, one of them being his buddy, he'd get patched in as a Jackal."

"He must've really wanted to belong."

"It was a double-edged sword—he either slew the Shadow Riders and earned his patch, or refused and was dead. At least that's Allison's take on his story."

"Why would they threaten to kill Carbon?"

"We've learned, Carbon had only loose connections to the gang before this all happened, just hanging around the fringes. He had some mechanical skills and worked on the bikes and such. Perhaps couriered drugs past security into the oil field work camps. With no proven loyalty to the gang, if he'd been told about the planned attack and subsequently refused to participate—"

"That would've made the Jackals uneasy," Shrug interrupted. "They had nothing on him to make sure he didn't run to the cops with the story."

"Exactly. Prior to the massacre, his hands were dangerously clean."

"Making him perfect for the job in some ways. No criminal record, not bein' watched by the police. Best of all, the involvement of a guy like Carbon with no known connection to the Jackals would've made it easy for the gang to distance themselves from the kill should somethin' have gone wrong."

"You're right. That would've befuddled the cops."

"And reduced the risk of retaliation by the Shadow Riders," Shrug added.

Kindle sighed, as if in resignation. Shrug understood the discouragement. Despite all they'd done, the risks they'd taken and the intel they'd gathered, the violence continued. On all fronts. He picked up a pen from Kindle's desk and clicked it against the wooden arm of the chair. Though battle-weary, Kindle wouldn't give up and neither would he.

"To us, Carbon might look like a perfect candidate to murder on behalf of the Jackals," Shrug said. "However, gangs don't generally use outsiders for such sensitive activities. There must've bin somethin' else happenin' between the Jackals and Carbon."

"There's the matter of a woman."

"That would do it!" Shrug leaned forward. "Tell me."

"According to Allison, Carbon was caught in the sack with a leading Jackals' lady. Although he insisted to Allison it was consensual, records show the woman filed an assault complaint against him. She retracted her story before the investigation got far. We don't know what her reward was for shutting up, but Carbon was offered forgiveness in return for taking out the top tier of the Shadow Riders."

"They set him up," Shrug muttered.

"Pardon?"

"I've seen it before—convince some biker bitch to tweak his dick and then use that to pressure him into doin' their dirty work for 'em."

"You think the woman was in on it?"

"Likely. Lendin' your woman to facilitate gang business is common and the ladies are willin'—makes 'em feel important."

"The Jackals were smart enough to plan something as convoluted as that?"

"Don't underestimate the cleverness of a biker gang. They didn't want Carbon tied to them in case somethin' goes wrong but they need somethin' on him, some hold over him. An indiscretion with a powerful gangster's woman serves that purpose well."

"I suppose it would." Kindle again took to staring out the window.

"I've gotta ask," Shrug said, breaking the silence. "Is there any indication either gang knew that Cory was a police informant?"

"Allison never heard any mention of that."

"Is Carbon the only suspect we have?"

"Although according to Allison, there were other Jackals on the scene, Carbon didn't give her any names. So, unless he gives them to us, it's not likely we can charge anyone else in connection with this case. The Crown Prosecutor says we have enough to proceed against Carbon since the bullets were all from his gun, he had motive and he knew where the missing body was. We have the DNA and prints. I spoke to Corporal Stanley in our Gang Unit and he says if there were other Jackals there, they likely weren't there as backup but more to make sure Carbon did what he was supposed to. Since he wasn't a full-fledged Jackal, there wouldn't have been a lot of trust."

"So we don't want to try plea bargainin' with Carbon in exchange for information on who all else was involved?"

"The general consensus is it would be a wasted effort. The code of silence among bikers is too strong. He'd be signing his own death certificate if he were to name names. We have a strong case against him, do we want to water it down on the faint hope we can uncover other guilty parties?"

"So we'll be happy with six dead and one guilty?"

"It appears we have no choice. It's better than being left a cold case and no arrests. It'll send a message to the gang we're watching and yes, we can solve their crimes. Gang violence, even against other gangs, won't go unpunished."

"How do you get the jury to buy the scenario a lone gunman killed six burly, heavily armed, paranoid bikers?"

"Allison said Carbon got the top Shadow Riders together under the pretence the Jackals wanted to join forces with the Riders. When they arrived to iron out the details, he slaughtered them."

"That story's weak. I can't imagine the top tier of a seasoned gang like the Shadow Riders walkin' into a trap like that."

"Our informant told us a few months before the murders that the Jackals approached the Shadow Riders to unite. Having evidence from another source that there'd been talk of a merger strengthens Allison's story."

"We know there wasn't a fuckin' chance in hell of a merger. As Cory Ash told us, the Jackals' offer to unite, had his Riders pumped because they took it as a sign their rivals were losin' steam and the time was ripe to take over the West."

"Perhaps for both gangs the talk about merging was rhetoric. Maybe both arrived in White Rock under the guise of uniting but with the intention of decimating. After all, there was more artillery found on that hill than the Canadian army took to Afghanistan. It may have boiled down to who had the quickest draw."

"Or which side planned the best ambush," Shrug said. "The fact that the Shadow Rider's weapons were left with the bodies and not confiscated by the winnin' team, backs the theory there might have been a lone gunman."

"We just might have to concede we'll never know exactly how it happened and we'll never be able to prosecute all those with blood on their hands."

"Bad guys kill bad guys," Shrug muttered. "What else you got there, Sarge?"

Kindle pulled a new sheaf of papers to him and coughed uncomfortably. "It was Allison who breached the security of the safe house."

"Allison?"

"She found Carbon online."

"She confessed to that, or our computer techs eventually tracked it?"

"A bit of both." Kindle cleared his throat and tapped his pen. "It wasn't the computer you confiscated that she used. It was one Katrina lent her."

"Katrina lent Allison a computer?" Shrug openly bit his tongue and rolled his eyes.

"There's no way Katrina could've anticipated her goodwill would lead to trouble, Shrug. She wasn't privy to the investigation and didn't know you'd caught Allison searching for Carbon."

"I take it you don't want me sayin', *'I told you so'*."

Kindle's face reddened. "Go ahead if it'll make you feel superior; I like my officers having abundant self-esteem."

"That's all you have to say to me? You go against my advice, resultin' in our prime witness endin' up two-inches shy of death, and all you have to express is concern about my self-esteem?" Shrug rose and paced to the window. He could see nothing outside that might have fascinated Kindle. The parking lot was all but empty, the sky grey, the trees bare.

"My decision to involve Katrina was based on sound judgement," Kindle said. "This result was unforeseeable."

Shrug abruptly turned from the window and strode to Kindle. Bending over him, he hammered his fist on the desk so hard the phone jangled in its cradle. "How was it that I foresaw it, then?"

"Perhaps you're psychic! Or maybe it's just your direct link to the Lord. Or, the fact your IQ hovers a hundred points above mine. Maybe, Shrug, you're just a much better man than I!"

Shrug backed away and lowered his voice. "I wasn't aimin' to insult you, Sarge. I was aimin' to point out that, contrary to your opinion on the matter, my assessment of Katrina is accurate. The girl's a she-devil and it's time you faced that fact."

"Stop the name calling; there was nothing devilish about what she did. As close a call as it was, the shooting got us what we wanted—Allison talking. Let's quit quibbling and take the gift handed us."

"Fine," Shrug said, with a quick nod. He lowered himself into his chair and took a deep breath. "How's Allison doin'?"

"She's out of the hospital and we've put her up with Tim. She assured us that since she didn't know until now where Tim's safe house was, she couldn't possibly have intentionally or otherwise revealed anything about his location to Carbon. They're engaged to be remarried."

"Tim and Allison?" Shrug felt a rare flush of pleasure. "Hot dog, that man knows how to romance."

"He's a little less sure of the situation than you and Allison are. She proposed to him in her hospital bed after the shooting and he's a bit nervous that she doesn't really mean it."

"She means it. That's not psychic, that's my direct line to the Lord."

"Either way, it's good news for us. With Tim in the picture, it's bound to chip away at her loyalty to Carbon. She'll be strong for us on the witness stand."

"Where's Carbon being held?" Shrug asked.

"Why? You have that look in your eye again."

"Remand Centre?"

"What are you up to, Shrug?"

"Just wantin' to talk to the man."

"He's already well-lawyered up. Even you won't be able to get past his attorneys. He won't talk."

"Not wantin' him to talk. Wantin' him to listen." Shrug rose. "Don't need a lawyer around for that."

"What are you wanting to tell him?" Kindle asked suspiciously.

"That I'll never forgive him, but God might." Shrug strolled from the room.

"Is Tim the proper replacement for Carbon, Allie? Your relationship with him didn't work the first time." **Dr. Erica Freid**

"I don't know." **Allison Montgomery**

"Why did you propose to Tim when you're not sure?"

"I...I...I don't want to be alone. Tim loves me—that I know for sure. At least I will be with someone who loves me."

CHAPTER 18

"You seem so distant," Allie complained to Tim.

"I'm only four feet from you!" Tim muted the TV and looked over at Allie. She had a paperback open on her lap but hadn't turned a page for fifteen minutes.

"You know what I mean."

"I suppose I do."

"In bed..." She paused to pick some lint off her sweater. "Does it bother you things are different?"

"To be honest, it did at first. But I've decided I like it. The differences. They're good."

"You're sure? I don't have to...the oral stuff, you know. We could just do it, like before."

"It's okay. I like it."

"You're sure?"

"Do *you* like it?"

"Yeah," Allie said, embarrassment reddening her cheeks.

"Then, it's not a problem."

She closed her paperback. "What *is* the problem?"

Tim sighed and closed his eyes. "You told me in the hospital you were scared of growing old alone. Does that mean you regret not having children?"

"I wasn't thinking of children in the hospital. I was thinking of having no man at my side. Sleeping alone. Having my morning coffee alone."

"Not having kids doesn't bother you?"

"It did when we first separated. I was hitting menopause and realized how final the decision was. But as Fran and Missy said, it's better to regret not having children than to regret having them. It hasn't been in my thoughts much since."

"You do know I would've considered adoption or any of the other options we looked at."

"Yes, I know. I was blaming you for a while after we split but I knew I wasn't being fair. We'd talked often about having a family. You were always open to the idea. It was, without a doubt, a mutual decision not to. I'm harbouring no resentment."

Tim straightened and squinted across at her. "You're sure?"

"I'm sure."

Tim paused. *How important is the past? Should I just let it be?* "I wouldn't have minded having kids, you know."

"You wanted to be a father?"

"Yeah. But we were so busy, it's okay. Our lives were full. Maybe too full. Is that why you didn't want to reconcile, you were frazzled?"

"I can't remember why I didn't want to reconcile. I can't remember much of anything about that time in my life."

"You accused me of having an affair—"

"I know that."

"I wasn't."

"I know you weren't. We had that sorted out before the divorce. I realize I said otherwise when I first arrived home from Korea with Carbon. And I know I said some real mean things about your manhood, Tim. But although I meant it all then, I certainly don't think the same way now."

"Okay. So if it wasn't because I couldn't father children and wasn't because I was having an affair, what was it, Allie? Why did you want a divorce?"

"I don't remember. Honest, I don't. I mean, other than us both travelling so much for the business and stuff like that."

"I'd offered to change that. I wanted to make it work. I hadn't realized how unhappy you were. I'd thought you were enjoying what you were doing. You were certainly good at it. You were ninety-percent responsible for the success of Mahogany Imports."

"I did enjoy my job," Allie said, furrowing her brow, as she concentrated on her memories. "I don't understand what was making me unhappy."

Tim sighed deeply. "Are you happy now?"

Allie set aside the book and curled her feet under her. "I would be, if I thought you were."

Tim kicked out the footrest and reclined his chair. "It's not that I'm unhappy. I'm just worried about you." Folding his hands across his chest, he closed his eyes.

"Are you worried I'll collapse on the witness stand when I see Carbon? That he'll arouse my feelings for him and I won't be able to betray him?"

"Does that worry you?" She took too long to answer and he peeked over at her. She was playing with the diamond on her finger.

"I bet it worries the Crown Attorneys," she finally answered.

"And...?"

"Probably worries Shrug." She stopped her fiddling and looked to him. "I guess I'm disappointed it worries you, though."

"You're saying it shouldn't?"

"I can understand your distrust. After all, I've backtracked on our love before, right? Refused to reconcile. Professed my love to you the night Shrug's guys came and took me to the safe house and then reneged a week later. I thought I was the one who had to relearn trust but I guess we both have to."

"Did you have something going on with Carbon before the kidnapping?"

"No! Why would you ask that?"

"There were several texted messages from him on your cell phone. Calls from him. You obviously had given him your number. Fran said—"

"I didn't give him my number!"

"Okay."

"Tim, it was just before our divorce was to be finalized that I first met him. I was at the bar with the girls, celebrating or grieving, or whatever. I was showing them my photos of my Korean vacation and, you know Fran. When it came to pictures of Haesindang Penis Park, she starts shrieking. I thought that's what drew Carbon to our table. It wasn't, though, as I later learned. He'd been stalking me all along, sent by the Jackals to recruit me."

"Fran said he bought you all drinks and then—"

"He later told me he'd fallen in love with me that night. I, however, was just plain terrified of him. His strange eyes. Tattoos. Dropped a fifty on the waitress's tray and told her to keep the change. Even though I was pissed out of my mind, I knew he was danger."

"After the girls left, you stayed. Is that when you gave him your number?"

"I said I didn't give him my number! I had my phone attached to my purse on the table and I remember him fiddling with it. At the time it didn't dawn on me, but he was probably looking up my number. I was just wondering how the hell I was going to get away from him, since Fran and Missy, the good friends they were, had abandoned me there with him. Tim, I'd never seen the man before in my life. Honest."

"At some point, you started liking him."

"Yeah, Tim. At some point. Some dark point."

"Facing Carbon in the court room doesn't worry you?"

"It does, but not for the same reasons it's worrying you."

"Tell me your reasons."

"I have good ones." Allie stretched out on the sofa and plumped the cushion under her head. "That man has devil eyes. They shine in the dark, I swear. He can make them say whatever he wants, regardless of what's in his heart or his head. He's one of those guys who could fool a lie detector."

"You won't have to look at his eyes in the court room."

"But I know I will. He could flash anything he wants to at me with those eyes."

"Like love?"

"That's not what scares me."

"What scares you?"

"I'm scared his eyes will laugh at me. Tell me what a dolt I was to fall for him. Brag about how grand he was at seduction. How easy I was. How funny it is that I now have to reveal my stupidity to the whole world."

"But none of that would be true."

"It would be. I knowingly fell in love with a mass murderer."

"He drugged you. Raped you. Threatened you. You weren't easy, Allie. It took damned near all he had to break you."

"The kidnapping trial will be the hardest. Having to remember. Having Carbon's lawyers question me, insinuate I was willing. Tim, I remember deciding the only way I'd be able to get home to Canada was to make Carbon fall in love with me. I set about to do that. I'm not sure I'll be able to defend that decision. And I'm not at all sure how I ended up being the one who fell in love. I hadn't planned that. I hated Carbon. Was terrified of him from the moment we met. The only reason I didn't get a restraining order was because I was scared it would anger him and unleash the danger I saw in his eyes."

"It's something I think a jury will understand. With all the evidence of a kidnapping, there won't be any doubt you didn't go willingly to Korea. What happened after you got there, shouldn't much matter."

"They'll try to make it matter, though. Insinuate since I was so willing once I got there, Carbon had reason to believe I wanted it...somehow."

"Don't, Allie." Tim kicked in the footrest, rose and walked over to her. She motioned for him to sit with her. He took the spot by her feet and she crawled to him, laying her head in his lap.

"Why are they making me do this? I asked them not to. If they get Carbon for murder, he'll be behind bars forever. They don't need to get him for kidnapping, too."

"I know."

"Do you think they'll make me talk about personal...about what we did in bed?"

"I don't think so."

"Carbon might make his lawyers ask just to get even with me for betraying him, or to make me fold. I can see the defence pressuring me into saying I loved him."

"It wouldn't be allowed."

"How do you know?"

CHAPTER 19

"You're totally unhappy with everything," Allie surmised from her spot at the kitchen table.

"No. No, I'm not." Tim ceased his pacing. He noticed again the new furniture, although much more comfortable, looked so out of place. The rich, cherry wood table was straddling a tiny pool of dark blue where feet hadn't scrubbed off the lino pattern. Its carved legs were biting into the worn grey around it. The stylish ergonomic chairs Allie had chosen, matched none of the colours in the peeling layers of wall paint. Behind the fresh furniture, the old blind still hung crooked. Allie was grinning.

"You're laughing at me," Tim accused.

"You're so bad at lying. Always were."

"Okay," Tim conceded with a sigh. "I admit. I'm frustrated."

"It's good you're frustrated."

"Good?"

"It's been a long time since you felt comfortable enough to show your true feelings. You've been tip-toeing around me as if I am too fragile to deal with anything."

"Is that so?" Tim walked over and took a chair by Allie.

She reached for his hand. "It's a beautiful spring day. Enjoy it."

"Beautiful, eh? The snow's melting off the roof and the damned eaves troughs all leak and we have an Olympic-sized skating rink forming outside the front door."

"Another month and it won't matter—it'll all change to grass."

"Another month...we're always waiting for something, aren't we?" He let out an exaggerated sigh. "Why do the wheels of justice churn so slowly? Why can't the trials be over with so we can get our new identities, leave this hole and start our lives?"

"Shrug keeps reminding me I don't get anything until I testify. I'm sure these miserable conditions are his way of motivating me, ensuring I don't back down. It'll soon be over."

"It better be."

"I know why you're upset, Tim."

"Why am I upset?"

"You're upset because you were told you might be called to the stand, too."

"You can read minds?"

"Yes. And there's much more than that weighing you down." Allie glued her eyes to her coffee mug and ran a finger over the gold inlay. "Tim, you want out of this relationship."

"It's not that, Allie! It's just...everything else."

"I'm not the woman you married and this relationship is not at all what you were expecting."

"I'm sure it will be different, when—"

"Don't lie to me. You're wanting out. You allowed me a condition on my proposal, I'll allow you the same on your acceptance." She looked up at him. "If you're wanting out, Tim, go for it."

"Wow," he said, rising.

"Wow?"

"You're right I've been questioning things but I never considered what the option is. That's it, though, isn't it? If I don't like it, get out. Up and leave." Tim paced to the window and fiddled with the blind, trying to level the slats. The cord tassel came off in his hand. He stared at the sun-beaten strings becoming dust in his palm. *What if they force me to explain under oath how Allie has been changed by the kidnapping, what she was like before and after?*

"It doesn't have to be all or nothing," Allie said quietly. "If there are things I can change to make it better for you, I will. I get the feeling, though, that you're not really into making it work."

Tim rolled the tassel in his hand, then reached for the cord and studied the broken ends. *Perhaps I can tie it together.* "This discussion should wait until after the trials."

"Are you interested in someone else?"

"I'm not going to abandon you, Allie. When the stress of the trials and of hiding here is over, we'll have a much better idea of where we're at as a couple." He successfully tied the ends together and tightened the knot. "It can all wait."

He yanked at the cord to let some sun in and the entire blind clattered to the floor. He stared at the slats fanned across his feet. The convex sides were chalky, spotted with rust, two shades lighter than the reverse. He thought of Hannah, the Crown Prosecutor. Attractive, kind. Gentle. Always a smile.

Divorced—it had come up when Allie had mentioned their engagement. Never anything more than a professional interest. "There's nobody else, Allie. Don't start those accusations all over again."

"What's her name?"

Tim looked up at the holes where the screws once held the blinds. Red slivers of rotten wood splayed from the ecru frame. He kicked the blinds off his toes and, satisfied with the enormous rustle of metal against metal, turned to Allie. "Don't do this to yourself. You have enough on your plate without making up things."

"I wish I could read Tim's mind." **Allison Montgomery**

*"Can't you just ask him what he's thinking?"***Dr. Erica Freid**

"He says one thing but I know he's thinking another."

"How so?"

"It bothers him I slept with Carbon. I know it does. He pretends it doesn't and that drives me insane."

"Do you feel guilty about your relationship with Carbon?"

"I could deal with it if Tim would admit it bothered him. Then we could talk about it and work it through. As it is, I'm left on my own to deal with it. I'm so alone. Even when I'm with Tim, I'm alone."

"Consider it aloneness, not loneliness. Use your alone time to connect with your soul. Focus on yourself without distraction. Without obligations. You're strong enough to be alone, Allie. Be alone and heal."

CHAPTER 20

"Carbon, you didn't need to bring your lawyer here," Shrug drawled, glancing about. "I ain't gonna be askin' any questions. Just tellin' you shit." He wondered what psychology went into designing the interview rooms of prisons. *Do men truly talk more freely when confined in close uncomfortable quarters than when luxuriating in an open expanse?*

"Nobody speaks to my client without me present." Shrug glanced at the mousy man who'd spoken in a voice so weak and high it was almost falsetto. His nose was weighted down by a pair of dark frames that hugged thick lenses. Beside Carbon's bulk, he looked insignificant, almost comical. *Such a small man must feel quite important representing a Jackal.*

"Sit," Shrug invited, plopping a file onto the small wooden table. As they all settled into the austere prison chairs, Shrug leaned forward and put on his best preacher voice. "I've come to save your soul."

"There will be no soul saving," the lawyer piped up. "My client has not granted you that permission."

Shrug couldn't help but chuckle. "I promised I wouldn't ask your client any questions, but I got one for you—who the hell are you?"

"Krypton." The fellow stretched his hand across the table between them. "Anthony Krypton."

"Krypton?" Shrug shook his hand and chuckled again. "That a name you made up?"

"Funny to hear from a man named *'Shrug'*."

"Guess you're right," Shrug conceded with a grin. "Were you wantin' your soul saved, too?"

"Not likely."

"Because it's like this—if you step into another man's soul savin' experience, yours automatically comes up for renewal. So, unless you're wantin' that, I'm thinkin' it's best you remain silent."

"You talk as if you believe your own shit. You're as crazy as they say!"

"Does insanity intimidate you?"

"Unfortunately for you, no."

Shrug glanced to Carbon. His eyes were glittering with obvious amusement. "Carb," Shrug said, opening the file in front of him. "I've come to save your soul." He pulled out a paper and began to read. "Six counts of outright first degree murder. One count of kidnappin' along with nine associated crimes such as assault, sexual assault, forgin' documents, etc., etc. Plus, one count of attempted murder, which ought to have been first degree but your aim the other day was a few centimetres off."

Carbon started to speak, but Krypton growled and Carbon stifled his words with an apologetic grin.

"I won't be askin' questions," Shrug said, "but, you're free to speak. If I'm sayin' somethin' you disagree with—"

"There'll be no speaking—" Krypton cut in.

"All the truth so far, Shrug," Carbon said, overriding his lawyer. "Surprising for a man with your dubious reputation."

"Yeah, all the truth." Shrug tilted his chair. "As I see it, this 'truth' all started goin' bad for you when you went and yapped about White Rock to your woman. Can't figure why the hell you'd go and do that." He paused just long enough for Krypton to cast Carbon a warning glance. "It's got you in a hell of a lot of trouble." Shrug slammed his chair down, coiled his legs beneath it and leaned into Carbon. "You ain't gettin' off on any of these charges and you fuckin' well know that."

"Do I smell a deal in the offing?" Krypton asked.

"You've seen the overwhelming evidence; there ain't no judicial deal to be had. However, I do deal in souls."

"The attempted murder—" Carbon started, his words cut off by the resounding slap of Krypton's hand across his mouth. It was all Shrug could do to keep his jaw from dropping. It was not often someone manhandled a biker— and got away with it. His opinion of Krypton skyrocketed.

"You don't have enough on the drive-by shooting," Krypton said without pause. "We're ready to defend against it. All of it. There was a whole lot of funny stuff going on with the kidnapping evidence. The supposed victim is a convicted criminal, pled guilty to the drug charges related to this supposed kidnapping trip to Korea. There was no mention of kidnapping or coercion at that trial. It's all tainted evidence you have. It's not going to fly. None of it." He leaned his elbows on the table and glared defiantly at Shrug.

"Defendin' against our evidence and the woman's testimony will be a colossal waste of money," Shrug scoffed.

"I didn't shoot the woman!" Carbon broke in loudly. "I wouldn't do that to her."

Shrug raised his eyebrows and turned to Krypton. "If your client were to have information on the attempted murder..."

Krypton eyed him up expectantly. "If?"

"If he did, he could tell me."

"And? You would...?" Krypton queried.

"Write it down," Shrug said decisively. "And investigate it fully."

"And...?"

"And?" Shrug echoed. Carbon shifted restlessly, his eyes on the table. Shrug could swear he was focussed on some inner turmoil, unaware of the chatter swirling about him.

Krypton ignored Carbon and leaned eagerly toward Shrug. "Get the Crown prosecutor in here, now! I want to hear a legitimate deal."

"Told you there's no deals to be had. Other than savin' a soul."

Carbon rose and paced to the far wall. "Someone shot your woman, Carb!" Shrug bellowed at his back. "How does that make you feel?"

"I warned her," Carbon muttered. "I fucking warned her."

"*I* couldn't keep her safe," Shrug shouted. "*You* couldn't keep her safe— thanks to your Jackal pals."

Carbon stuck his hands in his pockets and pressed his forehead against the pale yellow brick wall. Shrug lowered his voice. "In Ontario in the sixties, a couple of young boys were having a hard go at it in a foster home. The older one, Jed—"

"That's enough, Shrug," Carbon interrupted quietly, scraping a shoe over the tiles.

"Is it? Is it enough? Jackals got to you with Jed. Got to you with Allie. They're some great pals, ain't they? You certainly wouldn't wanna turn on 'em and say anythin' about a drive-by shootin'. Nope. You'd rather take the blame and leave Allie thinkin' for eternity you were out to kill her. When is it enough, Carbon?"

"I didn't shoot her." Carbon strode to Shrug and slammed his fist to the table. "I DID NOT SHOOT HER!"

"The thought of testifyin' against you is rippin' her apart, buddy." Shrug slowly rose. "You're gonna waste a pile of money on a fruitless defence and make her take the stand against you. Make her talk about the most intimate details of your time together. Make her tell the world where exactly you touched her and how. You'd make her do that? For what? I came to save your soul, but I gotta find it first."

With his eyes glued to Carbon's, Shrug walked around the desk. "It ain't her fault you spouted off." Shrug crowded closer, almost toe-to-toe, forcing Carbon to step back. "It was your own idiocy, not hers, yet now she's compelled by law to tell us what you said. Compelled by her heart not to." Shrug paused and again lowered his voice to a whisper. "It's rippin' her apart."

"I'll plead guilty to the murders and kidnapping," Carbon said. "But not the shooting."

"You will not!" Krypton shouted, squeezing between the two men.

Carbon shoved him away. "What the hell, Tony? I'm not paying you to argue with me."

"He will not plead guilty to anything!" Krypton desperately grabbed Shrug's elbow. "He does not admit to anything."

"Seein' a lot of lost dollars, Tony?" Shrug asked. "Lost headlines? No sound bites on the evening news?"

"This is about justice, not dollars and publicity. My client has a right to a fair trial, whether or not that upsets your witness."

"Tony, leave it," Carbon said. "It's how it will be."

"No, Carbon. You'll be behind bars forever! We have a good shot at this. With all the funny stuff happening behind the scenes—incomplete Agreed Statements, the woman's guilty plea, witness coercion—we can wipe out a whole slate of their so-called 'evidence'. It's worth a try. What's the woman to you, Carb? She'll survive it. Shrug's lying. She's reunited with her husband. She's not ripped up about you."

"She's with her husband because she thinks I shot her," Carbon said.

"No, no. Long before that," Krypton argued. "Her heart's with hubby, not you, Carbon. There's no sense wasting your life on her."

"A man has a life and a man has a soul," Shrug drawled. "Pity to waste them both."

The sound of Krypton's heavy breathing pulsated through the room as he and Carbon stared at each other, one frantic and one resigned. "Tony," Carbon finally said. "We're not going to win. Why pretend otherwise?"

"You don't know that unless we try. Have faith in me."

"We didn't win the drug case," Carbon reminded him. "Guilty, all round."

"We'll appeal. Now, they will have to listen to our argument that the investigation was tainted. I'll get you out on bail until the appeal is heard. There's stuff... Lots of stuff we can do."

"She told them Jed's name and where the body was. How else would she have known that? They have me. No use arguing. Did it to myself. Not like I wasn't warned. Saber said I was falling for her. Told me she'd take me down. Didn't think it could happen to me. Didn't think I knew how to love..."

"But it's not love now!" Krypton protested.

"Tony, your client wants to save his soul," Shrug said, gathering up his file. "I suggest you let him."

CHAPTER 21

Shrug sat in his car outside the safe house pondering the words he would use. He did not want to say anything to reinforce Allison's dangerous love for Carbon, but that might be an impossible mission.

He thought of Project Casanova and the young officer secretly assigned to flatter and befriend Carbon's plain and socially inept wife, who happened to work at the West End Motor Vehicles Registry.

While Shrug would prefer letting Allison think it was Carbon who tracked her down and shot her, that didn't appear to be the truth. Rather it was a jealous wife reading love messages on her husband's computer who set up the attempted assassination. Exactly which lucky Jackal was the recipient of the information Mrs. Carbon had sleuthed from Allison's sunset photo and which one fired the shots wasn't yet known. Casanova was still working on finding out—a few more late-night dinners atop the revolving restaurant with a few more whispered words of affection and the love-starved lady would no doubt give his officer the name of the guilty. Shrug's money was on the name 'Saber'.

He sighed and clicked off the ignition. It seemed the older he got, the harder it was to lie. Perhaps because he'd learned over the years that lying, no matter how grand the motive, always had a downside, usually a steep and slippery one. With another deep breath he climbed out of the car and headed up the walk.

"Any preferences as to where you want to live with your new identities?" he asked when Allie opened the door for him.

She motioned him in. "We finally get to think about that?"

"Not just think, you can start packin'."

Allie gasped. "Before the trials?"

"Ain't gonna be no trials. Carbon's pleadin' guilty." Allie felt the blood drain from her face, as if her heart had stopped beating. There was only one reason she could think of that would make Carbon do that. *He loves me.*

Shrug hurriedly continued. "He's got himself a clever enough and honest enough lawyer to realize it's useless to fight the evidence."

"He's pleading guilty to all the charges? The murders? The kidnapping?"

"Looks that way."

Shrug brushed past her to the kitchen and joined Tim at the table. "Hey, buddy. Finally gettin' you outta this hole as I promised."

"I heard," Tim said. "We'll get protection even though we don't need to testify?"

"Oh, yeah."

Allie shut the door and walked over to the men. "We can choose where we'll live?" she asked Shrug.

"A protection expert will be in touch. They know more about that shit than I do. Are you guys gonna tie the knot before or after you get your new names?"

Allie and Tim cast each other a quick glance. "Still undecided," Tim finally said.

"What's goin' on here?" Shrug was making no effort to hide his disenchantment. "Don't be tellin' me we're gonna be lookin' for two different locations."

"Perhaps," Allie said quietly.

"What's gone wrong?" Shrug asked. His expression reminded Allie of his jail visit when he'd told her she shouldn't cooperate with the murder investigation just to please him, then followed up with a judgmental stare so severe it crushed the breath right out of her.

"We've discovered we're two very different people than we were before—" Allie started.

"Or too much the same," Tim cut in. "It's not working out."

Shrug stared at his shoes. "I thought it would. I really did." His voice was unbearable heavy.

"Perhaps, it will," Allie said. "When this stress is all over."

"Allie!" Tim quietly objected.

Shrug straightened. "I'm sorry for both of you."

"Anyway," Tim said, heaving a sigh. "It's for sure Carbon's pleading guilty?"

Shrug nodded.

"To *all* the charges?" Allie asked again.

Shrug shifted uncomfortably. "Well, not the attempted murder."

"No?" Allie gasped.

"Why not?" Tim demanded.

"Because it wasn't him," Allie said softly. "He didn't do it."

"Don't know why not." Shrug glanced at his watch and rose. "I've gotta go."

"They're going to drop the attempted murder charge, aren't they?" Allie raced after him as he headed to the door. "You were lying when you said Carbon pled guilty because his lawyer told him to."

"I didn't say his lawyer told him to." Shrug had his back to her, struggling with the sticky door latch. "I dunno what his lawyer told him. That's confidential between an attorney and his client."

Allie tugged at Shrug's sleeve. "He did it for me, didn't he? So I wouldn't have to testify."

"Can't read a man's heart." Shrug reefed on the door and it creaked open.

"He loves me," Allie whispered. "Always did."

"Allison, there's a problem with Carbon's kind of love." She followed Shrug's gaze outside to the snow banks, brilliant white tops beneath a high March sun, muddy grey melt water beneath. The trash of an entire winter peeking through the undersides. He turned to her. "He tends to kill those he loves."

"I just want it to have been that way, to have been love, so it all makes some kind of sense."

"Leave it behind! That kind of love never makes sense." He walked out the door, bounded down the three risers and strode toward his car.

He was leaving her.

"Shrug," she pleaded so quietly that she was startled when he stopped and turned.

"Yeah?" The expectation was again in his eyes. What tense had he used when he told her his wife couldn't tell if he lied? What was it Tim had told her, Shrug was divorced? Said he hadn't done very good at his own marriages? Perhaps he expected too much of all his women, like he had of her. She'd never forget that powerful look in his slate grey eyes, totally convinced she was as morally upright as he was and would give him the convictions he wanted.

That unrelenting expectation, as tough as it was, had eventually pried her free of Carbon—almost. Now, Shrug was again waiting for her to do what was right. Waiting in the cold, two steps from his car. His eyes on her.

"Is it true you were once a minister?" she asked.

Shrug could see into people's souls. She was pretty darn sure it was that ability, not any lawyer's fast-talking, that had wrested those guilty pleas from Carbon's lips. Shrug had known, when nobody else did, that Carbon really did love her. And he'd known how to use that to benefit her so she could…so she would—

"Still am," Shrug drawled.

"So you can perform marriages?"

The anticipation that had been tightening his brow, melted into pleasure. He grinned. "You and Tim?"

She nodded. "You'll have to give us time, though."

"All the time you want, Allison. All the time in the world."

"I could have gone back to Carbon. He loves me. Always did. I believe that totally." **Allison Montgomery**

*"But?"***Dr. Erica Freid**

"When Shrug pointed out Carbon's definition of love, I realized how twisted it is—his entire way of life is twisted."

"How so?"

"Shrug said gangs aren't like families, they don't exist to support their members. In order to belong, people must sacrifice themselves to the gang. Unlike families, gangs don't help members who are weak or hurting—they get rid of them. The Jackals might view Carbon's love for me as a weakness, especially if I were to keep hanging around him."

"That's why you chose Tim, so the Jackals won't kill Carbon?"

"I sometimes tell myself that's the reason; it makes it easier somehow. But I know it's not true. Carbon belongs to a gang and that's where his loyalty will always lie. In my head, I know he pleaded guilty not just for me, but for the gang."

"For the gang?"

"It ended the investigation, closed the file. Any other Jackals who might have been involved in the massacre were freed from repercussions." Allie sighed. *"It would be nice to believe he did it for me."*

"But, he didn't."

"No, he didn't."

"Tell me about your relationship with Tim."

"I have been treating Tim as if we're gang members, expecting him to devote himself to the cause and offering nothing in return. But Tim is my family. He sacrificed a hell of a lot for me and now it's time for me to give something back."

"I see."

"With Tim, I actually do know how to love him and that's a very peaceful feeling."

Author's Afterword

The unsettling feeling that Allie just might change her mind and once more return to Carbon's arms is justified.

In real life it takes a woman on average, more than twenty attempts to end an abusive intimate relationship. In addition to the factors compelling Allie to stay with Carbon, abused women often must deal with financial constraints, child care issues, addictions, medical problems, mental health issues, lack of support, lack of knowledge and the fallout from traumatic childhoods.

It's my hope Allie's story helps both the victims of domestic violence and their communities understand the mental and emotional processes involved in the bonding between abused and abusers. May this understanding empower victims to break free and encourage us all to support them until they find the strength to do so.

* * *

The depiction of South Korea is based on my interpretation of its geography, people and culture during my trip there in 2006. For realism with other story elements, I called on my experiences as a volunteer with the police, my past career as a psychiatric nurse and interviews with the staff at the Columbus House of Hope Women's Shelter.

* * *

The movie, DISPASSIONATE LIES, to which the lyrics, *I don't know how to love you*, are attributed, is a fictional film based on my novel of that name.

* * *

If you'd like to read more about Shrug, Sergeant Kindle, Katrina and Chad, their stories are featured in my ongoing *BackTracker* series.

About the Author

Eileen Schuh is the author of the ongoing *BackTracker Series* which includes THE TRAZ, THE TRAZ School Edition, FATAL ERROR, FIREWALLS, and the soon-to-be-released OPERATION MAXTRACKER. As well, she has two adult SciFi novellas to her credit, SCHRÖDINGER'S CAT and DISPASSIONATE LIES.

She was born and raised as Eileen Fairbrother on a small farm near Tofield, Alberta and now lives with her husband in the remote northern boreal forests of Alberta, Canada. Drawing inspiration from her family, her community, and the wilderness she creates entire universes populated with fascinating characters doing intriguing things.

Schuh recently retired from a life of careers that varied from nurse to journalist to editor to business woman. In addition to writing, she remains involved in her adopted community of St. Paul, Alberta and enjoys speaking to youth and adults about the magic of writing and the social and personal issues addressed in her novels.

She invites you to visit her online:

Blog: http://eileenschuh.blogspot.com
Website: http://www.eileenschuh.com
Facebook: http://www.facebook.com/EileenSchuhAuthor
Twitter: http://twitter.com/eileenschuh

The year is 2035 and the world's emerging from the devastating collapse of cyberspace. Computer guru, Ladesque, finds her task of restoring the world's internet capabilities, dull until...

She's approached by Paul, an attractive FBI agent intent on recruiting her to an ultra-secret project. There's a problem, though—the asexuality she was born with thirty-five years ago, vanishes.

While struggling with the unfamiliar power of libido, she uncovers encoded clues to the truth behind the stolen sexuality saddling her generation of women. However, uncovering facts proves difficult in an age where hackers have corrupted all digital records.

In order to save the world, she puts her personal quest on hold and joins Paul's secret project. Moral dilemmas abound as mating instincts kick in, technology and politics collide, and Paul and Roach, the two men in her life, both begin courting her.

She wonders if it may all boil down to intellect rather than emotion when she's commissioned to assess the risk of the explosive new technology she finds in the vault. To make her job that much harder, she discovers it's a risk that might also unravel the mysteries of her past.

Book Club Discussion Questions

1. Shrug says, *"There's a problem with Carbon's kind of love."* Is love an absolute, or are there different kinds of love? Do different cultures define love differently and hold different expectations of 'love'? In your mind, what are some of the 'right' components of love and how do they compare to the various views of love offered up by the SHADOW RIDERS' characters?

2. Just like most perpetrators of domestic violence, Carbon offers justification for his abusive behaviour and is eventually able to convince Allie that his excuses have merits. What factors play into Allie's acceptance of Carbon's explanation? Are there parts of his excuse that you are willing to accept?

3. Fear, physical allure, depression and loneliness help nourish Allie's growing attraction to Carbon. What factors, the same or different, play into the establishment of an ordinary romance? Do some of these factors make us all vulnerable to abuse?

4. Did Carbon really love Allie? Why is the answer to that question important to the story? To Allie? To us? From your point of view, if Carbon loved Allie, does that make his abuse more abhorrent or less so? How about from Allie's point of view?

5. Abusers often isolate their victims from the influence of family and friends in order to tighten their control over them. How big a role did isolation play in Allie and Carbon's relationship?

6. Several times in the story, the justice system is manipulated. In the end, was everyone treated fairly by the courts? Should justice be malleable like this in order to adapt to circumstances or does that increase the possibility that not everyone will be treated equally under the law?

7. Allie refused to cooperate with investigators. With a few exceptions, Canadian law doesn't require people to report illegal activities or answer police questions about them. Discuss the effect this has on justice. (One exception requires certain professions to report suspicions of child abuse.)

8. Communication and transportation technologies are making the world a much smaller place. Both legitimate and illicit business is commonly conducted across borders and jurisdictions, and 'off shore', where no country has legal jurisdiction. To adapt to technology, what changes to national and international legal systems are needed? What are some changes that have recently been made?

9. Allie appears confused about when it was that she fell in love with Carbon. In your view, which scene was the turning point in Allie's feelings toward Carbon? What were the deciding factors? Is there a point in the story when *your* feelings toward Carbon changed dramatically? How about your feelings toward Allie?

10. Carbon stirs Allie's sympathies with his tearful tale about the massacre. Discuss why this sharing of his emotions and 'secrets' works so well to bind her to him.

11. Carbon uses a sly mixture of truth and lies to manipulate Allie. Her distrust of his honesty initially prevents her from falling for him. Does Allie's love for Carbon and her trust in him, evolve in sync? Which scenes increased your trust in Carbon? Decreased it? Do you agree with Shrug when he tells Allie that '*damned near everything*' Carbon told her was a lie? Discuss the positive and negative roles dishonesty plays in all relationships.

12. What do you think was the most helpful thing a character said or did to assist Allie in breaking free of Carbon? Which parts of Allie's story most influenced your feelings toward women in abusive relationships? Would you feel confident in offering support to a friend experiencing domestic violence?

13. In real life, it takes a woman an average of twenty attempts to break free of an abusive relationship. So...is Allie eventually going to go back to Carbon? If she were to go back to him, would you understand why? Which character would likely be least surprised if she made that decision and why? Do you want her to stay true to Carbon? If Allie gives Carbon the chance, shows him trust and love and loyalty, how likely is he to become a non-abusive partner? What other factors play into the likelihood that he'll change or not change?

14. There are several well-developed characters in this novel. Which one is your favourite and why?